Close to the Wind

Close to the Wind

Zana Bell

Published 2013 by Choc Lit Limited
Penrose House, Crawley Drive, Camberley, Surrey GU15 2AB, UK
www.choc-lit.com

A CIP catalogue record for this book is available
from the British Library

ISBN 978-1-78189-026-4

Printed and bound by CPI Group (UK) Ltd, Croydon, CR0 4YY

*To Geoff, our kids, the mokopuna and the rest of
the crew who all mean so much to me.*

Acknowledgements

I'd like to thank Gill and Iona for their invaluable feedback in the early stages of the book. Thanks also to Rob and Jo, Kali, Derry and Michelle for their nautical input, and to the Voyager New Zealand Maritime Museum and Equestrian Sports New Zealand for their advice.

A special mention must go to the wonderful Kath who is canny in her suggestions, dedicated in the pursuit of obscure detail, and tireless in pouncing on grammatical glitches.

And of course my great gratitude to the Choc Lit team who have welcomed me aboard so warmly and who have provided such wonderful support throughout the process.

Chapter One

England, August 1868

It was midnight when Georgiana swung herself up into the oak tree that grew outside her bedroom window on the third floor of Ashton Hall, her blood fizzing with exhilaration. She'd just given her final performance as Dick Turpin and the rousing applause of her bucolic audience still rang in her ears. It had also been a splendid ride home, a moonlit gallop through the silvered countryside, lying low over Sheba's neck. Her boy's cap had whipped off and her hair had tumbled down. It would take hours to comb out, but she didn't care. Tonight, nothing mattered. Soon she would be married and escaping Aunt Ashton forever.

But even as she began to climb the very familiar branches, she saw light spilling from the billiard room immediately below her room. Georgiana pulled a face as voices wafted down to her through the open windows. So Lord Walsingham was still visiting. She paused on a branch almost level with the room and heard the click of billiard balls. 'Jolly good shot,' she heard Jasper say. 'I fear I'm on the ropes.'

Jasper was a master at billiards, so he must be throwing the game. Georgiana wished he wouldn't. She wanted him to defeat his employer. Despite his affability, she had taken a dislike to their guest who'd arrived unexpectedly that afternoon. Lord Walsingham was short and rotund, the buttons on his waistcoat straining when he sat, and though he smiled often, his eyes were unnaturally sharp. Jasper liked to boast that Lord Walsingham and his partner Lord Iver were the backbone of the nation's tea industry and that he was their right-hand man. But her cousin, usually so urbane, had laughed a little too loudly at Lord Walsingham's quips over dinner. He'd fidgeted with his knives and been short with the footman.

Another click of the balls and Jasper cried, 'Well done, sir. You've vanquished me. Shall I get us a brandy then rack the balls again?'

'Yes, do that. I have at least one more game in me.'

Georgiana frowned, mistrusting the smooth-toned humour and shrank back against the tree trunk. She was loath to climb past while they were so close to the window. It was irrational but she couldn't help feeling that Lord Walsingham would detect the slightest unaccountable noise. The thought of being discovered made her shiver.

There was the rattle of balls being racked then broken. 'Nicely done.'

Did Jasper hear his sycophantic tone? Perhaps, because he went on to speak with elaborate airiness. 'I confess I was a little surprised – though delighted naturally – to have you visit today, Lord Walsingham. It was lucky business should bring you to this neck of the woods.'

Lord Walsingham chuckled. 'Ah, my boy, that's why I employ you. You aren't a fool. I do in fact need to have a talk with you. Besides, I was curious to meet your fiancée.'

'Indeed?' Jasper sounded guarded.

'She's not—' Lord Walsingham paused and Georgiana couldn't resist leaning out at a perilous angle to peer through the leaves. Walsingham was lining up his shot, his small round eyes fixed on the far pocket. 'Not in your usual style, but no doubt you will deal well together.'

How strange, that's what Jasper had said. *Marry me, Georgie, I think we'll deal well together.*

'Thank you.'

This colourless response tugged her heart a little, but her mind was quick to point out that, in fairness, he had never spoken of love. Neither had she, though since his proposal Georgiana had been trying to kindle suitable wifely emotions. She was certainly grateful, for Jasper would take her away from Ashton Hall and her carping aunt, his step-mama. They'd live in Shanghai for some of each year, just as he did now. That would be exciting. Besides, she was fond of Jasper. He'd always been tolerant of his two young cousins and since Charles had disappeared to the goldfields of New Zealand, he'd been the only one to show any interest in her, offhand though it was.

'She'll tolerate your, er, interests, I suppose?'

Jasper was a compulsive gambler. He was also known to appreciate the company of dashing young widows. However, marriage was preferable to the certitude of another failed season and a life sentence with Aunt Ashton.

'She's not in a position not to.'

Jasper was only stating the truth. It would have been nice though, if his answer had been different.

'No. I can see that. With her looks and manner ...' Lord Walsingham didn't say any more. Didn't need to. Georgiana was well acquainted with her faults, though Aunt Ashton never missed an opportunity to point them out.

'The wedding will take place within the next month.' Lord Walsingham's voice was affable, but this was unmistakably a command. Startled, Georgiana almost slipped and had to quickly pull herself back.

'Next month? That's impossible!' Jasper exclaimed. 'How would I explain such a rushed affair?'

'Very soon, you'll be recalled to Shanghai where you'll remain for the foreseeable future. It's only natural, therefore, that you'll wish to take your bride with you.'

There was silence. Then Jasper spoke, voice wary. 'I don't understand, sir. You have my word that I won't renege on our agreement. I'll marry my cousin and half the gold mine will be yours.'

Gold mine? What gold mine? Georgiana had the strangest feeling she'd just walked into the wrong play.

'I know that, m'boy. I've paid so many of your debts, you should be grateful that I'm settling for only a half-share.'

There was a click of balls.

'The mine is only a part of it,' Walsingham said. 'Events are moving swiftly and I've taken action to ensure they advance our cause.'

'*Our* cause?'

The inflection was not lost on Lord Walsingham. He sounded amused. 'Yes, *our* cause. Your future is now locked in with mine, make no mistake.' His tone became brisk and businesslike. 'Iver is determined to finish the company, so he needs to be removed.'

'What?' Jasper sounded astounded. 'Why on earth …?'

'He's become squeamish about trading opium for tea since his boy Eddie became so foolishly addicted.' There was a pause and a click as another shot was taken. 'Threatens to bring the whole industry down. Just waiting for "proof" to arrive. Apparently Eddie'd been recording our actions in the war and has sent his papers back to England. I believe they are on their way, even as we speak.'

Jasper made a choking sound.

'Just so, m'boy. Three hundred women and children killed outside Shanghai. Imagine if that became public knowledge. As soon as Iver receives Eddie's papers, which he says are due any day from China, he plans to go to the Prime Minister.'

'Oh my God.'

Georgiana heard the splash of more brandy being poured, the clink of a bottle put unsteadily back down on the table.

'Indeed,' said Walsingham. 'Hence the need to move swiftly.'

Now Jasper's voice held both fear and suspicion. 'You said *removed*?'

'When the papers arrive, he'll contact me. So far, I've been very sympathetic with Iver's *volte face*. But when I get word, I have a man ready to destroy the papers and deal with Iver.'

There was silence. Everything was very still. The smell of jasmine wreathed the air. The full moon shone bright and cold. The night was warm, but Georgiana realised she was shaking. None of this was real. It couldn't be. The script was more melodramatic than any play she'd acted in. She waited for laughter, for Walsingham and Jasper to reveal it was all a hoax.

But Walsingham continued in the same inexorable way. 'Once Iver has been dealt with, my man will leave England immediately. It's sensible, therefore, to kill two birds with one stone, as it were.' There was a note of ironical humour that curdled Georgiana's blood. 'He'll find your cousin in New Zealand.'

Georgiana pressed her hand very hard against her mouth, teeth sinking into skin.

Jasper sounded shaken. 'There's no need, sir. I told you, he's fatally ill.'

Ill? Impossible. Charlie never got sick. Why did she know nothing about any of this?

'So you said.' There was another click of balls. 'My man will simply ensure your fiancée does indeed inherit the mine.'

Jasper made another choking sound. 'Marriage for gain is one thing, but I won't be party to murdering my cousin.'

Lord Walsingham sounded both amused and sympathetic. 'You don't have any choice. The debts you owe me are considerable. Besides, I know about the Chinese girl.'

There was a stunned pause. 'What? How?'

'I have eyes everywhere.'

'It was only a bit of fun,' Jasper stammered. 'I never guessed – I mean, how would anyone? – the silly girl would kill herself!'

'A daughter of a high-ranking dignitary at that. Imagine the scandal. Go against me and you won't escape justice, you know.'

There was a long silence and when Jasper spoke again, his voice rasped. 'You won't get away with this.'

'No? I think I will. All you need do is marry your cousin and sail away.'

'I want no part of this.' Jasper cried.

'It's too late,' Lord Walsingham pointed out. 'You're in over your head. Take this lifeline or you will drown, my dear boy. I guarantee it.' And he chuckled.

Unable to take any more, desperate to escape this nightmare, Georgiana climbed swiftly and vaulted into her room. Back to the wall, she slithered to the floor, pulling her knees in tight. She could feel the wild pace of her heart. Nothing made sense; it was all unbelievable. One fact burned. Charlie was in danger. He was very ill and an assassin would soon be after him. She had to get there first. But how? He was at the bottom of the world. She had no money, no friends. If she told her story, Jasper would deny it. Walsingham would simply laugh. No one would believe her.

She dug her fingernails into the knees of Charlie's old trousers. Trousers. Slowly she looked down at the boy's shirt she wore on her escapades. The idea was preposterous. Yet she had fooled audiences for some months now. She could do this. She could – for Charlie.

Chapter Two

The wind was picking up outside and Harry glanced from the cards in his hand to the small tavern windows. The long summer twilight had softened into night and it must have been an hour since a lad had lit the two small gas lamps on the walls of the anteroom and provided a branch of candles for the table. Soon Harry would need to get back to his ship, but he was loath to leave this haven of peace and camaraderie. Sitting here with his friends he was almost able to pretend yesterday hadn't happened.

He spread his cards out over the scarred boards of the table. Tristan took one look and swore, throwing his own hand down with such force that the candle flames danced. 'Christ, you really do have the luck of the devil, Harry.'

Old Willy gave a crack of laughter around the pipe lodged in the corner of his mouth. 'T'aint luck, lad, 'tis skill.' His grizzled ginger beard compensated for his bald pate above.

Bernard cocked his head to one side, his teeth white against his gleaming black skin. 'But does the skill lie in the playing of cards or the handling of them? Let us check your sleeves, Harry, for I swear you're hiding a few aces up there.' His voice held the velvet notes of his Jamaican background.

Harry laughed as he scooped his winnings towards him. 'Poor losers, the lot of you.'

'Well, it's time one of us beat you. And to think it was I who used to be the reigning champion when we were at Harrow.' Tristan shook his head, then flicked fluff from his immaculately cut jacket. 'Your vagrant life has taught you wicked ways, Harry my lad. Speaking of which, surely you aren't serious about taking your leaky old tub all the way down to New Zealand.'

For a second, violent images from yesterday flared and Harry's fingers tightened as though once more around that old bastard's neck. His smile was easy however, as he forced his fingers to relax.

'A comment like that could find you facing my pistols at dawn, Tris. *Sally's* a grand vessel and has been around the world more times than you've been to Scotland.'

He gathered the cards together and began to shuffle them.

'But *New Zealand*?' Tris eyed Harry. 'What are you up to? Surely you aren't planning to join in this latest gold rush?'

'He's not so daft,' Willy scoffed.

Tris raised a brow. 'You don't think so? Harry's the prince of madcap schemes.'

'That's because poverty,' said Harry as he dealt the next hand, 'is only noble in fairy tales.'

'So you're planning to become a miner?' Bernard was incredulous.

'No.' Harry paused. His mission, even to himself, sounded insane. So far he hadn't told anyone, even the crew. He'd just announced to them this morning that they'd be leaving for New Zealand the following day and to ready the ship for the voyage. He looked around at his friends' curious faces. 'I'm looking for a man,' he temporised and was saved as a knock at the door distracted his companions.

'Bring in the brandy,' Tristan called out.

It was not the publican, however, but a youth clutching a bundle. For a second he hesitated in the doorway, eyeing the four men grouped around the table littered with cards and glasses. Then his gaze fixed on Willy and with a deep breath he stepped forward.

'I'm looking for Captain Trent.'

His well-modulated voice was curiously at odds with his travel-stained, ill-fitting clothes, and Tristan cocked a brow at Harry as he leaned back in his chair.

'Not me,' said Willy, taking his pipe from his mouth and pointing at Harry. 'Him.'

The boy turned and his eyes widened as they travelled up the length of Harry's outstretched legs. Harry was amused as the boy continued in his unconscious, somewhat censorious examination, taking in the rolled sleeves and unbuttoned neck of Harry's shirt before finally coming to rest on Harry's face.

'Captain Trent?' He sounded uncertain, as if suspecting a prank.

'That's right,' Harry said. 'Why do you want me?'

The boy paused and then, coming to a decision, he stepped closer. His face was white and strained, but there was a determined set to his mouth. 'I'm looking to work my passage to New Zealand and the chandlers in the lane said you were headed there.'

Harry strummed his fingers on the table as he surveyed the boy. The youth held his ground, staring steadily back. He was probably about sixteen, Harry surmised, with long slender limbs not yet hardened with muscle. Yet there was something in his stance that bespoke a firmness of intent beyond his years. His eyes were his most striking feature, wide, clear, and unusually sensitive for a boy as they gazed out somewhat defiantly from under a roughly-chopped mop of brown curls.

'What's your name?'

'George. George – Miller.'

The hesitation was barely discernible.

'And why do you want to go to New Zealand?'

'I'm going to look for my brother on the goldfields outside Dunedin.'

Harry shot out a hand and caught George's wrist, turning it over to inspect the palm. 'Just as I thought. Your hands are as soft as a girl's. You've never done a day's work in your life. Go home, boy.'

Harry dropped the wrist and George, flushing, stuffed his hand in his pocket. His chin jutted as he replied, 'Your hands might have been just as soft when you were my age.'

Taken aback, Harry laughed. The boy was quick, apparently drawing his own conclusions based on Harry's speech which still held traces of his Cambridge education. 'True. But I learnt fast.'

'And I will too,' George said stubbornly.

His pluck amused Tristan. 'Why not give him a chance, Harry?'

At this unexpected support, the boy looked hopeful. Harry, however, was not in the habit of encouraging youthful miscreants and spoke in dampening tones. 'Because I don't believe him, Tris. I think Master George *Miller* here – and don't for one minute think I believe that's your real name – has run away from school and that his family is sick with anxiety even as we speak. Go home, George. There's no berth for you on my ship.'

Harry turned back to the table and picked up the cards Bernard had in the meantime dealt, signalling the end of interview. But even as George began to protest, the door was flung open and a child stood panting in the doorway.

'Captain Trent, Mam said to come warn you.' His voice, coming in gasps, was shrill with urgency. 'The law's asking for you everywhere.'

Harry went very still. The old man – it had to be. Events had moved fast – faster than he'd expected. Just as well *Sally* was all set to go.

'How far away, Joe?'

'Just behind me. They've already asked at the forge.'

'Thanks. Take this for your trouble.' He tossed a coin to Joe, who exclaimed with delight when he caught it. 'Now run away. Your mother will be after me herself if you get involved. Go.'

But even as the door slammed behind Joe, an authoritative voice rang out in the room beyond. 'I'm looking for a Harry Trent.'

'You're popular tonight,' Bernard remarked as Harry sprang to his feet, looking around to room. The windows were far too small.

'What on earth have you been up to this time, Harry?' Tristan demanded.

'No time to explain. Damned if I'm going to be taken though.'

'The chimney,' Willy hissed.

In two bounds Harry was at the hearth and as he hitched himself up, he saw Master Miller toss his bundle under the table and take his place in front of Harry's winnings.

The air inside the chimney was gritty and clogged Harry's nostrils as he scrambled to find a point of balance on the sweep's narrow ledge – no easy feat given his height and width of shoulders. He straddled a corner, but as he braced his hands, he dislodged a tiny amount of soot. It floated down into the hearth and Harry cursed soundlessly.

The door burst open and a belligerent voice cried out. 'Harry Trent?'

'No,' said Willy sounding surprised. 'He left a while back.'

There was a hesitation then Harry heard the officer say in a voice heavy with suspicion, 'You're mighty young to be playing cards here, laddie.'

'I came to find my grandfather and took the captain's seat. See how well I've been doing? My grandfather says it's just beginner's luck, but I don't think it can be, do you?'

The boy's voice contained just the right amount of jaunty pride and despite his reservations, Harry had to admit Master Miller was a remarkably quick thinker for his age.

A younger officer spoke. 'Did Trent say where he was going?'

'No – though I fancy he may have gone to find some,' Tristan fished for the right expression, 'female company.'

There was a choke of embarrassment from the younger officer who muttered apologies and it sounded like he was backing out of the room. Harry held his breath.

But the belligerent one must have spotted the soot.

'Search the chimney!'

With a silent oath, Harry dropped into the hearth. The older man shouted for reinforcements as the younger officer rushed towards the chimney. Harry swung a punch that caught him squarely on the nose and sent him flying backwards.

The card table somersaulted, dowsing the candles as Tristan leapt at the door through which poured a number of uniformed men. Within seconds, blows were flying in all directions. Harry was a marked man with two officers trying to bring him down. Fortunately, they hadn't the advantage of backstreet fighting in Brazil, and Harry laid both out in quick succession before scanning the room.

Tristan was landing one beautifully balanced punch after another on a hapless, stout young man. Bernard had two men hanging from his black neck, trying to pull him over. Some hope, Harry thought. Bernard was strong as an oak. Several officers were hopping and clutching toes as old Willy wielded his crutch and bounced on his peg leg. But where was the boy?

Then Harry saw George, fists bunched but looking around wildly. An officer came running up behind the lad.

'Watch out, George!' Harry yelled.

George glanced around and doubled over just as the man launched himself.

Unusual, thought Harry as the man flew over the crouched figure and crashed into the wall, but effective.

A blow to his own back had him spinning on his heel to look up – and up. Harry fired two quick blows, but the giant just laughed as the punches pinged off rib and jaw. Then he lifted one huge paw and landed a massive blow to the side of Harry's head. Harry staggered, ears ringing. The man laughed again, showing the stubs of only two teeth in his entire mouth, and raised his arm again. Harry tensed, ready to duck another bone-shattering punch, but was amazed to see Goliath's leer fade into a beatific smile. His eyes glazed then closed as he folded to the floor in a heap of brawny limbs. George, looking aghast, stood behind, clutching the remains of a chair to his chest.

'Well done, George,' shouted Harry above the din.

'Harry, go!' roared Bernard, wrestling fresh arrivals.

'Yes, get going,' cried Tristan, his jacket torn, his neckcloth askew and his eyes dancing with fierce delight.

'Find out the damage, Tris. Message in a bottle.'

'Got you. Now go!'

Grabbing George's arm, Harry shouted, 'Come with me.' The boy caught up his bundle as Harry hauled him away.

The taproom was a melee of fighting, flailing bodies. Any excuse for a good fight, Harry thought grimly, keeping a tight hold on George's arm. It was no place for a boy to be. A man lurched forward, trying to rip the bundle out of George's hands, but the boy retaliated with a sharp kick to the shins. The man swore as Harry's right jab dislodged a tooth and they left the would-be thief mashing his jaw.

Falling into the warm, summer night air was bliss. Harry leaned over, hands on thighs, to draw in a couple of deep breaths while George hugged his bundle to his chest, his breaths short and sharp. Wincing with bruised ribs, his head still pounding from the Goliath blow, Harry straightened.

'First tavern brawl? Well, you kept your wits, lad.'

George smiled but as his lashes swept down Harry knew his suspicions had been right. The boy *was* hiding something. Then he lifted his eyes again and Harry was struck by the hope and trust he saw in them. George was clearly not going to quit his ridiculous plan and if left alone – with those eyes, that mixture of bravado and innocence – he'd land in trouble. Serious trouble. Not Harry's problem. He had more than enough of his own as it was. Which is why he couldn't believe his own ears when he heard himself say, 'You can't stay here alone. You'd better come with me.'

George's face lit up. 'Really?'

The boy was far too expressive for his own good. Harry was severe as he added, 'But we've got to run so you'd better keep up. I'm not waiting for you! Come on.'

They sprinted up the main street until a shout from behind had them swerving down an alley that led to a narrow lane. They vaulted a wall then tore across the fields beyond. The moon was buried in clouds and several times George stumbled and would have fallen if Harry hadn't caught him by the elbow. The boy was game, but Harry heard his breathing grow ragged as they fled along the brow of the cliffs, then dashed down into the bay where he'd left his dinghy on the beach.

'Push,' Harry ordered, and together they heaved it into the water. George tumbled into the stern, his breath coming in shuddering gasps, one hand clutched to his shirt as though trying to contain his heart. Harry seized the oars and began rowing as hard as he could for *Sally*, anchored further out. Just as the first silhouetted figures reached the brow of the cliffs, Harry felt the wind lift his hair from his forehead and it splintered the water around them. His legendary luck had not quite deserted him after all and he laughed. Let the bastards try to catch him now.

'Well, we're out of that frying pan, George.'

Georgiana stared, for at that moment the moon slid out from behind the clouds. Silver light reflected off the captain's tumbled black hair, and washed over the slants and planes of his face. Soot from the chimney streaked his skin like war paint. His eyes, a vivid blue in the candlelight, were now dark and glittering. Suddenly the well-spoken captain in the tavern resembled nothing so much as a wild pirate king.

'But into what fire?' Georgiana asked herself, and despite the warmth of the evening, she shivered.

Chapter Three

Even as they climbed aboard, the captain began shouting orders.

'Haul up the anchor. Release the mainsail.'

The crew sprang into action, their movements far more disciplined and well ordered than their scruffy appearances suggested, while the captain strode over to the man at the wheel. Georgiana saw surprised looks surreptitiously exchanged, though no one questioned the commands. Reeling from the swift turn of events, she struggled to believe she was here, actually here, on a ship bound for New Zealand. Yet it had to be true, she thought, as she watched the sails drop from their lashings then billow with the night's wind.

The events of the last forty-eight hours suddenly overwhelmed her. The flight from home had been followed by a day of jarring coaches. Then came the long search through this busy port for a ship bound for New Zealand. She'd begun to despair until her late query at the chandlers had led to the tavern, the fight and now the ship. For a second the world misted and she swayed. A hand caught her elbow and the captain was beside her, looking down into her face.

'Boy, you're all in and you'll just be in the way on deck. Get below and we'll talk in the morning.'

She blinked. 'I'm fine. I can help. Tell me what to do.'

'I just have,' he pointed out. 'Go below, I have no use for you tonight.' Turning, he shouted, 'Alec!'

A grizzled man with white whiskers materialised at his elbow. 'There's no need to shout. I'm right here.'

'Take this boy below and find him a hammock.'

Alec looked Georgiana up and down. 'What're we taking him for? We're not needing another lad.'

The captain glanced down at her. His eyes were very dark, but his cheekbones and jaw were rimmed with the silver moonlight. A breeze carried the musk of his sweat. He smiled and her heart did a small, unexpected flip.

'Damned if I know,' he admitted. 'It just happened that way. He wants to work his passage to New Zealand.'

'New Zealand? Setting sail *now*?' Alec's mouth clamped in a thin line.

'Yes, we are. Madeira will be our first port.'

The lines of disapproval deepened. 'Message in a bottle?'

The captain laughed and Georgiana thought she'd never heard such a splendidly reckless sound.

'Yes, message in a bottle. Little gets past you, old man.'

Alec shook his head. 'I knew no good would come of that Shanghai deal.'

'Stop your gloom-mongering. It's nothing we can't handle. Now get this pup out of the way.' Turning, the captain called, 'Stephen, I'll take the wheel.' With that he was gone.

Alec made no further comment, just indicated for Georgiana to follow him with a jerk of his head. She picked up her bundle and followed him down the ladder. At the bottom, she paused to let her eyes adjust. There were only a couple of lanterns in this dank lower deck, their weak pools of light barely extending into the blackness. The stench was overpowering: damp timber, food stores, stale air and that unmistakable edge of male odour. They pushed their way through a number of hammocks and threaded their way around barrels, trestles and other shapes hard to discern in the dark.

Alec led her to the far end. 'I'll give you a hammock in the corner here, out of harm's way. It's an old one, but being a bantam weight, you won't go through it. Come here and pay attention, I'll only be showing you this once how to tie it, so mind you learn.'

He unearthed a dirty hammock and showed her how to fix it to the beams. 'See, there's a bowline at this end, you do it like this. Then at t'other end here, it's a round turn and two half hitches. Now you try.'

Understanding this was a test, Georgiana was determined to do a good job though it hadn't been easy to follow the movements of the sailor's broad fingers in the twilight of the lantern. The rope was stiff with salt and tore at her fingers, but she persisted and Alec only intervened once.

'No, you need an extra loop there or you'll be flat on your arse. Yep. Like that. Not tidy but it'll do. Store your things in that corner.'

'I'd like to help.'

'Best help you can be is staying out the way. Don't know why he brought a pup still wet behind the ears.'

'Actually he did refuse,' said Georgiana with rueful honesty, 'but when the law came and there was a fight—'

'The *law*? What in God's name—?' he shot her a look. 'There's bad business here, I can smell it. You hold your tongue with the others, mind. It's none of their concern. Understand?' Georgiana nodded. 'Now turn in. It's bilges and potatoes for you tomorrow. That'll keep you out of mischief.'

Left alone in the gloom, Georgiana looked about her with a sinking heart. Clearly the crew ate together, slept together. She hadn't thought of that. Face it, she hadn't thought through anything. Now, listening to the men's feet running on the boards above her head, feeling the lurch of the ship beneath her, the enormity of her plight came home to her.

What on earth had she been thinking? It was one thing to play at being a boy for a few hours, even a day perhaps, but such a guise was surely impossible to maintain over weeks, let alone months. If her true identity was ever discovered … Ugly, half-formed images rose before her but, as panic welled, unexpectedly she remembered the captain's smile. Instinctively she felt she could trust him – then gave a hollow laugh. Was she mad? The captain was a fugitive from the law.

Georgiana swung herself into the hammock and its canvas sides enfolded her, the swaying motion foreign. Everything, in fact, felt and smelt and sounded foreign. The blackness stretched around her as she forced her breathing to slow down. Rightly or wrongly, she had chosen this path and now she had no choice but to follow it through to its end.

She remembered her father teaching her to somersault many years ago in the circus. 'Once you have begun the move,' he'd told her, 'there is no going back. Lose your courage halfway …' and he'd grimaced.

In the darkness, Georgiana set her jaw. Nothing was going to stop her from finding Charles and warning him – providing he was still alive. What if the illness had already claimed him? With a groan, she rolled onto her side, clamping her cheeks between her palms as if to crush the terror that gripped her at that thought. The malodorous canvas pressed against her features like a shroud. Be strong. She must be strong. Focus. Above all, keep her head.

She wondered what cousin Jasper was doing right now and, despite her dire situation, she felt a small flare of triumph. Ha! He'd never find her here, and he'd never think to look for her in disguise.

What a fool she'd been. As if Jasper, tall and languidly elegant, would have proposed to his gauche cousin without some good reason.

Gold, she acknowledged, was a very good reason. But the thought still stung. True, she hadn't loved Jasper either, but she had trusted him, had seen him as her way to escape. Well, she'd been a fool but had learnt her lesson. She would never allow herself to be duped like that again. Or to be trapped again.

Memory of her aunt's face puckered with dislike, her jowls heavy with disapproval, suddenly made the mildewing hammock seem almost like a sanctuary. Her hands relaxed as she recalled the exhilaration she'd felt two nights before when finally galloping away after years of resentful docility. Was that how her mother had felt the day she'd run away from her own domineering parents to join the circus?

The hammock creaked as Georgiana flipped onto her back again and wriggled to ease the cloth that bound her breasts. The thick belt holding up an old pair of Charles's trousers dug into her waist and her unnaturally short hair rasped against the canvas. For a second she fingered the ragged edges of what had been her only beauty, but this was no time for regrets. Having no money of her own save for the few guineas she'd taken from Jasper's desk, this masquerade was the only way she could work her passage to New Zealand.

It was when taking the money that she had suddenly thought of looking in the drawer Jasper always kept locked. While he was careless with his money, he kept what he termed *vital documents* in this drawer, the key to which hung on a hook concealed beneath the desk top. He never knew his young cousins had discovered it soon after their arrival, when they'd sought refuge under the capacious desk to escape their aunt's tongue-lashing for a misdemeanour. While Georgiana had felt no compunction over the guineas she knew Jasper could well afford, she'd felt furtive as, with shaking hands, she'd fumbled the key into the lock. These last qualms had immediately vanished, however, as she pulled open the drawer and spied Charlie's letter lying on the top of a pile of papers. Terrified of being caught, she'd only skimmed it before putting it back and hastily returning the key to its hidden hook. Taking the letter would have only aroused Jasper's suspicions, but she'd seen enough to convince her this situation was all too horribly real and put iron into her resolution to foil Walsingham's dastardly plans.

Theoretically, Charles should even now be safe as Walsingham no longer had any reason to unleash his assassin – so long as he heard about the broken engagement in time. But she could take no chances. If Walsingham *hadn't* called off his man then she would do everything within her power to save her brother.

Her hand moved down and her fingers curled around the gold griffin which lay hidden under her shirt. Her grandmother had given it to her when she was a child, explaining that it would be her talisman through life, and its weight now comforted her. Into the darkness she whispered, 'Come on Charles, fight the fever. Forget what the doctor said. I'm on my way.' She refused to think that even now, her irrepressible sibling might be dead.

The deep-bellied swaying of the ship was strangely soothing; the wash of water running past lulled her. The hoarse, unfamiliar cries of the men dimmed and become indistinct from the creaking of the timbers that embraced her. In her mind's eye she saw the sails billow white under the moon, carrying her away from all she hated, and towards her beloved brother. The exhaustion she'd been keeping at bay stole over her and as Georgiana finally surrendered to sleep, her last thought was to wonder how Jasper had taken her disappearance.

Not at all well, as it turned out. Jasper had been irate when woken at some ungodly hour by an urgent message that Jet, his beloved Arab stallion, was missing.

'Missing? What do you mean, missing?' he'd said, rubbing his eyes and rueing the amount of brandy he'd consumed the night before. 'That's impossible.'

But when he'd flung on some clothes and gone down to the stables, it seemed that Jet had indeed vanished. Manners, the groom, was mystified.

'It don't make no sense, Mr Jasper. I groomed him meself and put him into his stable same as every night.'

'This is ridiculous. Horses don't disappear. If he'd been stolen, the dogs would surely have barked.'

'Perhaps they was drugged.'

'Drugged? Drugged? Good God, do they look drugged?' Exasperated, Jasper flung a hand towards the three dogs who were straining on their chains, stridently barking and wagging their tails. Manners begged pardon and drew a line in the dust with his toe.

'Could it be possible that Miss Georgiana ...' he trailed off.

Jasper was thunderstruck. 'She wouldn't dare!'

Manners' unhappy face suggested that yes, she most certainly would. Jasper knew she would, too.

'I'll horsewhip the girl myself if she has,' he vowed as he strode back to the house to find his unruly cousin. He still found it difficult to think of her as his intended bride.

'Jet'll be in good hands,' Manners called after him.

As Jasper entered the house he heard his step-mother cry out, appalled, 'That wicked, wicked girl!'

Running up the stairs two at a time, he found her in his cousin's room clutching a letter.

'Will you just look at this,' she cried, thrusting the page at him. 'She's gone back to the circus. Well, good riddance. I did my best, but she's defied my every effort these past seven years and humiliated me more times than I can say. She's nothing more than a common circus brat – just like her father. Not that my sister was any better. Like mother, like daughter I always say.'

Jasper, having heard similar tirades over the years, paid

no attention as he skimmed the note. It was short and to the point.

Dear Aunt

I find I cannot marry Jasper after all. I do not think we will make one another happy. I know I have always been a trial to you, so I've decided to rejoin the circus. I heard they are up in Scotland so will make my way there. Tell Jasper I am sorry that I've had to take some of his money. I will borrow Jet, but he's not to worry, I'll leave him with the constable in Knavesby.

Thank you for all you have done for me and I am sorry for all the trouble I've caused you over the years.

Georgiana.

He went quite cold, despite the mild summer morning. If they didn't marry, he'd never get his hands on the gold and Walsingham would be furious. Dimly he was aware of his step-mama still babbling on.

'That ungrateful hussy! How will we explain her disappearance? Not that I'm not very pleased that you won't be married, now. I never understood why you proposed to her in the first place. Even though you are only cousins by marriage, it still seems so very odd, you know. Celia Chasborough is by far more suitable in every way.'

Disregarding his step-mother, Jasper ran downstairs to the second floor to his desk in the alcove of the billiards room. Sure enough, the money he kept in the lower drawer was gone. He stood, frowning. A glint of metal under the desk caught his eye and when he stooped down, he saw it was the key to the top drawer. It must have fallen from the secret hook where he always hid it. But Georgiana could never have known about it – could she? A tickle of fear ran down his spine as Jasper thought rapidly. Georgiana was not one to suffer from bridal nerves, so what really had precipitated this flight? Jasper slowly unlocked the drawer and opened it. There was Charles's letter to Georgiana just as he'd left it last night. Jasper didn't need to read it; the words were engraved in his mind.

Georgie

New Zealand is a splendid place and I've struck gold! We're going to be rich, wildly rich. I'm just writing to tell you this because I'm wretchedly ill and the doctor – an old pessimist – told me to set my affairs in order. So if I shouldn't make it, I want you to know that I've made my will out to you. You'll have to come out here to Dunedin, but the journey will be worth it. Of course, I've no intention of dying and missing out on the most glorious adventure of a lifetime, but I am stupidly weak. Will write again when I'm on the mend, but if you don't hear from me in six months, use the papers enclosed.

Charles

Georgiana had never seen the letter. It had arrived a few days earlier when she was out riding and, idly curious, Jasper had opened it, the seal being poorly fastened. That afternoon he'd proposed to Georgiana, with the letter and ownership papers in the pocket next to his heart.

Jasper stared at the letter now, thoughts in tumult. Surely she wouldn't have looked in the drawer. But how else to explain the key fallen from its hook? He had double-checked it as he always did when he'd last used it.

What on earth had made her decide right at this moment

to run away? After all, she couldn't have overheard his conversation with Lord Walsingham last night. Georgiana was not the sort to skulk at keyholes. She was far more likely to be out, roaming under the full moon as had been her custom when young. He recalled how Charles would wait for her at the bottom of the tree, both thinking none knew of their midnight adventures. Jasper had known but had kept their secret. Their exploits had amused him because they annoyed his step-mama so.

Apprehension mounting, Jasper crossed the room to the window. It had been hot last night and the windows had stood open as they'd played billiards – as they'd talked. Right outside was the oak tree Georgiana had always used to get to her bedroom above. Was that why she'd taken Jet? Had Sheba been tired after some midnight excursion?

Jasper drew his hand down his face. If she'd heard, then she would know everything. He would have to warn Walsingham and Walsingham would be livid. The mere thought of his employer's wrath made Jasper swallow, but his mind was moving swiftly. Not all was lost, not yet. Charles was almost certainly dead from his illness – Walsingham's assassin was surely just an unnecessary precaution. Jasper had never meant to bring harm to Charles. Everything with Walsingham had just got so out of hand – but it was no use thinking about it now. He had this appalling mess to sort out. Bloody girl. What the hell did she think she was up to? His fingers crushed the letter, but Jasper forced his mind to stay clear.

With Charles out of the picture – one way or another – he could talk Georgiana back into marriage. No woman could resist him and she'd be all alone in the world. He just needed to find her and not for a minute was he buying the story of the circus – he knew exactly where she was going. If he could beat her to New Zealand, be the shoulder for her to cry on when she discovered her brother was dead, all would be saved. It would. Feverishly reassuring himself, Jasper once more ran up the stairs to his step-mother, calling, 'I think I know where Georgiana is headed and I'm going there to bring her back.'

Chapter Four

Georgiana woke with a yelp the following morning when her hammock was flipped, tumbling her onto the boards below.

'Up you get, boy. The captain's on the foredeck, waiting for us.'

She scrubbed a hand over her face and staggered to her feet. The night in the hammock had left her feeling stiff. Her mouth was dry, she felt filthy, but otherwise she was still in one piece. She must have slept like the dead for she hadn't heard the sailors coming down to their hammocks, nor rising for their watch. Her nightmares had been vivid though, of dark chases and unknown assailants. Charlie had been there too, but always in the far distance and though she'd been screaming to him, he hadn't heard her warnings.

'Come along,' the sailor growled with a jerk of his head for her to follow. Despite his considerable girth, he was nimble as he threaded his way through the barrels and chests and judging by the pungent trail he left in his wake, Georgiana was not the only one in need of a wash.

On deck, Georgiana joined the jostling crowd of men. They were oblivious of her, but she couldn't help eyeing the brawny arms, the tattoos and the long tangled hair with some awe. Several men sported wicked looking scars, but the general feeling was of rough companionship which reminded her of the circus men she'd known as a child. From this she took small comfort.

A strong voice rose over the creaking of the timbers, the sound of wind and water. 'Right. Your attention, men.'

The crew immediately fell silent and Georgiana looked up to see Harry standing astride above them on the small foredeck. His black hair was tossing in the wind, which also moulded the soft, worn material of his shirt to his chest. Trousers rode loosely on his hips, his legs looking even longer than she'd remembered. Etched against a huge sky, he rode the pitching of the ship easily.

'Having set sail for New Zealand sooner than anticipated, we are now headed to Madeira where we'll pick up provisions.' He paused, his smile wry. 'I must tell you that I have made an enemy and left England with the law on my heels.'

There was laughter and catcalls.

'Nothing new in that, Cap'n.'

'Wha'? They still remember us from a few years back?'

Harry shook his head. 'No, this is unrelated to past activities. At this stage I am not prepared to say anything more except the stakes are high. If my mission to New Zealand is successful, I'll have enough money to restore *Sally* and there'll be double pay for everyone.'

The men sent up a cheer, but the captain sliced this with a swift chop of his hand. 'However,' he continued, 'I will not mislead you. My enemy is a powerful one and the odds are stacked heavily against us. If I fail, the voyage will have been for nothing and the coffers will be empty. Added to that, while I believe in the old girl,' and here he slapped the railings affectionately, '*Sally* is not, as you all well know, in the best of shape to go around the world. Therefore, if any of you would prefer a more secure future, I am happy to pay you out in Madeira.'

Mutterings and head shakes broke out around Georgiana and she frowned. Was the man mad? Honesty was all very well, but what if the crew took him up on his offer? Unknown missions with little chance of success might be the stuff of adventure novels, she thought as she hitched her brother's trousers a little higher, but they were hardly sensible undertakings in real life. If there was a mass exodus in Madeira, where would that leave her?

Then the seaman who'd woken Georgiana called out, 'Tisn't the first time we've left a port with the law chasing us, Cap'n, and it won't be the last. But you've never steered us false and I'm willing'—he looked around at the nodding heads—'we's all willing to stay.'

There was a general noise of agreement and a few 'hear, hears' tossed in.

Georgiana should have been relieved by this loyalty from such an unkempt, hardened crew. Instead she now had to wonder what sort of men they were to so enthusiastically embark on a wild goose chase to the other end of the world just because the captain – a man wanted by the law, no less – thought he might find an unspecified fortune in an unspecified way? Then Captain Trent – fists on hips, legs astride – looked down at his men and grinned.

Her breath hitched.

It was a grin that invited camaraderie, promised adventure. There was suddenly about him a reckless insouciance that reminded her of the heroes of her childhood: Raleigh, D'Artagnan, Robin Hood. A man who laughed at risk and danced with danger.

'Thanks, Bert, thanks all of you,' Harry cried out. 'To New Zealand it is, then!' and he raised his fist in a warrior gesture. 'May fair winds bless our voyage.'

The men cheered, punching the air above their heads, but as they quietened, Harry was serious as he added, '*Sally* and I are indeed lucky to have such a loyal crew. I assure you, I will not let you down.'

It was just a trick of the light, she knew, but it seemed at that moment he gazed straight down into her eyes and she experienced a strange breathlessness that had nothing whatsoever to do with the band tightly binding her breasts.

'Back to your duties.'

The men dispersed and this time she most definitely did catch the captain's attention, for he frowned down at her. 'I'd forgotten you, Master Miller. Come up here.'

Georgiana scrambled up the ladder, collecting her senses as she went. She was George. George the schoolboy. There could be *no* momentary lapses for the sake of a raffish grin. Charlie's life depended on it. Harry must never, even for a second, suspect anything.

It was not easy to maintain her masculine façade, however, as she looked into the captain's face and experienced a most decidedly feminine breathlessness all over again.

Piratical stubble darkened his long jawline and squared chin, though his high cheekbones and long nose lent his face a certain autocratic severity despite his careless appearance. But when she looked into his dark blue eyes she was dismayed to find the reckless adventurer seemed to have been replaced by a displeased school master.

'I can't think what madness made me bring you along last night, George. However, you are here now and you're about to find out what life on board is really like. It won't be pretty, I can tell you that now. The crew won't accept you for a start. They don't like little *gentlemen*.' Harry's own tone carried disparagement on the last word.

'But you're one.' The words were out before she could stop them.

For the briefest second, she thought she saw something flicker in his eyes. 'Not quite,' he said coolly, 'and not for many years. The men have long since learnt to accept me.'

'And they'll learn to accept me as well.'

He stared at her for a moment. She glared back. The corner of his mouth twitched.

'We shall see. So Master Miller, tell me now what use you can be. I take it you've never been out of England before?'

Georgiana shook her head.

'Nor on a ship before?'

'No.'

'Ever worked at anything apart from school books?'

She hesitated, then said, 'Not yet, but I'm about to.'

Humour sparked in his eyes, but his tone was pointed as he asked, 'Is there anything you *can* do?'

Georgiana thought for a second. 'I can climb.'

He nodded. 'Let's see you go up the main mast, to the crow's nest, then.'

She swarmed down the ladder, ran across the deck to the base of the mast and looked up. The crow's nest seemed very small in its wide frame of sky, but she remembered her father's advice.

'The height, it does not matter. It is all in your head. There is no difference between walking the rope a foot off the ground or thirty feet. Only your head and your heart tell you differently.'

Even as a young child, she had climbed the trapeze with her father to perform simple somersaults. Without hesitation, she began scaling the mast. Little Monkey was what her father used to call her, and as she went higher and higher up the rope ladder, Georgiana relished the sensation of stretch and balance. For once she was glad of her height and long limbs as she reached for secure foot and hand holds, trying to accommodate the unfamiliar rocking of the ship with every shift of her weight. The deck was far below, but she only noted the height with interest, not fear.

She swung herself into the crow's nest with a grunt of satisfaction and looked out. Below her the sails billowed while the sea and sky stretched seamless to the horizon. The breeze was steady and strong and she drew in a deep breath. Ashton Hall seemed a million miles away.

Impulse seized her and she pulled off her shoes before

climbing onto the railings of the crow's nest. For a second she squatted, getting the feel of the sway of the vessel. Then slowly, she stretched her arms out and rose to her feet. Her concentration was absolute and only very distantly was she aware that far, far below the crew had stopped work to watch. Eyes forward, Georgiana took a step, feeling the railing under her toes. She took another, then a few more. *Sally* shivered as it hit a larger swell, the reverberation carrying up the mast, amplifying as it went. Quick as a cat, she leapt back into the crow's nest.

Her descent was swift and within minutes she was back at the foot of the mast where the captain was waiting. Flushed with pride at having passed her first test, she couldn't help grinning. Some of the crew laughed, but Harry's eyes narrowed into furious slants of blue.

'What in all hell were you playing at, you little idiot? You could have killed yourself. What would've happened if you'd suddenly lost your nerve?'

'I wouldn't,' she assured him. 'My father made sure of that.'

'Your *father*?'

'Roderigo da Silva, the Human Swallow.'

Harry looked bewildered.

'Famous trapeze artist,' she added helpfully.

'Your father was a trapeze artist?' His tone was incredulous.

'I know, it seems a bit unbelievable,' began Georgiana.

'*A bit*?'

'But,' she continued, 'it's true. I was raised in a circus until I was twelve.'

Harry rubbed a hand over his eyes. 'George Miller, none of your stories makes sense. For a start, if your father was *da Silva*, how on earth can you be Miller?'

Aunt Ashton had made Charlie and her relinquish their father's name when they'd gone to live with her, replacing it with *Bellingham*, their mother's maiden name. They couldn't have such a heathenish surname, she told them. Georgiana took some pleasure in claiming it back now, even though it did not help her convince the captain of her identity.

'It was the first name that came into my mind. If I'd told you last night that my name was *da Silva*, you would never have believed it.'

Harry grunted and propped a shoulder against the mast, folding his arms across his chest. 'I'm not sure I believe you now. So your father was Portuguese?'

'Actually, he was born in Spain – but you know how it is with circus folk. They move around. I have no idea who my grandfather was on that side. My mother's side is different – English right back to the Domesday Book.'

His expression remained sceptical. 'Where are your parents now?'

'They're dead.' She spoke the words baldly. Even after all the years, she still found it hard to speak about. 'They both died when I was twelve. I've been raised by my aunt ever since.'

The captain's gaze was unwavering, but his voice was less brusque as he asked, 'So why are you running away?'

His eyes looked into hers, pulling her away from painful memories, back into this sunlit world. It must be the depth of colour, she thought, that made it seem that his eyes could look right into her soul.

'I'm not,' she began, but as his mouth tightened she modified her story. 'Well, not really. My brother truly is on the goldfields, but he's ill and I need to help him.'

'Does your aunt know where you are?'

'No.'

'She'll be mad with worry.'

'No, she won't. She always said she didn't deserve to be saddled with a couple of circus brats.'

Harry raised a brow. 'Is that what she called you?'

Georgiana shrugged. 'When she was angry.'

'And what did you do to provoke this anger?'

'Nothing!'

Now both brows arched. The captain was clearly not a man to be fobbed off with half-baked replies.

'Well nothing serious at any rate,' Georgiana amended. 'For instance, she once became furious when the groom caught Charlie and me walking along the ridge of the stable roof.'

'Such behaviour might indeed be cause for some concern,' Harry suggested.

'It wasn't *dangerous*, if that's what you mean. We could have done it blindfolded. Besides, we hadn't deliberately set out to annoy her – we were just practising our tightrope skills.'

Harry shook his head. 'One of you, I can already see, is a handful. Two brats must have been a nightmare, poor woman.'

Despite the severity of his tone, Georgiana saw humour glint in his eyes and couldn't help smiling back. 'She certainly made it clear there was no pleasure in raising us.' Then she became serious again. 'Even so, she was appalled when my brother went to New Zealand. She'd never have allowed me to join him.'

The humour had disappeared. She could see the captain was still unconvinced.

'Can't you see, I *had* to run away. He hasn't got anyone else to help him.' To her horror, her voice caught in her throat. Drawing herself up, she added half-defiant, half-imploring, 'You'd do the same for your brother – anyone would.'

For a second Harry went absolutely still as he stared out over the ocean. It was as though he'd forgotten all about her, but when he did turn back, she was surprised by the bleak intensity of his expression.

'I've never known what it is to have a brother,' he said. 'Perhaps you are right – blood ties may prove thicker than I know.' He paused, then became brisk. 'This madcap adventure of yours will lead you into all sorts of trouble, you know.'

Georgiana squared her shoulders. 'I'm not afraid.'

The captain was unimpressed. 'That just shows how rash and foolish you are. Still,' he said as he straightened up from the mast, 'seeing as you're hell-bent on going, I'll take you to New Zealand.'

Relief flooded her. 'Thank you!'

Her errant heart fluttered too, though she tried to ignore it.

'But,' he added sternly 'you'll work hard, learn the ropes and not do anything foolhardy. There are many ways to die at sea without pulling stupid stunts. Understood?'

'*Absolutely.*'

Amused curiosity crept into the captain's eyes as he stuck his thumbs into his belt. 'By the way, how did you sort things with your aunt?'

'I left a note saying I'd run away to my old circus.'

Again he surveyed her. 'You are nothing if not enterprising, but do you have any regard for the truth?'

She was affronted. 'Of course. Apart from my name, everything I've told you is the truth.' And it was, she comforted herself. She'd just omitted some details ...

Harry glanced sideways at her. 'Hm, time will tell. In the meanwhile you can learn to swab the deck as soon as you've eaten. Go find Alec in the galley.'

Harry scratched his throat as he watched George go. There was something indefinable about the boy that made him uneasy. In many ways he was no different from a dozen other such lads Harry had met on his travels, runaways in search of adventure. George was a particularly engaging example of these scamps. He was still young and stupid enough to be fearless, though there was a resolution about him that was interesting. But it was more than that. With this boy Harry felt a strange bond that was almost unsettling.

He well understood how George and his brother would have provoked the aunt. Society ran on a web of invisible social codes, incomprehensible to those who had not been raised with them. Harry vividly remembered the shock of being whisked from his humble cottage to boarding life at Harrow when he'd been twelve. He'd had to learn quickly all the basics of life again: how to dress, how to talk, how to walk, even how to eat to avoid unwanted attention and disapproval. It appeared George and his brother had been neither so sensible nor so compliant.

You'd do the same for your brother – anyone would.

Young Miller was wrong. Most lads would have neither the courage nor the resourcefulness to undertake such a foolhardy expedition. Yet despite the boy's brave front, Harry had heard the catch in his voice, had seen the stricken look in his eyes. His brother really was all he had in a world that cared little for orphans.

Why then did his gut still warn him of trouble? The brat, with his expressive face and steady grey eyes, seemed guileless yet Harry's instincts were on alert. He knew deep down he should have just left the boy at the tavern.

Enough! Harry shook his head. He didn't have time to waste on a scruffy schoolboy. He'd keep an eye on young George but beyond that – well, time had a way of unravelling deceits.

Unbidden, images of subterfuge and betrayal rose in his mind and his hands tightened on the railings till his knuckles were white. Then he let out a long, slow breath.

Like a game of cards, life had to be played lightly.

A consummate player, Harry well knew that a man who

has nothing to lose can risk everything. For that reason he made it a policy not to care about anything – anyone – in his life. Except for *Sally* and his crew of course.

Yet ever since his fateful visit to Iver two days earlier had set off this lamentable chain of events, he'd been plagued by damnable feelings he did not want to confront.

You'd do the same for your brother.

Harry winced. Then he thought of the hovel which his gentle mother had called home and the bile rose in his throat. Turning, he looked up at the sails which were as threadbare and patched as a fisherman's trews. He knew of a dozen boards in *Sally*'s hull that had needed replacing over a year ago. Sailing the old girl now was a gamble, an enormous gamble. No one would buy her in her current state – she was ripe to be sunk. Yet the thought of her valiant decks wrecked upon the ocean floor squeezed his heart.

He scrubbed a hand over his face. Nothing needed to be decided yet. First he'd go to New Zealand and seek out his man. Then he could choose whether to follow through and become a rich man, thus saving *Sally* and his crew, or walk away – a poorer but better man.

He looked out over the water. The sea behind them was empty, his pursuers left many miles behind. Still the hair on the back of his neck prickled …

Fortified by cold porridge, Georgiana learnt to swab the deck. It took a while to do, but it wasn't so difficult, she thought as she stood back to admire her handiwork.

'Get rid o' tha' bucket o' water 'fore someone steps in it,' a seaman growled, jerking a thumb to the railings.

Picking up the bucket, she threw the water over the side of the vessel, only to have it promptly blown straight back, saturating her. Gasping, she still thought to pluck the sodden shirt away from her body so her bound breasts wouldn't be seen by the laughing crew. Humiliation took the form of attack and she rounded on the grinning men.

'You knew. Why didn't you warn me?'

One old seaman with an empty eye socket laughed. 'Consider yourself baptised. Ye'll not throw anything over the windward side again, will ye?'

Dirty water ran down her face from her hair. It smelt awful. Out of the corner of her eye she saw Harry, further down the deck, pause in his conversation. She forced a laugh. 'No, that's one lesson learnt.'

Harry gave a brief nod before turning back to Stephen, the helmsman. It was stupid, but this casual gesture of approval sparked a warm feeling in her heart as she wrung out the tails of her shirt and shook her head like a dog.

Still, the crew wasn't about to let the new boy off quite so easily. For the rest of the day Georgiana received a number of cuffs as the sailors sought to speed up her learning of the sails, sheets and winches. And it worked, she noted, rubbing her head after a blow which had sent her staggering for not noticing a rope trailing off the side of the deck. She'd never do that again.

By dinnertime, she was ravenous even though the glutinous stew didn't look appetising. Georgiana carried her plate to the table where the rest of the crew were already tucking in and squeezed next to Bert. Some glanced up and there was a strange air of jovial anticipation. Eric, a boy of about sixteen, was grinning.

'Tuck in, lad,' said Bert.

Suspicious, Georgiana picked up her spoon. The stew looked grey in the dim light, but she took a mouthful. Something squirmed on her tongue. She shrieked and spat it out, shuddering as a fat weevil crawled to the edge of the plate. The men erupted with laughter.

'What's the matter, boy? Doncha like fresh meat?' asked Bert. 'You've got yourself an Alec special there.'

She stirred the stew, seeing movement all through it.

'Eat the lot, or Alec won't be pleased.' Eric seemed delighted to have a new boy to take the brunt of the jokes.

She lay down her spoon. 'I'm not very hungry.'

'What – food not good enough for you? Or d'you need one of them butler men to help you? I'll feed you meself, fancy boy, if you can't manage.'

Georgiana looked across into Mack's small eyes and a thin, very cold trickle of fear went down her spine. Most of the crew were rough, but she sensed an underlying malice in Mack. The other men waited. They didn't seem to care if she ate or not, but clearly they wouldn't come to her rescue, either. Pulling the plate back in front of her, she picked up the spoon and took a mouthful. She couldn't bear chewing and it was hard to swallow. She retched, her eyes watering, but somehow she got it down.

Mack gave an ugly grin. 'That's it. All of it.'

She took another mouthful, coughed and retched. Think of Charlie, she told herself. Think of him. Doggedly she kept her head down, though out of the corner of her eye she saw Mack looking sour as she battled on. Just as she got to the final mouthful, Bert clapped her on the back, nearly sending her face down into her plate.

'Well done, lad. Lots of goodness in them critters. A few more of 'em and you'll be as big as me.'

He gave her a friendly grin that was minus several teeth. Mack gave no sign he'd noticed at all.

After dinner, the air soon became clogged with pipe smoke, causing Georgiana to cough.

'Here lad, take a shot of rum to clear the throat.'

She didn't want to but took the cup and dashed down a gulp with what, she hoped, would pass for boyish enthusiasm. It did not so much clear the throat as strip it raw and her subsequent choking was everything the grinning crew had hoped for.

'Go on,' Pete urged. 'Take another sip and drown the little bleeders in your stomach.'

But Georgiana, wiping her eyes, shook her head and held up her hand. 'I'm not about to provide the entertainment all the evening,' she said hoarsely.

'Oh but you are,' said Bert. 'New crew always does something to show what they're made of. Play the fiddle. Dance. Sing. Wrestle with one of the crew. You want to take on Big Jack here? Great odds offered.'

Georgiana's heart sank. What on earth could she possibly do? Her only talent was acting. Then she smiled and nodded. Shifting her position, she gave the impression of arthritic knees. Her face fell into dour lines and, squinting ferociously, she mimed trying to thread a needle.

'Why, it's One-Eyed Pete mending sails!' cried Eric, and the crew's laughter bounced off the beams.

'Go on lad, do another.'

She thought for a minute then rose, pretending to stir a pot. She gave a phlegmy cough, dropped invisible food on the floor then scooped it up, plopping it back into the stew. With a backhanded wipe to her nose, she bellowed, 'Dinner's up you good-for-nothings.'

The men fell about, eyes streaming with laughter.

'He's got your number, Alec,' wheezed Bert.

Harry dropped down the hatch, landing light as a cat. 'What's all the fun?'

'Ye must see the laddie – he's got a wicked talent, cheeky devil,' said Alec. 'Do another for the captain.'

Georgiana became a chunky boy creeping into the galley.

'It's Eric about to steal some biscuit,' cried Big Jack, 'I've seen him thieving a thousand times.'

Georgiana straightened and, pretending to be abashed, scratched her rump. Eric reddened as the laughter once more resounded and he received some good-hearted cuffs. Georgiana was happy to see Harry laughing, too.

'You've a fine talent there, brat. Let's see more.'

For the next half-hour Georgiana took off a number of crew and there were even cries for repeats but finally she pleaded, 'Enough. I'm worn out.'

'Yes, it's time for everyone to be turning in,' said Harry.

'You too, captain,' Alec said. 'You look worn to a rag.'

Harry stood and stretched. 'Bed will be good,' he admitted. 'There are a couple of things to attend to first, though.'

As he disappeared up the ladder, Alec watched him go with a shake of his head. 'Bad business,' he muttered, and Georgiana wondered again what crime the captain had committed. Who was the enemy he spoke of? The crew's easy acceptance of last night's escape did not alleviate her unease, though as yet she'd seen nothing to enhance it either.

The rest of the men were stringing up hammocks and Georgiana's skin prickled with a new apprehension. Would they undress? Would she be expected to? Why oh why had she fallen so fast asleep the night before? Hands clumsy with nerves, she busied herself with her own hammock as she watched surreptitiously. But as the hammocks were secured, the seamen rolled into them, many of them still fully clothed. Relieved, she soon had her own up, and worn out, she tumbled into it.

She did not fall asleep at once, however. Memories of the day crowded in and she was overwhelmed by overlapping images of decking and sails and ropes and sailors and barrels and buckets. A new world looped within a perfectly circular horizon, under the command of an autocratic captain whose smile could stop her breath. An almost forgotten emotion nudged at her and when she examined it, she realised it was, astonishingly and contrary to all evidence, hope. With a sigh, she stretched out long, clasped her griffin and fell asleep.

Chapter Five

Over the next few days Georgiana fell into the rhythms of shipboard life. She discovered that she loved sailing, loved the motion under her feet, the dome of sky and the endless stretches of ocean. Sometimes she threw her head back and drew in great breaths as though to rid her lungs of the last of the stifling air of Ashton Hall.

The underlying fear she'd betray herself was slipping away as daily she became more confident in her masquerade. Her use of the very unsavoury head, rather than relieving herself over the side of the ship as the crew did, was put down to her class and incited many ribald comments aimed to make a well-bred boy blush. The snores, belches and farts astounded her, but she was so exhausted at the end of each day that she just tumbled into her hammock and passed out.

Several days passed before they noticed she never stripped down to the waist on deck, as they did, for a daily wash. Harry insisted on a degree of personal cleanliness for each man and in return he ensured his crew didn't suffer from scurvy. It was seen as a fair trade though the crew thought him overscrupulous.

'Oi lad, niver seen you washing,' one-eyed Pete called out on the third morning.

'I did just now, on your blind side.'

'Come to think about it, you never wash,' said Bert.

'Can't in this cold wind,' said Georgiana, punching her breastbone. 'Weak lungs.'

'That explains your pitiful thin chest. You need to grow some muscles, lad.'

'Come here boy – time for a dunking,' said Big Jack, swinging up a bucket, but Georgiana dodged sideways and swarmed up the ratlines to perch on one of the yardarms, laughing at the older man who was far too heavy to come in pursuit.

'I'll get you later, young George,' he called up, but she knew he was only teasing.

Georgiana had fitted into the crew with relative ease for she was a quick learner and what she lacked in physical strength she made up for in spirit and was fearless aloft. Having endured constant rejections in the ballroom these past few years, she now basked in the grudging acceptance of the crew.

Jack put the bucket down and the men began to go about their chores so she descended from the rigging, dropping onto a barrel. Old memories stirred and, tensing her muscles, she did a back flip onto the deck. The men paused and a few laughed.

'You're a proper little monkey, you are,' said Bert. 'Go on, show us what else you can do.'

Her performer's blood stirred. Georgiana did two handspring somersaults – not easy on the cramped deck. She rose, a little breathless and giddy, to find Harry in front of her.

'The circus?'

She nodded. 'But I'm out of practice. When I was a child I could do six or seven at a time.'

He grinned, tousling her hair. 'You're still a child.'

'Not such a child,' she thought, as he sauntered over to Stephen. He said something and they both laughed. As always, he was dressed in salt-marked trousers, his shirt sleeves loosely rolled. His thick black hair was windblown, but he'd shaved this morning and Georgiana had the strangest impulse to run her finger along that strong jaw.

Unconsciously, she touched her hair where his fingers had been. Then she shook herself. *Stop that! He's the* captain *and you are nothing but a grubby schoolboy playing at being a sailor, George, my boy.*

These were words she'd told herself not just once but a score of times these past few days. The captain was, to put it frankly, a distraction. He was the fly in her ointment, the spanner in her works. She was vividly aware of him and whenever his shadow touched hers – as it did a dozen times a day – cracks threatened her carefully created façade.

Resolutely putting unruly thoughts from her mind, she picked up the bucket Jack had abandoned and swung it over the side of the ship to get more water. Scrubbing the deck was not hard, but it presented challenges in manoeuvring around the busy crew and the detritus that tended to strew the decks of a small working ship. Today someone had left a large barrel in her path which she tried to shift, her fingers scrabbling to find purchase on the fat, smooth sides.

'Out the way, George.' Harry was back beside her. 'You'll never move that.'

Harry always seemed to be everywhere at once, throwing himself into the hard physical side of work alongside the men: hauling on sheets, stacking the hold. Now she watched as he hoisted the barrel to his shoulder. His knees braced, Harry shifted weight until it was balanced then walked with lithe grace across the deck. She couldn't help but notice the play of muscles down his back under the worn shirt, the easy stretch of his long limbs.

'Thanks, Captain,' she called out in a gruff voice as he set it down and the offhand smile he tossed at her before he walked away again made unfamiliar but delicious things happen in her stomach. Sighing, she picked up the scrubbing brush and set to her task with frustrated energy.

Her guise was, she had to acknowledge, invaluable in more ways than one. Harry treated George with casual approval, but Georgiana, she knew, would have been overlooked for more beautiful girls. She could almost hear her aunt's querulous voice. *'If you don't learn to act like a lady, you will never attract a gentleman.'*

Was Harry a gentleman?

Georgiana still found it hard to place him. He had the voice and manner of a lord, but these were belied by his dishevelled appearance and his profession. Yet though he was only a sea captain while she was Miss Bellingham of Ashton Hall, he was far out of her league.

Self-hatred needled her heart. Even her own cousin would only marry her for gold. A man like Harry would never see anything in a girl like her. Better by far to stay George forever, she thought bitterly. Then, with a shrug, she managed a smile. After all, George was having a far more exciting time than Georgiana'd ever had in the past seven years.

As she was finishing up, Alec shouted, 'George, get me more salt. Move your arse, boy. I haven't got all day.'

Fetching things from the hold was one job she didn't like and she grimaced. The air was fetid down in the bowels of the ship, and as she descended into the darkness she could hear the scurry of rats. Georgiana groped her way through the barrels and had just reached the sacks with salt when she heard a heavy person drop into the hold behind her.

'What are you doing down here, fancy boy?'

Mack's voice was low and oily. The air down the hold suddenly seemed thicker; the rats fell silent. Georgiana backed away though she kept her own voice neutral. 'Just getting some salt for Alec.'

'Not thieving?'

She could see him approaching in the gloom, his bulk blocking out the thin ribbon of light that spilled down the ladder behind him.

'Of course not.'

'You could be punished for having your fingers where they don't belong.' His voice rasped with menace. 'Don't do for fancy boys to go where they didn't ought.'

Georgiana felt the damp side of the hold at her back, trapping her. Mack stepped closer and the sour stench of his sweat stung in her nostrils. Above she could hear footsteps and a man whistling, but he could have been a million miles away. Her heart was suddenly too big for her chest and air squeezed out of her lungs. Still, she strove to sound normal.

'You can get the salt if you prefer, but we'd better be quick. Alec doesn't like to be kept waiting.'

Mack hissed and moved even closer, his breath hot on her face. 'You telling me what to do? I'm not one of your lackeys, boy. We aren't in your world now.'

Georgiana pressed back hard against the timbers and hunched her shoulders as she saw his hand clench. His fist rose with the slow, deliberate control of a bully out to extract every ounce of fear. Her breath caught as violent images surged into her mind, Mack jumping on her fallen body and discovering—

The sailor's fist was now in direct line with her face, his arm pulled well back to maximise the punch. Georgiana flung up her arms to ward off the impending blow at the very moment a voice, brisk and impatient, called down the ladder.

'Mack, I need you on deck now!'

Swift as a snake, his hand shot to her neck, pinioning her. Her throat constricted and convulsed, but it was impossible to make a sound as Mack called back, 'Aye, Captain.' But in the gloom she saw his glittering eyes had not left her face for a second. With his free hand, he placed his finger to his lips, not that it was necessary. In a malevolent undertone he added for good measure, 'Not a peep out of you. Understand?' She nodded, fighting to swallow. His words curdled almost soundlessly in the stale air. 'We'll talk again later, cos we aren't finished, you and me.'

'Oh but you are.'

The voice was very soft and spoken directly into Mack's ear. With an oath, Mack spun around to find Harry right behind him. Georgiana was startled too, not having heard or seen the captain's descent.

Harry's voice continued soft but threaded with threat. 'No member of my crew is to be harassed at any time, in any way. Is that understood?'

Mack was silent.

'Is that understood?'

Each word was spoken with icy deliberation and though they were not aimed at her, Georgiana shivered. The piratical menace in the captain's voice was even more frightening than Mack's threats.

'Understood,' Mack muttered.

Harry stayed very close for another second, then stepped back. 'Take the salt with you to Alec.'

Without a word, Mack stooped and swung the bag of salt onto his shoulder. Head averted, he made his way to the ladder and disappeared up into the square of sunlight.

Harry turned back to Georgiana, still flattened against the sides of the hold. Her knees threatened to buckle as she fought a craven desire to sink down and burst into tears. She forced herself to stay upright but couldn't raise her head to face Harry. Humiliation, fear and relief were all too raw to expose to his searching gaze. When Harry spoke, his voice had returned to its normal tone.

'It won't happen again on my ship, but George, you're going to have to learn to look out for yourself. The only way to deal with threats is to meet them head on.'

Georgiana felt strangely ashamed. George would have been braver – but Georgiana couldn't afford to be.

A strong hand came down onto her shoulder and squeezed it. 'Don't look so crestfallen, boy. Mack is a lot bigger. Still, you are going to need to toughen up and learn to keep your wits about you.' Then he gave her a friendly shake. 'Get along, now. Pete needs a hand with the ropes and I've a pile of papers awaiting my attention.'

For Harry the incident was clearly over, but Georgiana was still shaken. If the captain hadn't been there ... Such a narrow escape. Yet how had Harry known? Bert said nothing on *Sally* slipped Harry's notice and so it seemed. She'd have to be doubly careful – not only of the crew but of Harry's uncanny instincts as well.

It was a relief being back in the open again and Georgiana gradually regained her equilibrium as she sat in the sunshine with Pete, learning to splice ropes.

'How long have you been with the captain?'

Pete grunted. 'Nigh on three years.' Though his fingers were as thick as sausages, they were deft in their movements. After a pause he added, 'Won us all, he did – *Sally* and crew – in a game of cards in South America.' Georgiana made a disbelieving sound and Pete squinted at her with his one eye. 'Don't believe me?'

'Go on then, tell me how it happened.'

'We-ell, at the time he'd hardly tuppence to rub together, picking up work where he could get it in almost every corner of the world, far as I could tell. Anyway, he got into a game of poker with our Captain Belcher – a mean old bastard if ever there was one. They was both used to winning and as the night wore on they drank more and more and the money kept passing between them. Then Cap'n Trent hit a winning streak, massing up all the money they both had in one pile in front of him and he said, 'I'll bet it all against your ship.'

'Now Belcher, he could never resist the promise of a quick

win. 'All right,' he said, 'but if you win, you take the stinkin' crew wiv you. I'm not paying 'em off.'

'Agreed!' said the cap'n.'

'He risked everything?' Georgiana was incredulous. 'But he could have been left penniless again.'

'Aye, he could. But that's how he lives life, laddie. He risks everything for what he wants. No price is too high when he's a mind for something.' He shrugged and grinned. 'Such pigheadedness usually pays off for the cap'n and it did this time too. It was close, but he won. *Sally – The Lady Sarah,* really – is nuffing more than an old tub, but he won't hear a word against her. The love of his life, he reckons. Mind, she's bound for Davey Jones' locker if some repairs aren't made soon. The cap'n doesn't say a lot, but I know it plagues him.'

Georgiana held her splice out for Pete to check and was surprisingly proud of the curt nod it received. 'How does he intend to find money in New Zealand, do you think? Surely he isn't thinking of gold mining.'

Pete blew out through his lips. 'I've been wondering that, meself. Whatever he's up to must be important or he'd never risk *Sally* in them southern oceans. But it ain't like the cap'n to be so secretive.'

The garrulous sailor didn't seem to mind questions so, as though only mildly interested, she asked, 'Any idea why the law is after him?'

Pete shook his head and grimaced. 'Damned if I know that either. It's not the first time of course, but he was only on shore for not but a couple o' days. Wouldn't have thought a man could get into that much trouble in so short a time.' Then he shot her a look. 'Still, it's not our business, boy, and the cap'n will see us right. There's never been a tight corner he hasn't been able to pull us out of. He has the luck of the devil, that one.'

He seemed unperturbed and Georgiana couldn't help asking, 'Have you always had such faith in the captain?'

Pete's eyebrows quirked. 'Nope. At first, some of us didn't trust Cap'n Trent's nice-talking ways at all. Twice men challenged him and in both cases the cap'n sorted it out, one on one.' He chuckled. 'He had them over the side of the ship in no time. Niver seen any fighting so quick and efficient-like.'

She laughed. 'What happened to them?'

'One was left in Brazil – resented losing too much. T'other' – he glanced sideways at Georgiana – 'was me. I'm happy to stay with a cap'n what can beat me in a fair fight.' He paused then added, ''sides, I'd rather have the captain on me side than against me. He's not one to be trifled with.'

Georgiana's thoughts winged back to the hold; his silent speed, the naked threat in his voice. 'I can imagine.'

'Aye, some are deceived by his gentleman manner, but the cap'n is a dangerous man when someone gets in his way.'

What would the captain do with a girl who had tricked him?

'Does he get very angry?' she asked in a small voice.

Pete shook his head. 'No, that's what makes him so dangerous. He's one who fights from the head, not the heart, see. He has a temper, but when it really counts, he goes as cold and hard as steel. He don't go looking for trouble, but trouble usually finds him. He's got a nose for it though, smells it as it sneaks up on him, then he deals to it, quick and final.'

She could hear the admiration in Pete's voice, but anxiety prevented her from sharing it and Georgiana decided she really did not need to know one thing more about how the captain coped with trouble. She changed the subject.

'What sort of cargo does *Sally* carry usually?'

Pete shrugged. 'All sorts. Whatever the cap'n can pick up.

We did a fair bit of smuggling in the early days.' His eye gleamed, then he sighed. 'But the need for smuggling fell away and 'sides, the cap'n was restless – he's like the wind, that one – so off we went to the far ends of the earth. We're a small ship so we can take the ends of consignments or small, one-off jobs. It's taken us to some pretty strange places – the West Indies, Australia, Shanghai.'

A shadow fell over them and Eric stood over them.

'The captain wants you in his cabin immediately, George.'

Her heart bucked against her ribs. Had he guessed her masquerade?

Chapter Six

Filled with trepidation, Georgiana knocked at the door, but when Harry bade her enter her fears were instantly allayed. He was mopping piles of papers which sat in pools of wine on the table. His shirt, stained red, clung to his chest.

He glanced up, eyes narrowed in annoyance. 'Eric, the bloody idiot, has just knocked a decanter of wine all over me and my paperwork. The writing has begun to run as you can see and I want you to make more copies before they're illegible. You did learn that much at your lessons, I take it.' She nodded and he grunted, 'Well, at least we've found another use for you. Here, take over while I change.'

As she took the cloth from him she saw it was a large handkerchief with the monogram HT embroidered in one corner. It was clearly a labour of love and she was surprised by a stab of a new emotion as her fingers turned to claws around it.

Harry saw her examining it as he put his hands to the back of his collar and began to pull the wine-stained shirt over his head. 'My mother was a seamstress and monogrammed all my handkerchiefs when I went to school.' His voice was slightly muffled by the cloth. 'I was teased unmercifully and hated them, but now she's dead, I can't bring myself to throw them out, threadbare as they are these days.'

Georgiana scarcely heard his words. Unlike most young women her age, she was well acquainted with male bodies. Growing up in the circus, she was used to seeing the torsos of working men and acrobats. Practising gymnastics with Charles had brought her a clear understanding of the differences between men and women, especially when one day she'd accidentally kicked him between the legs. There were also the daily sluice-downs of the crew on deck.

But this was different. As his shirt rose, she glimpsed his taut stomach, the broad lines of his chest, the bands of rib and sternum overlaid by lines of muscle. Then the captain's head emerged and Georgiana, cheeks hot, looked hurriedly away and began mopping the wine.

'What school were you at?' she asked, fighting to keep her voice casual.

'Harrow.'

'But how on earth did—' she broke off, realising it was not the place of the youngest crew member to question his captain. Harry, however, did not seem to mind.

'—the son of a penniless seamstress go to such an illustrious school?'

She nodded, as she continued to wipe, not trusting herself to speak. Her tongue had a worrying way of running ahead of prudence.

'We are not so different, George, you and I,' he continued. 'We were both whisked out of one world and dropped into another.'

Georgiana glanced up and for the briefest second their looks tangled. After so many years of being viewed as an oddity, the seduction of being understood was almost too strong to resist, and she immediately dropped her eyes. If she wasn't very, very careful, she'd be blurting the whole truth before she knew it.

Luckily, Harry seemed to take her silence for boyish reticence. As he balled his shirt and flung it into a corner, he changed the subject. 'You've a long job there thanks to Eric, the clumsy oaf! I should use his hide to scrub the keel. I was up all hours last night doing this tedious stuff and was just putting the finishing touches to it when he ruined the lot.'

He strolled over to rummage in a chest and Georgiana

paused in her mopping to steal a look at the lean lines of his back, the long indentation of his spine as he pulled out a shirt and shrugged into it, tucking it into the waist of his trousers. He turned to her.

'I can't face doing it all again. Up to the task, brat?'

He'd taken to sometimes calling her that, his teasing tone robbing it of all its previous sting. In fact, in some strange way, it had formed a bond between them.

'Absolutely,' she said promptly, 'but …' and she stopped and grinned.

Harry cocked a brow. 'But?'

'Alec told me to clean out the bilges when I finished the ropes.'

Harry laughed. 'Ah, the perfect job for Eric! Seems the boy has done you a favour. Now, here's the pen, ink and paper,' he said, putting them in front of her. 'I'll be back later to see how you are going.'

For the next hour Georgiana recorded cargo deliveries and ship stores. It was not always easy to read the sodden pages. The wine had washed away some of the firm but flourishing handwriting. One page was particularly hard to make out so she took the paper over to the porthole to see it better. A shelf of books to the right, caught her eye. Virgil, Plato and Horace all had the look of well-read books. There was also a book of verse which included poems by Byron, Wordsworth and Shelley. She smiled. Was the captain a secret romantic? Then she noticed several Shakespeare – *Much Ado about Nothing*, *Macbeth*, *Richard the Third*, *Twelfth Night*. With a glad cry, she took the last from the shelf and began scanning it.

At that moment Harry walked in and said with an edge in his voice, 'I don't remember including reading in my orders.'

Georgiana jumped and dropped the book with a clatter.

'Careless, too,' Harry said as he bent to pick it up. He glanced at the title and was surprised. '*Twelfth Night*?'

'Sorry, Captain. I shouldn't have touched them, I know. I came over to the light to read that page,' she indicated to the abandoned sheet, 'but your books caught my attention.'

Harry eyed her as he propped against the table. 'Are you a reader, George?'

She felt uncomfortable under his gaze and decided honesty was the best policy. Little escaped Harry. 'I enjoy it, yes. Particularly plays.'

'Even Shakespeare?'

'Especially Shakespeare.'

'Hm.' He regarded her for a minute. 'Unusual choice for a schoolboy.'

She felt her cheeks flame. 'Poetry is unusual for a captain.'

He lifted a brow. 'Why? Do you think captains care only for seas and sails?'

There it was again, that autocratic hauteur, despite his shabby clothes and lines of humour in his face. Georgiana, ever alert as an actress, couldn't identify what it was. The set of the shoulders? The timbre in his deep voice? No, she thought, it was something more profound. It was as though the ability to lead and command were ingrained in him.

'I can understand the pleasure the *Odyssey* might have for you,' she said, 'but I confess I was surprised to see the sonnets. I hadn't pegged you as a romantic, Captain.'

This made Harry smile. 'No, I would certainly not describe myself as one, either. I don't read them often but my father gave them to my mother.' His fingers touched the anthology as he spoke. 'She told me to always keep them safe.'

'Oh, I thought perhaps you might ...'

'What? Have a love in my life that I sigh over when reading the poems? Not a chance of it. I have nothing to offer a wife. I'm a captain and a woman has no place on a ship.'

Georgiana forced a laugh. 'You don't think so?'

'Absolutely not! This is a working ship. Having a woman around would be courting trouble in all sorts of ways. For a start, the crew believes women bring bad luck to a ship.' Georgiana winced but Harry didn't notice as he tapped his chest in light self-mockery, '*Sally* has complete possession of my heart, you know, and she won't surrender her sovereignty easily. Besides, no woman with proper sensibilities would enjoy a life at sea.'

Proper sensibilities? She should just get over her infatuation right now, for as her aunt would no doubt have been happy to point out, Georgiana had never had a proper sensibility in her whole life.

'Some might find it a wonderful adventure.'

She herself could think of nothing more splendid.

Harry shook his head as he rose from the table and crossed to the bookshelf, replacing the play. 'No lady could, nor should be asked to tolerate the discomforts and dangers of ship life. Only a man lacking every bit of consideration would expect his wife to traipse around the world with him. Keep that in mind when you begin growing face hair, George. Women are a softer sex and need looking after.'

He was right next to her and she didn't know whether to step back or obey her desire to get even closer. Harry smelt of the sea and the wind. 'Surely not all of them.'

'All of them!' Harry said with finality as he propped a shoulder against the panelled wall of the cabin. Then he looked at her more closely and changed the subject. 'So why do you like plays?'

Georgiana hesitated. It was dangerous, she knew, but the urge was strong to share with the captain that which was dearest to her heart. 'I love acting. I used to sneak out of my aunt's house at night to act in a neighbouring town.'

'George! You were obviously a trial to your aunt. Couldn't

you just tell this hapless relative of yours what you were up to?'

She shook her head, resisting the urge to smile back into his blue eyes where laughter lurked. 'You have no idea how impossible it would have been for her to accept the notion of her nie-ephew acting in a town hall for farmers.'

'Shakespeare for farmers?'

'No, alas. I read those plays for pleasure and would dearly love to try them. The plays I was in were all rollicking adventures. *Pirates of the Main, Dick the Highwayman* that sort of thing – plays with plenty of action. I was usually the hero,' she concluded, casting her eyes down modestly.

Harry gave a shout of laughter. 'Yes, I can just see you swinging from the rafters, George. But how on earth did you come to be an actor in the first place?'

'Chance. I was out riding on the far end of the woods near my aunt's house and came upon a small town.' Deliberately Georgiana left out the name. 'I happened to see a notice cancelling the afternoon's performance due to an actor's illness so offered my services. They were desperate and I fitted the bill. I learn lines fast and I'm quick on cues.'

What George couldn't tell Harry was that the manager had first laughed uproariously at the young lady's suggestion, but when she cajoled him into letting her say a few lines for him, he'd been convinced. She was the best actor he'd ever seen and her height and athleticism allowed her to play male roles far more convincingly than the wooden young man he had been using. He agreed to keep her identity secret and was quick to shake hands on the arrangement. It was only later that she realised she hadn't even thought to discuss payment.

He had, however, provided her with several disreputable caps to cover her hair, and dressed in Charlie's cast-off shirts and trousers she had been able to attend rehearsals with no one suspecting her true identity.

For six joyous months Georgiana went to rehearsals under the pretence of going for long rides and on the weekends she went to bed early so she could sneak out, down the oak tree by her bedroom window. Dressed as a boy, she would ride to the theatre where she played to cheering audiences and it had all been a grand adventure right up until that fateful night when she'd overheard Jasper talking to Walsingham …

'Well, that explains the mimicry and your quick thinking in the tavern when you picked up my cards,' said Harry. Then he looked at her with narrowed eyes. 'And yet there is still something about you, George, that I can't make out.'

She felt the colour rise in her cheeks and suddenly the light from the porthole seemed too bright, the cabin walls too close. The floor tipped and tilted under her feet with the motion of the ship. Too late she regretted her impulse to confide. Striving to sound offhand, she replied, 'I'm just a boy who likes acting, nothing more. Now, I've finished all the papers save for that one there, and I should probably go to the galley – Alec told me he has a sack of potatoes reserved for my attention.'

Harry's blue eyes held hers and she tried to be guileless as she returned his look. He wasn't fooled.

'Secrets, George,' he warned her, 'have a way of coming out at the most inconvenient time.' She remained silent so, with a wave of his hand, he dismissed her. 'Go on. Cut along to Alec.'

As the door closed behind George, Harry looked down at the papers the boy had handed him. He wrote well, though his writing was a trifle careless as could be expected of a schoolboy. Yet when the lad had spoken of acting it had not been with a child's enthusiasm but with the passion of someone more mature. He thought about the way George's eyes had lit up, his face glowing.

Such a curious mix of parts, this child. He could climb to the outer reaches of the rigging without curling a hair yet also loved Shakespeare. And though he answered all Harry's questions readily enough, he always seemed to be keeping something back. Again Harry wondered what the youth was really up to. Clearly he had no regrets for the life he'd left behind and Harry smiled, shaking his head, as he imagined the aunt trying in vain to instil gentlemanly behaviour into a couple of circus brats.

The affinity he felt for the boy surprised him. The sense of protectiveness which had begun in the tavern had re-emerged forcibly in the hold when he'd been a whisker away from laying Mack out cold for threatening the boy.

Harry was not a fool. He'd noted the way George watched him covertly and ascribed it to the hero-worship he'd inspired in the younger boys at Harrow. Then he'd played up to it, enjoying the admiration of boys for his prowess in sports, his easy success at his studies. The young Harry had used this adulation to shield himself from his own fears of being one day found out to be the imposter he really was: the son of a penniless widow – or worse, illegitimate.

As he crossed the cabin to put *Twelfth Night* back onto the shelf, Harry paused, looking out of the porthole. He thought again of George's unequivocal loyalty to his brother and experienced a sudden, sharp pang of envy. How lucky both boys were, to be tied by such fierce bonds.

Since his mother's death and his decision that day to quit Cambridge and walk away from everything he knew and loved, Harry had always felt he had nothing left to lose. This he had seen as his source of freedom, the willing price. But now he was not so sure. George's love for his brother, far from being the anchor holding him at bay, was his rudder, steering him into new waters. Perhaps there was a lot to be said for that. He smiled to himself, thinking of the adventures the boys would have together in New Zealand. Harry always travelled alone.

Then he braced his hands on either side of the porthole. The waters behind them were empty. Just as they were whenever he checked – which was considerably more often than usual.

A fortune beyond his wildest dreams was suddenly possible. But at what cost? Could he bear living with the consequences? And could he ever reconcile himself with the man it would turn him into?

Chapter Seven

That evening some of the crew were up on deck, smoking and playing cards after dinner. Georgiana showed herself to be a dangerous opponent in poker, Bert being her first victim.

'There you are with that innocent boy's face and the soul of a gambler, and I bought it!'

'More fool you,' she retorted as she scooped up her winnings. 'I grew up learning card tricks at the maestro's knee. He could pull four aces out of any pack you gave him and with one hand behind his back.'

'Goin' to fleece all the miners there in Noo Zeeland are you?'

'Maybe,' she said, 'if you don't warn them off. How long will it take to get there?'

Pete blew out his lips. 'A few months, depending on the winds, but rest assured, the captain's powerful interested in getting there as quick as can be.'

'I'd give a monkey to know what happened at that Lord Iver's house to put him in such a hurry,' Bert said.

At the name, Georgiana started in shock and dropped some cards. Surprised, Bert looked at her. 'What's the matter with you, boy? Looks like you've just seen a ghost.'

Georgiana gave a shaky laugh as she retrieved her hand. 'Alec's stew is not agreeing with me. Lord *Iver*, did you say?'

'Yup. Why? You know him?'

'I think I – I may have heard the name.'

It was engraved into her memory, as everything else was from that unreal conversation she'd overheard. But surely it couldn't be the same Iver that Walsingham's man was going to *deal with*? There was no way that Harry could be involved with a dangerous snake like Walsingham.

'Very likely. A famous man is Iver. The cap'n delivered this box to him just a few days ago from his dying son. Got well paid for it too, but Alec didn't like it from the word go. Warned the cap'n against shady businesses, but he's stubborn once he's set his mind to something and said it was a dying man's wish and he'd honour that.'

'What was in the box?'

It was hard for Georgiana to speak, for her mouth had gone dry.

Bert shrugged. 'Nothing special. Just some papers this young cove was sending to his father.'

'To Lord *Iver*?'

'Yup, Iver, that's right.'

She assumed casual interest. 'So how did the captain come to get the job?'

'Well, that's the funny thing, it was when we was in Shanghai. One evening we walked into a Chinese dive and the captain was greeted by this young gent like a long-lost friend. Cries out, "Phillip! Haven't seen you for years. Did my father send you to check up on me?" But the cove was away on opium and when he got up close, he saw his mistake, apologised saying the cap'n was a dead ringer for his neighbour. Still, he insisted on buying the captain a drink. Draped his arm round the captain's shoulders, and asked him to deliver this box.'

'To the young man's father? Lord Iver?' She had to make sure she understood properly.

'That's what I said didn't I?' Bert was impatient now. 'Anyway, course, we all knew the name – Iver and Walsingham are the bigwigs of the tea trade, y'know. The captain asked why the cove needed him when he had his father's ships there in the dock. He got all wild-eyed and said there were spies everywhere and he didn't trust no one. Then he named his price.'

Pete laughed softly. 'We knew then that he was barking mad. It was more money than we'd earned in the last year. The captain's always one to take a gamble. When he went round to pick up the box, he found the man was del— what was that word?'

'Delusional,' Bert supplied, taking up the story again. 'Too much opium. Dying of consumption as well. So the captain took him to a hospital, but the doctors said he wouldn't see the next day. That settled things. Dying man's wish, see, plus the cap'n felt it was – what'd he say? – *incumbent* on him to tell Iver how his son died.'

'Then what happened?' Georgiana's nails bit into the palms of her hands though her voice remained light.

Bert shrugged. 'We got to England. The captain left in the morning in good spirits, box on his shoulder. Came back late that night, three sheets to the wind and in a powerful ugly temper—'

'And that's not like the captain,' Pete cut in.

'*Anyways*,' said Bert, determinedly ignoring the interruption, 'next thing we knew, he was telling us we was off to New Zealand, leaving as soon as possible.'

'Weren't you surprised?'

'Course we were, but he didn't say any more and from the look of him, wasn't about to either. None of us was going to ask any questions with him in such a mood. Now we knows of course that that's because he'd made this enemy what's got him worried. He went ashore next night to play cards and came back with you.'

He bit down on his pipe, and shook his head. For a minute they were all silent, then Bert threw off his ruminative air. 'Well, boy, are you going to cradle those cards all night or are you going to give me a chance to have my revenge?'

After a few more hands, the last of which she deliberately lost to keep the older men happy, Georgiana escaped to the stern. She leaned her elbows on the railings, watching the wake foam white under the waning moon. Iver, Walsingham. Oh yes, she'd heard those names before and she shivered, despite the warmth of the night.

Somehow Harry had insinuated himself into this fantastical story. He had seen Iver. He had been the carrier of Eddie's papers – but surely nothing more. Yet something, someone, had suddenly set him on this path to New Zealand. The law was after him. Who was this enemy he spoke of? What had he done?

Suddenly cold, Georgiana rubbed her arms as she remembered the admiration in Pete's voice as he described Harry's ability to fight. She herself had seen how easily he'd dispatched opponents in the tavern, had dispensed with Mack. The pirate king. Yet he'd been protective of a circus brat and his men trusted him. There were, after all, many reasons to go to New Zealand. Gold, for example. He might just be going for the gold. Nothing more.

Georgiana shook her head, shutting down her mind to conclusions she couldn't bear to think about; her every instinct cried against them. She felt sick to her stomach though, with unvoiced fears.

Touching the griffin about her neck she whispered into the darkness, 'Grandmother, why have you led me here? Who can I trust?'

Chapter Eight

Georgiana woke alert at dawn. Nothing seemed amiss. The ship was sailing an easy course. She looked along the rows of hammocks misshapen with their loads. One man farted as he turned over and another muttered in his sleep, but everything else was tranquil.

Unable to get back to sleep, Georgiana slid out of her hammock and scaled the ladder to the decks. Burt was at the wheel, Dougal on watch. She nodded to them as she slipped up to the prow where she was hoping to enjoy the dawn in solitude. She was surprised, therefore, to find the captain sitting there, back against the foremast, arms resting on his bended knees.

'Sorry,' she said, backing away as he glanced up. 'I didn't think anyone—'

'—would be here, I know,' Harry gave her one of his swift smiles. 'Neither did I. But now that you're here, come and take a seat, George. It'll be a stunning sunrise.'

At the sight of his smile, all the ugly thoughts of the night before evaporated. Impossible that he could be a murderer. She was being ridiculous. Even more ridiculous was the sudden urge to tame her curls which were dancing in the wind, to flatten them more becomingly behind her ears. Lord, she had to be so careful around Harry not to betray herself with unconsciously feminine gestures.

Harry shifted over but still it was a squeeze for Georgiana to sit beside him. She could feel the warmth of his body and when he stretched one leg out flat next to her, the lean muscles of his thigh were hard against hers. Beside him she noticed a bottle of port. He took a swig and passed it over to her. She hesitated then took a sip. The port burned and she coughed.

'You'll have to get used to grog if you want to be a sailor, George,' Harry mocked.

'It's a bit early for me.'

'Me too.' His smile was wry as he took another pull. 'Why are you about at this hour?'

'I woke and couldn't go back to sleep – I don't know why.'

He nodded. 'There's a storm in the air.'

'A storm?' Georgiana was disbelieving.

The black of the night sky had already surrendered to deep blue, though fading stars still glimmered. The sea was as smooth as a satin sheet. Harry smiled and she watched the faint lines around his vivid blue eyes deepen. The half-light accentuated the planes of his face. Shadows lay under his high cheek bones, while the long, strong lines of his nose and jaw stood out in contrast. A breeze lifted his tousled black hair from his brow. Realising that she was staring, Georgiana hastily pulled her woman's eyes from his face to look out over the ocean.

'It's hard to believe,' Harry agreed, 'but there's a stillness I don't trust and the barometer is dropping fast. I didn't sleep much last night. I'll get the men up soon to batten down the hatches and make ready. You'll be surprised when you see how swift and fierce the storms are in the Bay of Biscay. Frightened?' he asked, glancing down at her.

'Not at all,' she replied with all the confidence she did not feel.

He looked to the horizon and took another drink. 'You're a fine actor, I'll say that for you.'

She went very still. 'What do you mean?'

'I felt you shiver when I spoke of the storm.'

Georgiana became aware again of their touching arms and thighs. She must have leaned into him unconsciously and now tried to ease away.

Harry smiled down at her. 'You've nothing to fear, George.

I've never lost a man overboard and I'm not about to spoil the record by losing a circus brat.' He passed her the bottle and the port went down easier this time.

'Have you been through many storms?' she asked, then winced at the stupid question. Of course he must have.

Harry laughed. 'Oh God, yes. Thought I might die several times, especially when I went round the Horn a few years back. Didn't think any of us would come out alive but we did. The thing to remember is storms always blow over eventually. Like life,' he added, and Georgiana threw him a sideways look.

'It isn't just the storm, is it?'

He looked down at her, his dark brows drawing together in question.

'The reason you couldn't sleep,' she added.

'Ah.' He took another drink from the bottle. 'No, it's not just the storm.'

She waited, willing him to confide in her. For a second he was silent then he asked, 'How're you fitting in with the crew?'

'Fine, I think,' she said, bewildered by this change in tack. His tone was almost too casual. 'I like them and I think they don't mind me.'

It was impossible to read his face as he nodded. 'They've certainly accepted you, but you are not of their world. Do you mind that?' He turned to look at her and she wrinkled her nose reflectively. 'Well?' he prompted.

Georgiana didn't know how to answer. What would Harry say if she told him who she really was; that she felt more herself posing in boy's clothing than she had ever felt dressed up at balls, trying to please young men for whom she felt nothing but scorn. Miss Bellingham of Ashton Hall. She hadn't even been allowed her real name.

'I didn't fit my aunt's world either,' she temporised.

'Because of the circus?'

She nodded. 'It made me think differently and no matter how hard I tried to appear the same as everyone else, they still knew I wasn't and disliked me for it.'

Harry nodded. 'From two worlds and not of either,' he said. 'We are not so different, George.' She couldn't place his tone. It wasn't bitter or angry but it had a distinct edge.

They looked out over the flat sea and watched as the sun split the line between water and sky with a shaft of gold. Georgiana's thoughts were not on the sight in front of her, however, but on the books in the captain's cabin, on Harry's effortless charm, and his natural sense of command. She thought of herself sitting with her aunt at balls, her card only half-filled, and felt a surge of bitterness.

'Not quite the same. You could belong to whichever world you choose,' she said.

Harry shook his head. 'Not when I know myself that deep down I don't truly belong to either.'

Perhaps he was the illegitimate son of some aristocrat. It would explain the education and explain his inability to find a proper footing in England.

'Is that why you sail?'

He smiled. 'It is why I first set sail. Then I found I liked it – I belong on *Sally*.'

'But she's a very small world,' Georgiana said. 'She cannot remain your world forever.'

Yet even as she spoke, she thought of the sense of freedom she'd enjoyed these past few days, despite the long, unaccustomed hours of work. It was amazing how easily the world did indeed shrink down to the dimensions of the ship.

'No? Maybe not. I used to think she would, but just recently—' he broke off.

They sat for a few minutes. Georgiana bubbled with questions that George could not ask his captain. Was the smallness of his world beginning to irk? Was he bothered by his belief – a gravely mistaken one – that he had nothing to offer a woman?

'If you could find a way to belong – would you take it?' he asked.

Georgiana could feel the importance of this abrupt question but did not know how to reply. She had been prepared to marry Jasper to escape, but she'd never imagined ever actually belonging anywhere.

'I don't know,' she said. 'I think it would depend on what I would be required to do.'

Harry sighed. 'Therein lies the rub,' he agreed. Then softly repeated it, as if to himself. 'Therein lies the rub.'

Despite the rising sun, it seemed a shadow passed over his face as he tipped up the bottle and drained it in an angry, almost contemptuous movement, setting her instincts on alert.

What have you done, Harry? her mind asked. What is it that you don't want to do?

Georgiana wasn't sure she wanted to know the answer.

When he turned to her, she knew any confidences he might have been on the point of sharing had been put aside. He smiled and tousled her hair.

'Don't look so concerned. I'm just talking. Now, you be off and raise the alarm. See, the first cloud's already gathering on the horizon. The others will be massing soon.'

The moment was passed and Georgiana hastened away to do as she was bid, though questions still burned inside her head. What was eating at him so?

Touching her griffin through the fabric of her shirt, she stifled the words welling up. 'Oh dear God, don't let it be anything to do with Charlie.'

These thoughts were driven out, however, as she scrambled

with the rest of crew in readiness of the storm. By mid-morning the sky was black, but all sails were reefed, sheets secured and the men, though tense, were confident. The captain had acted in good time.

At eleven o'clock, however, a fresh alarm was sounded. High in the crow's nest, Eric cried out, 'Captain, there's a ship on the horizon headed straight for us.'

Harry looked through the telescope. 'A naval ship. She's carrying a lot of sail in the teeth of a storm. I wonder what the hurry is.'

Within the hour both storm and ship were bearing swiftly down upon the *Lady Sarah*.

'What the devil is she up to?' Harry demanded.

'She's signalling, sir. She wants us to heave to, Captain.'

'The hell we will.'

The ship continued to bear straight down on them.

'I don't like it, Captain,' said Burt.

Harry's face was inscrutable. 'Neither do I, let's lose her.' He turned and bellowed, 'Loose the sails – we'll have to run in front of her.'

The men were alarmed but only Alec had the courage to voice their concerns. 'It's suicide, Captain, to carry heavy sail in these conditions. She can't take it.'

'We know what we're up against with the storm, whereas we don't with that ship. I know *Sally* well enough to keep her safe. Now *move*!'

At the crack of his command, the men snapped into action. A wild wind presaging the storm hampered their movements and nerves made some fingers clumsy.

'Come on!' cried Harry, grabbing the wheel from Stephen. 'She's gaining on us fast.'

With a cold feeling in the pit of her stomach, Georgiana watched the ship bearing down on them. It was a huge vessel and its sails ballooned white against the black bank of clouds. Lightning lit up the sky and seemed to fork from the ship itself. The men were apprehensive.

'It's a man o' war – why would she bother with us?'

'No time for questions,' Harry shouted. 'Just get those sails up. She may be big but we're more manoeuvrable.'

The wind whipped and whined and as soon as the sails unfurled *Sally* leapt ahead. The sea was now heaving black waves laced with angry yellow surf and the valiant ship heeled as she ploughed through it with terrifying speed. Yet she was not fast enough. To the crew's disbelief, the huge ship bore down on them with great speed and drew up alongside, even in the heaving seas. She was so close that they saw the cannons lined up against them. 'She's going to fire!' someone yelled.

'Keep your heads down!' Harry spun the wheel hard so the ship moved downwind to port just as the cannons went off and the heavy clouds burst directly above them.

Georgiana could make sense of nothing. Cannon balls roared, lightning flashed, and torrents of rain swirled both vessels into the whirlpool of the storm. A cannon ball hit one of the upper yardarms, splintering the end and causing the topsail to flap wildly.

'Secure the sail!' Harry bellowed above the roar of the storm. The two vessels were so close now that musket balls began to rain onto the deck.

Sally was dwarfed by the lurching man of war but the storm, initially so feared, now became their ally. More manoeuvrable, *Sally* skittered up and down the mountainous waters while the man of war wallowed. Despite the waves that rose high and crashed deafeningly on deck, and the rain which pelted in their faces with the power of small stones, Harry's hold on the wheel never faltered. He seemed to move as one with the deck, the wind and the waves, his body always in balance. *Sally* ran the gauntlet of the storm valiantly and the distance between the ships began opening up.

'Secure that bloody sail,' Harry roared. Several of the crew sprang to the rigging, but Georgiana was fastest as she began scaling the treacherously slippery ratlines. Never had she been more petrified yet more focused. Hands slipping on the wet ropes, rain drumming her eyes, she climbed until she was on the level with the wildly flapping sail. It snapped and whistled like some wild creature. Holding tight with one arm, she swung out, caught a corner and wrestled it in. She had to fight to secure the rope, her legs wound around the yard arm, arms shaking with exertion. But her mind remained trained on the task in front of her. She scarcely heard the sounds of the storm and certainly didn't hear the whistle of one of the last musket shots loosed before the naval ship lost *Sally* in the next huge waves.

The ball scorched her arm and Georgiana jerked back in shock, her hand instinctively going to the wound. Blood. Then she felt herself slip. Ignoring the searing pain in her arm, she grabbed for a rope, but it was too late. Like a wounded bird, she fell, twisting and helpless, to crash onto the deck below.

Chapter Nine

The world was black when she came to. Disorientated, she began to struggle up, but Alec's voice penetrated the mists in her mind.

'Lie down, girl. You need your rest.'

As she slipped back into oblivion, the word *girl* strummed in her head.

The next time she opened her eyes, the world was light again, but blurred. Her head pounded, her arm still burned. Blinking, she tried to focus. Then a blessedly cool cloth pressed against her forehead.

'Patience, lass. That was a quite a blow you took to your head. You've got a thick skull to survive that fall.'

'My arm?' Her voice sounded pathetically weak.

'Aye, you were shot but it's a flesh wound, no more than a scratch. It'll hurt but it'll heal.'

These words gave her some comfort. 'What about the storm and the man of war?'

Alec gave a creaky laugh. 'The storm saved the day for us. The captain is in league with the devil himself, the luck he carries with him. The storm pitched their ship just as the cannons fired which saved us from too much damage. Later we managed to outrun them. Eric swears he saw one of their masts go in one of the gusts for they were carrying way too much sail. We didn't see them again in the next six hours of the storm and there's not been a peep of them since it ended, so it seems that for the moment we are safe.'

'Why were they chasing us?'

'That the captain doesn't know, girlie.'

Suddenly it dawned on her and she flushed. 'You know?'

'Aye, well I could scarce not now, could I. They brought

your body down like one dead and when I took a look at your arm—' Alec broke off and shrugged.

Her hand went to her chest but the binding was comfortingly in place.

'Does the captain …?'

'Aye, he does. Soon as we were clear of the storm he came down to see how you and the others were.'

'Others? Are any badly hurt?'

'No, I told you. The captain has a pact with the devil. Just bumps and cuts, most of them. But I had you moved to my cabin, away from the others. Said you was badly hurt – though I thought the concussion would lift. Anyway, I've explained the problem to him.'

Georgiana's voice was very small as she asked, 'Was he very angry?'

'Didn't say much to begin with. Just stared down at you and muttered something about being a very fine actor indeed – but not in an admiring way, you ken.'

Georgiana nodded dolefully. Yes, she *kenned* all right. She knew very well the captain's views about having a woman aboard.

A smile stole over Alec's grim features. 'Then he swore in Spanish – it was particularly colourful, you might say.' His tone was appreciative.

Georgiana winced. 'Then what?'

Alec shrugged. 'Nothing. Told me to keep you in my cabin and he went away again to sort *Sally* out. She took a right hammering. Kept the crew busy for hours. He swung back at midnight but you were still out and he was the walking dead by that stage.'

For a second Georgiana closed her eyes, wishing she was dead herself. 'What'll happen, Alec?'

'I don't know, lass, I really don't. The men could go wild if they hear there is a woman aboard, not just because—'

here he coughed, reddened then went on. 'Well, they're a superstitious bunch, you know, and a woman aboard is terrible bad luck. *You* could get blamed for that man o' war and storm.'

'But I never—' she protested.

'I know, I know. I'm not saying that they *would*, but they *might*,' Alec shook his head. 'But if I were you, it would be explaining to the captain that I'd be worrying about. He's terrible put out about it and no wonder.' Then seeing her face, he seemed to relent. 'Best eat this porridge up, girl. You'll need something to strengthen you. The captain'll be awake before long. I'll go now and see how he's faring this morning.'

Harry was pulling himself out of his heavy sleep with an effort when he heard a tap on his door. He swung his legs over his bunk and sat there for a second, arms braced either side of his body, regrouping his strength.

'Come in.'

His voice was hoarse from hours of shouting over the storm. As Alec entered his cabin, Harry shook his head to chase away his fogging exhaustion before pushing himself onto his feet, where he swayed for a second. Then he saw Alec holding out a cup of coffee.

'Now there's a welcome sight,' he said with a grateful smile. 'I need something to get me going this morning, Alec. How are things up top?'

'Right as rain, Captain. No sign of Her Majesty's ships nor nothing.' Alec handed him the cup. 'She's awake now.'

'What?' For a minute Harry was quite blank but then he remembered and closed his eyes. 'Oh God! What am I to do with her?'

'Talking to her would be a start.'

Harry grimaced. 'And that's just one reason why I *don't*

have females on board. Starting the day with a *talk*! I don't know if I've got the stomach for it at this hour of the day.'

'Don't know that she's much relishing the prospect either,' Alec said with a glimmer of one of his rare, grim smiles.

Georgiana was alarmed when Alec returned to say the captain would be along in a few minutes. She struggled up into a sitting position and the world swam.

'Easy girl,' said Alec, catching her under the elbow. 'Best lie back.'

Fighting nausea, Georgiana shook her head. 'I will face him standing.'

Alec shook his own head at her stubbornness but helped her to her feet. He was awkward around her now and she wished he would go back to his gruff, bossy self.

'I truly am sorry, Alec. I didn't mean to cause trouble.'

He cleared his throat. 'But you have, all the same.' He shot her a look under beetling eyebrows and added in his dour way, 'George was all right, you know. Pity he turned out to be a pesky girl.'

Just as she laughed wanly, Harry arrived at the cabin door. It was clear the captain's temper was under close rein as he paused in the doorway. Alec glanced from the captain to Georgiana.

'Well, I'll be leaving the two of you to it, then.'

Georgiana tried not to feel abandoned, but there was silence for a minute after his departure. She was shaky, but keelhauling wouldn't have dragged an admission of such weakness from her. While she had been waiting for Alec's return she had been thinking. Until she knew what had taken place between Harry and Lord Iver, she had to be very careful.

'Ma'am,' said Harry, indicating a stool, 'would you please take a seat.'

His tone was polite but icy. Georgiana's heart sank. She had never seen the captain look so forbidding. 'I'm fine standing, Captain.'

'Nevertheless, I insist.'

'Nevertheless, I wouldn't dream of sitting down in front of my captain.'

'Oh for God's sake, George,' snapped Harry, descending rapidly from the lofty to the irate. 'Sit! You're swaying as it is and I won't have you fainting on me.'

She sat down and though her heart was hammering, she felt relief that his cold demeanour had shattered so quickly. For a minute he towered over her, then seemed to realise for he perched on the berth and spoke in a slightly less forbidding manner. 'Let's start with the basics. What is your name?'

'Georgiana da Silva.'

'So, the Spanish father is true?'

'Yes.'

'The circus?'

'Yes – everything I told you was true.'

He laughed, but there was no humour in it. 'Apart, of course, from your sex.'

Georgiana remained silent.

'And why are you intent on going to New Zealand?'

'I told you, my brother is sick.'

'Why couldn't you travel as you are – a concerned sister going to help her brother?'

'My aunt would never have let me go so I ran away. I thought I would be safer travelling as a boy than a girl.'

Harry's eyes flashed. 'What on *earth* made you think that you *stupid* child? Don't you realise what an impossible situation your charade has landed you in?'

Georgiana's chin lifted. 'Would you have taken me on as a girl?'

'Of course I wouldn't. Can't you see how — ?'

'I needed passage as quickly as possible. I had no money. What else could I do?'

Harry was silent. Georgiana pressed home her advantage. 'All that I told you about the acting was true, too, so you see I knew I could convince people I was a boy. *You* believed it!'

He gave a bitter laugh. 'The more fool me.'

'It wasn't just you – the whole crew believed it. I've lived with you all for days now and nobody guessed, or would have guessed, if I hadn't fallen.'

But mentioning the crew was a mistake. Harry's temper snapped. 'Can't you see how foolhardy the whole masquerade was? If they'd for one minute suspected —'

'But they didn't!'

'One female among so many men! You paid no heed at all to the consequences, little caring that you were a liability to any captain fool enough to take you on.'

'I never thought —'

'That's plainly obvious!' Harry interrupted.

For a second they glared at each other.

'If you only knew,' Harry said in measured tones, 'how my fingers itch to wring your neck, George. You have put me in an abominable position. What am I to do with you?'

'Nothing,' she replied. 'Why change anything? Only you and Alec know. The rest of the crew don't need to be told. Why can't things go on as they have?'

Harry's eyes rested on her face, but he was acutely aware of how long her legs were in their men's breeches. Knew that under that loose shirt … He remembered her leaning over the table to mop the wine, the line of back curving down into thigh. Saw her lithe body flipping in a somersault. Expressive grey eyes, fringed in long lashes, now burned both in defiance and entreaty under a curly mop of chestnut hair. Her slender hands were curled into fists, but he recalled how fine the fingers were, the palms soft and white, and he cursed himself. Had he been blind? What in the hell sort of an idiot had he been to be so easily fooled?

'Knowing changes everything,' he said with finality.

She made a gesture of despair. 'What can I do, then? How will I get to my brother?'

'Did the naval ship yesterday have anything to do with you?' he asked.

She looked at him bewildered. 'No! What on earth made you think that?'

'I've been wondering why a ship of Her Majesty's was so keen to stop us despite a storm brewing right behind us.'

'It wasn't me the constabulary were seeking that night in the tavern,' Georgiana pointed out.

'I'm well aware of that,' he said shortly. Had been thinking of little else, in fact. Was this whole accursed mess because of the old man? 'Still, I have to make sure your aunt does not have connections in high places.'

Georgiana shook her head. 'My aunt believes me in Scotland with the circus – I told you. You have nothing to fear. No one will follow me because no one knows where I'm headed.' She looked at him, head high. 'We had a deal.'

'I had a deal with George, not Georgiana.'

'But I have to get to my brother.'

It was a cry ripped from her heart and it stopped Harry short. She was still not telling the whole truth, he was sure of it, but he did believe her love for her brother lay behind all her mad, ill-considered, foolhardy, idiotic – but strangely quixotic – actions. She really was the most astonishing female Harry had ever encountered. Her brother was a lucky bastard to have a sister who loved so fiercely.

In silence, Harry surveyed her. She was very pale, but there was a proud tilt to her head. Her shirt was grubby, and soot and blood stained the sleeve. Her top buttons were undone and Harry glimpsed a gold chain.

'What's that around your neck?' he asked.

She looked taken aback but drew it up so he could see. 'A griffin. My grandmother gave it to me to protect me.'

'A griffin? How fitting with its dual nature.'

She flinched at the intended slight but was not going to be intimidated. 'It's also the symbol of wisdom and strength.'

'Yet you display none of the former and your sex prevents the latter.'

She must have been more shaken by her fall than she'd let on. Instead of one of her ready comebacks, it was as though her mettle suddenly deserted her and her shoulders slumped. 'I know. Perhaps that's why she gave it to me,' was all she said as she slipped the trinket back down under her shirt.

Dammit, now he felt like a bully. What the hell was he going to do? His entire world had been off kilter from the day he'd met her. She was just one more complication in his already far too complicated life. Yet here she was and short of throwing her overboard, here she had to remain.

'Rest now,' he said gruffly. 'I'll get Alec to bring you a clean shirt.'

She began to protest, but he'd had enough and ran roughshod over her. 'We'll reach Madeira in a few days. First I will find out why the hell the Navy is interested in *Sally*. After that, I'll decide what to do about you. For the moment you will remain in Alec's cabin. The men will be told that you're still in a bad way and you'll do nothing that will draw attention to yourself. Is that understood, George?'

'Absolutely,' she said, but he saw hope light her eyes.

'Don't push it, Miss da Silva,' he warned, his voice dangerous. 'I expect you to follow orders to the letter.'

'Of course.'

Her face was instantly serious, but still he was wary. 'I

mean it,' he said, fixing her with a look that could subdue the roughest crew member. But though she nodded meekly, still he couldn't help doubting its efficacy on this wayward slip of a girl.

As he quit the cabin, closing the door behind him, he paused. Despite his anger, his exhaustion and the impossible predicament she'd put him in, he couldn't prevent a grudging smile. He was still furious with her, as well as furious with himself, but her mixture of valiance and vulnerability was hard to withstand. It appeared that Miss Georgiana da Silva was going to prove to be even more irrepressible and unpredictable than Master George Miller. Heaven help him – heaven help them all!

Chapter Ten

The following days were a trial for Georgiana. Although her head ached and her arm was painful, she couldn't bear the enforced inactivity, so Alec put her to polishing brass fittings and cleaning out the lamentable galley. Still she felt claustrophobic and cramped and missed the camaraderie of the crew.

In order to allay suspicions as to why the young 'un was being pandered to for a mere bump on the head and a shot arm, Alec had muttered dourly under his breath about infection and dirty young scamp, implying some sort of horrible complaint the men might catch. Consequently she was given a wide berth by all and ate and slept alone in Alec's tiny cabin. She scarcely saw Harry either. Sometimes he dropped by to check on her, but their exchanges tended to be abrupt and awkwardly formal, leaving Georgiana to lament the loss of the casual, teasing relationship George had enjoyed with the captain.

She had plenty of time to consider her situation. The facts spoke for themselves. Harry had been with Iver and was now wanted by the law. Not only that, immediately after the meeting he'd embarked on a secret mission to New Zealand. Though it plainly caused him grave misgiving, the only explanation he'd given was that it might pay well. Very well, indeed.

There was only one, rational, unavoidable conclusion. But every part of her cried out in rejection. She replayed images of Harry rescuing her from Mack, Harry tousling her hair, Harry laughing with his crew. There was nothing sinister about this man, nothing duplicitous. His crew trusted him absolutely. Besides, he'd seemed as confused as everyone else as to why their ship should be attacked. Yet what did she really know about the captain? What did she know of men? After all, she'd already been deceived by Jasper, her cousin whom she'd thought she knew so very well.

What, after all, did a murderer look like?

Not Harry, her heart cried out. Not Harry.

Reason insisted that she stay with Harry. If he were the assassin, she needed to keep an eye on him.

Her heart, in this regard, was in agreement – which infuriated her rational brain even more.

She felt relief, therefore, when she looked out one afternoon to see the outer islands of Madeira slipping past the porthole. Finally she might be freed from this captivity and her restless thoughts. Georgiana was admiring their beauty when the cabin door opened and she turned to see Harry's tall frame in the doorway.

'May I come in?'

'Of course.'

She didn't show how much she hated his studiedly polite manners. He crossed to the porthole and leaned one shoulder against the cabin wall to look out with her.

'They're lovely, aren't they?' she said to ease the moment. Harry seemed to fill the tiny cabin.

'Mm.' But she could tell his mind was elsewhere. The sun fell onto his face, lighting the swooping planes of his cheeks, catching dark lights in the thickness of his hair. As always, it was impossible to guess what he was thinking. His eyes, the same glorious deep blue as the ocean, stared out and she wondered what it would feel like to trace his beautifully shaped lips – looking always halfway to a smile – with her finger.

Harry glanced down at her. 'George,' he said, then paused.

Her pulse quickened with relief. It was the first time he'd called her this in the past few days. She hated being addressed as Miss da Silva.

'You and I will get off at Funchal for a few days. I have a friend there we can stay with. *Sally* will go into hiding in one of the bays further around the island until I can discover what the hell is going on and decide what to do about you.' His eyes lit with something of his old teasing and her heart did a tiny flip. 'The men won't be surprised that you're going ashore too, given your ghastly infection.'

To share the joke, she assumed an expression of outrage and was rewarded by one of his smiles, but then he became serious again. 'Bring all your things with you.'

Suspicion immediately set in. 'Why? Have you decided against going to New Zealand?'

There. If he didn't go, he must be innocent.

But then, if he didn't go, what would she do?

Harry shrugged. 'Nothing is decided until I learn more, but it's wise to prepare for all eventualities. I'll be taking some things with me, too – just in case.' He straightened and reached out as if to tousle her hair, but then his hand dropped. Still, his wry smile had more warmth as he added, 'Don't look so concerned, George. We'll find a way through all of this. Be ready to go when you hear us drop anchor.'

She watched him go, her heart in tumult. She hated to leave *Sally*. Despite Alec's and Harry's misgivings, she had felt surprisingly happy and safe, once Mack had been set down. She wanted to stay. She needed to stay. She didn't want to lose the captain. Couldn't afford to until she knew what game he was playing. At the same time, he'd said *we*, and he was calling her George again. She couldn't suppress the welling happiness she'd felt to see his teasing look return. Perhaps the hated Georgiana could be forgotten, after all.

They anchored off Funchal in the dead of night so no one would see their arrival. Georgiana was feeling faint, and her head was pounding as it had done every evening since her fall. Nothing would force her to admit it, though. Alec came into her cabin.

'Time to go, lass.'

'Will I come back, do you think?'

He shrugged. 'It's hard to see how you can. This is no place for a girl, even one as unnatural as you. But you've not been a bad hand, when all's said and done.'

'Oh Alec, that's the nicest thing anyone has ever said to me,' said Georgiana, tears welling up. 'I'm going to miss you.' Dropping her small bag, she enveloped the cantankerous old man in a hug.

Awkwardly, he patted her on the back. 'No need for scenes, girl, and no more harebrained schemes, you hear. Listen to the captain and mind what he says.'

'Of course I will,' she assured him, blinking back her tears as she stooped to pick up her bag.

He eyed her. 'I mean it, girlie. No more daft notions.'

This made her laugh and she dropped a kiss on his wrinkled cheek. 'Your grumpy manner doesn't fool me. You've been like a father to me these past few days.'

'Ah well, I've never had no children of my own that I know of, but if I do happen to have a daughter, I just hope she isn't as pesky as you.'

Her laughter mingled with her tears as she slipped away, so she almost missed his whispered, 'Godspeed, girl.'

The wharf was silent as they drew up to it in a dinghy and in minutes she and Harry were watching Pete row away into the dark. Feeling desolate at leaving *Sally*, where for such a short time she'd been happy, Georgiana nevertheless kept her voice light as she asked, 'Where now?'

Harry swung up their bags. 'Good girl, that's the spirit. It's not far. We'll be there in ten minutes or so.'

The town was in darkness and Georgiana found it hard to

make out much at all, but Harry, with his catlike eyes, had no difficulty in leading her through a maze of tiny, twisting and incredibly steep roads. Her legs were rubbery as she struggled to walk on land again and her feet slithered on the cobbles. Her head was beginning to spin when Harry shifted both bags into one hand and put an arm about her.

'Here, George, lean on me. We're nearly there.'

'We'll look strange to anyone who sees us.'

'There's no one about, but if there were, they'd think I was helping my very drunk young friend back home to bed.'

'Thank you very much!' But despite her feigned indignation, Georgiana leaned against him. It felt oddly natural to let her throbbing head rest on his shoulder. Through the thin shirt, she could feel warmth and muscle. He smelt of the sea, of the brandy he must have had with dinner, and something less tangible but distinctly male that awoke her senses with disturbing new awareness. 'Where are we going?'

'I told you, a friend.'

'Won't he be surprised to be disturbed at this hour?' Georgiana looked at all the shuttered windows. In the whole town not a single soul appeared to be awake.

'She. Consuela Dias. No, she's used to unusual hours.'

Georgiana raised her brows but said nothing. In a few minutes Harry was rapping at the door of a small pension tucked at the end of one of the back streets. Silence. He knocked again, louder, but still with no real force so as not to wake the neighbours. An upstairs shutter was flung open and a woman's nightcapped head looked out.

'*Quem e?*' The woman's whisper sounded alert even though she'd obviously just woken.

Harry stepped back so that he was visible and called up softly. '*Boa noite*, Consuela. It's me.'

'Harry?' The voice was tinged with delighted surprise and Georgiana felt something twist inside.

'Consuela, I have a friend here and we are in dire need of a room. Is that possible?'

'*Claro*. Wait there.' The shutter closed softly and in a minute the front door was opened by a beautiful woman. The cap had been flung off and Consuela's luxuriant black hair tumbled to her waist. She'd wrapped a richly embroidered shawl around her shoulders and the candle she held lit her creamy complexion and caused her large dark eyes to glow.

'Harry!' Stepping forward, she placed a hand on each of his shoulders and stood on tiptoe to kiss him on both cheeks. She was so petite that he had to stoop to receive these salutes. Georgiana suddenly felt very large and gauche – just as she'd felt at every hated ball in England.

'Ah Harry, so good to see you again, my friend. But what a strange hour to visit. Could you not wait until tomorrow to see me?'

Her voice was dark as molasses and both caressing and teasing at the same time. Georgiana did not know whether to nurse her embarrassment or study this fascinating creature to enact her one day. Consuela arched her brows and threw a saucy look at Harry. 'I am respectable now, you know. There is no entertainment at my little guesthouse these days.'

Harry bowed and laughed softly. 'Truly, it is only a bed we seek, Consuela, for my friend here. And for myself, if that is possible.'

'For your young friend?' Consuela turned and smiled at Georgiana. 'Come into the light so I may see you, friend of Harry.'

Georgiana stepped into the glow of the candle held aloft and for a moment Consuela surveyed her. The initial smile of welcome faded and Consuela's eyes narrowed. With some haughtiness she turned back to the captain. 'What is this, Harry? I told you. I am now respectable.'

'No, it's not like that at all. Let us come in, let me get the child to bed and then I will explain.'

'Child?' Though the tone was ironic, Consuela considered for a moment then nodded and waved them in. Feeling larger and clumsier by the minute, Georgiana followed their diminutive hostess into a parlour with whitewashed walls and elegant furniture.

'Sit, sit,' Consuela urged as she lit a gas lamp on the table. In the flare of light, Georgiana saw that their hostess was not as young as she first seemed. The skin on her face was soft and faint lines fanned her eyes. Still, she moved with the grace and lightness of a girl as she poured them each a glass of Madeira wine. Then she settled herself on a chair, arranging her nightdress so it fell in flattering folds about her. Georgiana noted the filmy lace that hemmed the garment and thought how the nightdress alone would have cost more than her best ball dress. This reflection did nothing to lessen her awkwardness and resentment against Harry for putting her in this position.

'So, Harry, what is this about? It is not like you to bring a girl to me.'

Harry smiled. 'You were never one to be fooled, Consuela. My apologies for the lateness of the hour and the lack of notice, but I did not know where else to go and I know I can always count upon you.'

This caused her to lose a little of her haughtiness and she inclined her head. Still, her eyes lingered on Georgiana who, unable to meet her gaze, stared into the ruby contents of her glass.

'So,' Consuela turned back to Harry, 'what is your story?'

With remarkable economy, Harry explained his flight from England, Georgiana's mission to find her brother, the storm and the discovery of Georgiana's true identity. Consuela did not blink or exclaim once during this recital and Georgiana wondered what Consuela's own story might be that she was so unshockable.

'Having left England with such unseemly haste, I have a few things to attend to here in Madeira – and you, my obvious sanctuary. We are throwing ourselves on your mercy,' Harry concluded with humorous humility, but an underlying thread of sincerity.

Consuela nodded slowly. 'Still, you have not told me *why* the law was chasing you, Harry.'

His mouth tightened and Georgiana held her breath. 'That, Consuela, I cannot tell you. However, it appears that I've made a powerful enemy.'

'*You?*' Now Consuela was surprised. 'It is true you like to play dangerous games, but it is not like you to make enemies. What did you do?'

Harry leaned forward and rested his forearms on his thighs as he cradled his wine with both hands. For a minute he remained still, staring into the glass, then he looked up to meet Consuela's eyes. 'I'd rather not tell you the full story for now, to be honest,' he said. 'It's a sordid business but I need to play it to the end. Will you trust me, Consuela?'

Her lovely dark eyes searched his face. While she was obviously fond of Harry, it was also clear that she operated from her head. What she saw must have reassured her, for the last of her haughtiness fell away. 'Of course! You are my friend and we have shared many years, no?'

'Yes, many years indeed,' he said, his smile answering hers. Georgiana felt a pang of exclusion.

'So,' said Consuela turning back to Georgiana and spreading her hands wide. 'My pension is your home. What do you need?'

'Firstly, a bed for the night – two beds that is,' he added, as her eyes went speculatively to Georgiana.

'That I will do immediately, for the *child*,' she stressed the word with humorous irony, 'looks not at all well.'

Georgiana rose, putting the almost untouched glass of port down. 'Thank you. You are very kind.'

Consuela inclined her head and murmured, 'Pretty manners – a lady then, no?'

Georgiana managed a smile. 'No, not according to my aunt and certainly not at the moment!'

Harry laughed and shook his head at her while Consuela's eyes also lit with laughter. 'I like you,' she pronounced. 'At first I thought you were not respectable and I, you see, now am. You are just a little crazy, I think – like Harry. Come, but be quiet for my guests are asleep.'

Harry rose and said softly, 'Sleep well, brat. I'll see you tomorrow.' The reassurance in his smile once again melted her defences. Surely no murderer could smile like that.

Consuela led Georgiana up two flights of stairs and into a tiny bedchamber which, like the parlour, was simple yet elegant and very comfortable. The bed had a white lace cover and was piled high with a seemingly indecent number of pillows. In the corner stood a washstand with a pitcher and a bowl decorated with bright flowers.

'It's beautiful!'

Consuela smiled. 'I like my guests to be comfortable. Now take off your boots and I will return.'

She disappeared out of the room, but her perfume lingered. Turning her head, Georgiana lifted one shoulder and sniffed. She definitely needed a wash before she could go near the inviting bed.

'Here is a nightdress.' Quiet as an evening breeze, Consuela wafted back into the room with a foamy white gown over her arm. 'It will not be a good fit, but it is something. Now you must sleep. Tomorrow we will talk and you will tell me how you fooled all those men for so long.'

There was a naughty twinkle in her eye as she slipped away, holding up a hand to stem Georgiana's stammered thanks. As soon as the door closed, Georgiana stripped down. It felt peculiar to unbind her breasts and she shivered as the night air fell upon them. Even in Alec's cabin, she'd not dared to fully undo her bindings – just enough to strap her breasts up firmly again. Now she washed thoroughly, relishing the freedom of being able to do so. The water was cold but the night was warm and she felt infinitely better for her ablutions. After a second's hesitation, she slipped into the nightdress. It was clearly not one of Consuela's for it was far too wide and only a little short on Georgiana, but still the most feminine garment she had ever worn. She twirled to make the lace flutter and mimicked Consuela's widespread hands, her inclined head.

'How lovely,' she whispered, 'and *most* respectable.'

Chapter Eleven

The smell of fresh coffee and hot rolls woke her. Opening her eyes, Georgiana saw Consuela put a laden tray down on the table beside the bed before crossing the room to fling the shutters wide. Sunlight painted a broad path through the room and with a start, Georgiana realised it must be quite late. She struggled into a sitting position, then winced, her head resenting the sudden movement. 'Have I slept long?'

Consuela smiled. In the daylight the fine lines about her eyes were more pronounced and there was a softness around her chin, but still she looked fresh and charming in a dress of rich blue over a crinoline which swayed and dipped with her movements. No sign of her disturbed night could be detected in her face. 'You have slept a long time. I thought you might be dead, but Harry said the days have been tiring and, of course, your head is still a problem.'

'Tiring? Yes, but even so, it's unforgivable to sleep this long and I certainly never meant for you to wait on me.'

Consuela disregarded these protestations and just laughed as she rearranged the pillows, helping Georgiana to sit up more comfortably. 'I am feeding you here, in your room, so that my guests will not see you until you are respectable.'

Georgiana suddenly realised the position she was in – they all were in – and she coloured. Consuela, seeing her blush, nodded. '*Bem*, now eat.'

Shyly, Georgiana turned her attention to the breakfast tray now placed in her lap. Everything tasted wonderful, especially in sharp contrast to Alec's cooking.

'You like that?' asked Consuela. 'My, but you English girls can eat so much!' She smoothed the folds of her dress down her tiny form. 'Now, I have a surprise for you.'

She whisked out of the room and in no time returned with a maid, both of them laden with clothes. Georgiana's eyes widened and she began to protest, but Consuela cut her short. 'Harry says the masquerade is over and I must agree with him. It does not do to be a man any longer.'

'But what about New Zealand?'

'But nothing. Harry will have a plan – he always does – and if he thinks now you should be a woman, you may be sure he is right.'

This faith in Harry's judgment caused some resentment to burn in Georgiana's breast, but before she could protest further, Consuela was laying out the clothes, explaining them. 'They are a leetle old from my past. I had girls, you know.' She turned and faced Georgiana who looked politely interested. 'That was a long time ago, but it made me money to be respectable. I kept the dresses because who knows how life goes. Maybe I need them again one day – and see, now I do!' She was watching Georgiana who, though puzzled, smiled and Consuela continued. 'Some of the men liked the *governess* who, by good fortune, was tall like you. They liked being reminded of what bad boys they were.' Georgiana still didn't grasp what Consuela was talking about so pointedly. 'Others liked the young maid. Some preferred only stockings and corset.'

Suddenly – horribly! – Georgiana understood. Her shock must have shown in her face, for Consuela said, 'Ah, now you know. *Muito bem*. We must understand one another, you and I. It is best that we do.'

Feeling shaky, Georgiana pushed the tray away. Consuela, still watching, nodded as if to confirm something and then moved forward to put a hand on Georgiana's arm as she drew the sheets up as if in protection.

'No, you are safe. Now I am sorry. As I say, I am respectable these days and I wanted to make sure you were not – not—' she stopped, her English failing her in this delicate situation. 'My guests, you see,' she said by way of explanation. 'I cannot have them shocked.'

For a minute Georgiana stared up into the apologetic, lovely dark eyes as a myriad of thoughts bubbled in her head. What would her aunt think? What an appalling situation she had got herself into. How *infamous* of Harry to have brought her to such a woman. Impossible to stay under this roof, and as for wearing the clothes – never! But as these thoughts jostled for expression, she looked past Consuela and her glance fell on her discarded boots and trousers. Consuela followed her look and smiled.

'You see,' she pointed out, 'I am not a lady, but I am respectable, while you ...' She left the sentence dangling.

The absurdity of the situation suddenly hit Georgiana. That she, Miss Bellingham of Ashton Hall should have to prove *her* respectability to a – well – to the sort of woman of whom she'd only ever heard the vaguest of references! Bubbles of hysteria began to rise in her and as she relaxed her grip on the sheets, all her pent-up, confused feelings of fear and outrage gave way to a peal of laughter. Consuela began laughing too, sitting down on the bed so they could enjoy their merriment together.

'Oh *senhora*,' said Georgiana weakly, trying to compose herself, 'forgive me for putting you in such a position.'

Consuela made one of her graceful flying gestures. 'It is nothing. I am happy to help a friend of Harry's. Now we must fix this dress. You may put it on behind the screen.'

Georgiana felt bashful rising in the too short nightdress and she retreated behind the exquisitely carved screen in the corner, but Consuela, oblivious of any embarrassment, chatted as she passed first the undergarments, then the crinoline and petticoats and lastly the dress over the screen.

'Do not fear, the chemise, corset and drawers are new. I

sent the maid out early this morning to a little shop where no questions are ever asked. I guessed your size. I hope they fit. The crinoline as you see is modest – as it should be for a young lady. It may be a little short for you are so tall, but no matter. Now come out and I will help you.'

Feeling shy and clumsy to be in women's clothes again, Georgiana came from behind the screen. Head to one side, Consuela looked her up and down, then smiled and nodded.

'The blue is very good for your eyes. They take their colour from your clothes, yes?'

'Yes. By themselves they are just a boring grey.'

'Grey is a good colour. They go blue with one dress, green with another. You are lucky. Me, my eyes always are brown.' She sighed in mock despair then went back to the task at hand. 'The dress is too loose and too short. How tall and slim you are. I can see how you could be a boy.'

'But you knew immediately.'

Consuela smiled mischievously. 'Ah, but I know men.'

Georgiana could feel herself flushing again but had to smile too. Consuela was a most remarkable woman.

The maid was summoned and a small bath was brought up to the room. Behind the screen Georgiana had the luxury of washing in hot water brought up in steaming bucketfuls, while Consuela and the maid made hasty alterations to the *governess* as Consuela continued to call the dress. When Georgiana tried it on again, it fitted perfectly. She tried to express her thanks, but Consuela just laughed at her.

'It is nothing. We did this work all the time, before. How lovely you look, but now we need to do something with the hair. Come sit here in front of the mirror and I will try to make it look better.' She picked up a brush and went to work on the wet locks. 'It makes me want to cry to look at it. It was beautiful before, no? Thick and with such curls. How could you cut it?'

Georgiana shrugged. 'I was desperate at the time, so I just hacked it off as quickly as possible.'

'So the story about your sick brother is true?'

Their eyes met in the mirror. 'Yes. I'm very worried about him.'

'Harry told me some more last night after you left us. He wanted me to understand what sort of girl you are. But still, I wanted to see myself. You are as he described, I think.'

'And how was that?'

'Thoughtless – what was the word? Rash? Ah, yes, rash. Also naïve. Young and naïve. Too innocent for your own good.'

'Oh.' Harry's description had a dampening effect on Georgiana's spirits.

Consuela looked at her and added, 'But he was angry with you because he wants to protect you.'

'I don't need protection,' said Georgiana, tipping her chin.

Amused, the older woman regarded her. 'You are very innocent,' she said flatly, 'to go among so many men in such a disguise.' Her face grew curious. 'What was it like to live like that?'

Georgiana considered for a moment. 'It felt strange to begin with,' she admitted, 'and I was frightened. But you know, after a day, I began to feel like a boy. There was so much to learn, so much work to do. Everything was new. I was just George.'

'Even around Harry?'

Georgiana looked up at the reflection of the older woman, but she seemed intent on the curls she was trying to coax into some order.

'Mm, well, he was the captain,' she said evasively.

Consuela smiled. For a minute Georgiana watched the pretty, dark face above her own and then asked, 'Have you known Harry long?'

'Why yes, many years. No! Not like that. I see what you think on your face. We did business. He brought me wine for my customers. He was like a brother to my girls – not that they wanted him as a brother!' She smiled. 'Of course there were some women in Lisbon … Harry can charm any woman, but he never gives his heart. I have watched them try to win his love and never, never did they succeed.'

Georgiana didn't know if this information made her feel happier or not.

'There were some that thought they might tame him,' Consuela went on, 'but though he would stay a bit, he always leaves in the end. Still,' she added philosophically, 'he always made sure they were left well.'

Georgiana was surprised. 'What do you mean?'

'Harry looks after people. He does not stay, but he always provides. For one girl he found enough money to set her up in a shop making hats – now all the fine ladies in Lisbon go to her. Another swore she would love Harry forever, but he just said she could do much better and next thing she was marrying one of his crew!' Consuela laughed. 'They are very happy and their baby is named Harry after his godfather. Harry plays, but he never loses his heart and he always leaves. He is a good man – but a wild one.'

Georgiana played with a hairpin. 'Why doesn't he give his heart, do you think?'

Consuela shrugged and gave a grimace that on an English woman would have been ugly but on her it was charming. 'A man cannot love until he knows himself. Or perhaps it is through love he learns of himself? Harry, he is like a tiger with his tail on fire, always running ahead, taking his past with him.'

Georgiana was mystified. 'What do you mean?'

Consuela paused for a moment 'Our past makes us what we are, who we are. We cannot change it. Me, I have left mine but still I know what I am, who I am. Harry is a man without history. Ask him about his past, he makes a joke or changes the subject. There are problems there – problems he will not face, I think.'

She gave another couple of twists to the curls and said, satisfied, 'There. It is finished and looks not bad, eh? If anyone asks, we say you cut it when you were sick. What do you think?'

Georgiana looked at her reflection. Her hair was different of course from when she was in England, but still she felt a wave of revulsion for the young woman looking back at her. Just as the skirts hampered her movements, she could feel her life closing in again, pinching at her. Without thinking, she crossed her eyes and stuck out her tongue at her reflection.

Consuela was shocked. 'Why do you do that?'

'I *hate* being a dull young lady – and people hated me when I was one. It was much more fun being a boy.'

The vehemence with which she spoke surprised them both.

Consuela looked thoughtful then said, 'You must learn to like yourself as a woman, *senhorita*. That is what you are. You cannot hide in man's clothes all your life.' She smiled. 'There are good things in being a woman – you will discover. You have played the boy, why not a woman? You do not have to be only a dull English girl, you know. There are other ways to be a woman – many exciting ways.' Her eyes, full of mischief, met Georgiana's in the mirror. Intrigued, Georgiana was going to ask more but Consuela was giving her curls a final twirl. 'Now it is time for you to go down. Harry is waiting below to take you to see Funchal.'

Georgiana leapt to her feet. 'He's been waiting all this time? You should have told me. I would have been quicker.'

'Do not look worried. Now you are not George, you are Miss Miller. Yes, Harry thinks that Miller will cause less interest than da Silva. So you are Miss Miller, just arrived from England. Walk slowly. It does not hurt a man to wait for a lady, you know.'

Her voice was soft but reproving. Georgiana couldn't help smiling and she smoothed the dress down. It was ludicrous, of course, to think of herself as a lady worth waiting for, but perhaps Consuela was right. Perhaps she could treat it as a role – act the part as she had as a boy. Her thoughts must have shown in her face because Consuela nodded and said, 'Remember, if you feel beautiful, so you will be. Go. I will follow in a minute.'

Head held high in her best Consuela imitation, Georgiana went down the stairs. Harry was in the small parlour they'd been in the night before, reading a newspaper and, like Georgiana, he'd washed and wore clean clothes. His jaw was freshly shaven and his hair combed back into smooth waves. Georgiana paused in the doorway, suddenly shy, but he must have felt her presence and glanced up. She did not miss the look of surprised appreciation as he rose, but it disappeared almost immediately as he moved forward.

'Miss Miller, you are recovered I trust.' Alerted by his formal tone, Georgiana looked around the room and saw an old man tucked into a wing-backed chair near the window. Picking up her cue, she came forward in a swirl of skirts.

'Fully recovered, thank you Captain Trent.'

Consuela appeared in the doorway. '*Senhorita*, here is a parasol. You must take it for the sun is very strong in Madeira.'

Georgiana took the flimsy umbrella. With this prop, her costume suddenly felt complete and she could feel herself grow into her new role. 'Thank you, *senhora*,' she said in her most gracious tones.

'Would you care to explore the town a little?' Harry asked.

'That would be charming.'

'Let's go then,' he said, smiling as he offered his arm. 'Consuela, we will eat at Pedro's.'

Consuela nodded approvingly. '*Muito bem*! Have fun.'

'My compliments,' Harry murmured as he passed the small Portuguese woman, 'the *governess* looks splendid.'

Chapter Twelve

Funchal was a delightful town. The sharp-edged relief of the thickly wooded, volcanic mountains provided a perfect backdrop to the small town clinging to the lower slopes. The cobbled streets rose steep and narrow between quaint, flat-faced buildings with thick walls and bright shutters. Brilliantly coloured flowers hung from balconies and flights of steps, as well as framing doorways. Arm in arm, Georgiana and Harry strolled along the dockside of the port which, while small, was busy.

Georgiana had to adjust her stride to a more feminine step and the thin line of lace at her neck tickled. However, she did get to hold Harry's arm and though she knew it was only social convention, she was vividly aware of his sleeve under her fingers.

'It's all so beautiful,' she couldn't help exclaiming. It was head-spinning to think just a few weeks earlier she had been in England, preparing to be a bride, totally unaware this world even existed.

Harry smiled down at her. 'It's one of my most favourite places in the world.'

'Do you come here often, then?'

'Been in and out of it for years.'

His attention was caught by an old woman, sitting in her sun-filled doorway, making lace, and he raised his hand in greeting. 'Maria,' he called out. 'Good morning.' Then he said to Georgiana, 'I must just have a few words with her. I hope you don't mind.'

'Of course not.'

They crossed the tiny cobbled street and after introductions, Harry and Maria chatted in Portuguese while

Georgiana looked about her as she twirled her parasol, enchanted by the narrow streets, the donkeys, the warmth of the light breeze and the brilliant blue of the sea beyond. The chatter in Portuguese reminded her of the Spanish her father and grandmother used to speak, making her feel strangely at home in this sunny town. Then she was aware of the old woman's eyes upon her and she said something, jerking her chin at Georgiana. Harry laughed.

'What did she say?' Georgiana smiled at the old woman but was wary.

Harry shook his head. 'I can't tell you, it'll go to your head.'

Georgiana looked again at the old woman who waggled grizzled eyebrows and said something else. It was amazing how arch a wrinkled old woman with a hairy mole on her chin could look. Harry laughed again but this time his ears went red. Maria winked at Georgiana who couldn't help laughing though she wasn't sure at what.

'Time to be going,' Harry said very firmly and bid farewell to Maria, dropping a kiss on her weathered cheek. She clapped a hand to the spot and kept it there, smiling as they walked away.

'What was all that about?'

'Nothing.'

Georgiana threw him a sceptical look and he added with a shrug and forced laugh, 'She's the town matchmaker and said I'd done her out of her commission.'

It took a second for Georgiana to understand, then it was her turn to blush. 'Oh.'

Her unruly heart whispered, *If only*.

She was glad Harry immediately changed the subject, telling her about Madeira's history and economy. He proved to be an informed and entertaining guide and Georgiana plied him with questions. She was impressed at how much he had picked up on his travels, his clear understanding of the more subtle aspects of the island. However, when the subject of Madeira had been well explored, she couldn't resist turning her curiosity in new directions.

'Where is *Sally*, now?'

'In a tiny bay where no one will trouble her.'

Harry looked young and carefree and Georgiana couldn't help but notice the glances he drew from other women. The feeling was bittersweet; this most attractive man was with *her*. At the same time, she was reminded that he was only here because she had put him in an impossible situation, and he was far too much the gentleman to abandon her – yet.

'You're looking relaxed,' she ventured.

Harry looked startled, then smiled. 'I suppose I am feeling happier now I know that for the moment *Sally* and the crew are safe. How's your head today?'

'Much better.'

Georgiana realised he didn't want to pursue the topic. 'When did you first come here?'

Harry pursed his lips. 'Six or seven years ago. But it's changed, even in that time. More visitors seem to come every year.'

'Is that when you met Consuela?'

He glanced down at her, but she kept her expression demure. 'Consuela was in Lisbon when I first met her,' he said cautiously.

'And were you looking for a governess or a maid?'

She squealed as he pinched the fingers that were lying in the crook of his arm.

'George!' He sounded shocked. Then severe. 'And what, young lady, do you know of governesses and maids, anyway?'

'Not a lot,' she admitted, laughing. 'But how can you

sound so disapproving when it was you who introduced me to Consuela in the first place?'

His grin was rueful. 'I know, it's appalling that I put you in such a position, I am truly sorry. It was the only thing I could think of, given the circumstances. It never occurred to me that Consuela would let slip to you.'

'She was testing me, to see if I was – ah, how did you put it – young and *naïve*.'

Harry either didn't notice or chose to ignore the edge in her voice as he nodded. 'I should have guessed she wouldn't necessarily take my word for it. She is careful that no one pulls the wool over her eyes. I thought she'd trust me more, however.'

'Oh, she's clearly very fond of you. It was *me*, she wasn't sure of. I suspect she was making sure I wasn't somehow fooling you. She wanted to see if I was respectable.'

Harry laughed and Georgiana's heart skipped. This new, carefree Harry was even more irresistible.

'That rings true. Consuela's respectability is very important to her, especially in Madeira. She moved here a few years ago and people believe she is a widow.'

'And she isn't?'

He shook his head. 'No, she's just being pragmatic as she has to explain her wealth somehow.'

Harry hesitated and looked down at Georgiana as though unsure whether to continue.

Georgiana peeped up at him from beneath her parasol. 'You don't know how to talk me, do you?'

Her frankness made him smile. 'No,' he admitted. 'Not a week ago I was bossing around a scruffy cabin boy. Seeing you now, kitted out in female rig—' He shook his head. 'I'm finding the transition unsettling to say the least.'

That makes two of us, she thought.

'Consuela said you used to supply wine to her.'

'Consuela obviously said a lot. Women. But she must have liked you to say so much. Yes, I used to bring her wine. I like her – what's more, I admire her.'

'Why?' Georgiana sought to understand the relationship.

Harry paused. 'I think it's because she's a survivor. You see, she came from a poor family and watched both her parents work themselves into early graves. She decided very early on she wasn't going to do the same so she used her only assets – her beauty and her business sense. I admire her courage, her determination. However, I must apologise if you—'

'No, don't apologise. I like her. She has been nothing but kind. And you're right, our own circumstances were … unusual. Besides, people are usually harsh in their judgment of circus folk too, you know, without really knowing anything. My mother caused a terrible scandal when she ran away with my father. If I'd become all missish with Consuela, then I would be behaving just like my aunt – a terrible thought! But what I don't understand,' she continued a bit shyly, 'is why you wanted me to become Miss Miller. I was happy to continue being George.'

'Well, I wasn't.'

She was surprised to hear the emphasis in his voice and stole a look up at his face. His expression was again hard to read, and she thought how adept he was at concealment. A tingle of warning went down her spine, but she disregarded it.

'Was it really that much of a problem?'

'I told you before, a woman has no place on a ship.'

'But I worked as well as any boy and you said yourself I was one of the best in the rigging.'

'That's not the issue.' Harry sounded impatient. 'It was your safety I was worried about.'

'Oh but none of the men would have—' she began to protest then broke off, remembering Mack.

'And it's ideas like that which prove just how naïve you are, George.'

'Miss Miller!'

'Miss Miller,' he agreed, a smile dissolving his severity. 'Now, would you care for something to eat? There is a particularly fine little restaurant near here.'

'I'm famished,' she said with the most unladylike emphasis.

They sat outside under the shade of a large tree and chattered on a range of topics as delicious dishes were set before them. All constraint between them fell away and Georgiana was surprised to discover there was a freedom in being a woman again, in not having to keep her identity a secret any more. Harry too, seemed free for the time being from whatever demons had been haunting him. The pervasive holiday mood was enhanced by the sun and the perfume of flowers that scented the air.

Towards the end of the meal, Harry leaned back in his chair. 'Now George, you must tell me how it came to be that you were raised in a circus. It's been a question I've wanted to ask for some time. It's such an unlikely story.'

'Why?' She laughed at him. 'Lots of children are.'

He smiled into her eyes. For a second she felt quite faint and took a sip of wine.

'Minx. You know I was referring to your undoubtedly good pedigree.'

She wrinkled her nose as she leaned forward, one elbow on the table, her chin on her fist. 'What a disagreeable thought. Just like a dog. But I am a mongrel then, I suppose. You're right, my mother came from a good family, but my father was a child from the back streets of Madrid. My grandmother never spoke of who his father was but she joined the circus when he was a tiny child – she had the second sight, you see. She told fortunes.'

Harry raised a brow. 'Is this the grandmother who gave you the griffin?'

Her hand went to her talisman, lying hidden under the dress. 'Yes.'

She half expected him to pass it off with some humorous remark, but he just said, 'She must have loved you very much. Griffins protect treasure.'

There was no irony in his tone and she felt her cheeks grow hot. She'd never had anyone give her anything like a compliment before. Harry rescued her from tongue-tied embarrassment.

'So tell me how your parents met.'

Georgiana pulled herself together. 'Mama was what her family always termed *wild*. She was a great horsewoman and would slip away to ride about the countryside. Of course my grandparents would be furious but she said it was intolerable to be always holding back for other riders. One day she took a particularly high hedge – my aunt told me that Mama always rushed at things without thinking through the consequences.'

Harry's mouth twitched, but he made no comment as he leaned forward, selected a peach and began peeling it. It was clear though, from the tilt of his head, that he was listening closely.

'She didn't realise there was a circus camped on the other side and, as her horse came over the top, it nearly landed on one of the performing dogs. The horse stumbled and Mama was thrown. Papa saw the whole thing and came running. At first he thought she must be dead, but she was only stunned and, as he lifted her head, she opened her eyes and said, 'How is my horse? How *stupid* of me.' He used to say that he fell in love with her at that very moment. The horse was fine, but she was shaken so he took her back to the camp where my grandmother could tend to her.'

Georgiana paused, seeing the scene in her mind's eye. She'd imagined it countless times over the years so now it felt almost like her own memory. 'As soon as my grandmother saw my mother coming towards her, leaning on my father, she went forward and kissed her on each cheek saying, "Welcome, daughter." The second sight, you see.'

Harry slanted a look at her, but all he said was, 'Of course,' as he sliced the peach with deft movements. 'But how did your other grandparents feel about this? Surely it didn't have their blessing?'

'Far from it! They ranted and raved, but Mama was very headstrong. Once her mind was made up, it did not matter what anyone said. When the circus moved on, she slipped away with them. Of course she was disowned and never saw her family again.'

'From your blithe tone, I gather that was no great loss.' Harry smiled as he rinsed his fingers in the bowl provided and dried his fingers on his napkin. Then he passed the plate of peach slices and Georgiana took one. It made her feel special to be fed in this way.

His expression became more serious. 'You told me your parents died when you were twelve.'

'Yes.' She took a bite of the peach as a way of ending the conversation. She was used to telling only bare facts of her parents' death and usually people backed away, as though in some way embarrassed by her loss. But as the peach slipped down her throat, sweet and cool, she glanced at Harry. In his face she saw an understanding that went far beyond the usual muttered expressions of sympathy. He seemed to be waiting for her to continue and she experienced an unexpected urge to share that terrible evening with him. Clearly he had suffered in his life; he would understand. Laying down the rest of the slice, she dried her fingers on her napkin, hardly knowing what to say.

'They died one night in a fire,' she began, then faltered, and Harry reached out to cover her hand on the table with his. His clasp was warm and strong. She could not look at him, she felt too exposed. Instead she focused on his hand. It was brown, the fingers long and lean. She could feel the rough hardness of his palm. This was a hand that harnessed winds, that commanded ships at storm, that fought when necessary and that knew how to be gentle. From it, she drew strength to continue.

'The fire broke out in the barn where the horses were being kept. It was probably started by boys from the village who had been seen about earlier in the evening, smoking and drinking. No one from the circus was stupid enough to have a flame near the horses. The barn went up in a huge fire and we could hear the horses inside.'

Georgiana paused. She could almost smell acrid smoke, hear the terrified whinnies above the crackle and roar of the flame. Images that had haunted her in nightmares for years. But now she was aware of the strong hold on her hand. His fingers tightened as if in reassurance and she drew a deep breath. 'Of course everyone was running, shouting about saving the horses. The men managed to get a hose to the barn, but it was clear one stream of water wasn't going to dowse the flames. Mama cried out that someone would have to go in, but everyone said it would be suicide. She wouldn't listen to reason – she never did – and rushed into the barn. She was so sure she could save them. Papa ran in after her.'

It was impossible to talk any more. There were no words to describe the tearing grief and horror when she'd realised neither parent would be coming out. Harry seemed to understand, for when he spoke his voice was low, but matter-of-fact, pulling her back to the happier present.

'And after that you went to your aunt's?'

She opened her eyes to find him steadily regarding her.

She became aware again of the sun on her back, the dappled shadows on the tablecloth, the warmth of his hand covering hers, and she smiled. 'Yes, my mother's sister. She'd never forgiven my mother for the scandal she left in her wake and was in terror that my brother and I would bring shame upon her a second time. She was determined to mould us into respectable young persons and spared no effort to do so.'

'She would appear to have failed dismally.' Harry's tone was dry but his ready smile hovered as he released her fingers and sat back again.

'Yes,' said Georgiana, and though she still felt shaky, she couldn't help chuckling. 'My poor aunt. Seven years of misery, as she constantly pointed out.'

'Seven?' Harry looked sharply at her. 'You said your parents died when you were twelve.'

'That's right.'

'So you're nineteen?' His surprise was evident.

She straightened and bit her lip. 'I know what you're thinking. I'm a disgrace, as my aunt always told me. Two failed seasons.' Then she looked at him defiantly. 'All I can say is that I was as unmoved by all the young men I met as they were by me!'

His eyes rested on her face, but he did not seem to be judging her. 'Tell me about it.'

She shrugged and leaned back in her chair, hands in her lap. She didn't want to talk about her failures to Harry. 'What's to tell? I'm too tall, I'm not obliging and I won't giggle.'

'No wonder your poor aunt despaired.'

She cast him a sidelong look. Laughter danced in his eyes. Encouraged, she confided, 'The boys always used to boast about how fast they could ride.'

He shook his head. 'Tsk. And let me guess. You are an accomplished horsewoman?'

She puffed up in mock consequence. 'I am my mother's daughter, I'll have you know. I did my first somersault off a horse's back when I was five.'

This drew a laugh as she'd hoped it would. Why, oh why, hadn't she ever met someone like him at one of her aunt's balls? But, of course, men like Harry were not confined to English drawing rooms but were away, roaming the world, having adventures.

'So you are older than I first thought.'

'Certainly not the child you thought I was.'

'I realise that now.' His eyes swept over her. 'Your aunt *should* be worried to have you running loose.'

It was a particularly male comment. Georgiana had heard a lot in the hold that had shocked her, despite having grown up with a brother, but this was the first time anyone had ever referred to her in that context. Suddenly she *felt* older. Felt female. She laughed to disguise the strange feeling it gave her. 'Oh no, she'll be happy to have me out of her hair. She really did *not* want to have me as her—' Georgiana broke off before she could say 'step-daughter-in-law'.

Harry prompted her. 'Her—?'

'Her companion forever.'

Georgiana flushed under Harry's searching look. To distract his attention, she took some of her discarded bread roll and leaned down to offer some to a small bird who was hovering nearby.

Harry sat back in his chair, his fingers playing with the stem of his wineglass as he watched her. Rays of sun slipped through the dense canopy of leaves above their heads and glinted red and gold in the rich brown of her hair. The blue of the dress reflected in her eyes as she smiled, coaxing the small bird closer.

Her lack of social success was not surprising. Georgiana

was quite right; she did not possess the pink and white delicacy, the plump softness of prettiness. Her features were all a trifle overdrawn. Her nose had a strong Spanish line, her mouth was too wide though her bottom lip was lovely. Her smile was infectious but it was *not* decorous. Mischief too often lurked beneath. Her curls were already springing free of Consuela's ministrations. Harry liked them but he could see she would not suit the demure buns so favoured in England. Her chief beauty lay in her eyes which showed her every mood. Now they were gentle as she smiled to the bird, but Harry had seen them dance impishly, flash in fury. When she had spoken of her parents' death, he had glimpsed the ragged depths of the anguish and loneliness this girl had suffered. First her parents had died, then her brother had left her. No wonder she would risk everything, having nothing to lose. How much pain her flippant courage concealed.

She had the face, he suddenly realised, of an actress. Small wonder the girl – young woman – had slipped away from the harness of her aunt's attention to seek the stage. Showmanship was in her face, in her blood. On stage all those features, far too strong for a Victorian drawing room, would radiate emotion to the far corners of a theatre. It was a pity for her that she was a lady, but she was and shouldn't be encouraged to flout convention any more than she already had. More than anyone else, he understood the cost if she did. He could never allow her to suffer the social ostracism he'd condemned himself to.

He watched as she tugged in a most unladylike way at the lace at her throat, and couldn't help but smile. George was not happy to be in skirts again. They did her no justice. The damned cage women insisted on wearing swung strangely on her tall frame. It was designed to be worn by women taking small, gliding steps. George matched his own strides easily. Callow youths could never guess at the beauty of her strong, young body hidden under all those absurd layers. For a second he saw again the graceful arc of her body as she somersaulted off the barrel.

An image he immediately quashed. It felt wrong even to begin that line of thought. George – Georgiana, that is – was under his protection. The weight of her reputation rested in his hands. And, while definitely not the child she had first seemed, she was still naïve. Very, very naïve, little realising how completely in his power she was. Luckily for her, Harry did not have dalliances with innocents.

Not that *innocent* described her exactly. She'd deceived him once already and while one secret was out, he couldn't shake the feeling she was still hiding another.

'Why didn't your aunt share your concerns about your brother's health?'

Georgiana glanced sideways at him before transferring her gaze back to the bird. 'Sh-she thought he was probably making a fuss over nothing. She was sure it was not serious.'

There it was again. This continual dissemblance which, coupled with her mix of trust and caution, was as infuriating as it was impenetrable. Why the hell couldn't she be compliant as befitted most girls of her age and breeding? Harry found himself quite in sympathy with the aunt. He could not let her see his frustration, however. She would retreat back into her guileless pretence and then he'd never learn what this girl was up to. Didn't she know how dangerous such games could be?

'But you believe it is serious enough for this mad dash across the world, all alone?'

'Yes.' For a second Georgiana was silent, then she looked into his eyes. 'I really fear for his life and believe I should be with him. He only has me, you see.'

And you him.

Still Harry worried about her reputation. 'Are you

completely sure that no one will tumble to your plan and come after you?'

'Absolutely. My aunt will be glad to see the back of me. I doubt she'll make the slightest move to find me. She will wash her hands of me as my grandparents did my mother. I didn't make too much of his illness because I didn't want to bother her any more. I made it seem that I'd accepted it when she said he would recover.'

Clearly Georgiana wasn't going to confide further. He was surprised at how much it offended him. In a brittle, light tone, he said, 'Well, ten to one your aunt is right, of course. If your brother is at all like you, I'd lay a bet he is already recovered.'

Georgiana did not look convinced but said, 'I hope so. At any rate, my aunt won't be surprised I've gone off to join the circus. She always said there was too much of my mother in me.' She took a sip of wine, then made a slight grimace. 'That's enough wine for me, I think.'

'Is your head starting to ache again?'

'A little.'

'Then let me take you back to Consuela's. You should rest, have a siesta while I go and see if any messages have arrived.'

'Messages?'

'Yes, I'm hoping Tristan will have sent word.'

She wrinkled her nose as she thought. It was endearing, but he could imagine her aunt reproving her for the gesture. 'Tristan? Wasn't he the one in the fight?'

'That's right. Remember he shouted about a message?'

'Message in the bottle – I remember. It didn't make sense.'

'That's good. Hopefully it won't have meant anything to my pursuers either. But it's a code. Madeira – port – bottle, see? We used to use it when in tight situations.'

'What tight situations?'

'Nothing important,' said Harry, ignoring her unladylike

curiosity in clearly unsuitable subjects. 'But it means that with luck, Tristan will have found out what sort of trouble I'm in and will have telegraphed it to a contact in Lisbon. He'll send it over on one of the ships.'

'Very neat,' Georgiana commented drily. 'Obviously a well-tried system.'

It was clear she didn't like having him skirt the truth any more than he liked her evasions. Well, good!

'It's certainly proved handy on the odd occasion,' Harry agreed. 'We'll have dinner at Consuela's and afterwards we will talk of New Zealand.'

Damned if he knew what he was going to say then, though. She really had put him in the most impossible situation.

As she lay down on the bed in the dimness of the shuttered room for an afternoon sleep, Georgiana relived the past few glorious hours during which she and Harry had somehow slipped into the role of friends. She could not pick the exact moment it had happened, but there was a warmth between them that was even stronger than the friendly solicitude he'd shown George. Now when he looked at her – she couldn't explain it but somehow it felt like he really was seeing her, Georgiana, as she was and that he still liked her. Accepted her.

It was absurd to suspect that Harry, with his smiling eyes, could have anything to do with the murky business Walsingham talked about. Harry had only visited Iver to tell him of his son's death and to deliver the papers. When there, he must have seen something, heard something just as she had and this was what was worrying him. After all, he'd denied knowing what all the trouble was about in the tavern. Perhaps together they could unravel what had happened. There were too many secrets. Tonight she would tell him everything. Georgiana heaved a great sigh, awash in a sudden surge of something that felt very close to perfect happiness.

Chapter Thirteen

Georgiana woke with a start as a hand came down over her mouth. She immediately struggled but stopped when Harry whispered, 'It's me. We need to talk.'

He removed his hand and she wriggled into a sitting position, pulling up the sheet around her neck, for she was dressed only in chemise and drawers. She, too, spoke in a whisper. 'Harry, what on earth are you doing here?'

He passed her the lacy dressing gown that Consuela had provided when she'd gone up for her siesta. 'Here, put this on. I didn't mean to catch you like this.'

He walked over to the shuttered window while she pulled it on and came to where he was standing. Georgiana realised she must have been asleep for some hours for the light that now filtered through the shutters was soft. Then Harry turned and when she saw his face she faltered, her hand coming up to clutch the wrap at her neck. There was no trace of her carefree lunchtime companion. Grim lines of resolution bracketed his mouth, his eyes the same brooding blue as a lake in winter.

'What's wrong? Message in a bottle?'

He nodded. 'Yes, and as a result I've sent *Sally* away and I'm going on alone. Leaving for Australia in an hour.'

She must have misheard. '*What?*'

'Shh. Consuela's guests, remember. Look, I haven't much time, so listen. I've made arrangements for you.' He spoke in staccato as though an hourglass were in the room and even now he was watching the sands slip through. How could everything have changed so much in just a few hours?

'I don't understand. Why *Australia*?'

He shrugged. 'I have to move fast and it's the first ship

going in the right direction. It's only a small vessel but it'll do. From Australia I'll get a boat to New Zealand.'

He would not meet her eyes and she struggled to make sense of what was happening. Was he leaving her? Just like he'd left all the other women? When she spoke, her voice was hard with accusation. 'What arrangements? You said you'd help me get to my brother.'

'George, I—' For a second his icy façade slipped. Was that regret in his eyes? He lifted a hand as though to touch her but then let it fall. 'I'm sorry.' His voice was strained. 'I shouldn't have said I could help you.'

'Why? What have I done?'

'It's nothing you've done. It's what I've done – or they say I've done.'

Her stomach clenched. 'Why? What have you done, Harry?'

He hesitated. Then, taking a paper from his pocket, he threw it on the washstand. 'Read that.' A muscle ticked in his jaw.

Georgiana picked up the telegram.

```
IVER STRANGLED ON EIGHTH STOP
HANDKERCHIEF NEAR BODY STOP FLY STOP
```

For a moment she could only stare at the paper. Her mind refused to work. Then she remembered his monogrammed handkerchiefs and the hairs rose on her arms as though brushed by a ghost. No wonder they'd tried to arrest him in the tavern. But now there were other questions, questions she wasn't sure she wanted answered.

'This Iver, why would someone think you killed him?' she asked in a voice that shook.

'I made a delivery to his house, on the eighth. The opportunity was there.'

There was no evidence of guilt in his manner but there wouldn't be – not if he was as cold-blooded as Walsingham. 'But you didn't—?' The words jammed in her throat.

'What? Kill him?' His eyes held hers for a minute. 'Do you really have to ask, George?' She flinched at his tone but held her ground. With a shrug, he turned away. 'He was alive when I left him.'

'And the handkerchief?'

'I left it at Elrington Manor where I met another man, Lord Walsingham.'

Walsingham.

At the name, the pit of her stomach fell away. She'd so hoped, had *believed*, it would never come to this. It was all a nightmare with no possible chance to wake. Georgiana's hands shook as she put down the telegram. 'How can you remember so clearly what happened to your handkerchief?' She forced her voice to stay neutral.

He never looked at her. 'I lent it to someone.'

She knew then he was definitely hiding something.

'Why did you visit Walsingham?' Her throat was so constricted it was hard to speak.

Harry's jaw hardened. 'I had – business there.'

'What sort of business?'

Harry shook his head as he ground the words out. 'It's of no consequence, but if I hadn't gone there, I wouldn't have been caught up in this bloody mess.'

The suppressed rage radiating from him frightened her. Still, there was information she desperately needed.

'Why are you going to New Zealand?'

He turned back to face her, his expression inscrutable in the soft light seeping through the shutters. 'I have to find a man.'

Any answer but this. It was almost impossible to breathe, let alone speak, but she had to continue. 'You said going to

New Zealand could make you rich. Is it linked with finding this man?'

'Yes,' he said in a low voice, 'if I find this man, I could be very, very rich. Rich enough to save *Sally*.'

Could he see her heart beating through the thin material of the gown? Still, she had to make sure. 'So is the man you seek in New Zealand to do with Walsingham?'

He hesitated and ran his fingers through his hair. 'Yes, but there's no time to explain.'

She made an inarticulate sound which had him immediately looking at her again and for a second the familiar Harry was back. 'Georgie, are you all right? You've gone white as a sheet.'

He took her hands which, despite the warmth of the evening, were icy. 'Your fingers are freezing,' he said, his voice remorseful as he rubbed them. 'It's all my fault, I've upset you.'

Unable to bear his touch while so many thoughts were whirling in her mind, Georgiana snatched her hands away. He flinched as though she'd struck him across the face and he took a step back. 'Oh for God's sake, George, I would never hurt you.'

She couldn't bear to look at him. Yet she couldn't afford to let him out of her sight. Couldn't allow him go across the world without her – to Charlie.

'Then take me with you.'

'Impossible!' he said. 'Don't you understand? This is why *Sally* was fired upon. Iver was a very influential man. His murderer *must* be brought to account. I'm a danger to everyone around me – I've sensed it from the moment we left England. As a consequence I've sent *Sally* to South America where she should be safe until I can sort this damnable mess out. It would be madness to take you. The journey is risky enough as it is without having to worry about looking after you. You'd just be a liability. So as I cannot take you with me, I am compelled to send you back.'

'Back? Back where?'

He would not meet her eyes. 'Back to your aunt.'

Her hands balled into fists. 'But you can't. You promised.' Even to her own ears, it sounded like a wail.

Harry's tone took on the patience of one talking to a petulant child. 'Look, if you go back now, no one will ever know about what you did. Your aunt will be able to scotch any rumours and your reputation can be saved. You need never fear indiscretion from myself or any of my crew.'

Furious, betrayed, fearful, she turned away to lean on the windowsill. 'I don't care about my reputation.'

'That's because you are a green girl.' He sounded impatient. 'You simply have no idea.'

She remained obdurately silent.

'Georgiana look at me.'

When she didn't move, a hand came onto her shoulder. It wasn't heavy but the pressure was inexorable and slowly she turned. His eyes bore into hers and his voice was low and urgent.

'There is no other option, can't you see? You can't travel with me and obviously you cannot go alone. You must go back. Don't turn your back on all that your aunt can offer you. I realise it isn't easy or enjoyable, but believe me, the alternatives are worse, infinitely worse.' His grip on her shoulder tightened. 'The world is very harsh, especially towards women. You can ask Consuela about that. I know. My own mother led a wretched life. I would never abandon you to such a miserable fate.'

Then his hand dropped away and he stepped back a pace, becoming brisk and businesslike. 'By good chance I met a captain this afternoon with an excellent reputation. He has agreed to take you back to England under his protection on the *Marigold* and will ensure your safe delivery to your aunt.'

'No!' Georgiana cried, but Harry did not pause. Used to being obeyed, he simply overrode her objection. 'I've paid your passage and he'll call on you tomorrow morning to finalise things. Consuela has found a couple of dresses for you so you'll have some clothes for the voyage.' He dug into his pocket and pulled out a wad of notes which he held out to her. 'This is the money you earned as a ship hand. You'll be able to buy a few things you'll need for the trip home.'

Georgiana made no move to take it so Harry reached for her wrist and pressed the money into her palm. Unresisting, her fingers closed around it. Everything was happening too fast. She needed to think. Some of her bewilderment and perhaps her fear must have shown on her face, for Harry's voice softened.

'I'm sorry it isn't more. I'm sorry about this whole damnable mess.' Then he became brisk once again. 'But listen, Georgie, give me your brother's details and I'll find him for you. I'll make sure he's safe and well and will send word back to you, I promise.'

He hadn't made the link! Georgiana felt limp with relief as her brain finally began to work again. Why should he? Whatever she did now, she mustn't arouse Harry's suspicions. He must never suspect, not for a second, her brother's true identity. Squaring her shoulders, she drew in a breath.

'Don't apologise, I understand. You said on the ship that I was a liability. Well, I won't continue to be one. You have more important things to worry about. As for my brother, I have to confess he isn't quite as ill as I'd pretended. I'd really just wanted to escape my aunt. I'll write when I get home and arrange to travel out as you suggested, as a sister, not a boy. I see now I've been very foolhardy.'

Her voice was steady but the strain of tamped down

emotions could be heard in it. Suspicion and relief warred in Harry's expression. He did not trust her sudden capitulation but she could see he wanted to. With a shaky laugh, she picked a flower out of the vase in front of her to play with so she need not meet his eyes. 'Who knows,' she said, 'we may yet meet up again in New Zealand.'

Harry took the flower out of her hand and pulled her close. Putting his fingers under her chin, his eyes searched hers. She was conscious of his height, the strength of his hold, though his hand was gentle. Warmth emanated from his body, but she could not be distracted, not even with his beautiful mouth only inches from hers. Not for anything would she give Charlie away. She looked back with deliberately wide, innocent eyes. Harry would never take advantage of a naïve girl.

For a minute they stood thus, the tension between them unbearable. Could he feel her heart with its slow thud? He bent his head and for a wild moment she thought he might kiss her, but his lips only brushed her ear as he whispered, 'I wish it could have been different. Take care of yourself, Georgie. And no more foolhardy schemes, promise.'

She nodded.

His voice was hoarse. 'Promise!'

'I promise,' she whispered and heard him sigh.

'Good girl,' he said. His fingers slipped from her chin to touch the chain around her neck. 'Remember, the griffin guards treasure.' In the muted light it seemed that his smile, whilst ironic, was also tipped with tenderness.

Then, with a light tousle of her hair, he was gone.

She listened to his soft footsteps go down the stairs and waited for the muffled click of the front door before she slowly uncrossed her fingers – the child's way out of a promise. It felt as though a part of her had just been ripped out. The telegram still lay on the table. Greater than her grief, however, was cold resolution. On no account could she return to England while he set sail. If he should beat her to finding Charlie ...

She shuddered and turned to the window where she leaned her forehead against the glass to look out into the swiftly gathering twilight. How long ago their meal together now seemed. Had she really thought she might confide in Harry? What a narrow escape, but now there seemed no hope of either stopping Harry or of reaching Charles. Slowly she closed her fingers over the gold griffin.

'I've lost him, Grandmother,' she whispered, but she wasn't sure whether she was speaking of Charles or Harry. She began to cry in great wrenching sobs which were partly out of desolation, and partly out of fury with herself for having craved the kisses of a man who might even now be on his way to murder her brother.

Chapter Fourteen

The next morning Georgiana was up at sunrise, emotionally wrung out. Throughout the long hot hours of the night she had swung from despair, to fury, to grief. It was impossible to say which was strongest; her terror for Charlie, her rage at having been abandoned or her pain at losing Harry. She was also furious with herself, having sworn after Jasper never to trust a man again. She'd come close, so perilously close, to confiding in Harry. As it was, she had no one to blame but herself for her pathetically bruised and aching heart.

By dawn, however, these violent emotions seemed to have consumed each other and she was left with nothing but a yawning emptiness where just yesterday there had been levity and hope.

Having nothing better to do, she slipped out of the pension and walked listlessly down to the harbour. Seagulls wheeled in a grey-tinged sky, their cries shredding the air. The berth where Harry's Australian-bound ship had been was now empty. A few new ships which must have come in during the night were anchored in the bay, and further down the wharf she could see the *Marigold*, a large, solid-looking ship.

Beyond the harbour, vast oceans wrapped around the earth and at the far end of their reach lay Charlie, battling illness and ignorant of plots for his murder. She had completely failed him. There was a small hope that if she sent him a letter it might reach him in time. But would he believe it? He was far more likely to greet such notions with a shout of laughter and treat the whole story as a hoax. Indeed, even having overheard Walsingham, having read the telegram, it all still seemed fantastical.

For the umpteenth time she did the calculations in her head. Walsingham had visited Jasper on the 7th. Iver had been murdered some time during the 8th, the day she'd spent travelling towards Scotland then doubling back. Georgiana felt pangs of guilt. She should have realised that *dealing with* meant killing Iver. Could she have got a message to him, saved his life? She had barely spared him a thought, being entirely focussed on Charlie ... Well, it was too late now.

Her thoughts veered horribly towards conclusions she still fought. She could no longer deny that Harry was somehow embroiled. She thought of Harry's long fingers and imagined them closing around Iver's neck, choking the life out of him. He undoubtedly had the physical strength, but surely he wasn't capable of doing such a thing. He'd also denied it. But of course a murderer would never confess his crime. And what was this secret that filled him with such repugnance? Had his own actions appalled him?

Suppose Harry were the assassin. Then clearly Walsingham had not alerted him to her disappearance. Yet, she couldn't just tell Harry of her true identity in hopes of convincing him that there was no reason to kill Charlie because she'd never in a thousand years contemplate marrying Jasper now. An assassin surely had to kill anyone who knew his identity. But just as surely, her heart whispered, Harry could never kill *her*. He could never murder anyone. The fact, however, remained. The law believed he was their man and had the evidence to prove it.

Utterly defeated, Georgiana sank down onto a bollard and buried her face in her hands. Why did everyone she love, leave her? With her parents' death, she'd lost half her world. Then when Charlie went to New Zealand, she'd been bereft and deserted. And now Harry had abandoned her. Not that she loved him of course. But an immense loneliness, such as she'd never experienced before, now engulfed her. Never had she felt quite so abandoned and so completely without hope.

Grandmother, what now? she thought. *Where is the path I need to take?*

A shadow fell over her and a voice asked, 'Excuse me, but are you all right?'

Caught by surprise, Georgiana's head jerked up as she tried to see who had spoken so solicitously. A man was standing above her with the sun behind him, and for a split second all she could see was his black silhouette. Then he dropped to his haunches so his face was level with hers.

'Sorry, I didn't mean to startle you,' he said, 'but when you sat down so suddenly like that, I thought you were about to faint.'

He was a tall, strongly built man with a friendly face – square, ruddy and finely freckled. His voice carried the warm tones of the Norfolk countryside. Georgiana tried to smile. 'Thank you for your concern, but I'm fine.'

He smiled back at her. 'Would you be terribly offended if I told you that you didn't seem to be?'

This made her laugh shakily. 'I was just feeling a bit … helpless, that's all.'

'We all feel like that sometimes. Could I be forward and ask what the matter is?'

Georgiana hesitated, but the need to confide in someone was too great and the man seemed genuinely concerned. 'I was travelling to New Zealand to join my brother, but the ship I was on sailed without me.'

'Oh?' The stranger sounded surprised, but he was gentle as he continued. 'Well now, why don't you tell me the whole story. Maybe I can help, for you see, I'm headed that way myself.'

'Really?' Hope flared in her voice and the stranger smiled. 'But yesterday there were no ships going to New Zealand.'

'Aye, we came in last night. It's only the briefest of visits, for we sail again in the evening. Now, you say the ship left without you?'

'Yes, that's right. I was travelling with my cousin who became sick and had to go back to England. I didn't want to go back with her so I – I found a captain who said he would take me, but he sailed off a day early with my fare and most of my belongings.'

It was the weakest of stories and inwardly Georgiana winced. If only she'd had some time to think up something more convincing.

The man was appalled. 'That's terrible! What was the name of the ship? Have you reported it to the police here? We need to track this captain down immediately. When did he leave?'

'No! I don't want the police,' Georgiana said hastily. 'I don't want to get caught up in investigations. He's probably halfway to the Caribbean, by now. I don't mind about my things – I still have a few clothes with me. I really just need to get to New Zealand.'

The man regarded her for a minute and then, as though he'd made up his mind, he patted her hand. 'Well I just may have the answer to your problem. I take it you don't have enough money to pay another fare to New Zealand?'

'I have some money, but I don't think it is enough.'

'On our ship there is a widower, a Mr Taylor, with two children. They are … a bit of a handful, shall we say, especially as Mr Taylor is inclined to seasickness. I think that he – and all the other passengers, I might add – would be grateful if they had someone to take care of them. Do you like children?'

'Why yes – well, to be honest, I don't really know. I've not had much to do with them, but I'm certain I could manage.'

'Then I'll go and talk to Mr Taylor and the captain right away. Will you wait here for me?'

'I won't move an inch until you return,' promised Georgiana, her heart fluttering with newborn hope.

The man nodded and began walking away, then suddenly turned around and put out his hand. 'I'm forgetting my manners,' he said. 'I'm Tom Mellors. I'd better know your name before I go offering your services.'

Georgiana rose, shaking the proffered hand. 'My name is Sarah Trent.' She was surprised at how quickly and easily the name slipped into her mind.

'Miss Trent, I'm very pleased to make your acquaintance.' He had a kind smile and Georgiana couldn't help warming to him.

'Not as pleased as I am to make *yours*,' she assured him. She could not believe her good fortune in meeting this man. Her grandmother was still there, guiding the way.

'Wait here,' he said, 'and I'll be back as soon as I can.'

'I won't stir a step until you return!' She watched him go, her mercurial spirits already beginning to soar.

Well, Captain Harry Trent, thought Georgiana as she leaned against the railings of the large ship, watching Madeira recede into the distance. With luck, it might go even faster than Harry's vessel. *You should see me now!*

She felt both triumphant and energised, once more sure she was following the right path. It had all been arranged so easily that surely it must be fate. Mr Taylor had evidently leapt on the suggestion with great gratitude and insisted on paying her passage. The captain had been easy to persuade, for Tom Mellors had solved the problem of finding an extra berth by offering to share his cabin with Mr Taylor. Georgiana could thereby sleep with the children, Julia and Sebastian, aged ten and six.

Consuela had been disapproving when Georgiana had begged her to turn the captain of the *Marigold* away when he came to visit later in the morning. 'This is not what Harry arranged for you.'

'I know, but then Harry did not arrange things the way I wanted them to be. I'm not going to be one of those women who simply accepts his arrangements for them before he disappears out of their lives. I can manage my affairs quite well enough on my own.'

The older woman was troubled. 'So you will go your own way, all alone, with no one to look after you? Think. These decisions will affect your life forever. There will be no going back.'

The world is very harsh, especially to women. I know. My own mother led a wretched life.

But she was in no mood to consider, even for one second, the words of a certain lying, treacherous pirate. This time she was most certainly done with all men. For all time. With a toss of her head she'd said, 'I don't need looking after. Please don't look like that, Consuela – this time I'm not going to do anything shocking or dangerous. I'm going to be a governess. What could be more respectable than that? And I have just the dress for it!'

This drew a laugh from Consuela and she dropped her disapproving manner. 'Will you see Harry in New Zealand?'

'If I never see Harry Trent again in my life it will be too soon!'

Consuela didn't say anything, but her scepticism was plain as she turned to the subject of buying more undergarments, collars and cuffs, and toiletries for the voyage. The money Harry had left came in very handy. She shook her head as she watched Georgiana pack her male attire.

'Why not leave those things here? You won't need them again.'

'You never know.' Georgiana spoke lightly to disguise the fear that still lodged in her stomach, despite her rising hope.

She had no idea what she was going into. More than that though, at this moment she needed something tangible of Charlie's. Somehow, his old, castoff clothes forged a link with him and she couldn't bear to leave them behind.

As Georgiana was leaving, Consuela gave her a large bag.

'There are two dresses which will have to do until you can get some more. One will be good on the ship, but the other,' she said, looking mischievous, 'is for when you want to be beautiful. It is not for governesses, nor for girls who dress as boys, you hear.'

'Oh Consuela, I'm afraid it will go to waste, then. You know I can't be that sort of woman.'

'Then you must learn, *senhorita*. It is there, in you. Let it out.'

Georgiana took the package and hugged the little Portuguese woman. 'I don't know how to thank you.'

'Then, let your hair grow,' Consuela advised her, 'for I do not like it short. And always remember – if you believe yourself to be beautiful, others will believe it too.'

'Miss Trent,' little voices called out. When Georgiana didn't react, the voices grew more urgent, 'Miss Trent!'

Georgiana suddenly remembered her new name and turned to the bright young faces which were now at her elbow.

'Didn't you hear us calling you?' Julia sounded surprised and a little aggrieved.

'I was daydreaming. Now, what do you need me for?'

'We don't exactly *need* you,' said Sebastian, who liked to be precise, 'but we thought—'

'—thought you might like to see the picture of our mother. We have one in the cabin. Her brother drew it of her when she was young. Would you like to?'

'I would love to,' said Georgiana and allowed herself to

be towed to the cabin she would share with her two young charges. She admired the picture of their mother who had died four years earlier, and was then introduced to Julia's doll and Sebastian's dog, made out of rags by a kind housekeeper. Soon it was time to straighten clothes, brush hair and make their way to the dinner table.

As they were leaving the cabin, Georgiana squared her shoulders, drawing in a deep breath. She had never been a governess before, and she was not sure she would be able to carry it off. Yet another new role to assume. Could she convince them? She touched the griffin under her dress. *Remember, the griffin protects treasure.*

Julia noticed Georgiana's hesitation and slipped her hand into her new governess's. 'Don't be shy. Sebastian and I will look after you.'

Georgiana laughed. 'I'm supposed to be looking after *you*. But I admit I am a little nervous.'

'Don't be. Everyone will be so pleased to have someone new to talk about,' Julia assured her. 'They'll want to know *everything* about you!'

Thus thoroughly un-reassured, Georgiana went forth to face her new companions.

Chapter Fifteen

As Julia predicted, the passengers were delighted to have someone new to the table and Georgiana was plied with questions. She smiled and answered best she could, though inwardly she cursed. She had picked a ridiculously flimsy story to explain her predicament. Captain Dunn, who sported a magnificent pair of mutton-chop whiskers, was most perturbed by her story.

'What a scoundrel the fellow is. What was his vessel called? What was his name?'

She shrugged and looked helpless. 'He was French – I can't quite remember. Dubois? Dupont?'

'French! Well, that explains it. Bounders, the lot of them, and that captain ought to be keelhauled for stealing all your belongings. No honour at all, these Frogs.'

'It's a terrible situation to be left in,' said Mrs Roper. She was a widow travelling out to join her own brother, which perhaps was why she looked at Georgiana with such sympathy. 'Now Miss Trent, I have a length of material of entirely the wrong colour for myself – blue-grey. I don't know what I was thinking of when I bought it, but it will suit you well. We'll make it up together.'

'I couldn't possibly—' but Georgiana's protests were cut short.

'Nonsense. I mean it. I would never wear the colour myself, and you must not deprive me of the pleasure. I have never had a daughter, you see.'

'Then I am truly thankful for your generosity and kindness,' said Georgiana with a smile.

During all these questions, Tom Mellors, the architect of her good fortune, had been listening quietly as he ate. From their first meeting, he had shown her nothing but consideration and practical assistance. He had even carried her bags to the ship, then shown her around. She'd been horrified to discover he'd given up the privacy of his cabin, but when she'd tried to thank him, he'd raised a hand in protest.

'Please, Miss Trent. You were obviously in a difficult situation and I'm only too delighted you allowed me to help you. Let's say no more on the matter.'

Now, as he sat opposite her at the dinner table, she was aware of feeling strangely reassured to have his quiet support. When the meal was over and she rose to take the children to bed, he rose, too.

'Sleep well, Miss Trent. I look forward to renewing our acquaintance tomorrow.' His voice was cordial, but there was a note to it that caused Mrs Roper to look arch and Georgiana to feel flattered yet confused. Could it be that for the first time in her life, a man was actually showing interest in *her*? Ha, Harry Trent!

Fine weather enveloped the ship as it sailed down the length of Africa, and the days slipped by pleasurably. Georgiana's charges, though clamorous and demanding, were greatly taken by their new governess who gave them lessons but somehow also made them fun. Her lively imagination, coupled with her experiences in the circus and the plots of plays she'd acted in, helped her make up exciting stories. She was good at card tricks and even taught them a couple which they delightedly tried out on the other passengers.

Georgiana found that she, too, benefited. Julia was a self-possessed young lady and from the moment her eyes opened in the morning she began talking and did not stop all day. Her friendly nature took her around the ship and she returned to Georgiana with a fund of information about the passengers and crew.

'Did you know, Miss Trent, that those poor people in steerage have almost no light down below? Mary's my friend and even though she's twelve, she can't read and write. She took me down and the smell is terrible.'

'I hope you didn't mention that.'

'Of course not!' Julia was affronted. 'I told you, Mary's my friend. Her father says that they are going to a new life with golden opportunities. Is that why you are going to New Zealand, Miss Trent?'

Georgiana laughed. 'That's why my brother went! As for myself, I don't know. There will be opportunities, but whether they'll be golden or not remains to be seen.'

'When I asked Mr Mellors if he was looking for golden opportunities, he said that's what everyone is looking for.'

Julia also kept her informed about the ship's course, the captain being a great friend of hers as he had a daughter on shore much the same age. 'We've had exceptionally good winds,' she said with satisfaction one day, perching on the bunk across from Georgiana's. Georgiana was sewing the seams of the new dress that she and Mrs Roper had cut out. The colour was going to look well on her, and she felt the welling thrill of having one dress which would be truly elegant. Her aunt had always dressed her in frills and lace to try to make her pretty, but they'd looked ridiculous on her.

'Captain Dunn says he's never had such a smooth ride and that I must be his good luck charm. Am I your good luck charm too, Miss Trent? Do you believe in them?'

'Indeed I do. I've shown you my griffin – it directs my path. Look how lucky I've been to get this job with you and Sebastian. But perhaps Mr Mellors is also my good luck charm. It was through him that I met you.'

Julia pulled a face. Of all the people on board, Tom was the only one she hadn't warmed to, though Sebastian thought he was wonderful. 'Is that why you spend so much time with him?' she asked.

'I don't spend much time with him,' said Georgiana, turning to look in the sewing box so Julia might not see the blush stealing up her cheeks.

'Yes, you do. After our lessons he's always around to bump into you on the deck.'

'It's a small ship,' protested Georgiana.

'And he talks to you all the time at mealtimes.'

'We all talk at mealtimes!'

'But then you meet on deck to talk at night.'

'That's only because I enjoy looking at the stars and he enjoys a cigarette at that time.'

Julia wrinkled her nose. Like many of the other passengers, she disapproved of the habit. 'He also looks at you differently from the way he looks at others.'

'Nonsense,' said Georgiana. 'Now, can you thread this needle for me,' she asked, steering the conversation away. It had been too close to the truth for comfort.

In fact, Tom did seem to seek her out and, for her part, Georgiana was always happy to see him. His affable ways and tall, broad-shouldered frame were reassuringly solid. He had not been completely accepted by some of the other passengers who, judging him by his accent and his dress, thought he might be better suited to steerage. Though his manners were impeccable, and he'd obviously had an education, he carried his rural heritage with him not only in his voice, which was deep and slow, but in his looks, as well. There was something about his square, freckled brown face and halo of russet brown curls that brought to mind images of green fields and cattle. His hands were large and strong and could easily be pictured guiding a plough. But though he was clearly not born a gentleman, he was respectable.

Like so many others, he was travelling to New Zealand

for business purposes and though he didn't speak much about himself, Georgiana guessed that the new colony would grant a man of his class far greater opportunities than England did. She hoped he would find prosperity on those new shores. Not only was he a good man, he had become her friend. It eased the loneliness she'd had since Charlie had left. He'd accepted her for what she was, and it was impossible not to be flattered by his attention.

One night, tucked up in her berth, listening to the even breathing of the children, she thought about the way his eyes followed her, the way he sought her out. A woman would be lucky to have such a steady man love her.

What would it be like to be his wife? An agreeable image rose in her mind. She was laying out a meal for Tom and their children. He was smiling at her, and the domestic scene was so tranquil, Georgiana smiled into the darkness. Unexpectedly, there was a knock to the door and when Tom answered it, he stepped back to look questioningly at his wife. Harry Trent stood in the doorway. Furious with herself, Georgiana rolled over and clamped a pillow over her head as though to suffocate her ungovernable thoughts.

The following morning Georgiana and Sebastian were playing a vigorous game of snap when Julia raced into the cabin. 'You'll never guess. Mr Collins has taken ill, very suddenly. Dr Carmichael says it's ap-ap-appen-something.'

'Appendicitis?'

'Yes, that's it. Anyway, he has to have an operation in Cape Town. And Captain Dunn says he will have to look for a new officer in the port.'

'Oh, poor Mr Collins!'

He was a quiet young officer who sat on Georgiana's right at mealtimes. He scarcely talked to her and whenever she addressed him, he'd blush and stammer in reply.

'Yes, but isn't it exciting for *us*! We'll be seeing *land* again soon!' Seizing her brother by the hands, Julia danced him around the tiny cabin, their laughter expressing Georgiana's own bubbling excitement.

The news quickly spread and, although there was much sympathy for Mr Collins, the jubilation at being on land again far outweighed the inconvenience of a potentially longer stop than previously expected. On deck after dinner, Georgiana and Tom discussed this turn of events. The stars seemed particularly bright, but it might have been the general stir of excitement that added brilliance to the night sky.

'Do you think we'll be delayed long?' she asked.

Tom shook his head as he drew on his cigarette, causing the end to glow red. 'I don't know. He'll need to find someone of the same calibre which may not be easy. I believe Mr Collin's navigational and engineering skills are very good.'

'Oh.'

'You don't sound too happy,' he said, looking down at her hands playing restlessly with the fringes of a shawl that Mrs Roper had insisted she accept.

'Well, of course I'm excited to see land again, but at the same time I need to find my brother as soon as possible. Every day's delay ...' she trailed off.

'He's lucky to have such a devoted sister.' The note in Tom's voice caused Georgiana to blush.

'Oh no, I'm only doing what any sister would.'

'What, tearing off to the ends of the world upon hearing he was ill? I think that shows great devotion.'

Georgiana gave a little laugh which turned into a sigh. 'I'm also afraid he might be in trouble,' she said, then could have bitten her tongue off.

Tom looked concerned. 'What sort of trouble.'

Georgiana hesitated. Tom was so solid, so trustworthy,

surely she could tell him. But she'd thought the same thing of Harry Trent.

'Nothing in particular,' she said lightly. 'He's just always been a magnet for mischief. I'm probably worrying over nothing. What about you? Does the delay bother you?'

Tom shook his head and smiled. 'Since I met you, I haven't worried about time at all.' He looked into her eyes. 'I'd be very happy to help you look for your brother, Miss Trent.' As he said her name, he laid a hand right next to hers on the railing. Georgiana looked down at the large, capable fingers and her heart fluttered. Later she wondered what her response would have been if Julia hadn't arrived at her elbow.

'There you are, Miss Trent. I've been looking for you *everywhere*. Sebastian is so excited he says he can't sleep and is asking for one of your stories.'

Snatching back her fingers, grateful for the screening darkness, Georgiana turned to Tom. 'I'm so sorry, but I should go and see to him. I'll see you in the morning?'

Her voice sounded a little high, but Tom was matter-of-fact, despite his rueful smile. 'Yes indeed. Sleep well.'

'Yes of course. You too.'

'Why do you sound so breathless?' asked Julia.

'Do I? No reason.' Feeling very flustered, Georgiana ushered her charge away to their cabin.

Chapter Sixteen

Sailing into Cape Town was breathtaking. Table Mountain stretched long and flat against the brilliant blue of the sky. The harbour bristled with the masts of ships from all over the world and, as the sailors secured the vessel, Georgiana could hear other languages being shouted on neighbouring ships. The children were literally jigging for joy at the sight of land and, thanks to Julia's friendship with the captain, they were amongst the first passengers taken ashore. The ground pitched under their feet much to the children's delight.

'Why is the land moving?' Sebastian demanded.

'It's not – it's our legs,' said Georgiana, laughing. 'We have to get our land legs back.'

Mr Taylor, quiet as ever, smiled at his exuberant offspring, then turned to Georgiana. 'What would you like to do, Miss Trent?'

'Go exploring,' shrieked the children.

'Yes indeed, please.' Georgiana's fervent tones made his smile widen.

'Let us go, then,' he said.

Having been the centre of shipping routes for three hundred years, Cape Town was diverse and exciting in every aspect. The narrow streets were lined with two-storied houses with exquisite, wrought-iron balconies. Others had shutters painted jaunty colours. There were beautiful stone churches and small parks studded with shady trees and colourful birds.

The shops were a treasure trove of goods which came from all corners of the world, and in Market Square the stalls overflowed with fruit and vegetables of such size and colour that Georgiana found it hard to believe they were real.

Many were entirely foreign to her. One fruit smelt especially exotic and she closed her eyes as she inhaled deeply.

'Mango,' said the seller, picking one up and offering the large orange fruit to her. 'Very nice, you buy.'

'Oh *please*, Father!'

'Just this once,' said Mr Taylor, buying them all one. They sat in the shade of a tree to try eating them. Soon all were smothered in the sticky sweet juice which ran down chins and arms to their elbows.

'Mmm,' said Julia. 'I love Cape Town. I wish we could stay here forever.'

She didn't quite get her wish, but the ship did remain in port for several days. On the third morning Georgiana and the children were gazing into a toy shop window in Adderley Street while Mr Taylor was in the bank, when she saw in the wavering reflections the profile of a man who looked surprisingly familiar. He was standing with his back to them, but his face was turned sideways looking up the street. It simply wasn't possible of course but, as she leaned closer to see, it really did seem to be – Jasper? With a gasp, Georgiana whirled around. At that moment, the man spied a gap between the carriages and carts and dashed across the street. He was immediately swallowed up by the crowds and Georgiana was left gazing after him.

Disbelief warred with fear. The hairs on her neck prickled and her back suddenly felt terribly exposed. Turning back to the window, she tried to reason with herself. Jasper here? Ridiculous! He would never imagine his cousin would attempt to travel across the world by herself. Besides, even if the ludicrous notion had come to him, he'd have been so incensed by her disappearance he'd have washed his hands of her. Jasper never made a move unless it was in his own best interests. If she was not going to marry him, he had nothing to gain from pursuing her. Yet the memory of that profile, with its arrogant tilt to the jaw, filled her with a cold dread.

Abruptly, she turned to the children. 'It's terribly hot, I think we should go back to the ship.'

'No!' wailed Sebastian. 'You said we'd go see the monkeys.'

The gardens on the lower slope of the mountain were the haunt of opportunistic monkeys who came down to entertain the humans in exchange for food. The monkeys were so tame, they'd even accept food from the children's hands.

Julia was more observant than her brother. 'What's wrong, Miss Trent? You've gone awfully white.'

Georgiana managed a shaky smile. 'It's just the heat.'

'You *promised* we'd go today!' Sebastian cried again. 'You said if I was good and I have been good, haven't I?'

She looked into the angry little face and saw tears welling. How could she disappoint him? She was just being silly. Of course Jasper couldn't be here. Her aunt had always accused her of an overactive imagination.

'You're right, I did promise. Oh look, there's your father.'

Despite having the somewhat absentminded protection of Mr Taylor, for the rest of the time onshore Georgiana kept her face averted, snatching hasty looks around her when she dared. She never caught so much as a glimpse of Jasper again but was still relieved to return to the safety of the ship.

That evening, still feeling jangled, but angry with herself for her unfounded fears, Georgiana took her seat at the dinner table and saw that the place next to her was set once more. A replacement must have been found and speculation rippled up and down the table.

'Who is it?' asked Mrs Roper. 'Does anyone know?'

'Heard he's a remarkable young man,' said the colonel.

Relief washed over Georgiana. They'd set sail again and that man in the reflection – not that it was Jasper, of course – would cease to matter. Captain Dunn interrupted these thoughts as he arrived at the door.

'My apologies for being late, but I have good news for us all. I have just found a new officer of considerable experience, so our journey will begin once more. Ladies and gentlemen, I would like to introduce Mr Richard Miller.'

The captain stepped inside so that everyone could see their new officer. Georgiana whitened and she made a small exclamation which she quickly turned into a spluttering cough. Everyone turned to look at her as she took a hasty drink from her glass. It was just as well. Shocked recognition flared in 'Mr Miller's' face, closely followed by thunderous disapproval. Then his expression smoothed out and he stepped into the cabin.

'Let me introduce you to our companions,' said the captain. 'At the far end is our esteemed Doctor Carmichael and beside him is Mrs Roper,' and so he proceeded down the table until he reached Georgiana. 'And last, but by no means least, may I present Miss Sarah Trent.'

His eyes seemed to burn with suppressed emotions, but on hearing the name, Georgiana saw – and her wicked heart leapt – humour conquer them all as one black brow rose.

'Miss *Trent*.' The gentle emphasis he placed on the second word caused her to blush. 'I am very pleased to make your acquaintance.'

'You will certainly become well acquainted on the voyage,' said the captain. 'As you can see, this is your place by her side.'

'So it is,' he said, slipping into the seat. 'How delightful to meet you all,' and he smiled at the group. Was she the only one, she wondered, to see the impudence in that smile? To feel his boundless energy held in check? 'Please start your meal. I must apologise for having held you up. I needed to bid farewell to my other ship.'

'I can imagine you did, Mr *Miller*.' Georgiana, despite a tumult of emotions, took some relish in stressing his name. The lieutenant's small grin told her he appreciated the irony. 'Did you feel guilty to abandon the crew so abruptly?'

'Not at all,' he answered. 'The ship was bound for Australia, but New Zealand was my real destination. The captain understood that from the start. When I heard of the position offered on this ship, I jumped at the opportunity. There was no problem at all, for the captain was a reasonable man and I was easy to replace.'

'With all your experience?' Georgiana feigned surprise.

'I'd signed on as an extra hand because it was the first position I could find.' As Harry looked affably around the table, his foot pressed down hard on hers. She threw him a swift, burning look but fell silent. Turning to Colonel Briggs, he asked whether the colonel had been involved in the land wars in New Zealand and the conversation shifted to the safety of general discussion.

Georgiana, who usually tackled her food with robust enjoyment, only toyed with her meal and paid perfunctory attention to the conversation around her. Her thoughts and emotions were in a terrible tangle. At the same time, all her senses were suddenly, vividly, splendidly alive.

His arm lay but inches from hers and her foot still tingled with the pressure of his boot though he had not hurt her. She knew full well that Harry Trent had had to disappear, but his choice of surname made her blood run quick. Under the guise of asking for salt and pouring the children more water even when they said they'd had enough, she could not resist stealing glances at Mr Miller.

The salt-stained clothes had been replaced by an immaculate uniform and his normally tousled hair was swept back in sleek waves, but his voice, his laugh were as she had recalled so often to herself in quiet moments. When she raised her glass, she saw that her hand shook.

Harry meanwhile had recovered from the immediate shock of seeing her but was still battling a number of conflicting emotions. He was, of course, furious. Did the silly girl not possess one iota of common sense? One inkling of propriety? One whisker of self-preservation? Clearly not, given the way she had so calmly overturned his plans. He had sailed away, relieved to think that at least *Sally* and George were safe, little realising that once again she'd lied, pulling the wool over his eyes – fool that he was. Yet seeing her sitting there, demure and self-possessed in that damned governess dress, he was hard put not to laugh. And he hadn't laughed for weeks – not since that day in Madeira. She'd even had the audacity to take his name and the name of his ship. He'd hit on Miller as it was, he'd told himself, as good a pseudonym as any, but now they had swapped identities. Only Georgiana da Silva could get him into such a ludicrous situation.

She was looking well, though. Her hair had grown and the gaslight picked out the red and gold tints in her curls. Her extraordinary eyes were bigger and brighter than he'd remembered. But that was beside the point. There were issues that needed sorting. Her insubordination for a start.

'So Miss Trent,' he said, his tone carefully conversational, 'do tell me – how is it you come to be travelling to New Zealand?'

His eyes bore into hers. She met his gaze without flinching. 'I had the misfortune to be abandoned in Madeira,' she replied, equally lightly, equally pointedly.

The little girl with long plaits – Julia? – cut in. 'Yes, Miss Trent was travelling with her cousin to see her brother, but her cousin got terribly sick and had to return to England.

Then the captain of the ship she was on just sailed away with almost everything she owned in the world.'

Harry was startled. 'The ship sailed without you?'

'It was a French ship,' young Sebastian explained.

'A French ship?' Harry raised a brow. 'Ah, you should have stayed with the English then, Miss Trent.'

She clearly caught the edge in his voice because her eyes flashed, but before she could come up with one of her preposterous excuses, Captain Dunn came to her defence.

'Not her fault,' he pointed out. 'She trusted him, they'd had an agreement. The captain was a rogue, sailing off like that.'

Harry looked down at the roll he was buttering. 'He certainly sounds like it – but perhaps there was a reason?'

'None that I could see. I will never forgive him,' she said in a low voice.

She could never forgive? Her effrontery was breathtaking.

'Surely you should have returned to England with your cousin?'

'She didn't want to,' supplied Sebastian, 'because she absolutely must find her brother.'

Was Harry the only one at the table to find her behaviour outrageous? 'All the same, it is foolhardy to venture abroad alone.'

'But, she isn't alone,' Julia cut in. 'Mr Mellors rescued Miss Trent and now she is our governess.'

Governess? Again Harry had to repress a terrible desire to laugh.

Georgiana beamed at her benefactors. 'And I am extremely grateful to both Mr Mellors and Mr Taylor.'

'I was only too happy to be of service,' said Mellors. During the introductions, Harry had spared the big man with the farmer's countenance little thought. But now there was something in his tone that caught Harry's attention.

'Miss Trent has proved to be a godsend,' said Mr Taylor. 'She's excellent with the children.'

Rosy with gratification, Georgiana shot a triumphant sideways glance at Harry but he just said, 'A godsend? You must be a treasure indeed, Miss Trent.'

'Thank you,' she said. 'I'm just grateful I can be of help. I'd hate to be a *liability*, you know. Now, I must prove my worth, for I can see Sebastian and Julia have finished their meals and are almost asleep – it has been a busy day. I have a slight headache myself so will retire with them. If you will excuse me.' Georgiana gathered her skirts.

The men rose and the farmer said with unnecessary solicitude, 'I do hope your headache is not severe, Miss Trent.'

'Thank you, Mr Mellors. I'll be fine in the morning.'

'Good. Then I will look forward to renewing our acquaintance, Miss Trent,' said Harry with a meaningful look and a small bow. Oh yes, she could beat a retreat tonight, but they were going to be locked together on this ship for a good many weeks. He'd have plenty of time to get the full story out of her and this time he was damned if he was going to be fobbed off with more of her lies. Georgie, however, just gave a slight toss of her head.

'How kind of you, Mr Miller, but you must not trouble yourself. I know how busy you will be.'

'Yes,' Mellors added. 'We scarcely saw anything of Mr Collins, for he was often taken away by his duties.'

Harry turned back to the farmer. 'No doubt I'll find out how hectic my schedule is over the coming weeks.'

His smile was as false as Mellors as they locked eyes.

'Well, good evening to you all,' said Georgiana as she hustled the children away.

And Harry, for the first time in weeks, felt lighter in the heart, his predicament suddenly a little less grim and considerably more problematic.

Chapter Seventeen

The following day, Georgiana, her employer and her charges all went ashore for the final time. The children begged to go to the markets, but Georgiana needed to make some last minute purchases of a more feminine nature.

'Would you mind if I left the children with you?' she asked Mr Taylor. 'I'll only be gone ten minutes.'

He looked doubtful. 'I don't think you ought to be walking the streets unaccompanied.'

'You needn't worry,' Georgiana assured him. 'I know my way around and, besides, the town's filled with the ship's passengers. I'm only popping up Adderley Street.'

Mr Taylor looked uneasy, but his clamorous offspring grabbed his hands and began towing him away. 'Be careful,' he called over his shoulder.

The freedom of being alone, if only for a short spell, was a relief. She wanted to have a moment to think. The children, excited at the notion of setting sail again, had been hard to settle the previous night and had woken early. Georgiana had been spared the sight of Harry over breakfast, but still needed time to gather her thoughts. Fate had twisted their paths together once again and she did not know what to make of it. There was relief, of course, she told herself, now she knew he was no closer to Charlie than she was. There was apprehension too but not, she mused, fear. Excitement, rather. The mere thought of Harry in close proximity, day after day, made her stomach churn in a most unseemly and disconcertingly delicious way.

Oblivious of the people around her, Georgiana was making her way up Adderley Street when her arm was seized in a painful grip.

'Georgiana?' The voice was sharp with disbelief.

Her heart bucked. This was no wavering reflection in front of her and the fingers biting into her arm were real.

'*Jasper!*'

As always, he was immaculately dressed, brown hair combed back from his clever, narrow features. He laughed. 'What a giddy chase you have led me on, coz. What luck to meet you here of all places!'

If she didn't know better, she'd have thought she heard relief in his voice, and inwardly she cursed her stupidity in being alone. Harry's unexpected appearance had driven all other thoughts from her mind.

'What on earth are you doing here?' She tried to shake her arm free but his hold tightened.

'Looking for you, of course.'

'I left word I was headed for Scotland.'

'I know what the note said, but I'm not such a fool, Georgiana.' His smile did not reach his eyes. 'Come, we need to talk.' His tone was coaxing and very reasonable but still he did not relinquish his grip.

'I have nothing to say to you.'

'Don't be like that. I don't know what's got into your head, but I'm sure we can sort it out.'

'There's nothing to sort out. Leave me alone, Jasper.' Again she tried to twist free, but Jasper, after a swift look around, began dragging her into a side alley.

'Let go of my arm! You're hurting me!'

'Just a few minutes to explain,' he said, and though Georgiana struggled, his grip was remorseless. In seconds, she was out of the sunlit street, thronged with people, and in the dim alley where all sounds were suddenly muffled.

'What do you think you are doing, Jasper?' She tried to sound calm but her heart hammered.

'There's been a misunderstanding. I love you, and I've come to take you back with me.'

Georgiana hated the way he could talk of love when his eyes stayed so cold. She gave a brittle laugh.

'Misunderstanding? I don't know what you mean. I simply decided we would not *deal well* together, after all.'

'No, I know something happened to change your mind. What was it? You must know that all I want is to marry you.'

His lies were tinder to her temper. 'I know *exactly* why you want to marry me, Jasper. Nothing in the world would induce me to take you as my husband now.'

'I knew it. You read the letter, didn't you.' Her eyes widened involuntarily and he nodded. 'Ah yes, you thought you were being so clever, leaving the letter in the drawer, but you dropped the key.' He pulled her closer still, forgetting all about being placatory now. 'What I want to know is what made you look there in the first place?'

She remained defiantly silent.

'Did you overhear something?'

He was guessing and she pressed her lips tighter together, determined he would not discover the extent of what she knew about Walsingham's plans.

Her silence enflamed him. 'Dammit, Georgiana. You left me in a devil of a predicament with your games,' and Jasper twisted her arm hard. She cried out and lashed back with the only weapon she had available, her soft pouch. It whipped across his face and, though it weighed nothing, the tassels caught him in the eye. With a curse, he dropped her arm to rub his face. Immediately she turned to flee, but in a flash he'd grabbed her again.

'Try that again and I'll wring your neck.'

'I don't think so,' said a voice behind them. Jasper whirled around and a fist caught him square on the chin, sending him staggering.

'What's this? Another man wanting to throttle you, George?' asked Harry, as with his other hand he swept her behind him, away from Jasper. His voice was light but despite his uniform, Georgiana recognised this Harry right away. The pirate king was back. Dangerous lights danced in his blue eyes, his half-smile taunted. Light on his feet, every muscle corded, he was tense and coiled, ready to spring. This was a man who knew how to fight. A man, she realised with a shiver, who would kill if need be.

Jasper worked his jaw to check it wasn't broken. 'This is nothing to do with you,' he said. 'I am speaking with my cousin, who also happens to be my fiancée.'

The dangerous lights in Harry's eyes sharpened. 'You … surprise me.' His voice was soft, but edged. He circled Jasper, still keeping Georgiana behind him. 'However, it would appear that your fiancée does not wish to speak to you.'

Jasper swivelled on his heel, keeping Harry in sight, and pulled a gun from his pocket. Georgiana gasped. 'Jasper!'

He ignored her as he trained the gun on Harry. 'This has nothing to do with you,' he repeated. 'Leave now and you won't get hurt.'

With a derisive laugh, Harry lunged. The sound of the gun going off as Harry knocked Jasper's arm upwards was deafening. In a movement almost too swift for Georgiana to see, he'd twisted the gun from Jasper's grip and sent it spinning down the alley. Jasper leapt at Harry with an oath and the two men locked together in swaying combat. Georgiana looked wildly around and spied a broken piece of wood. Swinging it like a club, she brought it crashing down with all her might to hit Jasper. Except, at that moment, the men stumbled and Harry caught the ringing blow on the side of his head. Stunned, he lost his grip, staggered and fell. With a horrified cry, Georgiana dropped the plank. Jasper laughed.

'Much obliged to you, coz.' He scooped the plank up to hit Harry again.

'No!' cried Georgiana, springing at him, but she was too late. Another hand had grabbed Jasper's wrist.

'Drop it.'

'Mr Mellors!' Georgiana felt weak with relief.

Jasper whirled around and the sight of Tom stopped him short. 'What the—?'

He had no chance to say anything further, for Tom, using his considerable strength, forced the plank from Jasper's grasp as he growled, 'I don't know what's going on here, but you make yourself scarce, fast. The lady is safe with me now so you've no further business here, understand?'

For a second there was a stand-off, Jasper staring in furious disbelief at this new rescuer while Tom, unusually severe for a mild man, stared him down. Finally Jasper seemed to realise he was indeed outnumbered, for he nodded wordlessly, retrieved his gun and left without so much as a second glance at Georgiana.

Tom called after his retreating back, 'And if I ever see you again, I'll personally kick you around the market square at noon!' Then he turned to Georgiana who was already beside Harry, helping him to sit. 'Are you all right?'

'I'm fine but I'm not sure about Ha— Mr Miller.'

Harry's eyes were not quite focused, but he managed a smile. 'I'm not dead, despite your best efforts, Miss Trent.' All trace of the dangerous pirate had disappeared. Harry had turned once again into the equable officer, a thread of laughter running beneath his words. She was too relieved, however, to wonder at this transformation. Instead she laughed, though filled with contrition. 'I am truly sorry. I just—'

Harry nodded and closed his eyes, '—rushed in without thinking. I know.'

Tom squatted down and checked the swelling coming up behind Harry's ear. 'It's a nasty one, but it'll heal. No doubt you'll have a terrible headache, tonight.' He helped Harry to his feet. 'What happened?'

Georgiana said quickly, 'I haven't been entirely honest. That man was my fiancé, but I don't wish to marry him. That's why I must get to my brother in Dunedin, for his protection. Jasper's quite unhinged when crossed.'

Tom whistled. 'Yes, so I see.'

'He's pursued me all the way from England, but it was bad luck that we met. He dragged me here and Mr Miller must have seen because he suddenly arrived and they fought and then you appeared – and I'm so grateful to the two of you.' Georgiana finished in a tumble of words.

'You've thanked me very well already,' said Harry a little unsteadily, but Georgiana was glad to see the corner of his mouth lift. 'You'd be a handy person in a tavern brawl I imagine, Miss Trent.'

She shot him a quelling look before turning back to Tom. 'But Mr Mellors, where did you come from?'

'I was walking up Adderley Street when I saw Mr Miller dart down this alley. Then I heard a gunshot. You don't have to thank me, I did nothing.'

'Nothing? You saw Jasper off before he could kill Mr Miller here,' she said, indignant at his modesty.

'You had already half-murdered me yourself,' Harry pointed out.

She did not deign to respond, and instead looked at Tom. 'You were wonderful.'

But Tom would have none of it. He held up his hand to stem any more thanks. 'Truly, not a word more.' Then he touched her arm. 'Are you all right? Did he hurt you?'

'No,' she assured him. 'Mr Miller arrived just as Jasper was turning ugly.'

'I'm relieved.' Tom smiled down at her, solicitude evident in both his eyes and his voice. Then he glanced at his watch. 'Much as it pains me to depart at this moment, I must beg you will excuse me, Miss Trent. I have an appointment I cannot miss. I hate to abandon you, though. Will you be all right?'

'Of course,' said Harry, straightening. 'I'll look after Miss Trent.' Tom hesitated, clearly unhappy at leaving her with the officer, but as he turned to go, Harry added, 'And Mellors, I believe I'm now in your debt.'

Tom smiled. 'Don't mention it,' he said and disappeared into the sunlight.

Harry offered Georgiana his arm as they began walking back down to the wharf. Though there was no sign of Jasper, Georgiana clung to the strength of arm and muscle she could feel through his sleeve. One thought went round and round her head. *He saved me. Harry saved me from Jasper.* She saw several women's heads turn as they walked past and had to smile. Wanted to laugh out loud. Only Harry Trent could come from a fight looking so splendidly tousled. Still she felt dazed with the swift turn of events.

'How did you know?' she asked.

'I was some distance down the street when I saw you ahead of me and alone. I thought we could talk so began making my way to you. Then I saw that man accost you – your cousin did you say?'

She nodded. 'Jasper.'

'Well, he's a most determined suitor to pursue you around the world. What happened? Lovers' tiff?'

Harry's tone was a shade too casual.

'He wants to marry me because he thinks I'm rich.' The bitter words slipped out before she had a chance to think.

Harry was surprised. 'And are you?'

'No! Well – maybe. My brother thinks he's found gold.'

She watched Harry, but he seemed genuinely perplexed. Surely Walsingham would have explained the situation to his man and Harry was quick enough to start making connections. Just at that moment, the town clock began striking the hour and Harry stopped dead.

'What is it?' she demanded.

'Twelve o'clock! I've just remembered I too have an appointment. Good, isn't that the Taylors over there?' He waved and Sebastian and Julia began running to meet them. 'I'm sorry, I must rush away, but you are certainly safe now,' he said softly. Then he vanished into the crowds, leaving Georgiana to stare after him, bewildered and furious with him and with herself.

He'd had the effrontery to once again abandon her in the most peremptory of fashions. Of all the unconscionable bounders, unspeakable curs – Would she *never* learn?

'Miss Trent, *there* you are!' said Julia. 'We've been looking for you *everywhere*. Where *have* you been?'

Chapter Eighteen

Georgiana did not see Tom or Harry again until dinner time. She hadn't mentioned the incident to anyone and she hoped neither man would either. Fortunately, they took their lead from her and nothing specific was said, although Tom could not help checking on her as the main course was being served.

'Miss Trent, I trust you found Mr Taylor in good time today and passed a peaceful afternoon.'

She could not suppress the feeling of warmth Tom's evident concern created, a sharp contrast to the stab of chagrin she still felt at being so summarily dropped by Harry. He hadn't even asked her how she was after her horrible ordeal – had simply plunged back into the crowd.

'Yes, thank you. We came upon one another shortly after your departure.' She did not look at Harry as she added, 'It was just as well since Mr Miller had to immediately rush away.'

The look of reproof Tom shot at Harry further gladdened her heart. 'Indeed? If I had known escorting Miss Trent was *inconvenient*, Miller, I'd never have left.'

Harry looked up from the cutlet he'd been struggling to cut. 'It wasn't inconvenient at all. I restored Miss Trent to the Taylors and still made my dentist appointment on time.' His voice was all airy unconcern.

Julia looked at Harry's teeth with interest. 'What did the dentist do? Pull a tooth out?'

'No, I just had a filling.'

'Did it hurt?'

'Like the dickens,' he told her with a grin.

'Then how can you eat such tough meat tonight?'

'I shouted so loud when he began drilling the dentist gave me nitrous oxide. It makes you laugh,' he added.

'I know *that*,' Julia said. 'Sebastian and I went to the dentist with our governess and she came out all silly.'

'Silly-er,' Sebastian corrected her. 'Miss Sackham was always silly even before the gas.'

'Thank you, that's enough,' said their father.

'Well, she was,' muttered Sebastian.

Georgiana intervened quickly to save her charges from being banished from the table before dessert. 'How about you, Mrs Roper? Did you purchase that silk you'd lost your heart to?' and the conversation turned to other matters.

They left Cape Town later that night and, as a special treat, the children were allowed to stay up – just this once. They danced at the railings beside Georgiana.

'Goodbye, Table Mountain!' shrieked Julia.

'Goodbye, monkeys!' cried Sebastian.

Goodbye, Jasper, Georgiana thought. I hope I never see you ever again.

The strength of her antipathy shocked her, but this was the first moment she'd had to take in what had passed that morning. After Harry had left her, she'd started shaking and had wanted to do nothing so much as either kill her cousin or sit down and indulge in a good bout of tears. Instead, Julia and Sebastian had swept her up in their usual cascade of questions and demands and there had been no time to privately reflect on the matter. Now, as she stood at the railings, watching the flickering lights of Cape Town slide away, she began to shake again and clutched her hands together. Tom appeared at her side.

'Miss Trent,' he said, 'I'm sorry I couldn't come earlier. Are you recovered from the appalling attack?'

'Yes, thank you.'

Her voice was steady, but something must have betrayed her. Remorse combined with Tom's look of concern. 'Oh Miss Trent, I should have stayed with you. I would have, had I known that Mr Miller was going to abandon you.'

'Not exactly abandon,' said Georgiana. 'He did take me back to Mr Taylor.' Why was she defending that pirate?

'Even so,' said Tom, and in her heart of hearts, Georgiana could not but agree. Even so! Then she chided herself. If Harry was the assassin, there was no reason why he would take care of her – it's just she'd become used to Harry looking out for her. Well, looking out for George at any rate. It was all very confusing.

'It is none of my business, of course,' Tom went on, 'and I don't mean to pry, but it appears your troubles are greater than you first admitted to, Miss Trent. If you should need a friend to confide in, I do hope you will consider me. You know I am wholly at your service.'

Tears sprang into her eyes and for a minute she was tempted to tell him everything, but here was neither the time nor the place. He seemed to read her mind, for his fingers closed over hers and he said, 'Of course, you may not want to speak about it just yet. But when you do, please know that I will be there, waiting for you.'

He squeezed her fingers then withdrew his hand just as Julia and Sebastian came running up.

'Oh Miss Trent, do come to the other side. The moon is coming up and it is enormous and *orange*.'

She and Tom both laughed, the moment broken.

Later, after she had the children in bed and asleep, Georgiana pulled a shawl about her shoulders and made her way across the deck to a quiet corner overlooking the wake. It frothed white under the moon, but black clouds were gathering overhead. Africa was merely a dark silhouette on the horizon. Jasper was now well and truly behind her.

At last she could give the incident proper thought. Harry had rescued her, as had Tom. If Harry was working for Walsingham, then he had unwittingly scotched Jasper's plan. Walsingham would not be pleased. The thought should have amused her but she could not laugh. It just didn't make sense. Why had Harry left her so abruptly and then made up that ridiculous story about a dentist? It must have been her mention of her brother's gold that had suddenly alerted him, making him realise what he had done. Had he gone in search of Jasper to sort things out?

'I've been watching out for you, wondering if you'd slip aft the way you used to on *Sally*.'

Harry's voice directly behind her made her jump. She hadn't heard him steal up on her. 'I've been wanting to find out exactly *what* was going on today, George, and what the hell you are doing on this ship.'

His manner was calm but with an undercurrent of anger which she instantly reacted against. 'Since you left me in Madeira, I can't see it's any of your business.'

'None of my business?' He caught her arm in a grip as hard as Jasper's and gave her a little shake. 'Some man claiming to be your fiancé tries to kidnap you and kill me and you say it's none of my business! You've been holding out on me.'

His grasp hurt and she clawed at his fingers. 'Let go of me!' Fury boiled over, swamping the fear that she'd been carrying around all day. 'Let go!' she hissed.

He dropped her arm, but said again. 'Tell me what this is all about.' His voice was low but, unlike Tom's solicitude, his tone was fierce. 'You've been telling only half-truths from the moment I met you and I'm tired of it, Georgie. I want to know what the hell is going on.'

'All right,' she spat. 'I didn't tell you the whole truth. I was running away from my step-cousin, my fiancé. I'd agreed to marry him, but then found out what sort of person he is. You saw how he behaved today. Can you blame me?'

Harry's eyes were narrow in the moonlight as they searched her face. 'No,' he admitted gruffly. 'But why didn't you just tell him you wanted to break off the engagement? Why this mad dash to New Zealand?'

'I couldn't just tell everyone I'd changed my mind. My aunt dotes on my cousin. There was no one – *no one* – who could help me, except my brother.'

'So you ran away?'

'Yes. I disguised myself and ran away.'

He sighed in exasperation. 'Why didn't you tell me all this before?' he demanded. 'How can I help you if I don't know the full story? If I had known about your betrothal, I'd never have tried to send you back to England.'

'Oh no?'

'No! What sort of cad do you think I am, George?'

An assassin, she thought.

Or maybe not, her heart whispered.

Georgiana stayed silent. Harry stepped closer and tipped her chin up with one hand, staring down into her eyes. At that moment the moon was blotted out by the clouds and the wind blew cold. Georgiana shivered.

'What else is there, Georgie?'

'What do you mean?'

'You know what I mean. You're still holding out on me and I intend finding out why.'

Georgiana's thoughts raced. If he'd found Jasper, then he must know who she really was. He would also know there was no point in killing Charles as the marriage hadn't taken place, and Jasper would never be in line to inherit the gold mine. But although she had no hard evidence about who had killed Iver, Jasper must realise she could implicate him and Walsingham. That was more than enough to put her own life in danger. Then an even more chilling thought struck her. If both she and Charlie were to die, her aunt would inherit the mine. Jasper would be rich, after all.

She searched Harry's eyes that stared so intently, so seemingly caring into hers. She could see no trace of the pirate, yet he was in there, somewhere. Summoning every ounce of acting ability, she grasped his wrist and widened her eyes. 'What are you talking about, Harry? You're frightening me.'

He held her look for a second, but she maintained her expression of bewildered alarm. The truth was, she did not have to fake her fear much at all.

A voice called out of the darkness. 'Mr Miller? Did I see you come this way? The captain's looking for you. The barometer is falling fast. A storm's on the way.'

Harry cursed then said, 'I have to go, but Georgie – don't get too close to Mellors. We'll talk soon.'

He slipped away, a black shadow in the light of the moon, and Georgiana fell back against the railing. Their thin support pressed into her back. The approaching storm was not the only danger on the horizon. Clearly Harry saw Tom as a threat and the thought of having Tom's strength at her service was very reassuring.

'Talk away, Harry,' she whispered. 'You'll learn nothing from me.'

Chapter Nineteen

The storm hit with unprecedented force later that night and raged for days. The ship, which had seemed so large and solid, was tossed as easily as a piece of driftwood in mountainous seas. The wind howled ceaselessly, shredding nerves. Waves broke with torrential violence over the decks. It was hard to tell which emotion was uppermost in the passengers' hearts – the fear of death or the longing for it as they stayed strapped to their bunks, struck down by seasickness of the worst sort.

Julia and Sebastian terrified Georgiana. They lay, clammy to the touch, with white-green faces and eyes black with misery. They had vomited and vomited until left with only dry retching that rendered them shivering and tearful.

'Make it stop, Miss Trent,' Sebastian whispered.

'If only I could,' Georgiana said as she smoothed his hair from his forehead, 'if only I could.'

Even Tom, usually so dependable, was stricken by the malaise and he and Mr Taylor could not leave their cabin. Georgiana visited all the passengers, making them comfortable where she could and earning the gratitude of Dr Carmichael, himself not faring well, for not only was he seasick but he'd sprained a wrist when he slipped on the wave-swept decks.

'Most obliged, Miss Trent,' he muttered, 'most obliged,' as she took away his bowl of vomit.

For several days she did not see Harry and when they did finally meet one dinner time at the empty table, she was shocked. Harry's face was white, his jaw stubbled, his eyes dark with fatigue. He started to rise but Georgiana motioned for him to remain sitting and he sank back. When he picked up his glass, she saw that his hand shook.

'Have you had any sleep?' she demanded, forgetting her resolve to treat him with indifferent cordiality.

He shrugged. 'The odd hour or two, but you know most of the crew is down too.' Then he looked at her as though trying to focus. 'Poor Georgie. You look exhausted yourself. Have you been ill?'

She shook her head and slipped into a chair across from him. He served her some soup from a large bowl that swung in a cradle. 'Thank you. No, I haven't felt the slightest twinge. No sensibility at all, as my aunt always used to say.'

He smiled at her attempted levity. 'And the children?'

'Worn away to shadows. I'm terribly worried about them,' she admitted, and she tried a mouthful of soup. 'Ugh, it's not very hot.'

The smell of mutton and vegetables cloyed.

'I know, but we have to keep our strength up. Go on, try some bread.'

He held out the basket and she took a roll but only nibbled on it. Though she did not feel sick, she had no appetite. Harry watched her. 'Here, drink this water and get it all down.'

When he was apparently satisfied that she was trying, he returned to his own bowl, eating slowly but doggedly. She knew the determination it took for him to eat when all he obviously craved was sleep. As if feeling her eyes on him, he looked up and smiled. 'Don't look so worried, I'll be right in a tick. As for the children, soon as this storm blows itself out, they'll bob up like corks, you'll see.'

'Thank you, that does set my mind to rest a little.'

Harry broke a roll in half and dipped some into the soup. Toying with her spoon, she added, 'It just all feels so empty, doesn't it.'

They both looked down the length of the table, usually thronged with passengers.

'They aren't dead, just ill. They'll recover too, you know. In a few days all will be back to normal, I promise.'

'A few days! That still sounds forever away. I'm sorry, I don't mean to sound fainthearted but you haven't seen how everyone is suffering.'

'Haven't I?' he asked dryly. 'I'm helping tend the crew as poor old Carmichael is so laid up.'

'Are you?' The idea entertained her. 'Nurse Harry?'

Their eyes met.

'Dr Harry, you disrespectful circus brat!'

They laughed, constraint and exhaustion falling away as they swapped nursing stories and then tried to remember the worst they had ever felt.

'I think it was that morning after I fell and you came to talk to me. My head was pounding, my arm on fire and I was in such a quake I could barely stand.'

He smiled. 'You disguised it well then – you seemed a trifle weak but as impertinent as ever and no sign of penitence at all.'

'Penitence! I was only doing what had to be done. I'll bet you've been far rasher than me in your adventures.'

That made him laugh. 'Perhaps Georgie, perhaps.'

'What about you? What was your worst moment?'

She was expecting a flippant sea story, but Harry went unexpectedly grave and said, 'Coming home from prison to find my mother had died the day before.'

'Oh, I'm so sorry.' Georgiana's spoke softly, partly in sympathy and partly to encourage confidences Harry had never offered before. She thought he might yet retreat but Harry, staring into his soup, continued in a low voice.

'I've never felt sicker than when I knew I'd failed her when she needed me most. She killed herself for me, you see. Died trying to put me through a fancy Cambridge education and I was so callow I never even knew.' His eyes were filled with pain.

'Perhaps she didn't want you to know.'

He glanced up at Georgiana. 'You're right, she didn't. All the same, I should have guessed all her talk of rich uncles was poppycock.'

This was a new Harry. The light-hearted confidence he wore as armour had been ground away by the storm. Here was a man driven beyond exhaustion. She remembered Consuela saying Harry never talked of his past. Was this her opportunity to discover the real man? Tentatively she asked, 'Why were you in prison? I don't understand …'

For a second Harry was silent as he stirred the soup with his spoon. 'It all seems such a long time ago now,' he finally said, looking up, eyes clouded with memories. 'It was my second year at Cambridge and I got a message to say my mother was dangerously ill. I travelled as fast as I could, but when I arrived at our cottage she was delirious, talking wildly of *them* and how she'd never meant to lie. There was other stuff about my father, how she'd deceived him. Normally she wouldn't talk of him at all, you know. She'd only say that he'd died before I was born. Of course in our village tongues were always wagging, especially when I was suddenly whipped out of the local schoolroom and sent to Harrow. She told me a rich uncle overseas was paying and, like a fool, I believed her.'

'There was no reason not to,' suggested Georgiana. She had never seen him show vulnerability before, reveal any sense of powerlessness. There was no sign of the humour that all too often lurked in his good natured face. Instead there was regret and self-disgust.

'Maybe, but I also didn't want to believe the explanation the gossips came up with. Anyway, there she was in our miserable cottage, tossing and turning and going on about how she had done a terrible thing because she loved my father, and begging my pardon. She kept insisting I take care of her poetry book. You remember it?'

Georgiana nodded. 'The Romantics.'

'That's the one. Well, I tried to reassure her that she'd been the best of mothers and the book would always be safe. It helped, but still she was terribly agitated.

'Bet, our neighbour who was tending to her, said she'd got sick after being caught in a snow storm in London. That made no sense. I'd never known her to leave the village, let alone go as far as London, but Bet told me that since I'd been at Cambridge, my mother had been up several times.

'At that moment the door burst open and in came two officers to arrest her for pawning stolen jewellery. I thought the world had gone crazy, but clearly I couldn't let them take my mother. I said I had stolen the jewellery and that she hadn't known where it came from. So they arrested me, and that was the last time I ever saw her.'

For a second Harry was silent, staring into his soup.

'What happened next?' asked Georgiana.

Harry glanced up, eyes blue-black in the lamplight. The pain in his face was speedily erased however and she saw his defences go up as he shrugged. In a matter-of-fact tone he continued his story.

'I spent the next two days in prison. I was lucky to have some coins in my pocket which bought me a private cell. I spent my time wondering what to say when my trial came up. I had no idea what I was supposed to have stolen and wondered how the hell my mother had come into possession of such jewels.' He gave a grim laugh. 'I still couldn't accept the most obvious explanation.'

Georgiana imagined how that time must have been for Harry; fearful for his mother, fearful for himself. His legitimacy, indeed his whole life, nothing but a series of questions.

Our past makes us what we are, who we are.

How did it feel, to not know who you really were? What a false position for Harry, of two worlds and of none. At least she knew who she was. She also had Charlie. Harry, usually so invincible, suddenly seemed very alone.

He took up the story again; his voice, though jagged with tiredness, still had that deep underlying strength that Georgiana always found reassuring. 'On the third morning the guard told me I had a visitor. I thought it might be Bet, but instead this cloaked woman swept into my cell. Her hood was pulled low so I could not see her face, but from her bearing I could tell she was someone of consequence. She demanded to know who I was. I bowed, gave my name and asked who she might be. She replied, "Impertinent boy! It was my jewellery that was recovered."

'I should have expected it, I suppose, and realised I'd have to be very careful. I began to apologise but she cut me short and ordered me to come closer so she could see me.

'I hesitated, aware that I must smell terrible and she said impatiently, "Don't be afraid. I won't hurt you."'

Georgiana laughed and Harry's eyes crinkled at the corners. 'I know, I laughed too at that and began to like her, despite her highhanded manner. I explained that I thought my presence close up might be offensive, but I moved forward into a strip of light from the window so she could see me. She took one look and recoiled. I must have been a terrible sight, dishevelled and unshaven, but it seemed to be more than that. Her hand went to her throat as she asked me to repeat my name. I did and she took a step forward to look closer at me. Her hood slipped back and I found myself looking into this haughty face with remarkably sharp eyes. She demanded I describe the necklace I'd stolen.

'I knew I was on thin ice so tried to bluff my way out by saying I couldn't talk about my case, but she refused to be put off, pointing out I'd already confessed.'

Georgiana laid down her spoon, put her elbow on the table and leaned her chin on her hand, caught up in the story. She was no longer aware of the storm raging outside. It was as if there were only the two of them in the whole world, trapped in the small pool of light from the kerosene lamp that swayed on the wall. 'So what did you do?'

He gave a half-smile. 'Oh, I made a great pretence of trying to remember by saying I couldn't quite recall which one was hers, having stolen so much. I asked her, "Was it the one with the diamonds?" Not clever, I know, but really, she had taken me so completely by surprise.'

'Did she believe you?'

Harry shook his head. 'I should have known from her eyes she was no one's fool. She just gave a crack of laughter, said she'd raised two boys and knew I was lying. I decided to give it one more try and said something like, 'The emeralds?'

'I thought she would be furious, but for a minute I swear she looked almost gentle. Then she cried, "Enough! It was taken twenty years ago. I did not think to see it again but it is returned and I am satisfied. I'll see to it you are released, and that all charges are dropped."'

Georgiana sat back, eyes wide. 'Unbelievable. You must have been thrilled.'

Harry's eyes met hers. 'I was dumbstruck, to be honest. I laughed because it all seemed so unlikely, but when I tried to thank her she just said she didn't deserve any. Then she asked if I was well and healthy.

'I said I was, wondering where on earth that question came from. She nodded and said that was all she needed to know. Then she said, "Goodbye, Mr Trent," and that was that. She just turned and left.'

Georgiana shook her head in wonderment. 'And you were released, just like that?'

'That very day.' His face had lightened while telling of this strange encounter – clearly he still felt some fondness for the old woman – but now it darkened. 'I arrived home just in time to bury my mother.'

'I am so sorry.'

'Don't be. It was all a long, long time ago.' Harry's manner changed and he laughed self-consciously. 'I should never have lingered so long and certainly shouldn't have bored you with my stories.'

'You didn't bore me,' Georgiana protested, but she could see he had already retreated, just as Consuela had said he did. Georgiana's mind buzzed with questions, but Harry's moment of confiding was clearly over. She became aware once more of the howling wind beyond the flimsy walls, heard the creak of timbers under strain. Smelt the fumes from the gas lamps.

'Did you ever see the old woman again?' she asked. 'Did you ever find out who she was?'

But Harry had already pushed back his chair and risen. 'I'm sorry, I can't stay any more. Forgive me for abandoning you, Georgie, but I've been away from my post too long.' He looked down at her. 'If you hadn't disregarded my plans, you'd be safely back in Britain and would have been spared this storm. This is exactly the sort of thing I tried to save you from.'

'How could I return—' she began, but he raised a hand to stem her protests.

'I know, the irate fiancé. Even so—' he paused. 'Even so,' he added softly, 'I am glad to see you again, Georgie.'

Several emotions chased across his face but they were swiftly banished. He stepped back, gave a small, formal bow. 'Miss Trent,' and was gone.

Chapter Twenty

The storm did eventually blow itself out – or they outran it – Georgiana wasn't sure which, but just as suddenly as it had arrived, it departed. People emerged white and frail into the sunshine, disbelieving that they were still alive. Sebastian and Julia bounced back as quickly as Harry said they would, and Georgiana was in awe of how much food the two children put away.

'Do you have hollow toes?' she demanded of Sebastian as he returned for his third helping of porridge.

'Every part of me feels hollow,' he explained. 'Even my teeth and hair.'

Mealtimes were back to being lively events, although the seat on Georgiana's right was often empty. At breakfast one morning, Mrs Roper asked the captain why Mr Miller was absent so frequently.

'That young man has become my right arm. I've never had such a fine officer,' the captain beamed. 'Many things shook loose or broke in the storm and Mr Miller is personally overseeing all repairs. I told him he'll make a fine captain one day. He only laughed, but I was being perfectly serious for he has a natural air of command, you know.'

Georgiana hid her smile by sipping her coffee just as Tom said in a low voice so only she could hear, 'He certainly does have a very high-handed manner.'

She was surprised. 'Don't you like him?'

'There is something about him—' Tom began, but he was interrupted by Sebastian.

'Mr Mellors, do you remember you promised to play deck quoits with me today?'

He turned to Georgiana's young charge and smiled.

'Of course. Did you know you've got porridge on your chin?'

While Sebastian scrubbed his face with the back of his hand, Mrs Roper leaned forward to gain Georgiana's attention. 'My dear, can I count on your company for a turn about the decks later this morning?'

Georgiana smiled. 'Of course. You know how much I look forward to our walks.'

Since the storm, Georgiana had been overwhelmed by the warmth of her fellow passengers, warmth sparked by the care she'd given them during those turbulent days. The captain was not above giving her cheek a paternal pinch from time to time, commenting on what an invaluable help she'd been. Dr Carmichael, more circumspect, had embarrassed her greatly with an earnest speech expressing his gratitude for her ministrations. Most heart-warming of all was the motherly interest to which Mrs Roper now gave free rein.

Their walk that morning, however, was interrupted by Julia racing up, crying, 'Oh Miss Trent. Come quickly!'

'What is it?' Georgiana's mind immediately filled with terrible images of Sebastian covered in blood.

'It's Muffin!' said Julia, agonised.

'Muffin?' Georgiana was mystified.

'The cat. Something awful's happened to her leg.'

Georgiana looked at Mrs Roper who smiled, making a shooing gesture. 'Go and help the poor creature.'

Julia seized Georgiana by the hand and dragged her to where Sebastian was standing by a nest of ropes. There lay the cat, sides heaving, eyes clouded in pain. Its lower back leg stuck out at an awkward angle.

'Oh, poor thing,' said Georgiana, falling to her knees.

'Can you fix it?' asked Juliana.

'I don't know.' Georgiana stared helplessly, then

brightened. 'Julia, go and get Mr Mellors. He grew up on a farm and knows all about animals.'

Julia scampered away and Sebastian squatted down next to Georgiana. 'We will be able to help her, won't we?'

She couldn't bear the entreaty in that small voice. 'Of course. Mr Mellors will know exactly what to do.'

But when Tom arrived, he glanced down, pursing his lips. 'It's broken. Best to put it out of its misery.'

'How will you do that?' Sebastian asked.

'He means we should kill Muffin, don't you, Mr Mellors?' Julia's face was pinched with fury.

'No,' Sebastian said, 'he wouldn't do that. Miss Trent said he'd fix her.'

Georgiana looked up at Tom. 'Please, isn't there something you can do for her?'

He shook his head. 'No. I'm sorry, Sebastian. But I promise I'll dispatch it quickly and painlessly – I'll break its neck.'

Julia looked at his hands and shuddered as Sebastian erupted, all previous hero worship forgotten. Flinging himself over Muffin, he shrieked, 'You won't murder her, you won't! Tell him, Miss Trent.'

Georgiana, trapped in the middle, didn't know what to say when Harry's voice cut calmly in. 'Sebastian, what's all this noise for, you abominable child?'

Immediately both children took it upon themselves to explain, gesticulating wildly first at Muffin then at Tom, who by this stage was looking harassed.

'It's what needs to be done,' he insisted.

Harry squatted down and ran a hand very lightly along the leg. Muffin hissed and spat. 'Language!' he said reprovingly, then looked sideways at Georgiana. 'The break feels clean, far as I can tell. It's a pity Carmichael's wrist is sprained, but I could try setting it if you can help.'

'Set it? Have you done it before?' Tom demanded.

'No,' Harry admitted.

'So what are you going to do? Maul the poor cat around, playing doctor to be hero?'

'Oh, Mr Mellors!' Julia was shocked at his tone.

'He didn't mean it like that, Julia,' said Georgiana. 'Did you, Mr Mellors?'

'No, I'm sorry I said that. But it riles me to see dumb animals mistreated.'

'I've no intention of mistreating, ah – Muffin did you say?' Harry looked at Sebastian who nodded vigorously. 'I haven't done this sort of thing myself, but I've assisted doctors setting bones. I've an idea of what must be done.'

Tom shook his head. 'Fools rush in. Trap a nerve and the animal will go berserk with pain. Set it wrong and it'll limp for life. It's a working cat, not a pet.'

Tears welled up in Sebastian's eyes. 'But I love her.'

'What do you think?' Harry turned once more to Georgiana.

For a minute she hesitated, but one look at Sebastian convinced her. 'Let's try.'

Harry nodded. 'That's the spirit! I knew I could rely on you.' The intimacy and approval in his smile caused her ungovernable senses to spiral giddily upwards. 'I'll go see John, the ship's carpenter, and see what he has that could serve as a splint. Do you have bandages?'

'I can get some.'

'Good. I'll meet you back here in ten minutes.'

Determined not to remain the villain of the piece, Tom volunteered to stay with the cat and children, and Georgiana was grateful not to have her charges with her in the cabin, asking questions as she pulled out one of Charlie's shirts to rip up.

She met Harry on the way back.

'John was most helpful and I think these will do,' said Harry, as he showed her two thin pieces of wood. 'Light enough for the cat to manage, but strong enough to protect the leg. Well, that's the theory at any rate. Now G— Miss Trent, could you hold Muffin in your lap? It might be an idea to use your shawl to control her front legs. Have you got a good grip?' His eyes were very blue as he smiled into hers. Georgiana's pulse tripped as she nodded. 'Right then, old girl,' he continued in a soft voice to the cat, 'no more of that language in front of the children.'

Julia and Sebastian giggled, but watched wide-eyed as his fingers very gently manoeuvred the leg until it lay on the splint at the correct angle and then bandaged it.

Time slowed as if under enchantment. Georgiana was vividly aware of the hot sun mantling them both and casting strong patterns as their shadows merged and mingled on the scrubbed deck. Harry was close enough for her to feel the warmth from his body, his thick black hair only inches from her fingers as he bent over his work. It took great restraint not to lean forward and inhale the smell of soap overlaid by the masculine tang of perspiration tinged with oil. His voice was low and mesmerising as he spoke to the cat.

On another level, life continued in real time. Muffin struggled and spat, but Georgiana maintained a firm grip and surprisingly quickly the cat, though very ruffled, was all trussed up. Harry stood and contemplated his handiwork. 'Not beautiful, but I think it will do.'

'Neat enough,' Tom admitted, having watched the proceedings. 'Seems I may have been wrong.'

Harry gave Tom a swift smile. 'No, you were right to have reservations. It could have all gone horribly wrong and then we'd have had to put her down, as you said. Still, it's always worth taking a risk I believe.'

'That is where we differ. I am a cautious man.'

'Oh, Mr Miller, you were *wonderful*,' Julia said.

'Thank you. Now sprats, Muffin will be off duty for the next few days and will require nursing – that's where you come in. Let's go find a place where she will be safe and out of the way and then we can discuss what you'll feed her. How good are you at catching rats?'

Picking up the cat, Harry smiled again at Georgiana, but there was something in his expression that caught her breath as she realised something had shifted in their relationship. When he'd first joined the ship, his manner still contained much of the captain dealing with an errant crew member. Today he'd actually deferred to her, giving her the responsibility for Muffin's fate, and together they'd worked to save the cat. Could he finally be seeing something more to her than just a troublesome girl? A strange anticipation – exhilaration – began bubbling up inside her as she watched him walk away, the children dancing beside him with suggestions of mousetraps and fishing.

Tom held out his hand to Georgiana. 'Well, I'm glad we didn't have to kill it.'

With some difficulty she pulled her attention away from Harry and accepted the hand up. 'Me too! The children would have been heartbroken.' As she shook out her skirts, Georgiana looked at him. 'Could you really have broken Muffin's neck, just like that?'

'There's no room for sentiment on the farm, Miss Trent. I've never shirked from what needs to be done, however difficult. You did a fine job holding it steady.'

Georgiana laughed. 'That was nothing. It was the cap— Mr Miller we have to thank.'

She glanced at Tom, but he was watching Harry go and didn't seem to notice the slip. When he turned to Georgiana, his face was troubled. 'Miss Trent, may I be frank?'

Georgiana was taken aback. 'Of course.'

'I may be sticking my oar in, but there's something I should perhaps have told you sooner, though there hasn't been the right moment what with the storm and all.'

'What is it?'

'That man – your fiancé.'

'Jasper?' she said. 'What about him?'

'I didn't tell all of the truth about that day. After my appointment, I chanced to see Mr Miller.'

Georgiana's heart stilled. She didn't want him to continue. Didn't want him to break the spell that lingered. Didn't want the harsh jarring of reality. 'I don't believe Mr Miller went to the dentist at all. You see, when I saw him, he was deep in conversation with your fiancé. Did he mention it to you at all?'

'No,' she said, 'he didn't. Could he have been warning him off?' Her voice sounded strained, even to her own ears.

Tom shook his head. 'I don't want to draw conclusions, but it seemed to me that they were quite chummy.'

'Surely you must be mistaken.' But Georgiana could see from his apologetic expression that he wasn't. Despite the heat of the sun, she shivered as memory of the pirate fighter flashed into her mind. How *could* she allow herself to be duped, yet again? She was such a fool!

'I wish I were. Maybe there's a perfectly good explanation, but it's strange Mr Miller didn't mention it.'

Georgiana was silent and Tom looked down at her. 'There now! I shouldn't have reminded you of that awful incident. I've upset you and I didn't mean to. I just wanted—' he broke off.

'Just wanted what?'

'Wanted you to be on your guard, that's all.' His words came out in a rush. 'I'm not wanting to insinuate anything and we don't want to go adding two and two and make five, but it is strange and would pay you to be wary.'

'Thank you, Mr Mellors, for your concern.'

Though stricken, she tried to smile, but her feelings must have shown, for he caught her hand and held it in his big, comforting paw. 'Won't you please call me Tom? We have been friends so long now, don't you agree?' Georgiana nodded and he smiled. 'And don't you worry, Miss Trent – Sarah.' His voice dropped gently on the word. 'If anything should happen – and I'm not saying it will, mind – but if it does, I won't let any harm come to you. You have my word.'

Georgiana looked into his eyes, so earnest and sincere. 'Thank you. It's good to have a friend – Tom.'

'There's one more thing. He might not like to know you have someone to protect you and try to drive a wedge between us. I'm not saying he will, but he might.' He patted her hand and smiled. 'You will be on your guard, won't you?'

'I will.'

Tom had no idea just how much on her guard she would be.

Chapter Twenty-One

As it turned out, Georgiana saw little of Harry, even at meal times, for his duties continued to claim almost all his time. She didn't know whether to be relieved or not. When he wasn't at the table, the conversation had less sparkle. But when he was there, it took all her resources to maintain a veneer of indifference.

The sensible thing, she knew, would be to tell the captain of Mr Miller's true identity. It was only right to clear up the situation one way or the other. She quailed, however, at the thought. If he was guilty of murder, he should, of course, be accountable for his actions. But then he would go straight to the gallows.

Over and over again she remembered his casual tousling of a cabin boy's hair, his punctilious manners upon discovering her sex, his leaping at Jasper's gun. His deep blue eyes with their lurking warmth, his beautiful mouth always slightly tilted in readiness to smile. She *must* be wrong. Yet what other explanation was there? What on earth would Harry have spoken about to Jasper? To warn him off ? Or to plot? Surely not. He had been, after all, the first to rescue her.

While there was a question in her heart, she could not betray him. Instead she surrounded herself with people to avoid any chance of being alone with him.

The ploy worked well and two weeks passed before Harry approached her on deck one morning. He must have been watching for the opportunity as the children had only just left her. His smile was warm. 'Miss Trent, you're looking very well.'

Suspecting a tease, Georgiana's hand went to her head

where curls had pulled free of their pins and were dancing about her head. But the expression in Harry's eyes was soft. Then he stepped closer, his voice low. 'I've been trying to talk to you for days, now. It's impossible to get you alone.'

She stepped back. She could not meet those blue eyes. Must not. 'Why?'

'Oh George, we have to get past these games. You still haven't told me the full story and I need to know. How can I help you if you won't trust me?'

He'd made a remarkable recovery from the shattered man during the storm. The sunlight gilded his face, casting faint shadows under strong brows, beneath high cheekbones, underlining the long jaw, the squared chin. He must have read the reticence in her eyes, however, for the habitual humour now faded from his face. He looked baffled but at the same time his mouth set in a determined line. Georgiana felt again an urge to run a finger over that firm lower lip. Then the image of Harry talking to Jasper came into her mind. 'What about you, *Mr Miller*?' she asked. 'What's your full story? Why don't you first tell me more about why you are going to New Zealand.'

His eyes slid from her face for the merest second. 'That's not relevant at the moment and has nothing to do with you.'

'Indeed?'

She loaded the word with scepticism and took perverse pleasure in seeing Harry, usually so unruffled, flinch as though caught on the raw. 'We don't have time for this. Look George, while you are my responsibility—'

'But I'm not.'

'The hell you aren't. Here you are, travelling alone—'

'I'm not alone,' she flashed and at that moment, almost miraculously, Tom appeared with Mrs Roper on his arm. The older woman greeted them.

'There you are, my dear. We've been looking everywhere

for you. Good morning, Mr Miller. We've hardly seen anything of you since the storm.'

'Mrs Roper.' Harry bowed, all frustration immediately erased from his face. Georgiana thought how good he was at dissemblance. Then, of course, he'd have learnt at school how to produce a façade that could both charm and conceal. She needed to remember this, whenever she felt herself begin to weaken. 'I've been very busy at my duties, but it's good to see you fully recovered, ma'am.' With a curt nod he added, 'Morning, Mellors.'

Tom's smile was affable. 'Good morning. Sorry to hear you've so much on your plate. However, we've come to beg Miss Trent's company in a game of cards, so we won't hold you up.'

His soft country tones neutralised any hint of discourtesy but left Harry little choice. Harry smiled – Georgiana was sure she was the only one to see the acid beneath it. 'Then I will wish you every pleasure in your game and return to work.' He bowed to the women. 'Your servant, ma'ams.'

'Such a gentleman,' Mrs Roper sighed, looking at his retreating figure, 'and so handsome.'

'Aye, pretty as a picture,' Tom agreed, but he threw Georgiana a look of concern. She smiled back, grateful for their arrival. When it came to Harry Trent, she simply had no defences. Tom, her self-appointed guardian, seemed to understand this. He would keep her safe from Harry – and her treacherous heart.

The pattern was set then, for the remainder of the voyage. Harry was very busy and on the occasions when their paths did cross, Georgiana forced herself to be cordial but distant. Good as his word, Tom was always quick to be at her side, forming a quiet but implacable shield. She was glad of this for it was impossible to stop her eyes from searching for Harry, to stop her pulse kicking whenever she did see him.

Impossible not to ache for their old familiar ease, to wish to recapture the closeness she'd felt when he'd confided in her. Because she yearned so much, she became far colder towards him than intended.

Initially Harry could not account for this change in Georgiana. Then as he thought back, he remembered the revelations he'd let slip during the storm when he'd been so tired. What a fool he'd been. She may have been born into a circus but she'd also been reared in drawing rooms these past seven years, and he cursed himself for confiding in a moment's weakness. What must she think? This was exactly why he'd left England. He hadn't wanted to see the cold distancing of former friends, once they knew he was either illegitimate or the son of a thief. Now, feeling humiliated fury whenever he saw Georgiana turn away, he knew he'd been right never to be completely honest in the past.

Rebuffed, Harry was forced to watch the growing closeness between Georgiana and Tom. He noted all Tom's tiny attentions towards Georgiana and her laughing acceptance of them. He saw their two heads bent together over Sebastian's drawings and burned at the sight of Tom's hand cupping Georgiana's elbow as she stepped over a coil of rope.

As if she needed steadying, Harry thought savagely, when she could cross the deck on stilts if she chose.

As the days passed, Harry's concern turned to anger and he itched to get Georgiana alone, to give her a good shaking. His tongue blistered with advice he knew she'd never take. He imagined the pleasure of planting a fist into Mellors' broad, good-humoured face. He was not the man for her, couldn't she see? Mellors thought he was courting a governess, for God's sake. What a dance she would lead him – lead any man rash enough to love her.

The sooner Harry delivered her to her brother, the better. Despite her protestations, Harry felt sure she was still up to mischief, playing a game beyond her league. The girl was a liability – but she was *his* liability. Not that he could say even that to her. As a man wanted for murder, Harry had no right to make even that claim over her. The thought that Mellors had more to offer, tortured him.

Before they reached shore, he had to somehow talk some sense into her.

The opportunity never arose, however, and New Zealand finally appeared as a streak on the horizon. Georgiana leaned on the railings, watching as the dark streak firmed to a black silhouette, then crystallised into the green hills and deep jade waters of Lyttleton, port to Christchurch.

I've made it, she thought with a flaring sense of triumph and jubilation. I've really made it! And somewhere, out there, is Charlie. Pray God he's still alive.

However, the joy of having finally reached her destination was eclipsed somewhat as the ship drew closer still and she saw that the hills, though beautiful, were dauntingly empty.

How on earth would she ever find Charlie in this vast, untamed land? She had focused so much of her attention on getting to New Zealand, she'd hadn't properly considered what she'd do when she actually arrived. Despite her determination, her courage quailed and she was suddenly filled with a despicable sense of desolation and helplessness which dimmed the day's sunshine and turned the hills from beautiful to forbidding.

It was with relief, therefore, she heard Tom call out, 'Miss Trent. Sarah. I'm glad to have found you.'

She looked over her shoulder to see him crossing the deck and was grateful for his company. 'Come and join me, I'm just admiring New Zealand.'

Tom came to stand beside her and leaned his forearms on the railings next to hers. 'I thought you might be packing.'

Georgiana forced a smile. 'I probably should be but was distracted by finally seeing our destination. It's even more beautiful than Madeira or Cape Town, isn't it.'

He half-turned, smiling back down at her. 'Aye, it's a bonny enough land.' Then he paused, clearly choosing his words, his manner serious. 'Sarah, I've been trying to get up my courage all voyage and I have to say it now. It would give me the greatest honour in the world if you would – would consent to be my wife.'

'Oh, Tom,' she began but, overwhelmed by such an offer, she did not know how to continue.

'If you're worried about my background,' he said, filling in the silence, 'I've good blood running through my veins.'

Georgiana gave a watery laugh as tears brimmed in her eyes. 'Tom, you know that is not an issue for me at all. You are a wonderful man, but ...'

'You won't accept, then?' Disappointment was written all over his earnest face.

'I'm so sorry, Tom, but until I find my brother, I cannot think about anything else. He's my first – my only – concern at present. I do hope you can understand that.'

'Of course I can. But then I must insist you will at least allow me to aid you in your search for him?' Tom said with an unexpectedly obstinate set to his jaw.

'I couldn't possibly trespass on your good nature.'

'It isn't trespassing. It would be my greatest delight to be of service to you.'

'I can't accept such a handsome offer.'

He laughed at this but said with finality, 'Come, you cannot refuse me twice in as many minutes. I will be quite undone if you do.'

She smiled, but shyly, and he took one of her hands.

'Sarah, I promise not to mention matrimony again until you are ready to consider the matter. But it's a new and raw land out there. Accept my help, for I won't rest easy until I know you are safely with your brother.'

'You are all kindness.'

'Damn my kindness! Just say yes.'

Was the sun suddenly warmer, the hills less intimidating? With Tom's strength to protect her, she could surely find Charlie and together they would finally be safe. Georgiana made her decision and laughed with relief. 'Yes, oh yes. Thank you, Tom.'

'Really?' His face brightened and he patted her hand. 'That's wonderful! Tomorrow I've business to settle in Christchurch and then we'll set off to Dunedin immediately after. Will that suit you?'

'Yes indeed!' She felt lightheaded as the terror of only moments earlier receded.

'Now, look at the time,' Tom exclaimed as he looked at the watch he'd pulled from his waistcoat pocket. 'Dinner is not too far away.'

'Then I must run. I've been loitering far too long. The children need to be dressed in their best.'

The final evening was to be a celebratory affair before all the passengers went their separate ways. As Georgiana hurried to her cabin, she tried hard not to dwell on the fact that this would also be the last time she'd ever see Harry.

Chapter Twenty-Two

Georgiana had just finished getting the children ready when there was a knock on the door. It was Mrs Roper with a silk dress in her arms. 'Miss Trent, I had my maid and a seamstress from steerage make this for you as thanks for all your help on this voyage.'

'But I've done nothing,' stammered Georgiana, though she couldn't take her eyes off the exquisite fabric she recognised as the silk Mrs Roper had bought in Cape Town.

'Nothing? Why you nursed me like an angel, read to me when I had my headaches and enlivened my days with your high spirits. You can't deny me my chance to say thank you. I had this made especially for you so if you won't have it, I'll have to throw it overboard for it'll never fit me, you know. Take it, please.'

She thrust the dress upon Georgiana who was both laughing and in tears. 'But how can I ever thank you?'

'By wearing it for me, my dear.'

Georgiana dressed with special care that night. Her eyes took their colour from the wild-sea-green of the silk and their sparkle reflected its sheen. It was cut lower than any dress she'd ever worn and she felt naked about her shoulders. Could she carry off a dress so feminine? Her answer came when Julia begged readmittance to the cabin.

'Oh, Miss Trent,' she breathed. 'You look beautiful.'

Georgiana blushed. 'It's just the dress—'

'No, it's not. It's you. Your eyes are so very green and your shoulders are as white as Mama's used to be. Please, please say I can help you dress your hair.'

Georgiana was not used to compliments and smiled to

cover her embarrassment. 'I'd be glad of your help. Could you hold the mirror? I can't see into it properly.'

She had only Julia's small mirror but between them they contrived to catch up her curls in a semblance of a bun, though tendrils escaped the hairpins.

'How good it is your hair is growing back. You are lucky to have curls. My hair is so straight!'

'But such a lovely colour – a mixture of corn, sunflowers and gold.'

Julia laughed and put her head to one side. 'And yours is a mixture of shiny brown acorns, red autumn leaves and orange flames.'

'Why thank you, Miss Taylor,' said Georgiana, sweeping her a magnificent curtsey.

'Why it's my pleasure,' said Julia, following suit. 'Do you have any diamonds or pearls?'

'No, why?'

'You should have something pretty around your neck. Where's your griffin?'

'I took it off. I thought it too unusual for a party.'

'But you are unusual, Miss Trent, and I don't think you should try to be like everyone else. There are plenty of ordinary people in the world.'

'How right you are, Julia,' said Georgiana, struck by these words. 'I shouldn't. Why did I never think of that before? I could have saved myself some terrible years trying to be like everyone else and failing miserably. The griffin, it is.'

As she clasped the griffin around her neck, she felt complete. She'd worn it throughout the voyage but only under her clothes. Though a trifle too large for most women, it sat well against the strong, graceful line of her shoulders and Georgiana drew herself up.

'Miss Trent, you look, look like'—Julia struggled for

words—'like a queen. Like Boadicea.' This made Georgiana laugh and she dropped a kiss on Julia's head.

'You are a darling. Now we must hurry for we're late.'

Everyone was seated as they arrived, a little breathlessly, at the salon and the men rose.

'By Jove,' said Captain Dunn. 'You look stunning tonight, Miss Trent.'

'An absolute picture,' agreed Mrs Roper. 'You carry that dress off superbly, Sarah dear.'

Tom and Harry both began to move forward, but Harry was the quicker. He stepped up to her and offered his arm. He was only funning, of course, for it was just a few steps to her seat, but she laughed and accepted. There was a curious smile in his eyes and her stomach fluttered as he leaned down to whisper, 'Gorgeous, Georges.'

His voice was deep and soft. Though she smiled at the silly rhyme, something caught at her heart, but he was already leading her to her place where Tom was waiting to kiss her hand and seat her.

'Bees to a honeypot,' she heard Mrs Roper murmur to the captain and saw the very slight wink he gave in reply. Georgiana's heart swelled.

Wine was plied generously, conversation flowed. Halfway through the voyage, some passengers had already had their fill of the others. Now all past differences were buried, and a few people even became maudlin.

'How I will miss the dear little children,' said Miss Trollope, dabbing her eyes. She appeared to have forgotten telling Georgiana the day she'd arrived that she was going to be governess to the most ill-mannered, *forward* children imaginable.

'Mr Mellors, you must come and visit our farm and give us some advice, eh,' said Colonel Briggs, all class differences set aside in the evening's bonhomie.

Tom's eyes declared his adoration of Georgiana and he was quick to meet her every need, filling her glass, passing her salt. It was all very gratifying and Georgiana, heady with the attention, became animated. Having seen the initial skirmish over her, she desired more. This was the last chance for Harry to – oh, she didn't know what. While not exactly flirting, she certainly demonstrated how close her connection with Tom was, and Tom was more than happy to respond in kind. The different courses came and went but apart from developing a dangerous edge to his smile, Harry seemed neither to notice nor care.

As second host to the captain, he played his part superbly and Georgiana was reminded that he was a man educated in all the social graces. He was gallant, but no more so towards her than to Mrs Roper or any of the other ladies present. In fact, his charm was so impenetrable that Georgiana began to wonder whether she'd imagined that whisper, that flaring heat in his first glance.

Tom pulled her thoughts back. 'Such sights we have all seen. I'll never forget the flying fish that only you and I, Miss Trent, were lucky enough to witness. Do you remember?'

'Of course! The memory of that night is imprinted into my mind forever.' Georgiana reached for her wine and threw Harry a swift, sideways glance. A muscle twitched in his jaw. A small, unworthy sense of triumph flared. Not quite so indifferent then, Mr Miller.

As the dessert plates were being cleared away, Julia exclaimed, 'Look! Sebastian's asleep!'

Everyone laughed to see the boy lying with his cheek pillowed on his bread plate.

'Oh, poor Sebastian, I must get him to bed.' Georgiana was overcome with remorse. 'The excitement has been too much for him.'

'I'll carry him for you,' Harry was already rising.

'No, I can,' said Tom, pushing his chair back.

'Don't worry, I have to check on a few things anyway.'

'Miller, relax, you—,' Captain Dunn began, but as his eyes went from Harry's face to Tom's, he coughed and added, 'Just so, indeed, just so.'

'Thank you, Mr Miller,' said Georgiana, and she smiled at Tom to reassure him as she also rose. He sank back into his chair, but didn't seem happy as he watched Harry scoop up the sleeping child. Georgiana turned to Julia. 'What about you, Julia? Are you ready for bed?'

'Oh *please* may I stay up for just one more half-hour,' she pleaded, and Georgiana looked to Mr Taylor. He crumbled under his daughter's beseeching eyes.

'Oh, just this once.'

As Georgiana led the way to the cabin she felt breathless. Her stays were obviously far too tight. They did not talk. As she stepped aside at the cabin door to let Harry past with Sebastian, she stole a glance at him. The clean lines of his profile were unreadable. The cabin felt very small as Harry lay Sebastian down, and Georgiana's arm brushed against his as she came forward to cover the boy with a blanket. She straightened to find Harry right beside her, his eyes very dark. But instead of speaking in that soft whisper he'd used earlier that had turned her innards to liquid, he said abruptly, 'About bloody time. Finally, George, I've got you alone. We have to talk.'

She instantly resented his tone. Here she was, dressed in her finery and still he talked to her as though she were a cabin boy. She realised suddenly, horribly, that all her efforts had been for him alone and still he couldn't *see*. What had she thought? That he'd kiss her? Absurd, and naturally she would have slapped him, had he tried. All the same, this was the last time they were ever going to see each other.

Didn't he care? Frustration and mortification combusted as she drew herself up tall. 'We have absolutely nothing to talk about.'

'I want to know why the hell you've been so damned frosty towards me over these past weeks.'

'I have not been frosty!' She bit the words out like icicles.

'The devil you haven't! George—'

'Don't call me that!'

'What would you prefer? Miss *Trent*?'

She hated his sarcasm. 'I'd prefer you to leave!'

She'd have been furious if he had. He stepped closer still, his eyes burning dark blue. Her heart began to thud.

'You will hear what I have to say whether you like it or not,' he said. She hadn't seen him lose his temper before, but instead of being frightened, she was appalled at herself for finding it rather thrilling. Her aunt had been quite right. She had no sensibility at all. 'Firstly, I will of course take you to your brother.'

Georgiana tossed her head in grand style. 'Thank you, but I don't need your help.'

'Oh come off from you high horse, Georgie. Mr Taylor remains in Lyttleton and Mrs Roper's brother lives up north. You can't travel alone, you absurd girl.'

'I won't be alone.'

His brows snapped together. 'Mellors?' He took another step closer, his legs pressing her crinoline back. She felt heat radiate from his body. His voice dropped. 'Look George, there's something about that man I don't like.'

'Possibly the fact that he likes me.'

His lips tightened and the muscle in his jaw jumped. 'Just listen, will you. He's up to no good. I'm sure I saw him in Cape Town coming from a meeting with your cousin.'

'What, did you see them actually talking?'

He hesitated. 'No, I arrived too late but I swear they

were walking in different directions from the same meeting point.'

'Nice try, Harry, but he tumbled to your game a while back and warned you might try blackening his name.'

Harry grabbed her by one arm and shook it. 'Can't you see he's up to something?'

His words stung. He obviously couldn't believe any man could be interested in her. The memories of many, many nights of failure suddenly came to the fore. She saw again Jasper's handsome, deceitful face. Her free hand came up and pinched Harry's restraining fingers cruelly. He swore and dropped his hold to flick his hand. Now it was Georgiana's turn to narrow the last remaining inch between them. She stepped so close that the bodice of her dress brushed his uniformed chest. She heard his sudden intake of breath but didn't care as she hissed, 'Why should he be up to something? You've no grounds whatsoever to make such a claim. Is it so hard to believe a man might find me attractive? Might like me just for being me?'

Harry began to speak but she was not in the mood for hollow protestations. She continued in a voice shaking with rage and hurt pride. 'I know your game, you don't fool me. I know exactly *who* you are and *what* you are, Harry Trent, and there is nothing that would make me travel a mile in your company. I despise everything you stand for. Let me assure you'—and here she prodded him in the chest with one furious finger—'I will do everything to ensure you do not succeed in this *sordid* business you won't talk about.'

His eyes blazed as he caught her wrist. 'That man—'

'—has done me the honour of asking me to be his wife.'

Harry dropped her hand and fell back a pace. For a second they glared at one another. The muscle in his jaw was ticking steadily now. His black hair fell across his forehead. Every plane and angle in his face was sharply defined. Even at the height of her fury and misery, she couldn't help noticing how splendid he was. Then, with a visible effort, he drew himself up and bowed.

'My felicitations, Miss *Trent*.'

And then he was gone, just like that. Once again – but for the final time – Harry Trent had walked out of her life.

Chapter Twenty-Three

The following morning, Harry felt possibly the worst he ever had in his life. He'd drunk considerable amounts of brandy that had left him with a pounding head but done nothing to alleviate the fury and humiliation in his heart. How on earth had Georgie discovered his motive for going to New Zealand? Couldn't she understand the reasons that drove him? Surely she had to see he had no choice now? And why – why in all hell – had she chosen *Mellors* as her companion? Her future husband. It was impossible to understand what she saw in the man.

The bright sunlight brought no answers. In fact it seemed to mock, dancing on the clear harbour waters and making Harry wince and squint.

'Bit the worse for wear, eh Miller?' the captain asked as they met by the gangway to bid farewell to the passengers.

'Just a little, sir.' Harry wished the soft shushing of the water beneath the keel wasn't quite so loud. Wished he hadn't allowed his jealousy to overrun his good sense during the one and only chance he'd had to talk to her. Throughout the long night he'd replayed a dozen different ways he could have spoken to her that would have led to her agreeing to stay with him, to her trusting him with her secrets. Instead he'd made a complete mull of things. Now he'd never know what the hell was going on in that stubborn, wayward head of hers. Would never be able to protect her.

She knew what he was and she scorned him for it. His soul writhed at the thought.

Out of the corner of his eye, he saw Georgiana arrive on deck with the children where she was enveloped in a warm embrace from Mrs Roper.

'Oh my dear,' Mrs Roper exclaimed. 'Such a sweet young woman. You must come and visit us. You have my address? Bring your brother too – I'm sure we'll love him.'

They parted with watery smiles and then it was time for Georgiana to leave the children. Harry could hear them weep as they clung to her, while their father stood to one side, nose twitching in embarrassment, saying, 'That's enough, now. Let Miss Trent go.'

'You will come and visit us and tell us your stories again, won't you?' Julia begged.

'And bring us some gold?' asked Sebastian, raising his tearstained face hopefully.

'Nuggets of the stuff, if I find it,' Georgiana assured him, laughing through her tears. 'And yes, I'll tell you my stories and just think – I'll have new ones to tell you, too.'

Harry felt strangely wrung as she said goodbye to her charges and motherly friend. She'd found a family of sorts on this ship. And now she was alone again.

Except, of course, that she was not.

In the end, it was Mellors – damn his eyes – who disentangled her from the children's hands and who, with promises to bring her back *soon*, propelled Georgiana to the gangway. Up close, Harry saw Georgiana had dark rings under her eyes and felt a stab of unkind pleasure. Good. He hoped she had spent as sleepless a night as he.

The captain clasped Georgiana's hands. 'It has been a joy having you aboard, Miss Trent. Best sense of balance I've ever seen in a woman. You could've been one of the crew the way you took to ship life.' He gave a braying laugh. 'You can sign on with me any time, my girl.'

'You cannot think how tempted I am,' she replied, and he pinched her cheek.

'That's my girl. You keep that spirit of yours and may you find your brother safe and sound.'

'Thank you,' she said. 'You've been so kind.'

Then she turned to Harry and held out her hand. 'Goodbye, Mr Miller.'

Her voice was very calm. Harry looked at her, keeping his own face and voice devoid of all emotion. 'Good luck and safe travels,' he said, just as he did to all departing passengers.

She murmured in reply but Mellors drowned her words with his own hearty farewells. He was as amiable as ever but Harry saw triumph in the farmer's eyes. Then they were moving away, side by side, down the gangway. Just like that, Georgiana was walking out of his life.

Harry watched, disbelieving. She really was leaving him. But it was *he* who usually left! As usual, Georgie had no idea of the proper order of things at all. His hands curled into fists though he'd have been hard pressed at that moment to say which was stronger: the urge to box her ears or punch Mellors on the nose.

The captain shook his head and glanced sideways at Harry. 'You shouldn't let her be escaping from you like that, m'boy. Thought you had more mettle in you.'

'She has become engaged to Mr Mellors. She informed me of that fact last evening.'

Harry's tone was carefully neutral but the captain snorted. 'And if you believed that, then I've vastly overestimated your intelligence. Rocks for brains if you swallowed that one!'

A few hours and one very bumpy but beautiful trip later, Tom and Georgiana arrived in Christchurch where they booked into a handsome hotel on the edge of the large, newly formed Hagley Park. Tom asked Georgiana if she would like to rest as she had been unusually quiet the whole journey.

'Rest?' Georgiana put on a good pretence of enthusiasm. 'Not at all. I can't wait to go exploring.'

He smiled down at her. 'Are you sure you do not want to take a long bath, sleep in a real bed?'

'This evening, certainly. But for now I would love to look about this city.'

She was determined not to be left alone with her thoughts. It had taken her all her self-control not to cry her eyes out in the carriage. Leaving the children had just been so hard, she told herself.

'In that case, let's leave our bags and go for a walk.'

'That would be wonderful, but don't you have business to attend to?' She realised that in all the time they'd spent together, Tom had spoken little about his own life. 'What exactly is your business, anyway?'

He laughed. 'I am in a partnership in a number of interests – there's a factory in England and some ventures in the Far East. I've been given the name of a man here – Malcom Sedgewick – who could open up more opportunities. New Zealand could be a very profitable country to invest in.'

This was a different Tom. Despite his farmer's mien, he was clearly a man of means and a man of vision, and for a split second she wondered if she'd been rash to turn down his offer of marriage.

'Do you want to contact this man now?'

'I don't imagine Sedgewick'll be home during the day. We can locate his house as we walk and I'll call again in the early evening. In the meantime we can discover the layout of the town and what pleasures it may harbour.'

'I'd like that above all things,' declared Georgiana. 'And I want to find out the best means of travelling to Dunedin. Captain Dunn thought I should go by ship, but I confess I'm quite keen to stay on land now, if it's possible. I want to see what New Zealand is really like.'

Tom smiled agreement. 'I'm glad to be on firm ground

again and will conclude my business as swiftly as possible. Then I'll be entirely at your service.'

'I can't thank you enough.'

'It's not your thanks I look for,' he said softly. Blushing, she looked away. Tom, seeing he had embarrassed her said, 'Come on, let's see what Christchurch is like.'

They passed the afternoon in exploration, enjoying the spring sunshine. It wasn't just the upside down seasons that surprised Georgiana though, everything about New Zealand was completely different from anything she'd experienced before. Even Cape Town and Madeira, while foreign, had at least the same feeling of having been established for a very long time. The buildings and faces might be foreign, but underneath ran reassuring weavings of customs and history which, once understood, were dependable.

In New Zealand everything was so – well, *new*. She couldn't help laughing at herself and her surprise. What had she imagined, after all? There were echoes of England everywhere – in the clothes, the accents, the goods in the shops. There were pavements and gas lamps in the main streets. Yet there were differences, too. For a start, the buildings were all wooden, like towns she'd read about in the Wild West. This made them seem temporary and reminded her forcibly of a series of flats in a theatrical performance. She kept feeling if she peeked behind the shop frontages, there would be nothing there. But of course there were shops and these were filled with many of the articles stocked in any small town in England.

Georgiana also couldn't help but notice that men considerably outnumbered women, and she encountered many speculative, sideways glances. They brought a blush to her cheeks and a rush of relief to have Tom at her side. He seemed so strong, so dependable in this new land. They stopped in front of one shop crammed with bed rolls, backpacks, picks, shovels, tin mugs and plates, and wide, shallow pans.

'A mining shop,' said Tom. 'Everything a man could need in his quest for gold.'

This made Georgiana look more closely. To think that these objects, so foreign to her, would be Charles's everyday possessions. All at once he'd never felt so close yet so far away. Her eyes misted and she blinked. Tom, noticing this, drew her hand through his arm and patted it.

'We'll find that brother of yours, I do assure you. I'm very keen to meet him myself. Now, is that a milliner's over there? Let's go and see if the London fashions have arrived here. Would you like a new bonnet to meet your brother in?'

This made Georgiana laugh. 'As if I'd waste my money on such a thing!'

So the hours passed pleasantly. Tom was a considerate, good-humoured companion, but Georgiana couldn't help being conscious of how different this day was compared to her first morning in Madeira. Tom was kind, but Harry had made her laugh and had entered into her spirit of enthusiastic discovery. Tom stood by and smiled patiently, talked patiently. It was not the same at all but, thought Georgiana as she gave herself a mental shake, Tom was all consideration, while Harry ... Her final image of him standing pale and removed, kept coming unbidden into her mind. She forced herself to listen to Tom.

'Mr Sedgewick's house must be in this road.' Tom was looking down at the paper in his hand on which the address had been written. 'Number eight.'

They walked along the dusty road with tiny cottages and gorgeous gardens crammed with English flowers. As Tom had predicted, no one was home when they finally located the house. 'Never mind, I'll come back this evening. How lucky it's just across the park from our hotel.'

'Will your business take long?' asked Georgiana.

Tom shook his head and pushed out his lower lip

thoughtfully. 'I don't imagine so.' He smiled. 'Then I will take you out for the finest dinner Christchurch can offer.'

There again was that soft expression in his eyes and Georgiana coloured as she looked away. Seeing her discomfort, Tom directed her attention to the willow trees growing by the river and so eased the moment.

In the late afternoon, Tom took Georgiana back to the hotel before setting off to conduct his business. Georgiana had thought she'd relax, enjoy a bath and a nap, as Tom had recommended. Once alone, however, she found she couldn't settle. She did wash, but it was an efficient rather than luxurious affair. She lay on her bed and her mind turned immediately to Harry – what would he be doing at this moment? Probably still on board. She had to stop such thoughts right now. Harry was out of her life forever. Charlie was ahead of her. Soon, God willing, she'd be with him again and starting a new life. Harry had no place in her future.

She wondered how long it would take to get to Dunedin. Tom was going to ask about a coach while he was out. He'd taken her money for safekeeping, conscious of safety in this town so filled with young men, and had promised he would buy tickets early the following day. That suited Georgiana well. Though she liked Christchurch, she was anxious to get to Charles. Just in case …

Restless, she rose from the bed and crossed to the balcony. The far, snow-tipped mountains seemed to call to her and she spent some time leaning her arms on the railings and looking at them. Images of Harry chased through her mind: drawn and white in the storm, concentrating as he set the cat's leg, eyes glinting as he whispered, 'Gorgeous Georges.'

That familiar feeling of desolation from her life in Ashton Hall after Charlie's departure stole up on her, the loneliness that she never seemed to be able to escape. What if she were wrong? What if Charlie was already dead? What if she discovered that anyone she ever cared for, would ultimately leave her? Was this whole journey one massive folly, a girl's fantasy to escape the inescapable fact that she was unloveable? Unloved.

With a cry of exasperation, Georgiana straightened. Instead of mooning around like a love-struck girl, she would go to meet Tom.

She knew he'd return across the park so, slipping a shawl over her shoulders, she made her way through the hotel and out onto the street. The twilight was deepening, the sky a rich dark blue, the first star a brilliant spark in the vast sky. Georgiana took in a deep breath, forcing herself to relax. Though she was not in love with Tom, he would help her. She should just tell him everything. She was tired of secrets and needed his calm, measured understanding.

The half-formed park, so lovely in the daylight, was now a little eerie, the trees throwing dark shadows. At times the bushes looked exactly like crouching animals or men. Georgiana pulled her shawl tight and her footsteps quickened even as she forced herself to concentrate on the softness of the air and to identify the scents of the flowers carried in the breeze. She'd just crossed a small, ornate bridge which spanned the river running through the park when she saw Tom walking towards her. She waved and called to him.

'Sarah?' He quickened his step and when he drew close, he caught her hands in his. 'What are you doing out alone at this time?' His voice was both happy and scolding.

'I was restless and excited – and just couldn't be alone so came to find you.'

He gave a soft laugh and his clasp tightened. 'I'm so glad to see you. Come, let's go back to the hotel and get some dinner – I'm starving.'

Suddenly all the menacing shadows had gone and the

evening folded around them as they made their way back to the bridge.

'How did you go? Did you find your Mr. Sedgewick?'

Tom shook his head. 'Apparently he left over a year ago for the better prospects of Dunedin.'

'Dunedin!' Georgiana couldn't keep the happiness out of her voice. In the last glimmers of the fading light, she saw him smile.

'We may leave as soon as you like,' he said. 'I have no further business here.'

'Good! Tomorrow then?'

'First thing,' Tom promised. He hesitated then asked, 'Sarah, would you mind if I had a cigarette? It's been a long day and I've been promising myself one these past few hours.' He sounded so apologetic that she laughed.

'Not at all! You've been so considerate and you must be craving one by now.'

They paused on the bridge while Tom pulled out his case and matches from his pocket. He didn't notice but as he did so, a piece of paper fluttered to the ground. Georgiana stooped and picked it up.

'You dropped this,' she said, then stopped short as the match flared, illuminating the words.

Malcolm Sedgewick, 8 Wye Road

And scrawled under that in pencil,

Charles Bellingham/da Silva. Dunedin
– possibly Gabriel's Gully

The match went out and she looked up into Tom's partially shadowed face. He was watching her. Very slowly, disbelievingly, she asked, 'Why do you have Charles's name?'

Chapter Twenty-Four

Tom drew on his cigarette then exhaled. 'To help you, of course. I've been making enquiries on your behalf.'

'But I never told you his name.' It was strangely hard to think, to speak. The stars seemed to blur and whirl behind Tom's head.

'Ah.'

The tip of the cigarette flared, then spun through the air as Tom flicked it into the river. He turned to face her. 'Your cousin supplied me with your real name and your brother's.'

'Jasper? But you said Ha— Mr Miller had spoken to him. Were you lying, then?'

She kept her voice flat and uncomprehending, but her brain was now beginning to work again. Every hair on her arms had lifted and she could feel the heavy thud of her heart.

'We all tell lies at some time, do we not, *Sarah*?' Tom's gentle emphasis on her name made her shiver. She pulled her shawl tighter about her. 'I'd suspected, of course – a young woman going to New Zealand in search of a sick brother. The coincidence struck me in Madeira, but it seemed so unlikely. Your cousin confirmed my suspicions, however, when we had our little chat. It was most illuminating.'

'But why did he tell you anything?'

Georgiana took a step back and felt the bridge railing behind her. It was hard to think coherently, but every instinct shrieked danger. If only she weren't wearing these cursed skirts. There was no way she could outrun Tom. He took a step closer. His teeth gleamed in the gathering dark. 'Jasper and I had met before, you see.'

'Where?'

'In Shanghai. We share a common interest.'

All at once she understood everything so clearly. 'You work for Lord Walsingham.'

'Exactly.'

How could she have been so stupid? So blind. Oh, Harry!

'I can assure you, you need never worry about your cousin again.'

Her eyes widened. 'You didn't—'

He laughed. How had she ever thought he had a nice laugh?

'No, nothing so final, my dear. I just ensured he returned to England where Lord Walsingham will take care of him. Don't worry, he will be sent away to somewhere quite remote – Northern China, I imagine, where he can't trouble us. He is no longer of any use, as I have the situation under control.'

Tom moved closer still. She tried to distract him.

'But why are you trying to help me find Charles? Surely you see there's no point because I didn't marry Jasper.'

'No, but I've been hoping you might marry me. Then I could become your brother's partner.'

She could smell the smoke on his breath as he placed a large hand on the railing either side of her waist, trapping her.

'I didn't want it to come to this,' he said gently. 'If only you'd agreed to marry me. It would have been the ideal solution.' His hands moved closer. His arms, strong as iron bars, pressed against her ribs. 'I like you, Sarah. I really do. We could have been happy together.'

'We still could be.' She hated that her voice shook.

'No,' Tom was regretful. 'You know too much, now.'

'No, I don't. I don't know anything. Besides, I'd never say a word about—' She stopped, but too late. In her panic, she'd said too much.

'A word about what?' he whispered in her ear.

Georgiana strained backwards. 'Nothing.'

He transferred one hand so it lay on her neck. His large index finger caressed her cheek. 'About?' he prompted quietly. 'What do you know? It's curious, you see, that you should have chosen the name Trent. A man called Trent was causing a spot of bother for Lord Walsingham until I dealt with it.'

She could barely swallow. 'How?'

A modest smile. 'Strategically placed evidence, that's all.' Then Tom's eyes fixed on hers. 'Why did you choose that name?'

'No reason,' she protested and his fingers tightened. She should have screamed earlier – not that it would have been any good in this deserted park. Now she could make no sound at all beyond a muffled squeak. She lashed out with a fist but could not reach around those broad shoulders to his face.

He tightened his fingers and she could only breathe in gasps.

'Tell me.' His voice stayed low, but the normality of his tone made her blood run cold. She suddenly remembered his calm offer to kill Muffin. Her hands clawed at his fingers then raked down his cheeks. He swore, jerking his head back. Then there were running footsteps and a blow caught Tom behind the ear. His hands dropped from her throat, and Tom lunged at his attacker.

In the dark, Georgiana could barely make out the two men locked in deadly embrace. They staggered, hit the low railings of the bridge and suddenly both tipped over the edge. There was a huge splash and Georgiana leaned far over the bridge to see. In the water they grappled and fought. Tom had the advantage of weight but the other was lithe and clearly equal in strength. Suddenly he got one arm free and dealt a ringing blow to Tom's jaw. Tom slumped and a rasping voice called up, 'Georgie, are you all right?'

'Harry! I thought it might – but then knew it couldn't – oh, fine, fine.' Wild bubbles of hysterical laughter threatened to overwhelm Georgiana as she ran down to the river bank to where Harry was dragging the unconscious body. With a heave, he managed to haul Tom half out of the river.

'I've a good mind to drown the bastard.'

'Harry, you can't!'

'No,' he agreed, 'but I'd like to.'

He threw his wet hair back from his face and looked at her crouching down, extending a hand to him. 'I don't need a hand,' he said, 'but you could give me your stockings.'

She gaped at him.

'To tie the man up,' Harry said impatiently. 'He could come around any minute and I don't fancy having him coming at me in a rage.'

As Georgiana hastily turned and pulled off shoes and stockings, Harry wrestled Tom's inert body up the bank and under the bridge. Georgiana passed him the stockings and Harry laughed. 'Good governess wear! Not from Consuela I take it.'

'No,' she retorted, 'and aren't you glad. Tom would make short work of silk stockings.'

'Very true.'

In a few minutes Harry had trussed Tom up, hands and feet neatly bound. He'd pulled Tom's jacket halfway down his arms to make struggling more difficult. Then he removed Tom's boots, flinging them into the night where they landed with a crash among some bushes.

'That'll slow him down,' said Harry with satisfaction. To finish, he removed Tom's handkerchief from his jacket pocket and crammed it into the unconscious man's mouth.

'Won't he suffocate?'

'No and it'll prevent him calling out for help. Mellors is on his own so hopefully no one will see his body here until at least sunrise, longer if we are lucky. Now,' he said, turning to Georgiana, 'we must get you back to your hotel and while we go, you can tell me why yet another fiancé should want to wring your neck.'

'He wanted to know—' she couldn't go on, and to her horror, she began to cry. Harry, oblivious of his wet clothes, pulled her into his arms and held her. She could feel the strength in his arms, the lean muscles running down his back and she relaxed into his embrace as her knees gave way.

'There, it's over. I'm here. But Georgie, for once in your life, tell me the whole damned truth.'

Her reason had played her false. Now she let her heart take over. 'Tom wanted to kill my brother for Lord Walsingham – they're in business together.'

'*What?*'

'And Harry,' she said, lifting her head to look at him. His face, inches above hers, was beautiful in the dim light. 'He must be the one who killed Lord Iver.'

Harry shook his head, his brows drawn together as he tried to make sense of her words. She wanted to put up a finger, smooth the line between them. 'For God's sake Georgie, what on earth are you talking about?'

'Walsingham ordered a man to kill both Iver and my brother. I overheard him telling my cousin Jasper one night. What's more, Tom was the one who framed you. He's just admitted to planting the handkerchief.'

Harry gave a low whistle. 'Can you prove it?'

She shook her head and pressed her forehead against his chest. Though he was soaking wet, she could feel his reassuring warmth, the strong, steady beat of his heart. 'Tom knows Jasper.'

'There! I did tell you!'

'I know. I should have believed you when you said you saw them together. Only he'd said the same about you—' she broke off in shame for having ever doubted Harry. He only laughed and tightened his arms about her for a minute before letting her go. 'Come on, we've got to move fast. We'll talk as we go.'

He drew her hand through his arm and set off swiftly down the path. She was grateful for his cat vision for now the park was in complete darkness and she pressed close to him. She could feel the damp seep into her dress but didn't mind. Relished it, in fact. This really was Harry, in flesh and blood, and soaking wet.

'When I saw them walking away from each other in Cape Town, it seemed very strange for men who'd been fighting just minutes before. I'd guessed something was up with that silly threat of Tom's to "Kick him around the market square at noon."'

For a second Georgiana was blank. 'What? Oh, Market Square, of course. How clever of you!'

He grinned. 'Wasn't it? But it's not flattering to hear such surprise in your voice, Georgie.'

She couldn't help laughing. 'I've underestimated you,' she admitted. 'But how on earth did you find us tonight?'

'I'd been looking for the man who drew me to this country in the first place and had learned he's moved away to Dunedin.' Georgiana gave a small exclamation and Harry nodded, continuing somewhat grimly. 'Ah, you've heard that one before. When I learned that, I enquired as to where I could buy a horse. It turned out there was one just around the corner for sale. You can imagine my surprise when, on completing the purchase, I chanced to see Mellors at the same door I'd been at half an hour earlier. I decided to follow him and saw you meet up in the park.'

Georgiana blushed in the darkness. 'It was forward of me

but I didn't like to be alone. But he wasn't – isn't my fiancé, you must know,' she added in a rush. 'He did ask, but I refused him.'

'But let me think otherwise.'

'I thought you might have been the one after my brother,' she explained.

'*What*?' Harry's head jerked back as if she'd struck him. 'What the hell—?'

And so the whole story came tumbling out as they made their way through the park: of Jasper, of Walsingham's plan and Harry's implication in Iver's murder. Harry heard it all out in silence, but at the end he stopped short and grabbed her by the shoulders to face him. His fingers dug into her skin. Even in the dark she could see the intensity of his gaze. 'Did you honestly believe I was capable of such things?'

'No, that's what made it all so confusing,' she said, hanging her head for a second. Then she lifted her chin, looking into the dark face above her. 'But you yourself told me you were searching for a man in New Zealand because Walsingham had sent you.'

He laughed shortly. 'Yes, I can see that. But you silly goose, I said I was going to New Zealand as a result *of my visit* to Walsingham, *not* that he had sent me.'

'Does it make any difference?'

'All the difference in the world,' he retorted. 'I loathe the man.'

For a second they stood looking at each other although there was barely enough light to make out each other's features. 'Oh Georgie,' said Harry roughly, 'I could have killed Tom even before he began strangling you.'

'Why?' Then she realised how it must have looked. 'Oh.'

'Oh indeed. He was your fiancé. He was entitled to flirt with you on the bridge. When I saw him come close, I nearly left. But then when I saw you hit out—'

'I've never been so glad to see anyone in my life. I really think – think he was going to kill me.'

Harry looked grim. 'Well, I'm not leaving your side now, no matter what you may think, until I can deliver you safely to your brother. Is that patently understood?'

How could such a severe tone flood her with rosy happiness? For once she had no argument. 'Absolutely.'

'Now is this your hotel? Meet me at the back in half an hour with your bags.'

'Right.'

She turned to go into the hotel, but he caught her arm and spun her around to look at him. 'And Georgie, no more slipping off alone. I want your word on that.'

'I promise.' There were no crossed fingers this time. 'I'll be waiting right here for you.'

And this time, when he left, she knew he'd come back.

Chapter Twenty-Five

In the hotel room, Georgiana pulled everything out of her bag to find, hidden at the very bottom, Charles's shirt and trousers. Within minutes she had transformed back into a young man and she smiled. Tom would be seeking a woman. Then she crammed her few dresses back into the bag, not caring about creases in her race to be gone.

Out on the balcony, Georgiana paused. No one was about. She leaned over the railing as far as she could then dropped the bag, wincing as it crashed into the bushes. Would the noise bring people running? But the only sounds were the raucous voices and laughter coming from the barroom on the other side of the hotel.

Reassured that no one was about, she swung her legs over the railings, hung for a moment and then let herself drop, landing in a crouch in the dust below. She looked into the shadows to see if anyone was there. All was still and the boisterous sounds from the bar seemed at odds with the stillness of the night air. She picked up her bag and withdrew into the sanctuary of the oak tree's deep shadows. This is how it all began, she thought. My hiding in an oak on a soft summer's night.

How long ago it all seemed now. She felt a different person – was a different person. At that time, she hadn't been out of England, hadn't walked foreign lands, hadn't worked as either woman or boy – hadn't met Harry. Events had moved so swiftly this evening that she hadn't had a moment to think, but now, as she waited, she was aware of a warm happiness welling up and filling every inch of her. It was as though the frozen core of loneliness that she had carried inside her had been finally burned away. Harry was not Walsingham's man. Harry had saved her not once but twice, and now he was going to help her find Charlie.

For a moment she thought of Tom lying trussed under the bridge. Very likely even now, he was struggling to free himself. How could she have ever been so misled? She closed her eyes in mortification. Fancy Julia being right in her mistrust.

The muffled sounds of horses' hooves caught her attention and she peered around the broad trunk of the tree. There, in silhouette, was a man on one horse, leading a second. She knew by the height, the easy grace, it could only be Harry. As she slipped out from behind the oak, he saw her and dismounted, putting out his hand to take her bag. When he saw her clothes, he nodded. 'Good idea. Tom never knew of your masquerade, I take it?'

'No, and I'm sure it'd never enter his head. He only knew me as the conscientious governess.'

'The *lying* conscientious governess,' Harry corrected, and she heard the smile in his voice. 'He knew there was more to you than your demure act suggested. There.'

As he'd been speaking, he'd fixed her bag to the second horse and now he looked down at her, the moonlight enhancing the slanting planes of his cheeks. Pirate king *and* white knight. 'Need to be tossed up?'

'No!' Indignant, Georgiana sprang into the saddle, gathering the reins in a manner that told the horse she was clearly mistress of the situation.

Harry laughed as he mounted. 'Of course, your mother. I can see you take after her.'

'Oh no,' Georgiana assured him. 'She was superlative.'

He just smiled, but she saw approval in his face as he checked her hands and seat.

'Where did you find this animal?' she asked as they picked their way down the dark road. Hotel bars were lively and lights glimmered behind curtains in houses but there were surprisingly few people in the streets.

'When I went to my hotel I saw a very drunk young man trying to mount his horse. I offered him a sum of money which made him think he was even drunker than he was, but when I pushed the notes into his hand, he was happy to pass over the reins. I only hope he doesn't lose it all before he sobers up. It's not the best animal I've ever seen, but it looks strong.'

Georgiana laughed. 'You did well to get one at all. I thought we might have to take turns riding one mount.'

'The thought occurred to me, too, but we need to put as much distance between ourselves and Christchurch as possible. Now, we take this road. The hotel owner told me we can't go wrong – only one road going south, apparently.'

They'd cleared the small town centre by now and were moving along a road which had only a sprinkling of houses, each well spread from the other. Fortunately the fat-bellied moon was gaining height and it was easy to see the way. In unspoken agreement, they kicked their horses into a canter, covering the next miles at a good speed. Glancing sideways at Harry, Georgiana saw that his style, though graceful, was unusual.

'Where did you learn to ride like that?' she demanded when they drew up, letting their horses walk again.

Harry lifted an eyebrow at her. 'Don't you recognise it, Miss da Silva?'

'It reminds me of my father in some way – yet it's not the same.'

'Close. I worked for some time with *gauchos* in South America. They are the finest horsemen I have ever encountered.'

Georgiana was intrigued. 'Tell me more,' she said, and their journey passed affably as he engaged her in stories of the wide South American plains, the strange animals and the *banditos* that he'd encountered. The moon passed its zenith and began slipping back towards Earth. They came to a wide braided river and splashed their way through to the other side where Harry reined in.

'I think we've made enough headway tonight. We'll stop and camp for the rest of the night.'

'Here?' Georgiana looked about her. The mountains were only just discernible in the far distance and the plains stretched wide and empty about them.

'Yes, it's a good spot. We've water for the horses and ourselves and we'll be on our way again at dawn. With any luck, Mellors won't be discovered until later. Why so dubious? Have you never camped out before, Miss Intrepid?'

Georgiana shook her head. 'Never. It'll be a new experience.'

'It is one I suspect you'll have to get used to,' said Harry as he swung down from his horse and began removing the saddle, 'if you plan to track down your brother in the middle of nowhere.'

While it was Georgiana's first camp, Harry was clearly at home. In less than no time, he had the horses loosely tethered and a fire going, with a billy filled with water over it.

'Tea?' he asked.

'Oh Harry! How *clever* of you. Where did you get all this stuff? I didn't give food any thought at all while I was packing, but now I could kill for a cup of tea.'

Harry laughed. 'I bought it all this afternoon. I knew I'd be off exploring as soon as my business in Christchurch was concluded. Only problem is I thought I'd be travelling alone. We'll have to share the cup. You go first.'

He passed her the metal mug and she wrapped her fingers around it with a sigh of pleasure. It was black, strong and very refreshing. She realised it'd been hours since she'd last eaten. Harry stirred the flames, the light playing on his cheeks and making dark hollows of his eyes.

'Harry?' He smiled up at her. Her heart flipped but she quelled it. There were things she needed to know. 'What *was* your business in Christchurch and how is it that you and Tom both landed up at the same house?'

He laughed and shook his head. 'At first I couldn't imagine, but now I know he's working for Walsingham, I suspect we're after the same thing.'

'So why are you here and how does Walsingham fit in?'

Harry stirred the embers for a second then settled back onto his heels and looked at her. 'It's a long story. Are you sure you want to hear it tonight?'

'I won't be able to sleep until I've heard it,' said Georgiana with perfect truth.

'Then we'd better get comfortable. If we sit back to back, we can share the bedroll and prop each other up.'

Harry wrapped Georgiana in a blanket and he pulled on an overcoat. Though it was late spring, the night was very chilly and Harry warned they'd soon feel cold. She leaned against the broad strength of his shoulders and felt the shift of muscle as he wriggled to be more comfortable.

'Settled?' he asked. She nodded. 'Right, remember when I told you about being arrested for stealing?'

'Yes, of course.'

'Well, I never quite finished the story. When I was packing up my mother's things I remembered my promise to look after her poetry book and wondered why she'd been so insistent. I flicked through it but there was nothing. Then I bent the covers back, looked down the spine and there it was – a piece of paper, hidden all those years. I can show it to you if you like.'

Harry wriggled his wallet out of his pocket and pulled out an old piece of paper which he handed to Georgiana.

Though the firelight was flickering, there was just enough light to make out the faded words written in old-fashioned, sprawling copperplate.

My Dear Wife (how strange and wonderful that phrase sounds)

Only a few days now until my brother's wedding and then we may astonish the world with our own glad tidings. No doubt you were right to caution secrecy so as not to upset the applecart for Alex, but I am impatient to acknowledge you openly to the world. Not long now.

Your loving husband.

'It pleased me to know my mother had always told me the truth about being married, though I couldn't say why it should matter. After all, I still didn't know who my father was, but I was sure that somehow he must have been known to the old woman I'd met in prison. She'd seemed to recognise me and my mother had once said I looked very much like my father. I'd always wondered if he'd stolen from her – had been her footman perhaps. If I wasn't the bastard son of a wealthy man, it could be the only explanation as to how my mother could afford my education.

He gave a shrug but she heard the self-loathing in his voice and snuck a hand down to his braced in the grass. Their fingers entwined and it seemed his tone was lighter as he continued with his tale.

'I went abroad because I couldn't bear the idea of returning to Cambridge, aping the manners of a gentleman when I could be the son of a thief. It was equally impossible to stay in the village, for I was well past being accepted as a fisherman.'

Georgiana didn't need to say anything. Harry had come from two worlds and belonged to neither. Perhaps he and Charles were not so different; young men of character who, rather than compromise, had sought adventure in the far-flung reaches of the world. For the first time, she felt she was finally meeting the real Harry who was neither the hero of her dreams nor the assassin of her nightmares but a man with both fine qualities and flaws.

'So what happened the day you went to see Lord Iver?'

'Did the crew tell you anything about it?'

'Some. They told me of your meeting with Iver and the delivery of the box. Alec was very grim about that.'

Harry laughed. 'Should've listened to him. But then, if it hadn't been for Iver, we'd have never met, Georgie.'

Hearing the casual warmth in his voice, Georgiana smiled into the darkness which nestled about them, marooning them in the pool of firelight. The river murmured as it flowed over the rocks and the smell of distant snow was clean and crisp on the night air.

Harry continued. 'Young Iver was wracked with opium and consumption when he met me in Shanghai, so I didn't pay much mind to his mistaken identity. But later, when I went to his father's house, I was surprised by Lord Iver's equally strong reaction. He invited me to take a seat and took the news of his son's death in his stride – had been expecting it, I gather. But I became suspicious when he started plying me with questions about my background. He kept darting looks at me and finally asked if the names Walsingham or Elrington meant anything to me. Of course I'd heard about Walsingham in Shanghai, but Elrington meant nothing to me. Iver recommended I visit Lord Walsingham who was his neighbour. He thought it would afford us both some interest. Looking back, I realise the old devil was stirring up trouble.

'My curiosity was up so after I'd left him – and yes, he was still alive when I did, Georgie! – I walked over to Elrington Manor. When the butler answered the door, my suspicions were further aroused because he went the colour of old pastry. I don't know why but I had a deep conviction the old woman was there and asked if I might see the senior lady of the house.

'While he went to enquire, I looked at the portraits in the hall. They were a grim bunch, but then I saw one of two brothers when they were about twelve years old. The younger brother could have been myself at that age, apart from his colouring. I have my mother's eyes and hair. I suddenly had the feeling I should leave at once, leave Pandora's box unopened.'

'But you didn't.' Georgiana leaned her head back into the nape of his neck where it fitted well. The sky was huge and splashed with stars, the Milky Way a river of silver-white against the blackness. She could feel the rumble of Harry's voice through her back, describing the scene so vividly that she could picture everything that had happened to bring him around the world to this night, beside this river. With her. Surrendering to the story, she let his words wrap around her, and pull her back to a world they had both left long ago.

Chapter Twenty-Six

The butler returned and led Harry upstairs to a drawing room where the old woman was seated on a canary-yellow sofa. Harry paused in the doorway. He forced himself to maintain an air of social calm, though every instinct was on high alert. He knew now without a doubt he was about to learn who he was, but he was not at all sure he was going to like it. 'Ah, my fairy godmother.'

Her face had been filled with anger and suspicion, but now she gave a harsh laugh. 'Is that how you think of me?'

'You came, freed me and left without telling me your name,' he reminded her, crossing the room and bowing over the hand she extended. 'I had to call you something.'

'I am Lady Elrington. How did you find me?'

'Fate.'

'And why are you here?'

'To thank you.'

'Impudent scamp. Do you hope to ingratiate yourself for a particular reason?'

'I doubt anyone has ever managed to ingratiate himself with you if you did not will it.'

'Not many, but my sons came close on occasions.'

Harry nodded. 'I'd like to ask you a few questions about them.'

'Indeed? Perhaps it is time after all these years. Pray, take a seat.'

He perched on one finely-turned chair while Lady Elrington surveyed him. 'Have you been seeking me?'

'Not at all. I have wondered, of course, over these past seven years, who you were and what your connection to my mother was, but I have been abroad most of the time.'

She tilted her head. 'And yet now you are here.'

'Fate, as I say. A delivery brought me to Lord Iver. His reaction to my appearance and his suggestion that I visit Lord Walsingham piqued my interest. I felt sure I might find you, for you too had seemed to know me.'

A shadow crossed her face. 'Yes, I knew you.'

'That's my father, isn't it, in the stairwell?'

'Yes, he was my younger son, Henry. His brother was Alexander. But why do you look so perplexed?'

'I don't understand, but perhaps you can enlighten me,' said Harry, drawing out his father's letter which he carried with him everywhere, and passed it to his grandmother. How unreal their unacknowledged relationship seemed. He scanned her face as she read. He had her cheekbones, he thought, but otherwise he could not see any likeness. Despite her rigid control, the colour drained from her face and tears welled as she lay the letter down in her lap once she'd read it. Harry produced his handkerchief, noting ruefully how grimy it looked. Only that morning he'd used it to polish the sextant. Her ladyship did not appear to notice its state, but she paused to look at the monogram sewn by his mother. She dabbed her eyes then looked back at Harry. 'Yes, it is Henry's writing.'

'But then I am not his bas—his illegitimate son?'

'No, you're not.'

'So why—?' he broke off, hardly knowing which of the thousands of questions he wanted answered first.

For a moment she regarded him before speaking reluctantly. 'You have a right to know everything, I suppose. It is God's punishment on me, for I have been a wicked woman. It began with your grandfather. He was an unsteady man in his time – a womaniser and a compulsive gambler. There were sideslips of his in the village for whom he paid upkeep. He also lost several small fortunes at the table – so much so that it became essential that our sons make good marriages. I did not see a problem with that.

'Both boys were fine young men and very amusing – no women could resist them. We should have curbed them more, though. I see that now. At the time, however, it was hard to resist their charm. They were only a year apart and were always daredevilling one another. Oh, the scrapes they got themselves into.' Lady Elrington broke off with a soft laugh. 'Both were reckless, heedless boys. It runs in the family.' She looked at Harry speculatively. 'There are some Elringtons who are steady, of course. My grandson is one. Oh, I can see from your expression you didn't know that I had another one. I'll come to him. Anyway, they were the best of friends but were always challenging each other to silly stunts. I thought marriage would steady them.

'Alexander, being the elder, was to make an advantageous marriage to the daughter of a man who'd amassed a fortune in coal mining. Alex was happy about it – like his father, he expected to have many mistresses so love did not enter the equation. Margaret was happy because she would get the title she craved. Preparations were made and during that time Henry was often off, roaming the countryside in sport – or so I thought at the time. Later I discovered that he was with your mother.'

Harry leaned forward. She had his absolute attention.

'The night before the wedding, Henry and Alex went off for some final high jinks together and, well, the story is legend in the village, now. They had a wager to climb the church steeple. Your father succeeded but your uncle slipped at the last minute. Henry lunged for Alex and caught his sleeve, but it was ripped from his fingers. The memory haunted him for the rest of his short life.'

She paused, her face drawn. After so many years, Harry could still see the memory pained her. His heart too went out to both his dead uncle and his remorseful father. What a terrible burden of guilt he must have carried.

His grandmother resumed her tale. 'In our grief, we lashed out at Henry, for the wager had been his idea. Later, when our pain and denial lessened, we knew we'd been wrong to blame him, but at the time ...' she shrugged and shook her head. 'Not once did he try to defend himself. We also insisted it was his duty to marry Margaret. The estate seemed so very important in those days. Now my two sons and husband are dead and I wonder why we fussed so. Henry initially refused. We were outraged and pushed and pushed until he became distraught, shouting, "I cannot! I'm already married."'

'It's hard to explain how we felt with one son dead, the other having made a disastrous marriage without our consent. I assumed he'd only married in order to have his way with some village girl who must have been a scheming wench to trap him thus.'

'She'd have never—' Harry began in hot defence, but his grandmother interrupted him by raising her hand.

'I'm sorry, Harry, that's just what I thought at the time. I'd watched my husband's small affairs for many years and was used to dismissing them. What we did next, I'm ashamed to say, was monstrous. Henry told us her name and where she lived in the village and that night we secretly visited her.'

The old lady paused and rubbed a tired hand over her eyes. 'The little thing was terrified. We swept in and told her she must go away. She cried and said she couldn't leave her husband, that she loved him. I pointed out that if she loved him, she could prove it by leaving. He was heir now to a vast estate. Could she be the lady of all that? He would be the laughing stock of the village. She could never maintain her role and he would learn to hate and despise her. The estate would fall into disrepair and pass out of our hands if an advantageous marriage was not forged immediately. I even said, God forgive me, their marriage vows were not sanctified because he had not received our blessing. Gradually she stopped crying and I could tell she was listening, though she would not look at us. Finally she just nodded and I was relieved she'd come to her senses. We told her we would arrange for a carriage at dawn to take her away and would provide her with a stipend, but she surprised us by slipping off alone sometime during that night. I realised at that time I may have underestimated her, but concluded it was too late.' She looked at Harry. 'I've often since wondered if she knew at that time she was with child.' Then, with a resigned shrug, she continued.

'Your grandfather, however, was always more sentimental than I, and his conscience clearly bothered him over the years, although he never confided this to me. Instead, he began a secret search for her which took years. I cannot imagine how he must have felt when he discovered there was a boy, but he did right by you, sending you to Harrow. Yes,' she said with a small, grim smile as Harry started, 'my husband paid for you to attend his old school. Our sons went to Eton, at my insistence. I only found all this out when I went through his papers after I'd visited you in prison. I'd never looked at them before, afraid of what I might find in the way of debts and poor decisions.'

'I thought some rich uncle paid for me. My mother would never talk about it.'

'Well, it was your grandfather. He died nine years ago, just as you were finishing school or no doubt he would have paid for your university too.'

Understanding dawned. 'Instead of which, my mother began selling jewellery. But how—?'

'Henry must have given her some necklaces and rings he'd inherited from his grandmother. It was very naughty of him, but they were ones I had never much admired and to be honest, I did not notice they had been gone for many months. When I realised what must have happened, I felt your mother had been well paid for her disappearance.'

Harry could hardly speak for the anger that choked him. 'She never wore them, not once. God knows where she hid them either, for we had precious little my whole life.'

'I'm sorry,' said his grandmother simply. 'If I'd known there was a child perhaps things might have been different ... But there is little point in dwelling on the past. I thought the whole matter ended until our family jeweller, who knows every piece he or his father ever made for us, reported the strange occurrence of a shabby woman selling a necklace he'd made some thirty years earlier.

'Unfortunately Margaret – your father's second wife – received the message and set the law upon your mother, thinking it right to retrieve family jewellery even though she'd never heard of this particular piece before. You see, she had never known about her husband's first wife and I only became involved when she told me that this woman's son had confessed to the crime. I *had* to see who the son was. Later, I told Margaret everything to prevent her from pursuing the matter further. Naturally she was beside herself with rage.'

Harry cared naught for the feelings of his father's second wife. One furious and bitter question dominated his thoughts. 'Did my father accept my mother's disappearance so easily that he was married a few weeks later?'

'Of course not.' Lady Elrington paused and sighed heavily. 'This part is hardest of all to tell. We knew if we said that she'd run off, he would search till he found her, so we had her cottage torched. He believed she'd died in the fire.'

Harry's fists clenched. 'What sort of people are you?'

She spread her hands. 'We did it for this.'

Unable to sit still any longer, Harry strode to the window and stared out. The shadows had lengthened over the immaculate green slopes of the grounds. The setting sun tinged the lake with fire as two swans glided across, their wakes smoothing out almost immediately in the mirrored surface. He leaned his forehead against the glass whilst his grandmother's voice picked up the story once again, listless yet determined to take it to its conclusion.

'The loss of his brother and his wife changed Henry. When the greatest despair had blown out, we were able to marry him off to Margaret quite easily. It was if he'd ceased to care about anything. He was like a man in a dream. Drank heavily. Never laughed any more. Rode his horse like a wild man through the forest until he took a tumble one day and broke his neck. When they brought his lifeless body back, I couldn't even cry. He'd moved beyond us and all I could hope was that he'd finally found some peace.' Her voice became defiant. 'But Henry had left us one final gift. Margaret was with child.'

Harry raised his head from the glass and slowly turned around. She nodded. 'Yes, you have a half-brother, Phillip. You are both the spitting image of your father though your eyes, your hair, are your mother's. Phillip grew up here and he loves the place.' Her voice warmed. 'He's always got several projects on the go and you should see the improvements he's made. The tenants adore him.'

But Harry was interested only in the immediate situation. 'So why did Iver tell me to seek Walsingham here? How does he fit in?'

'Margaret married Lord Walsingham, some fifteen years ago. He is our neighbour's business partner, you see. And though Margaret has never told Phillip about you, she did confide in her husband. I must warn you now, he is not happy about it.'

Harry's eyebrows knitted. 'What the devil has it to do with him?'

'He is, ah, somewhat possessive shall we say, of the manor. I believe he feels its size suits his consequence well. The family returned here after my husband's death. Phillip is the earl, though, in accordance with family tradition, he will only gain full control of the estates when he turns twenty-six. In the meantime, Lord Walsingham has been managing our affairs very well, but I have to say that he's—'

But whatever she was going to say was lost as the door opened to admit a rotund man in a fine silk waistcoat that strained at the buttons. When his round eyes fell on Harry they sharpened as he smiled. His snipped words, however, belied his genial manner.

'Ah, the bastard's return.'

Harry drew himself up and made a formal little bow. 'I am no bastard, sir, but the lawful son of Henry.'

'That cannot be,' Lord Walsingham replied, his smile not faltering. 'My wife was married to her first husband lawfully and in the sight of God.'

'Nevertheless, he was married to my mother first. The second marriage was nothing but a sham.'

Lord Walsingham's eyes travelled up from Harry's battered boots, to his faded trousers and shabby waistcoat and jacket.

'Forgive me if I do not immediately accept the word of a captain of uncertain means as he attempts what might well be construed as fraud and imposture on a rather grand scale.'

With those words he seated himself, crossing one plump thigh over the other, leaving Harry to stand as though a servant in the presence of his master. His gaze never left Harry's face.

'I understand your reticence to accept the facts,' said

Harry, maintaining his own icy civility. 'Perhaps this might enlighten you,' and he passed over the letter.

The silence stretched taut save for the ticking of the clock on the mantelpiece as Walsingham perused the letter. His face betrayed no emotion but Harry saw how the man's eyes flickered to the top of the page once he had finished reading the note. His lips stretched into a smile and he shrugged.

'This is nothing. There are no dates, no names even. It will never stand up in a court of law.'

Until this moment, strange as it later seemed to Harry, the enormity of what he'd learned had not yet dawned upon him.

'I'm the rightful heir,' he said slowly. 'I'm the earl. All this,' and he waved at the walls, his ancestors in their frames, the lands beyond the window, 'all this is mine.'

'But it is also my home,' his grandmother cried out. '*Phillip's* home. You cannot take it all away from him.'

Harry whirled on her, though he managed to keep his voice soft as he spoke through his teeth. 'It should also have been my mother's.' He locked eyes with his grandmother. 'You cheated her of her right and lawful place. You will never, *never* fully appreciate the appalling repercussions of your actions. If you only knew of the life you condemned her to because of your damnable pride and greed.' He made a gesture of contempt. 'I am ashamed to have the blood of this family in my veins.'

Walsingham rose now and crossed to the bell pull. All pretence at affability had vanished and Harry found himself looking into a face of implacable antagonism.

'If you do not leave now, I will have you tossed out as the pretender you are. You can spout your wild stories but all people will see is a bastard.'

Harry strode across the room and, despite his seeming complacency, Walsingham retreated a pace. 'I will not be evicted from my own home. I leave of my own accord but,' and here Harry allowed all the pent up rage to show in his voice, though he continued to speak softly, 'make no mistake. When I next come through those doors, it will be as lord and master.'

'A hollow threat,' jeered Walsingham, but his words choked in his throat as Harry grabbed his neckcloth, twisting it and using it to draw the older man close so they were nose to nose.

'You played no part in the original deception so I will not hurt you at this moment. However, if you try to stand in my way when I claim what is rightfully mine, it will be a very grave mistake. Do I make myself understood?'

Walsingham's eyes bulged as his face turned from red to purple, but hatred burned in their depths. He nodded and Harry released his throttling hold. Then he turned on his grandmother who had risen but had remained silent through this exchange.

'It is a wonder that you can sleep at all. If you knew of the life that you forced my mother to lead—' but here the words caught in his throat. Harry picked up the letter and brandished it. 'There may be no evidence, but in this room we all know the truth. God help you if I should ever find proof. I will take this house and its lands and turn you all out as you turned my mother out.'

Footsteps sounded outside and the door opened. Harry bowed. 'Lady Elrington, my time with you has been most edifying. I believe I can find my own way out.'

He swept past the footman without another glance at either his grandmother or Walsingham.

Outside in the driveway, he found his mouth was dry and his hands shaking. To have threatened a woman, his grandmother no less, was appalling. He longed for a man to fight, a storm to battle – if only Walsingham had taken a swing at him. There was no outlet, no relief for his feelings. But as he reached the gates, a page came panting after him and thrust a note into his hand.

'M'lady wanted you to have this.'

It was brief.

Walsingham is a dangerous enemy so watch your back. He will do everything in his power to protect his control of this estate. Malcolm Sedgewick was your father's most trusted valet. He may have the marriage certificate, for I never found it. Last heard, he was in Christchurch, New Zealand. I have done terrible damage to you all. Perhaps the truth can make amends.

Chapter Twenty-Seven

Georgiana was stiff and groggy when Harry shook her awake at dawn. They couldn't have had more than a few hours sleep, but as soon as she remembered that Tom might even now be escaping his bonds, she threw off her exhaustion. The mug of tea Harry pressed into her hands helped revive her.

She felt strangely shy, sitting there with the blanket wrapped around her shoulders, beside the glowing embers of the fire Harry had resurrected. The air was cold but the tea warmed her fingers through the thin metal of the pannikin. Just like the night before, the tea was black, strong and sweet, and she alternately blew upon it and sipped as she looked about her. The sky was very gradually lightening, dark shapes individuating into trees and bushes. The smoke from the fire rose in a thin blue ribbon, carrying with it the scent of ash. High above a skylark swooped, its tumbling song very pure in the clear morning air. Downstream, a hawk floated in lazy ellipses. What was it hunting? Mice? Rabbits? Did they have such animals in New Zealand? How strange to know so very little of the world that now surrounded her.

The scrape of spoon against pot drew her attention back to Harry, who was making porridge, and she watched his quick, economical movements. She was so used to thinking of him as a sea captain, it was strange to see how at home he was on land, rumpled and grubby as he was. How infamous but how *typical* of Harry that he should once again turn her world upside down. Or right it. She wasn't sure which.

Was he really an earl? It seemed absurd and yet, at the same time, perfectly believable. He would manage his estates with the same innate, easy air of command as he'd run *Sally*.

Feeling her gaze upon him, he looked up from his pot and smiled. His eyes were a startling blue in the early light – his mother's eyes. No wonder she'd caught Henry's attention as he roamed the countryside.

'Nearly ready,' he told her. 'Hungry?'

'Famished! I realise I didn't have dinner last night.'

He laughed. 'I've always liked your honest enjoyment of food, Georgie. Can't stand women who pick at their plates. Enjoy food, enjoy life.'

'Even if it's lumpy porridge,' she said, inspecting the plate he passed to her.

'The lumps'll give you sustenance for our long ride. Eat up.' He ate straight from the pot and Georgiana thought how they needed to buy a second plate, a second pannikin. Then she remembered. 'Oh no! I've been such a fool!'

'What?'

'Tom has my money.'

'What, all of it?'

'Yes, though it wasn't a huge sum. I gave it to him for safekeeping – it was his idea.'

'I bet it was.' Harry's voice was grim.

Georgiana drew a circle with her spoon in her porridge and tried not to sound defensive. 'At the time his reasons seemed sound enough. He'd heard there were many desperate sorts here who'd lost all their money on the goldfields and who'd have no compunction in robbing a woman alone.'

'It also ensured that you wouldn't be able to leave him either, once you were tied by the purse strings.'

'Do you really believe that was his motive?'

'Do you doubt it?' Harry gave a cynical laugh. 'He's a plausible rogue if, even now, knowing him for what he is, you are still willing to make allowances for him, Georgie.'

'Not really. I just hate ...'

'Hate?'

'Being such a gullible fool,' she said in a rush.

This time Harry's laugh bore a note of relief. 'Is that all? Don't worry. He had us all fooled.'

'Not you.'

'Well, seeing him with your cousin did raise my suspicions, but not to the extent that I'd have ever seen him as a murderer.'

'Julia didn't like him. She much preferred you.'

'That child,' said Harry, scraping the bottom of the pot, 'is possibly the most discerning young person I've ever met.' Then he dropped his teasing tone. 'If it's any consolation, I think you tamed the monster to some extent. He did ask you to marry him, after all.'

'For the gold mine!' Georgiana felt all the bitterness of a woman twice proposed to for mercenary reasons.

For a second Harry was silent before saying, 'Though I hate to take Mellors' side in any way, I do believe that his feelings for you were real enough.'

'Real enough to want to kill me as soon as his true motives were known!' She put her hand out for the pot, seeing Harry had finished.

'Well,' Harry's tone was bracing as he handed it to her, 'you can't expect the man to love you more than his own self-interests. The thing is, I've precious little money myself having bought my horse and gear.'

'And you spent more money in buying a horse for me.'

Georgiana was contrite, but Harry smiled as he rose. 'Best money I've ever spent. We'll worry about that later. For now, we must get moving and keep the distance between ourselves and Mellors. I have to beat him to Sedgewick.'

Georgiana began washing the utensils in the river while Harry began saddling the horses. The water was freezing. 'I suppose Tom is planning to buy the marriage certificate from Sedgewick.'

'I've no doubt that will be his first move. But if Sedgewick still proves loyal to my father, he might refuse, in which case Tom will probably feel it important to silence him. He's the only one apart from my grandmother who can testify that the marriage happened.'

Georgiana hadn't thought of that. She spoke in a small voice. 'Do you think Tom will want to kill you, too?'

Harry flung a saddle onto Georgiana's horse. 'At present, I'm still the main suspect in Iver's murder. We don't have any proof to the contrary and I can tell you now, I'd be laughed out of court if I tried to give my side of the story. It's so preposterous, no one would believe it.'

'Surely your grandmother would testify for you.'

Harry shook his head. 'I can't count on it. You forget that Phillip is the only grandson she has ever known.' Then he paused in tightening the girth strap and looked at Georgiana, his face grave. 'I hate to say this, Georgie, but not only is Sedgewick in danger for what he knows – you are too. You are in too deep for them to ignore. Tom is an ugly customer and the only way we can best him is by securing that marriage certificate before he does.'

Georgiana remembered the fingers around her throat, the naked menace in Tom's soft voice and shivered. 'In that case, let's be gone immediately!'

'Right,' said Harry, jamming a wide-brimmed hat on her head, 'but not before we hide your hair. Don't cut it again, will you, Georgie. The hat should do the trick until we get to Dunedin.'

Well-matched both in horses and horsemanship, they cantered side by side through the soft morning air. Despite the threat of Mellors, Harry relished the sense of freedom he always felt when giving a horse its head. Georgiana had clearly grown up in the saddle and he could tell by the way she leaned forward, urging her ungainly mount on, that she, too, was enjoying herself. The flat plains stretched wide and empty around them; the stunning flank of the far Southern Alps reaching down their western side. It was a glorious country and Georgiana must have been having similar thoughts, for when they reined in and dropped to a walk she said, 'Isn't New Zealand splendid?'

'It is.' Harry couldn't help smiling at her. She was flushed, her hair in wild tendrils, her eyes shining. She grew more and more lovely daily, dammit.

While she'd slept last night, he had lain awake for some time. His complicated life had just become a whole lot more difficult. It wasn't that he regretted having Georgie back as his responsibility. He was devilish glad. Too glad, and he recalled the almost murderous pleasure he'd felt in smashing his fist into Mellors. But what the hell did he think he was doing?

He was a man with a mission, a man who had to clear his name of murder and possibly claim an inheritance of staggering proportions. Was he being wise to take Georgiana with him? While he couldn't go to the police, she could and they would in all likelihood protect her from Tom and help her get to her brother safely. After all, he had absolutely no time for distractions and Georgie was, without doubt, one of the biggest distractions of his life. As he'd made very clear to her, there was no place for a woman in his life, and over the years he had perfected the art of extricating himself from liaisons when they became too complicated. This time, however, instead of letting Georgie go, he'd fought like a tiger to get her back.

The problem was, he didn't trust her safety with anyone but himself and was unable to rid himself of the deep-down conviction that somehow she was his. She wasn't, of course – but she could be. He'd seen it in her eyes. Yet there was not a damned thing he could do about it. For the first time since they'd met, she finally trusted him and was depending on him to help her find Charlie, to protect her from Mellors. How could he betray that trust which he'd sought for so long?

The future held far too many variables, the odds heavily stacked against him. In the past Harry had never cared, had played games out with all the recklessness of a man who had nothing to lose. But now it was different. The risks were not only for himself, and Georgiana had already lost far too much in her short life. Her feelings for him at present were nothing more than a green girl's infatuation. Harry had to make damned sure they didn't blossom into anything more.

She tipped her hat back now and asked, 'Which place have you liked best in all your travels?' That set the conversation rolling about the different countries he'd been to, the adventures he'd had, while Georgina had sat sewing samplers in her aunt's house.

'How much I envy you!' she sighed.

'There were many tedious hours too,' he told her. 'And the worst times were when there wasn't any work at all and the worry of where the next meal would come from.'

'I could cope with that, I think,' said Georgiana. 'It was knowing the next meal would be at exactly eight in the evening or eight in the morning that I hated. Every day was the mirror of the one before and the one to follow.'

Harry swatted away a fly. He'd never given much thought to the leisured lives of ladies before. 'That does sound pretty awful.'

'You have no idea! Sometimes I longed to shriek or throw plates or make a scene just to shatter that mirror.'

'So that's why you took to slipping out to act?'

'Exactly. I only felt I could breathe as I galloped away.' She laughed self-consciously. 'That sounds absurdly melodramatic, doesn't it?'

'Yes – but understandable, too,' he said. 'After your unusual childhood, it was mad to think you could settle to the routines of an ordinary young girl.' He glanced at her. 'What on earth possessed you to become engaged to your cousin if you hated that way of life so much?'

Georgiana paused, then said in a quiet voice, 'Desperation. Marriage would have bought me some independence at least, and I hoped that he'd take me to Shanghai. If nothing else, we'd have gone to London often. We would have done *something*. My alternative was staying with my aunt and growing old as I looked after her.'

'You might have met some other young man.'

Georgiana snorted. 'Have you seen the young men at country balls? They are all pink-faced and sweaty-handed with shyness.'

'Ugh, what an unattractive picture.'

Georgiana laughed, 'It's true!' Then she added more seriously, 'The most humiliating thing was that I couldn't engage the attention of even these dreary fellows. I have nothing to offer in the way of looks or manners, you know.'

She leaned forward to pat her horse's neck, her eyes averted, but he saw her flush under her hat and felt strangely wrung for the loneliness of the life she'd just depicted, the rejection and hopelessness she'd lived with for all those years.

To lighten the moment he said, 'Well, given that gloomy picture of country gentility, I think you did exactly right in casting all conventions to the wind, ruining your reputation forever and joining a shipload of disreputable characters to sail around the world.'

It worked. Georgiana gave a gurgle of laughter as she straightened and threw him a look of mock protest. 'That's not quite fair. Alec is extremely reputable and as for the rest, they were just following their captain's lead.'

'Brat! And just when I was about to suggest we stop so I can make us some tea.'

'Tea! Oh yes, please. My tongue's been hanging out this last hour.'

The rest of the day passed very amicably. The road was largely deserted though they passed a couple of Cobb & Co coaches which lumbered and groaned over the deep ruts. They anxiously checked the southbound coaches but never saw Tom's round country face sardined amongst the larrikin features of most of the travellers. They saw, too, a number of men walking, packs on backs and, as often as not, a gold pan hanging from the straps. They discovered there were a few hotels on the route; a rather grand title for the long, low wooden buildings. The larger rivers had punts which saved their horses from a swim and their belongings a soaking. They maintained a steady pace and felt confident Tom was still behind them as the afternoon shadows began to lengthen. Georgiana couldn't remember spending a happier day. There had been so many new sights, so many new experiences – and always there had been Harry.

'What will you say to Mr Sedgewick?' she asked.

Harry shrugged. 'To be honest, I have no idea. I'm hoping he'll recognise my father in me and that will make it simpler to ask if he can prove that my parents were married legitimately. If so, I might be able to clear my name, prove I was framed.'

'What I don't understand is why you didn't just tell us all the truth from the beginning. Why the big mystery?'

Harry brushed his hair back. It was glossy blue-black in the sunlight. He looked rueful. 'I didn't want to say anything until I had proof, otherwise it's such a preposterous tale. I mean, penniless captain discovers he's an earl. Come on, who'd have believed it?' He paused then looked at

Georgiana. 'I'm also still not sure what I'll do, if I do find the proof I need.'

She was taken aback. 'What do you mean? Claim your rightful inheritance, of course.'

'And destroy the lives of the only family I have?'

'They destroyed your mother's life and yours.'

'Do I want to be like that, though? I set out with a burning desire to avenge my mother in some way, right the wrong that had been done to her. Also I desperately wanted the money to fix up *Sally*. But as I calmed down I realised that what I was looking for was merely revenge. Both my mother and my father are dead. It's over.'

'Not for you.'

'No,' Harry admitted. 'Especially not with this damned murder charge. If it weren't for that, I'd be tempted to just leave the matter be.'

Georgiana pushed back the rim of her hat and looked at him. 'Really?'

He shrugged. 'Sounds crazy but my grandmother said my half-brother loves the place. He thinks it's his.' He added with a smile, 'Believe it or not, seeing the lengths you were prepared to go to for Charles made me think more about my brother, about how my parents would want me to behave towards him.'

'You don't even know him, though.'

'That's true, but if I hurt his family, take the only home he has ever known, I'll also be ruining any chance of us ever getting to know each other.' He gave a half-laugh. 'Of course, I can't be sure he'd ever want to acknowledge his relationship to a sea captain. His mother didn't. But then, she's a victim in all this too. As is, in a strange way, my grandmother. She has suffered a lot. The only real villain now is Walsingham.'

Georgiana suddenly understood some of the torment

Harry had been going through these past months; discovering he had family after all, only to find that to legitimately claim his place within it, he must destroy it. At the same time, a fortune dangled within reach. More than enough money to save *Sally* and provide for his motley crew who were, she realised, the closest thing he'd ever had to family. No wonder he'd felt embroiled in such a sorry, sordid situation.

She glanced at Harry. He was frowning, his eyes fixed on the road between his horse's ears though she doubted he saw it, for he added, 'To be honest, apart from clearing my name, I most want to talk to Sedgewick to find out what my father was like. Stupid really, for he's never been a part of my life.'

Georgiana had a flash of her father's laughing face and suddenly remembered how his moustache had tickled her cheeks when she'd snuggle into his lap for a story. 'Not stupid, natural. It must've been very hard not even knowing your father's name. Consuela says you have to know who you are and what you are, whatever your past.'

Harry's smile was regretful. 'I certainly never knew either – just those infernal whispers while my mother maintained her silence. I see why now, of course – what could she say? I was the only boy in our village who went to school past the age of ten, you know. When I came home for school holidays, I could never play with my old friends. They hated the way I'd learned to talk, hated my manners.'

'How awful.' Georgiana's forehead wrinkled in sympathy. 'At least I always had Charlie. Was it a relief to get back to school then?'

Harry shook his head. 'I didn't fit there very well, either. Always thought if they knew I was nothing but a fatherless son of a seamstress they'd turn on me, so I was determined to outdo them all in every way.' He laughed in self-contempt. 'Had to be the best at everything – sport, studies, dares. You name it, I was up for it. Same thing at Cambridge. Made lots of friends but while I could go and stay at their houses, they could never come to mine. It was a relief, really, when I left England and didn't have to worry about which world I belonged in any more.'

'But if you can prove you are an earl, you'll know where you belong.'

'Perhaps.' He didn't sound convinced. 'What about you, Georgie? Do you know who you are, what you are?'

A girl in love, she wanted to say. But at that moment they came around a bend in the road and she cried out instead, 'Oh look!'

Chapter Twenty-Eight

Ahead in the road was a cart, tilted at an awkward angle.

'Looks like a broken shaft, come on.'

They drew up alongside the man who was in the process of emptying the heavily laden cart. He looked up when he heard the horses coming and smiled ruefully.

'New Zealand roads!' he said by way of greeting.

'They are – interesting,' Harry agreed, swinging himself down and offering his hand which the man shook. 'Can I help?'

'Just unloading the cart. I've some tools which may help fix it up till I get home but I have to get the weight off it first.'

Georgiana dismounted too. 'Right, we'll help.'

'Well, I wouldn't say no to some extra hands as it'll be nightfall before long,' said the man. 'Jack Bulton's the name.'

'Harry Trent and my – young cousin, George.'

While George led the horses to a nearby stream, Jack and Harry set to work and within a short time they'd patched the shaft sufficiently to make it home.

'I'm most grateful,' said Jack, dusting his hands. 'You must come home with me and let me give you dinner.'

'There's no need—' Georgiana protested, as she handed the reins of his horse back to Harry, but Jack cut her short.

'No need, but I'd be insulted if you refused. My wife's an excellent cook.'

'In that case,' Harry said, 'we'd be delighted to accept.'

'Grand. Follow me; it's just a few miles beyond.'

Twilight was drawing in when they arrived at the farm. The house was small and made from sod, with a wood shingled roof. Jasmine wreathed the walls, smoke came from the chimney and hens scratched in the dirt. The domestic tranquillity brought a lump to Georgiana's throat.

'It's lovely,' she said, and Jack smiled.

'It's not bad,' he said, but his pride was very evident. 'Taken a bit of work to get it where it is, mind.'

'A bit? You must have worked like a slave to clear the land.' Harry looked about him. 'Did you have much help?'

'Not a lot,' Jack admitted cheerfully. 'We help each other out where we can but the other folk around here have their work cut out for them too. Ah, here's Maggie, my wife.'

A pretty young woman, far advanced in her pregnancy, came out to meet them, wiping her hands on her apron.

'I thought I heard voices. Visitors, how lovely!'

'I've asked them for dinner and the night.'

'If it's not too much of an imposition,' added Georgiana.

'No imposition at all. I'm delighted to see new faces. It can be a mite lonely at times. Come in, come in.'

After a brief discussion, it was decided Harry would help Jack offload the cart in the barn while George helped Maggie prepare a larger dinner. Maggie was shocked.

'Good heavens, I don't need a young man like you helping me. Do you know anything about cooking?'

'Not much,' admitted Georgiana, 'but I can peel potatoes. It wouldn't be right with the two of us landing on you like this, that your husband should get an extra pair of hands and not yourself, particularly as …' she trailed off. Maggie glanced down at her billowing skirts and torn between laughter and blushing, accepted the offer.

'You're an unusual young man, but come this way. The company will be welcome, at any rate.'

The kitchen was very plain like the rest of the house, with a large range and a table, but it was warm and comfortable and in no time Maggie and Georgiana were chatting away.

Georgiana asked all number of questions about life in New Zealand and Maggie, an old hand having been in the country five years, was delighted to share her experiences. She described how hard it had been when they first arrived; living in a tent, clearing the land by hand, being caught in terrible floods one year and a big snow storm the next.

'But we've survived and here we are today,' she said with a floury flourish as she put a hastily made apple pie in to cook.

'And what a lovely home you've created. It must be wonderful to think it's all a result of your own labours.'

Maggie laughed. 'Well, I don't like to say so myself but yes, I am proud of what we've achieved. It's better than anything I'd have had back home.'

This led to her telling Georgiana about her childhood in Liverpool, where she and her parents worked in factories until the day she'd heard that servants were needed in New Zealand. She'd caught the earliest ship out that she could.

'I was very frightened, but in a good way, if you know what I mean.'

Georgiana remembered the terrified elation she'd felt as she'd galloped away from Ashton Hall and said she knew exactly what she meant.

'Life is lucky though, isn't it? I met Jack on board – he'd bought the last available berth, just imagine!'

Georgiana wished she wasn't masquerading. She'd have liked to ask Maggie questions about how she had known Jack was the one. Had she been afraid to give her heart? Questions that would sound strange from a young man. Instead she turned the conversation to daily routines and that took them right up until the men came in, loudly proclaiming hunger.

'And we've fresh mounts for tomorrow, George, thanks

to Jack,' Harry said. 'I told him about needing to find your sick brother as soon as possible.'

'Really? That's wonderful.' Georgiana's gratitude nearly caused her to launch into most unmanly fervent thanks but fortunately Jack held up a hand.

'It's nothing. I just commented your horses seemed blown so Harry explained and well, there's no need to say more. I know you'll return them when you can.'

They dined well that night on roast lamb, fresh vegetables from the garden, followed by apple pie and cream, washed down by Jack's home-made ale. Harry amused his hosts by restricting the amount his young cousin drank.

'He doesn't yet know the punch home-made ales can carry.'

Jack laughed. 'Mine does at that. Got a kick like a mule, some batches.'

Georgiana was indignant, but as her protestations came over as a youth's frustration against adult interference, appearances were preserved. Maggie was sorry that their tiny house did not have a spare room and Jack offered the barn, but Harry said he preferred sleeping under the stars and Georgiana said she did too. Maggie did have plenty of blankets because of the very cold winters, however, and these were lent to make a very comfortable bivouac in the front garden. Rolled up snugly, Harry close to her on her left, Georgiana took a deep, blissful breath.

'Can you smell that bush, Harry? Isn't it heavenly? I wonder what it's called. So strange not to know so much. But you know, I think I'm going to be very happy living in New Zealand.'

'Envisioning yourself a farmer's wife, young George?'

'No-o. Not especially. But life is far more interesting in New Zealand. Can you believe it, Maggie makes everything – the butter, jams and preserves, quilts, even the candles and soap! She says her days fly by. She is far happier than my aunt who has everything done for her. I'm never ever going back to England now.'

Harry woke at dawn after a restless night. It hadn't been easy to sleep with Georgiana sleeping just an arm's reach away and now he lay on his side, watching her sleep. She had pulled the blanket tightly about her, curls a wild tangle above the rough material. Her mouth was slightly open, her breath slow and soft. It would be so easy to lean forward and kiss her. Harry shifted and the movement woke her. She opened her eyes which were misty grey in the half-light. For a second she was sleep dazed then he saw her gradually take in her surroundings. She smiled.

'Morning, Harry.' Her voice was gravelly.

He couldn't resist removing a leaf that was caught in her hair, his fingers brushing her cheek in the process.

'Morning, Georgie.' His voice was hoarse too, but it had nothing to do with sleep, and he saw that Georgiana must have sensed that too for while she smiled, a question began forming in those expressive eyes – a question he was determined would never come between them. He cleared his throat and tried for a lighter tone, 'Sleep well?'

'Mm, like a log.' She rolled onto her back and groaned. 'Oh lord, I'm feeling really sore this morning.'

That made Harry laugh. 'Me too.' But he sat up as he spoke, becoming businesslike. 'Don't worry, it'll ease when we start moving. We've a long day's ride ahead of us but Jack tells me we should make it to a town called Oamaru if we make good time.'

After an excellent breakfast of slices of mutton and fresh bread, they bade farewell to their kind hosts. The second day's ride was harder going. Georgiana was clearly tired, though nothing in her manner indicated this. Harry was impressed.

Most females would never withstand the punishing speed at which they were travelling, much less without pointing out all the inconveniences and hardships. But then, most females would not have travelled so trustingly alone in the company of a man – a man wanted for murder.

Unfortunately, moving about had not helped distract him. Even now, as they made their way along the deplorable tracks New Zealand called a road, Harry was all too aware of the set of her shoulders under her brother's shirt, the slender waist encircled by a large belt which held up trousers too big for her. The outline of her hips and thighs, the glorious length of her legs were all too discernible despite the bagginess of her pants.

Enough! he told himself savagely. George. He must think of her as George. George the cabin boy. The circus brat who trusted him and who now very slightly slumped with fatigue.

'This is a good place to stop,' he said. 'We'll take a break.'

Again, he had chosen a place by a river, with trees and plentiful grass for the horses. Somewhat stiffly, they swung themselves down and stretched aching limbs.

'It's so hot!' Georgiana fanned herself with Harry's hat. Her hair stuck in damp curls to her head and dust rimmed her features. 'If we are stopping for a while, I might wash in the river.'

Harry began loosening the girth straps. 'Good idea. I'll get a fire going and have tea waiting for you when you return. There's a bend in the river over there. You'll be quite private – no one's around.'

After she'd unsaddled her horse and left it loosely tethered to a tree, Georgiana pulled out a clean shirt and disappeared behind the curtain of greenery. He heard splashing and closed his eyes. Focus. He must focus. Get the fire going, fill the billy. The actions occupied his hands but he was all the time aware of the sound of splashes that floated in the hot noon air, above the sound of the cicadas.

Harry was squatting by the fire, tending the billy of water, when she returned, rubbing her wet hair with her old shirt. She hadn't dried properly and her clean shirt stuck damply to her. It was tucked in carelessly at the waist and she hadn't done up the top couple of buttons.

'The water is wonderful,' she said coming over to the fire. Harry didn't trust his voice and just nodded. Looking up, he saw a trickle of water run from her hair, down her neck then follow the line of her collarbone before disappearing under the shirt. His silence prompted her to add, a little shyly as if to explain her dishevelled appearance, 'I couldn't resist having a complete dip.'

Slowly he straightened from his squat to stand very close beside her. Her complexion was turning golden with her exposure to the sun, her Spanish blood he supposed. Her eyes were very clear, the lashes long and still with some drops of water clinging to them. As he stared down, he saw her pupils dilate slightly as she took a small, sharp intake of breath. The lid on the billy began to rattle as the water came to the boil.

Her throat was long and slender, disappearing into the v of her shirt. As if of their own volition, his hands came up and took hold of the loose folds of her shirt, either side of her collar. He gave a gentle tug and, unresisting, she came very close. One of the horses snorted. Was that sound in his ears the cicadas or his own rushing blood? With his thumb he traced the gold chain of her necklace. The griffin lay just out of sight, beneath the shirt. How well it suited her for she had the courage of a lion and claimed, as her right, the freedom of a bird. His head was drawn irresistibly closer until her lips were only inches from his. He felt her breath quicken.

At that moment the lid of the billy was dislodged by the force of the steam and there was a hiss as the water boiled over into the fire. The noise was just enough to jolt him back to his senses. Taking in a deep, shuddering breath, very slowly, Harry released his hold. His hands moved to the buttons and with great care he did the top two up before stepping away. The air between them thrummed. Two birds swooped overhead but neither of them moved.

'The water's very cold,' Georgiana finally said, as if unable to bear the tension between them any more.

'Good!' Harry's voice was hoarse and he strode away.

Chapter Twenty-Nine

The loud splash snapped Georgiana out of the spell Harry had somehow cast. Her heart slowed, returning to its regular beat. She became aware of being able to breathe once more. But though, almost sightlessly, she removed the billy from the flames, she was unable to complete the simple task of making the tea. Instead she sank down, her back against a tree.

Something was shifting. She'd known it from the moment she'd woken to find Harry's blue eyes burning into hers. He had been curiously preoccupied all morning and she had thought perhaps it was fatigue or worry. But in the last few minutes she had finally, almost disbelievingly, understood.

Georgiana had seen yearning in men's eyes before – but never for her. And when she'd felt the warmth of his knuckles so close to her skin, something inside her had kindled and caught with astonishing ferocity. Deep in the pit of her stomach, heat still surged, a glorious craving like no other. Every nerve ending was vividly alive and her breathing was erratic, as was the tripping of her heart and her fingers curled into her palms, her nails leaving crescents of pain to mark her deep, deep frustration.

Yes, there had been desire in Harry's eyes, but she knew him very well. He would never betray what he would see as his duty to protect her. Fool that he was! With a heavy sigh, Georgiana leaned her head back against the tree's trunk and stared up at the cloudless blue sky. How on earth was she going to get him to violate his own code of honour? How could she banish this horribly unwelcome gallantry?

Didn't he understand she was her mother's daughter? She may be innocent, but she was certainly not naïve. She realised now that somewhere between their first meeting in the tavern in England and this moment, she had grown up. Harry, too, sensed it but didn't consciously know it yet. Somehow she had to jolt him out of his carefully constructed defences. He must stop thinking of her either as a cabin boy or an impulsive younger sister. Time for her to show she was a woman. The thought both excited and scared her. She just needed to find the right opportunity ...

The late-spring twilight had already fallen when they finally arrived at Oamaru. The afternoon's ride had again been very quiet, conversation stilted and faltering. Neither of them referred at all to what had happened beside the river, but an unacknowledged thread of energy still burned between them.

In the gathering dark, they picked their way through Oamaru, a small town flourishing thanks to the gold rush. The very broad main road led them past elegant buildings and grand homes built out of a lovely cream stone. A huge cathedral was halfway to completion and some of the smaller backstreets had been cobbled. Entertainments of all types abounded – bars, saloons, dance halls and gambling dens. A ball was being held that evening in the large town hall.

Eventually they found lodgings with a greasy man and his worn wife in their rackety guesthouse, but Harry had only enough money for one room. It was stark: bare boards, wooden walls and two very narrow beds with straw mattresses. There was a rustle of rats in the ceiling above them. A lamp with a very sooty mantle perched on a three-legged stool, the room's only other furniture. Through the dusty panes of the sash window, a straggly back garden with a high fence could only just be discerned. At the far end was a small shack housing, Georgiana realised, the outside privy. The garden seemed private enough, which was good as there were no curtains.

While she claimed one of the cots by putting her bag onto

it, Harry lit the lamp. The smoke was acrid but the glow warmed the room marginally. Then he turned to Georgiana, his pack still slung over his shoulder. 'I'll sleep outside.'

'Don't be silly. There are two beds.' He opened his mouth but she rushed on, to forestall any argument. 'It'll raise awkward questions if you don't stay.' She could see from his expression that argument had gone home and she pressed her advantage. 'Stop worrying about my reputation, Harry. I've already slept many nights with several dozen men about me.'

'Don't remind me!' Harry's response was sharp, but he swung his pack down onto the other bed nevertheless. Then he straightened and ran a hand through his hair. 'Look, we'll worry about the room later. Our most pressing problem right now is money, but I think I have the solution. I'm going to need to leave you for a few hours, but you'll be all right on your own, won't you?'

'Why? What are you planning to do – rob a bank?'

His sudden, raffish grin made her knees weaken. 'Nothing so drastic. Cards. Thought I'd try my luck in that gambling hall around the corner.'

'Ah!'

The grin disappeared and Harry's eyes narrowed. 'Now why have you suddenly got that thoughtful look on your face, George?'

'What expression?'

'And it's no good playing Miss Innocent with me. What are you plotting?'

She smiled disarmingly as she opened her palms at him. 'Nothing. Really.'

But Harry had already guessed. 'No, you can forget any notion of coming with me right now.'

'I'm a good player,' she protested. 'We'd double our winnings.'

'Be that as it may, you are not coming. I am not taking a

woman into such a place.' He sliced the air with his hand to underscore the finality of what he was saying.

'No one will know. They'll just see me as a boy to be fleeced. It's perfect.'

Harry grabbed her by both shoulders. For the second time that day, his face was very close to hers, but this time there was nothing in his eyes but severity. 'No George, it's anything but perfect. You are my responsibility and I absolutely forbid it! You can't wear a hat tonight and your hair has grown. You can't pass off as a young man now, for any length of time. If anyone tumbles to the fact that you are a woman when there's so much alcohol around – it simply doesn't bear thinking about.'

That gave her pause for thought. 'No,' she agreed slowly. 'I can see it could turn bad.'

'*Bad*? It would be downright dangerous.'

She started pulling his fingers from her shoulders. 'Well, of course I don't want you to get hurt if fighting broke out.'

'It's not *me* I'm worried about, you infuriating girl!' He gave her a little shake before letting her go. 'Of all the stupid, madcap schemes.' He stepped back, his expression that of a captain addressing an irresponsible crew member. 'You will stay here. Is that understood?'

'Understood.'

Harry eyed her with suspicion so Georgiana sank down onto the bed as though overcome with weariness. 'I could do with an early night, anyway.'

Harry still regarded her with suspicion.

'I'm sore from the saddle,' she explained.

His expression softened and he smiled. 'True, it's been a long day, but you've been an absolute Trojan. I'll make sure I don't wake you when I return.' He tousled her hair – as if she were still a cabin boy! – and departed.

As soon as she heard the outer door close behind him,

Georgiana released her breath and began unpacking her bag. Trojan indeed. Another image shortly to be blasted out of the water, Harry Trent! A scheme was forming in her mind, though it made her tremble with trepidation. This was it. This was her opportunity – if she had the courage to see it through.

Her dresses were sadly crumpled, however, especially the green silk, and Georgiana sighed. Then, at the very bottom, she spied the dress Consuela had packed out of mischief. It was made of deep blue taffeta and wasn't as creased as the silk. Georgiana had looked at it before of course, but had thought she'd never have the confidence to wear it. It was cut very low and was both sophisticated and a little rakish. Now, as she held it against herself, Georgiana's smile grew.

Harry would be appalled, of course. Good. She wanted to break that damnable control of his. And this dress, she thought a short time later as she did up the outrageously tight bodice, would do the job nicely. She leaned around to shake the skirts into place and as she straightened, with the lamp behind her, she caught sight of her shadowy reflection in the window. Was that really her?

The dress was cut in the newest fashion, with a longer bodice coming down flat over her stomach, emphasising both her height and her slenderness. The skirts draped in rich swathes in the front and at the back gathered into a bustle which, Consuela had assured her, was most definitely going to replace the crinoline. The neckline plunged and her shoulders were bare above tiny belled sleeves. When she moved, the taffeta rustled alluringly. She drew her shoulders back and tilted her head in best Consuela fashion. Her ghostly self looked confidently back at her. This was a new Georgiana, far removed from both cabin boy and gauche debutante. Her heart beat stronger.

She wanted to see again that flare she'd glimpsed in Harry's eyes at the final dinner party on board. She hadn't known then how to take his frustrated possessiveness and turn it into passion. She didn't know if she could do it now but, looking at her reflection, she felt a welling hope. If nothing else, tonight any lingering confusions Harry might have about her and George, his youthful responsibility, must surely die.

At the same time, she knew she must be careful. She would be treading a very different sort of tightrope. But Charlie had once told her gloomily of a girl he admired who treated him like a brother.

'I tell you, Georgie, there's nothing more damned disconcerting for a fellow. Knocks me right back, every time. Dashed if I know how to make a move now.'

This, then, would be her defence.

Without further deliberation, she pulled her hair into a pile of curls on the top of her head, twirling coquettish ringlets about her face and leaving a few to lightly brush the nape of her neck. As she picked up her small pouch and wrapped a shawl around her shoulders, she trembled with the anticipation which always preceded a performance. This time, however, it was underscored by a feeling of dread. How would Harry respond? Was she mad? No, she told herself, she wasn't. Nor was she about to lose courage at this stage. After checking no one was in the hallway, she quietly slipped out of the house and into the street.

Georgiana was glad the hall was just around the corner, for already she could hear drunken youths further down the road. Though Oamaru was taking on an air of respectability with its lovely stone buildings, it was still a goldfields town largely peopled by wild young men who lived hard and played hard. At the door of the gambling hall she paused.

What if it went wrong? It wouldn't! Not if she played her part right. She could do this. She could. Quickly she pinched her cheeks, bit on her lips then, with a touch to the griffin at her neck, she drew in a deep breath and stepped inside.

Chapter Thirty

The room was hazy with smoke and filled with the rumble of a hundred men's voices. She was relieved to see there were a few women at the tables, although they were probably employed to be there. Without doubt, she was the most gloriously attired. She stepped forward, out of the shadow of the doorway. For the briefest second the noise checked before crescendoing into an almost deafening roar of approval as every man's head whipped around to look at her. It was the greatest entrance of her life.

Across the room she saw Harry in the act of raising a bet. At the sudden upsurge of noise, he glanced over at the door – and froze. For a second it seemed as though there was no one else in the room, just herself and Harry. His hand, full of counters, was still outstretched, his face blank with shock. Georgiana's head went up as she threw him a look, half apologetic, half defiant. Then three young men were descending upon her and time began moving again. She saw Harry throw down his cards and shove his chair back so violently that it fell, before she turned her attention to the men in front of her. Each was begging her mostly urgently for the pleasure of her company. None was much older than Charlie and she smiled radiantly. 'Thank you, but I've come to find my brother and persuade him to take me to the ball.'

The handsome, bright-eyed one spoke first, an Irish lilt colouring his voice. 'Your brother? Is he here? Sure, there's no need to disturb him. If you like ma'am, I'd be delighted to escort you to the ball instead.'

He was jostled aside by a man with freckles. 'You're not dressed for it, Mick, and besides, you're a disaster on the dance floor. May I offer my services instead, ma'am? Bobby Cracknell's the name.'

The third was already pushing Bobby aside and Georgiana couldn't help laughing. If her aunt could only see the attention she was getting now. There was no time to enjoy her popularity, however, for Harry, face livid, was bearing down upon her. The wrathful look he threw at her young admirers caused them to take an involuntary step back. 'Georgie! What the dickens do you mean by coming in here? I expressly told you that you weren't to come!'

Georgiana couldn't have hoped for better. His tone was thick with fury and threat and was exactly the same as the one Charles used to use when he caught her among his toys. There couldn't be a man present now who would doubt that she was anyone other than his sister. She dropped her head, the picture of dismayed contrition.

'Are you very angry with me?' she said in a small voice designed to goad him further.

'Angry? That hardly begins to describe how I'm feeling right at this minute. I gave you express instructions which you've chosen to flaunt!'

His fury was all she'd wanted. Instantly, half a dozen chivalrous souls were chiding him for being so harsh with his lovely young sister and begging to take her to the ball. Pretending to be overwhelmed, Georgiana held up her hands and laughed. 'Oh, you are all so kind. I'd hate to disturb you. The ball will be half over by now. But I wonder – if you wouldn't mind – could I possibly join in with one of your games? Harry has taught me how to play a little …' She let her voice trail off in pretty entreaty.

Immediately there was a fresh surge of chatter and a chair was pulled up at a table adjoining Harry's. As she settled her skirts, she couldn't resist shooting Harry a look of triumph under her lashes. He glowered back, his lips pressed white together. She could almost see him burn with the effort of withholding dire threats and admonitions.

'Come man, sit back down,' said one of the players at his table in placatory tones as he tugged on Harry's sleeve. 'She won't come to no harm right here next to you. You can keep an eye on her. You were about to bid, I believe.' Harry had to accept he'd been outplayed and subsided back to his game. She'd ruined his concentration, however, and he lost what he'd thought was going to be an easy win. Outwardly he struggled to assume his usual easy-going persona and merely laughed it off with a philosophical shrug. Inwardly he seethed, but not only with anger. There were several other emotions he was not about to name.

Never in his life had he seen anything so wildly audacious. The image of Georgiana, paused in the doorway, was seared into his mind. She'd stood, head held high like a goddess, the midnight-blue dress setting her magnificent figure off to perfection. Harry shook with a violent desire to kill every single man who looked at her with hot eyes – which meant, therefore, that he'd have to murder a whole roomful of people. Given his current frame of mind, the notion held immense appeal. Of all the infamous, impossible, ridiculous stunts. He'd expressly forbidden her to come and never dreamed she'd dare – but of course there was nothing, *nothing*, she wouldn't dare. Never had he felt more in sympathy with Aunt Ashton.

All the same, he had to pull himself together. They needed money; he couldn't afford to let her throw his game like this. He picked up his next hand, but the cards danced in front of his eyes. He heard her laugh and ground his teeth. If one of those mongrels even thought to … His fingers curled in savage anticipation.

Harry was not to have an outlet to vent his feelings,

however. Over the following half an hour he monitored Georgiana's movements and grudgingly had to admit she was playing her part to perfection. Her dress certainly threw several players right off their game, but her manner, innocent and very sisterly, was perfect at keeping any unwanted attentions at bay. Some men threw Harry measuring glances, but he glowered so fiercely they hastily looked away again.

Georgiana frowned at her hand, placing her fingers on one card, then changing her mind and pulling out another instead. She lost the first game which made the other players very fond of her and she was plied with good advice from all sides. The second game she played with more confidence and when she beat them in the third game, Harry heard their delighted praise. They were all immensely proud of their pupil's quick progress. Then a young man appeared at her elbow and begged she join their table for a few hands. She glanced at Harry. By now he was resigned to his designated part and grunted consent, clearly showing that all this fuss over his sister was ridiculous.

For the rest of the evening, though he pretended indifference, he watched her progress around the room, admiring the deft way she lost sufficient numbers of games so as not to arouse suspicion while steadily accumulating a handsome profit. Her frequent moves to other tables meant that no one realised just how much she had actually won over the course of the evening.

Harry's skills were more obvious and though he passed off his wins as a lucky streak, few who played him were deceived and he attracted the higher players, the more hardened gamblers. However, he was not out to amass a fortune and when he decided he'd won enough, he made his way to Georgiana's side.

She glanced up at him. Tonight her remarkable eyes were the same dark blue as the ocean under *Sally's* keel, and now they were alight with gaming's challenges and success. Her smile was dazzling. Despite his still smouldering fury, he couldn't help smiling back. She had been outrageous to come but clearly the night belonged to her. As soon as her game finished she rose, gathered her winnings into her pouch then thanked the men most warmly for their assistance. They all made their bows with fervent hopes that they might see her on the morrow.

'Unfortunately,' said Harry in quelling tones, 'we'll be leaving at cock crow. But thank you for allowing my sister to play with you. I only hope she hasn't plagued you too much.'

He was assured most heartily that she had not and it was only after some difficulty that Harry extracted his sister from her numerous admirers.

Out on the street she peeped up at him. 'Did you have a successful evening, Harry?'

'No thanks to you. You put me clean off my game,' he said, pulling her hand through his arm.

She leaned into him. 'Pooh, you shouldn't have taken my arrival so badly.'

'Badly! Do you know how ugly things might have got?'

'But you were there to protect me.'

He wanted to shake her, he really did. After he'd kissed her, as thoroughly and soundly as she deserved. 'The sooner I get you to your real brother's protection, the better. You are nothing but trouble.'

Merriment brimmed in her eyes. 'You haven't met Charlie. He'd have thought it a splendid idea – would probably have thought of it first, in fact!'

'The more I know of you and your brother,' said Harry roughly, 'the more your poor aunt has all my sympathies. You are entirely incorrigible, Georgie.'

She laughed and blushed as though he'd paid her a

compliment and he bit back a smile. It was impossible to dent her buoyant sense of triumph and suddenly he found he didn't want to. Spirit like hers was all too rare. Images chased through his mind of pressing her hard up against the side of the building they were passing and covering her beautiful shoulders and neck with kisses, firing her spirit even more.

When they reached their accommodation, however, he quenched all such thoughts in a superlative demonstration of self-control. Grabbing his bedroll and big overcoat, he headed for the door.

'Where are you going?'

'To the stables.'

'Harry! We've already talked about this.' She put a hand on his arm. 'You're being needlessly scrupulous.'

He paused, looking down into her eyes. There was an expression in them he couldn't place. All mischief had disappeared and for a second he thought he saw a woman's invitation there. Which only made it ten times worse.

'I can't stay.'

He removed her hand from his sleeve, then unable to resist, he pressed the inside of her wrist to his lips. He wanted to lick it, nibble it but let it go with a soft kiss. He had to leave, right now, before it was too late.

The door closed after Harry and for a second, Georgiana just stared at it, cradling the wrist which still burned with the imprint of his lips. Part of her yearned to run after him, pull him back. The other part let him go. Now was not quite the right moment. He was too torn, too conflicted. She sank down onto the bed, feeling both the exultance and the strange deep calm of victory. Finally, she had rattled Harry Trent out of every last vestige of his composure. Thank you, Consuela. But it was more than that. Something had indeed shifted. For the first time in their relationship, she felt the sense of power equalise. She was now as sure of his feelings as she was of hers. Tonight she'd shattered his defences. Now all she had to do was storm his scruples, the last stronghold of his heart.

Chapter Thirty-One

They were up before dawn, slipping through the silent streets so that no one would see Trent leave, not with a glamorous young sister, but with a boy with his hair too long.

'You look tired,' Georgiana ventured, glancing at Harry from under the brim of her hat.

'There wasn't much hay so I didn't sleep well.'

It hadn't been the hardness of the boards, though, that had kept him awake a large part of the night. It was something far, far worse. In the dark, fetid air of the stable, he had finally confronted the truth. He was a man in love. He didn't want it. Heaven knew he didn't need this added complication to his life. But Georgiana had never let the convenience of others dictate her actions. She had just come in and stolen his heart. It was as simple – and damnable – as that.

As a consequence, life suddenly arrowed down into a single goal. First and foremost, he had to prove his innocence. There was no question now of going on the run, should this venture be unsuccessful. He could never condemn Georgie to such a life.

Moreover, he knew now that if he did prove his legitimacy, he would have to take up his title and estates. A man had to have something more to offer a wife than life aboard a leaky old ship. But if he did that, everything would change. It was hard to begin to imagine what his life would be. Yet the thought of losing Georgiana was intolerable. Never had he so much to gain, or lose, in his life.

And because he loved her, Harry resolved not to talk of his feelings until he could come to her as a free man, a man without the shadow of the gallows hanging over him. The road ahead was still fraught with danger. Though he was sure Tom had not overtaken them, he was still out there, and Harry knew Mellors would stop at nothing to complete his appointed task – even murder. Harry couldn't embroil Georgiana any further. He would deliver her to the safety of her brother's arms, then go on alone in his quest. When – if – he was successful, then he would return to Georgie. Until then, the least said, the better. Only a cad would wake passions in an innocent girl then leave her to mourn his death.

Such had been his resolve last night, but it was proving devilishly difficult to maintain his friendly calm as they rode side by side.

Georgiana, too, was unusually thoughtful. The minx of the night before had been packed away with that outrageous dress. He glanced often at her but she rode steadily on, hat pulled low over eyes that stared only at the road ahead.

Why had she gone quiet? Had she retreated in embarrassment – either over her behaviour or his kiss? He didn't think so. There had been no shrinking shyness when they'd met at dawn. In fact, there'd been an almost tangible sense of resolution about her.

He did not know what to make of this new, poised, contemplative individual, but this was one of the reasons he loved her. Georgiana was not one woman, nor ever would be. A quotation tickled. What had Shakespeare said about Cleopatra? Something about age not withering her nor custom spoiling her infinite variety. He liked that. A man might be annoyed, frustrated, even infuriated by Georgiana, but he would never be bored. That seemed a very fair deal.

Georgiana's introspection only lifted at the end of their very long day's ride, as they finally drew into Dunedin. She stretched in her saddle and rose in her stirrups to look about her. 'Isn't it beautiful.'

'Stunning.'

The harbour spread before them, blue and luminescent as a stained-glass window in the early evening. Steep hills of brilliant green tumbled to the shoreline. The air was cooler down here, the bite of ice underlying it; a reminder the Antarctic was not so very much further south.

'It doesn't seem fair that New Zealand should have quite so many beautiful corners tucked away,' Georgiana remarked. Her contemplative self was almost visibly peeling away as she became animated, as always, by a new place to explore. That was another aspect about her Harry loved. He realised too that she must be looking forward to a reunion with Charles. His own role with her was nearly done. He was surprised by the pain he felt at such a thought.

Dunedin, heart of the gold rush, was both higgledy-piggledy and clearly booming. The streets ran up the sides of impossibly steep slopes and there was every stage of building to be seen. Muddy foundations sat next to beautiful stone buildings that looked like they might have been there for centuries. Other wooden buildings appeared to have been flung up within a few days. There were solid, worthy-looking banks, some elegant shop frontages, a large number of hotels, ranging from the grand to the deplorable, and numerous bars which were loud with custom.

Even more than Christchurch, this was a town of young men, generally very disreputable. They wore shabby clothes for the most part and many sported whiskers that had clearly not seen a razor for months. Harry, with his unshaven cheeks, looked right at home with this crew. Some hurried on seemingly urgent business, their strides eager and determined. Others lolled against street lamps, smoking and eyeing up the women who passed by with baskets of shopping, pretending they did not notice the hot looks that followed them. There were road stalls and wagons and newspaper boys calling out the evening headlines.

The town reeked of energy, although when Georgiana shared this observation with Harry, he suggested the reek emanated from the town's evidently poor sanitation.

But Georgiana was not to be put off. She was charmed by the town, though she could not say why. She relished the sense of jaunty opportunity and reckless energy that enveloped the town.

'We'll find a hotel for tonight,' said Harry as they threaded their way up what appeared to be the main street. 'What do you say to a hot bath and a decent meal, Georgie?'

'I've been thinking of little else.'

This was not true. Very different thoughts had occupied Georgiana all day. The thought of a bath sounded like heaven now, however. She twisted in her saddle to ease her back. 'It's time for me to become Georgiana again, isn't it?'

She cast him a look, but he was studying the double-storied hotel in front of them and his reply was non-committal. 'Yes, it'll be easier to ask around for Charlie. What do you think about that hotel?'

Georgiana leaned back in her saddle and pushed her hat back as she took in the wide flight of stairs and elegant balconies. 'Can we afford it?'

'We can, thanks to the gambling skills of my sister.'

She laughed but protested, 'You made far more than I.'

'I can cover all the necessities. Your winnings tip us into luxury. Come on, what do you say? Shall we treat ourselves? It may be our last evening together.'

He *was* planning to leave her again. She'd suspected as much during their ride today. He had been quite unreachable. Despair hollowed her resolution but she forced her voice to stay bright. 'In that case, yes indeed.'

'Good. Fortunately, it seems a popular hotel. With so

many people coming and going, no one will notice a lad going in and a lady coming out.'

Georgiana wasn't sure about that, but Harry proved to be right. Another scruffy youth went entirely unnoticed and she was able to slip into the room Harry had secured for her. For a second she stood still, hardly able to cope with the seeming opulence after the past days on the road, the past months at sea. The bed was large with a red coverlet and fat pillows. The curtains were thick and likewise claret-coloured. There was a carpet and rather bad watercolours of flowers on the walls.

For a second she thought she did not deserve such a splendid room. Then, with a shiver of delighted surprise, she realised that yes, she did. She had paid for this room out of her own winnings. She was a woman of independent means, even if only for a short time. It felt surprisingly good and she could feel her tired spine straighten as she walked over to the dressing table. One glance in the mirror, however, swept away any feelings of accomplishment.

With a moan of horror, she tossed the hat aside. Her hair lay in dusty, sweat-flattened curls. Despite the brim, she had caught the sun, her complexion colouring in a most unladylike way. Even worse, when she looked closer, she was sure she saw freckles! There was no time to despair, however. She needed to get ready for tonight.

She had been thinking about it most of the day. The time for subterfuge and masquerade was over. No longer was she Miss Bellingham, Master Miller or Miss Trent. If tonight was to be their last night, then she wanted Harry Trent to spend it with Georgiana da Silva.

When they'd met at dawn, Georgiana had seen instantly that her plan had not worked. She may have knocked Harry off kilter but it was quite clear to her that he'd regained his equilibrium overnight. The Harry who greeted her was as charming – and as infuriatingly controlled – as ever. This was the Harry who sailed the seven seas alone. If she wasn't careful, she'd land up with a millinery shop, a husband and a baby named after its godfather. Well, not this time, Harry Trent!

Georgiana had work to do; woman's work and it would begin with summoning a maid. With stern resolve, she tugged the tasselled bell pull before beginning to divest herself, once and for all, of her male garb.

Chapter Thirty-Two

When Harry knocked at Georgiana's door a few hours later, he was staggered by the stunning young woman who opened it. Georgiana was wearing her green silk and her eyes reflected the same wild-sea colour. She stood tall, her hair shining gold-brown, her face sun-kissed, shoulders white and smooth, the griffin standing in proud relief just above the neckline that skimmed the upper mounds of her breasts.

'My God, Georgie, you are beautiful.'

The words slipped out before he could stop them. After all his resolutions not to declare his feelings, he was perilously close to revealing his love to her.

Georgiana blushed but met his eyes. 'You are looking splendid yourself – but then, you always do.'

The urge to press her backwards into her room, kicking the door behind them, was almost overpowering. To offset the air that seemed to crackle between them, he said, 'And who are you being tonight?'

Her head lifted and she looked straight into his eyes. 'Tonight I am me. Georgiana da Silva.'

A strange happiness filled him; like the ending of a journey – or perhaps the beginning of one. He made a formal bow. 'I'm delighted to make your acquaintance, Miss da Silva. I believe I had the fleeting pleasure of meeting you once in Madeira.'

Her smile was blinding and she gave a small nod as if to acknowledge that he hadn't disappointed her. 'Indeed you are right, but what a long time ago that seems.'

He grinned back as he extended his arm to her. 'I see I will have to ready myself for more possible skirmishes with ardent admirers tonight. Is this to become a habit, Miss da Silva, that I must continually keep eager young blades at bay?'

She laughingly disclaimed and together they made their way down the stairs into the dining room. Being strangers in town, Harry was more than happy for people to mistake them as man and wife, especially as a quick glance informed him that he was indeed with the most beautiful woman in the room. A waiter darted forward, admiration of Georgiana clear in his freckled face as he led them to a secluded corner behind one column. Heads turned as they walked past and Harry knew it was because of the stately young woman on his arm. Georgiana seemed unaware. This surprised him as he was used to the self-conscious manner of beauties. Then it dawned on him that years of seeing herself as plain and awkward had left Georgiana refreshingly unaffected. Last night she'd been the gorgeous but impossibly disingenuous younger sister. Tonight, as herself, Georgiana was in a class all of her own.

She settled herself into her chair, sitting tall and graceful even though she must ache, as he did, after the long days in the saddle and nights of sleeping rough. There was nothing even remotely tired in the eagerness with which she perused the menu.

'I'm so starving I could eat a horse.'

'Given the nature of this town, no doubt it can be arranged. In fact, I suspect half the dishes on the menu may not be all that they seem.'

She made a small comical grimace but objected, 'Given the price you paid for our own horses, I very much doubt it. What are you going to have?'

They took their time over making their choices. The range of dishes seemed decadent and the food, when it came, was surprisingly well-cooked.

'I checked when I was booking our rooms and they assured me the chef was one of the best in the town. I wasn't sure what standards they were measuring by, but it seems Dunedin can boast a few decent meals at any rate. And I have a treat for afterwards. We are going to the theatre – I hope you aren't feeling too tired.'

Georgiana's face lit up. 'Tired? Not at all! Are you serious? They have a theatre here?'

He laughed at her delighted disbelief. 'Apparently they have several. Hard to believe, isn't it? But of course there are lots of young men with pockets of money and little entertainment other than drinking and gambling, so the enterprising are designing ways of alleviating them of a little of their wealth.'

'How wonderful! What is the play?'

'An opera, actually. *The Barber of Seville*, but don't get your hopes up too much. It'll probably be very amateurish.'

'I don't mind in the slightest! What a treat. Come on, we need to eat fast.'

'No, we have plenty of time, relax,' and Harry poured her some more wine, ignoring the waiter who was clearly wanting to serve the lovely young woman.

They chatted over the meal and later strolled arm in arm down the street to the theatre which was lit with hissing gas lamps. Like everything in New Zealand, the veneer of culture was paper thin as the cold light of day would have shown the curtains to be threadbare and the stage and chairs removable, as the theatre was also an auction room. But Georgiana was captivated by it all. She appeared oblivious to the musty smell of mice Harry could discern and seemed inured to the draughts that whistled around their necks. Instead she watched the performance with rapt, though measuring eyes. She hummed along with some of the songs and was enthusiastic in her applause. Harry watched her almost as much as he watched the opera.

As they walked back to the hotel along the street which flickered with shadows from the gas lights, Georgiana let out a deep sigh of satisfaction. 'What a *splendid* night. Thank you, Harry. I have quite put worries of Tom and Charlie from my mind.'

'Good. And tomorrow we will begin our search.'

'Yes.'

Was it his imagination or was her answer unusually subdued? It must be tiredness finally catching up, he thought, because Georgiana was uncharacteristically quiet for the rest of the walk.

They mounted the stairs of their hotel and Harry escorted her to her door. He bid her good evening and was just turning to go when Georgiana put a hand on his sleeve.

'Harry?'

She was suddenly looking very grave but determined, which perplexed Harry. She'd been in such high spirits most of the evening. 'What is it?'

She bit her lip. 'Could you come inside for one moment, there's something I want to say.' He glanced about them and she added impatiently, 'Oh for heaven's sake, Harry, no one's about. Come in quick.'

She pushed open her door and entered, beckoning for him to follow, and Harry, wondering what the hell she was up to now, stepped into her room and closed the door behind him.

Chapter Thirty-Three

While Harry went to the bedside table to light the kerosene lamp, Georgiana ran her palms down her skirts, drawing in a deep breath. This was it.

The light flared, illuminating his perfect features, and for a second her resolve faltered. Surely she must have imagined the expression she'd thought had been in his eyes all evening. A man like that could never seriously be interested in a girl like her. Fears of rejection and failure once more threatened to overwhelm her.

Her uncertainty must have shown in her face because, as he turned to look at her, Harry's wary look was replaced by concern as he took both her hands in his. 'Georgie? Are you worried about tomorrow? You have my word I won't rest until I find Charlie.'

'No, it's not that.'

His hands tightened on her fingers. 'Mellors, then. I promise I won't let that scoundrel within a mile of you.'

That made her laugh. 'I've scarcely thought about him since we left Christchurch,' she said. It was true. During these past few days with Harry, she'd felt as though nothing and no one could ever endanger her. Withdrawing her hands from his, she stepped away towards the window. For a second she pressed her fingers to her mouth. There was no role she could find for this moment. This had to be her. Georgiana da Silva. She turned and looked at Harry.

'I once told you I knew who you were and what you were.'

He flinched, the wary look back. 'Yes, I remember.'

'I was wrong then. Entirely wrong. I said terrible things that night. But now I do know. I know you, Harry Trent.' She drew in another breath and spoke her next words very calmly, very deliberately. 'I know who you are and what you are. And before we find out tomorrow about Charlie and Mr Sedgewick, I want you to know that I love you.'

A silence stretched and stretched about them. Harry's face was unreadable. She discovered her hands were shaking and clenched them hard. She shouldn't have said anything. Never before had she felt so exposed, so vulnerable.

Then Harry said, 'Oh God, Georgie, don't do this now.'

She made a small, helpless gesture. 'I have to.'

'You don't understand – I could be arrested any time, sent back to England to face the gallows.'

'I *know*. That is exactly why I am telling you now.'

He fell back a pace as though distance could stop her words. 'I will not have you giving your heart to a man wanted for murder.'

She took a step forward, smiling a little. 'This time you cannot forbid me, Harry. Your only choices are to accept it or not.'

Both his hands came up as though to fend her off. 'If I don't clear my name, I'll be on the run forever.'

'I don't care. I just want to be with you.'

'It will be different of course, if I'm an earl – but I cannot guarantee it, Georgie.'

She took another two steps forward. 'I don't need a guarantee.'

He shook his head. 'This is the wrong time, don't you see? At present I am nothing more than a penniless captain wanted for murder. I have *nothing* to offer you.' She heard the pain in this admission.

She reached up and put her hand on his cheek. 'I'm only a circus brat. All I want is you.'

He stood very still, his only movement the muscle twitching in his jaw. 'Georgie, stop now, I warn you.'

Instead, she took his face between her two palms and

gently pulled it down to hers. He didn't resist. Almost unbearably slowly, his mouth came down to meet hers.

His lips were very warm and firm against hers. For a moment they lingered and then, with a sigh of regret or reluctance or both, Harry began to pull away. Georgiana's fingers moved to his hair and she anchored his head, pressing her mouth more firmly against his. Instinctively her lips parted and, as the kiss deepened, she gave an involuntary sigh of pleasure.

It was as though that sigh undid all Harry's resolutions. He made a sound halfway between a laugh and a groan as his arms tightened about her, locking her to him. His mouth was no longer gentle as it took control with a new urgency.

Fire ran through her veins, awakening a hunger to match his. His hair was thick and silky under her fingers, his breath warm on her face, his mouth tasting both of danger and homecoming. She could smell soap and wine and Harry's own distinctive scent that always carried a hint of salt winds and sea.

Then his mouth left hers and soft, slow-burning kisses explored her face, her closed eyes, before travelling down to her shoulders, across to her neck. She wove her fingers tighter into his hair, binding him to her. And then suddenly he stopped, pulling away. Just like that. His breathing was ragged as he leaned his forehead against hers. She tried to pull his mouth to hers again, but he shook his head.

'We must stop now, Georgie.' His voice was hoarse.

'Why? I love you, Harry. I want to have at least one night with you. Who knows what will happen tomorrow.'

He straightened, his fingers touching her lips, then he stepped back. She could see he was shaking with the effort of his self-restraint. 'I will not seduce you, Georgiana. You deserve better than that. If I take you, I want to take you as my wife. And if – God forbid – I should swing, I want you to one day be able to go honestly to your future husband's bed. There'll be no shadow over your marriage, if anything happens to me.'

'Harry!' She could have stamped her foot at him. Was there ever such an infuriatingly honourable, noble *idiot*! But he had already stepped away and was running his hands through his hair, trying to steady his breathing. His eyes, the same blue as the centre of a flame, met hers ruefully. 'Oh God, Georgie. This is the hardest thing I've ever done. Will you try to understand? You came to me honestly, with your own name tonight. I want to be able to do the same with you.'

His body was taut as a drawn bow. If she made one movement, she knew his control would desert him. She ached to know how that felt, but his eyes beseeched hers. With a smile that broke halfway, she nodded.

Harry breathed out, long and slow. 'Georgie, you have tested me on more levels than any other woman I've ever known. But I swear, I will clear my name or die trying. I must go before I change my mind. Goodnight. Sleep well.' He gave a short, ironic laugh. 'I won't! But we have a big day tomorrow.'

'Goodnight, Harry.'

He crossed to the door, his hand went out to the handle. Then in two strides he was back before her. She looked up into his face. He smiled down at her, once more the man always in control of his feelings. Then he took her face between two warm hands and kissed her very slowly, very deeply. Once again her knees went weak, her senses swam. But this time she knew his kisses did not stem from uncontrollable hunger but from something far stronger, far more lasting. When he at last raised his head, he looked into her eyes. 'I love you, too, Georgiana da Silva.'

Chapter Thirty-Four

The following morning Georgiana was awake early. It had taken her a long time to get to sleep and now she luxuriated in a euphoric sense of wellbeing. Charlie would be found. Mr Sedgewick would be found and she and Harry could then marry and live happily forever. With difficulty she forced herself to stay in bed until she heard the hotel stir, then she rose and dressed. A soft knock some time later had her rushing to fling her door open.

'Harry! I've been waiting forever for you.'

He grinned. In the early morning light he looked more splendid than ever, especially as she could see happiness deep in his eyes. 'And I have waited an entire lifetime for you – a relatively peaceful, untrammelled life, I might add.'

Rosy happiness washed through her right down to her toes. 'Then you were in need of livening up, Captain Trent. But you know what I mean – I'm talking about Charlie.'

'I know.' He offered his arm. 'But the post office won't open for another half-hour yet. Breakfast?'

She shook her head. 'I can't even think about eating until I know how Charlie is.'

So they walked about Dunedin in the chilly, early morning air. Georgiana found it hard to describe how she was feeling. Apprehensive, excited but, above all, deliciously happy. She turned her face up to Harry and confessed somewhat shyly, 'When I woke up, I wondered if last night had been a dream.'

'Then let me dispel such notions.' He pulled her into an alley, away from the curious gaze of the early morning loiterers, and kissed her thoroughly. 'There, does that reassure you?'

'Hm,' she put her head to one side. 'Well, almost.'

Harry laughed and immediately took advantage of such an invitation. His fingers slid down her sides, over her bodice with its stays beneath and the ridges of the small crinoline. 'Damned feminine trappings.'

'I could get my trousers out,' she suggested.

His laugh caught in his throat. 'The sight of you in those were a torture to me.'

'Really?'

'Yes, really. And stop looking so pleased about it.'

She laughed, leaning her forehead into his shoulder and inhaling the delicious smell of maleness through the fabric of his jacket. His arms around her felt very safe.

'Will we find Charlie?'

'You can bet on it.'

'And Mr Sedgewick?'

'Without a doubt. My future happiness absolutely depends upon it.'

She raised her face and leaned back in his embrace so that he could kiss her again, which he obligingly did. A bell tolled.

'There. Nine o'clock.' Georgiana tore herself out of his embrace. 'We must go.'

'I feel so used,' Harry complained. 'Were you just filling in time?'

'We'll fill some more later,' she promised. 'Come on.'

When she walked into the post office to which she had sent so many letters from England, Georgiana found her heart racing. Her fingers tightened on Harry's arm and his other hand came up to cover them in a warm grasp.

'Now the clerk may not know anything about your brother,' Harry warned. 'He'll see so many young men he may not remember – but that might not mean anything, understood?'

'Understood,' she whispered.

They approached the counter and Harry addressed the bespectacled clerk. 'We are looking for a Charles da Silva. Do you know the name?'

The clerk was evasive. 'Who wants him?'

'Me,' said Georgiana stepping forward. 'He's my brother.'

'Is he now?' The clerk looked measuringly at her. 'He's talked of you. And where did you spring from?'

'She's come from England having heard her brother was dangerously ill. We need to know if he is alive.'

'Alive? Course he's alive. Was very sick mind you, but bounced back. Was here just a month ago and very disappointed he was at having no letters. As full of cheek as ever.'

Georgiana laughed aloud in her relief. She was not surprised the clerk remembered her brother. People always did, not just because of his unusual name but also because of his wide grin, his friendliness, his execrable jokes.

'I *knew* he couldn't be dead,' she said, but still she felt herself go limp and was glad to have Harry's hand lightly holding her elbow. 'Where can I find him?'

It turned out that Charles had decided to check out some land further south but where, exactly, the clerk did not know.

'But he said he'd be back in a month and that's some weeks ago so he may be returning anytime soon. He'll come by here, always does. You tell me where you are staying, I'll send him over to you directly.'

'I'm at the Provincial,' said Georgiana, 'and I won't stir from town till he's returned!'

As they quit the post office, Harry glanced up and down the street. It was busier now, but everything seemed normal. No sign of Mellors' hulking frame amongst the men going about their business.

'I can't believe I'm going to see Charlie soon. It seems unbelievable, incredible! I cannot tell you how relieved and overjoyed I am.'

Harry smiled. 'You don't have to. You are lit up like a candelabra. Happiness suits you, Georgie.'

And it did, but much as he loved to see her bubbling with delight, Harry was not at all comfortable walking through the town in broad daylight. If Mellors put the local police force onto him – and he was quite sure the man would do just that – he could be arrested at any moment. It was with an effort he walked normally without casting glances over his shoulder.

With his own brand of devil's luck, however, locating Malcolm Sedgewick's mining supplies shop proved to be far quicker and easier than they had ever imagined. Even as they began walking down Princes Street, there it was: *Sedgewick's* written in large letters over one doorway. They went into the cramped shop but, again, their quest proved unsuccessful. Sedgewick had just taken a large number of supplies up to the goldfields where profits were far higher.

'When will he be back?' Harry asked. 'It's urgent that I speak to him. Has anyone else been asking for him?'

The shop assistant shook his head. 'There's no one been asking for him saving yourself and I don't know when he'll be back. But he was going first to Arrowtown, I know that for a fact. There's a coach leaving in an hour you could catch if you've a mind to go after him.'

Harry stepped closer, his voice more urgent. 'If anyone else comes looking for him, don't tell them where he is, do you understand?'

The shop assistant looked anxious. 'Is there going to be trouble? I don't want no trouble – not here. I'm not paid enough for any sort of malarkey.'

Harry smiled reassuringly and slid several notes over the

counter to the man. 'There'll be no trouble as long as you hold your tongue.' The assistant picked up the notes, folded them and slipped them into the pocket of his waistcoat before nodding.

When they were back on the street, Georgiana was shocked. 'You bribed that man!'

'Mellors will be on our heels.' Harry couldn't keep the grim note out of his voice.

'Will it work?'

Harry shrugged. 'I don't know. Somehow I doubt it. That fellow has all the resolve of a wet straw.'

Georgiana tucked her hand into his arm once more. This time it was she trying to give comfort and he smiled down. Inside, his stomach twisted. The trouble with love, he discovered, was that suddenly he had so much to lose. If Mellors broke the shop assistant—

'You have to go look for Sedgewick,' Georgiana said abruptly.

'What?' He pulled himself out of his thoughts and glanced down at her. 'No. I told you, I'm not leaving you, Georgie, till I deliver you to your brother.'

'It's as good as done. The clerk said he would tell Charlie where I was staying the minute he came in. But you need to go.'

'I won't risk Mellors tracking you down.'

'Harry, stop being heroic. Think about it. Tom won't be bothering about me too much at the moment. He knows no one would ever take my word over Walsingham's. Sedgewick will be his first priority. With the marriage certificate destroyed and Sedgewick's silence ensured – one way or another – then you remain the number one suspect and he and Walsingham will walk away free. You *have* to beat him to Arrowtown. Everything – including Sedgewick's life – is at stake.' Harry was silent but she continued, 'I'll be fine here. It's a small town and the hotel is a reputable one. What harm could I come to?'

He smiled wryly at that. 'You would wonder, wouldn't you, but trust me Georgie, you could find trouble in a convent.'

But even as he was speaking, Georgiana's attention had been caught by an advertisement in the theatre window for actresses. 'Oh look!' she said, stopping short.

Harry took one look and said, 'No, Georgie, absolutely not. If I leave you, you must keep a low profile while I'm away.'

'Tom wouldn't be looking for me in a theatre, now would he? He knows nothing about my acting.'

'Be that as it may, I won't have you parading around with a dangerous man on the loose. It's inviting trouble.'

'Don't go using that high-handed tone on me, Harry Trent. It won't wash,' she said. 'Beside, I won't be parading around. Look, the theatre is just around the corner from the hotel. I could be there in a minute with no one being the wiser.'

'Georgiana, I won't have it, do you hear me! For once in your life, will you listen to reason!'

Her eyebrow lifted. '*Your* reason?'

For a second he glared at her. 'I completely understand why all the men of your acquaintance have a strong desire to wring your neck! I cannot go until I can be sure you'll be sensible and stay indoors where you will not be seen. Do you understand?'

'Yes, I understand.'

He didn't trust her compliant tone, but when they reached the hotel, Georgiana said very reasonably, 'Look Harry, you really do have to go. I'll be fine. Trust me. Charlie will be here in no time. You should leave immediately.'

Harry hated to leave but he knew she was right. 'Are you sure—'

'I'm sure!' She smiled. For a brief moment her gloved hand rested on his cheek.

Georgiana was not alone in her room for long. She couldn't believe how quickly Harry could pack. It seemed to be only minutes till again there was a knock at her door. She smiled as she opened it, hoping she could hide the pain she felt at his departure. This wasn't how she'd imagined things when she'd woken so full of optimism. Reality was cold and hard. Harry's life truly was at stake.

'Ready so soon? Good, you'll catch the coach, then.'

Harry stepped up to her and tilted her face up to his. 'Now listen, Georgie, listen very carefully. I won't leave unless I can be absolutely sure you'll be safe. I don't want you to go about the streets much. I know this will be dull for you, but I can't risk having Mellors find you. He'll probably just go straight to Sedgewick's shop and then follow me out to Arrowtown – he'll know that I'm ahead of him. If you keep your head down, he won't know where to look for you. Is that understood?'

She nodded and Harry bent to kiss her.

'When I clear my name—' he began, but she put her finger to his lips.

'We've already been through this. Harry Trent, I will love you forever, no matter what happens. Understood?'

He caught her in a fierce embrace, pulling her to him and pressing her against the length of his body as his mouth sought hers again. She wound her arms around his neck, her hunger equal to his. With a muffled oath, Harry finally tore himself away.

'Oh, Georgie, we must stop. Whatever you say, I'm only going to come to you as a free man. I won't leave a widow behind. I saw the life my mother had to lead.'

Reluctantly Georgiana saw how it was for him and

nodded. She pulled his head back down and kissed him one last time before giving him a gentle shove away. 'Then go. Go now and find Sedgewick. Don't let Tom beat you.'

He laughed and his eyes lit with a reckless joy. 'I'm gone,' he told her, 'for everything is at stake. I've gone from a man with nothing to lose to one who has the world to gain. Wait for me, and Georgie – don't get into any mischief!'

'I won't,' she assured him, but as he bounded down the stairs, she slowly uncrossed her fingers.

Chapter Thirty-Five

And she had meant to be good, she really had. The fingers had just been a precaution, but by lunchtime the following day Georgiana was desperate to escape the hotel. It was not in her nature to be patient and she was tortured by fears of having found love, only to lose it again. She should have gone with Harry. But then there was Charlie. She was torn in two completely different directions and could do nothing about either.

Finally she could stand it no longer. Grateful that it was drizzling, she threw a shawl over her head so her face was mostly obscured, and slipped along to the theatre. Her welcome there made her heart swell. They took in her height, her strong features and offered her a part in the evening's performance on the spot.

'But you haven't seen me act, yet,' she protested.

'Don't need to. You're a real woman. Got to be better than young Billy here!' and the owner of the theatre punched an adolescent boy affectionately in the back. 'He's been the heroine since Maud went down with flu last Tuesday. We haven't half had a few complaints. Don't worry about learning your lines – we'll stick cards around the stage. Can you begin rehearsals now?'

'Absolutely!'

She was greatly encouraged to discover it was a rococo farce and that her costume included a huge wig and lashings of make-up. Harry couldn't object for even he would have been hard-pressed to recognise her that evening, she thought, as she stepped out of the wings and onto the stage. All feeling of trepidation fled and as Georgiana faced the darkened auditorium, she knew, with deep certainty, this was what she'd been seeking all her life. Though the play was excessively foolish and she missed some cues and ad-libbed outrageously for others, the whole performance went with a swing.

'My girl, you are *splendid*,' one of the actors whispered to her as they made their final bows to an ecstatic audience. She wished Harry could have heard. A boy appeared at her elbow bearing a huge bunch of flowers. Management knew how to exploit their new find. The audience went wild as she accepted it graciously, threw one rose out into the crowd and then, with a final curtsey, made her escape from the stage. The cast all clustered about her, excitedly chattering, exclaiming at her radiance, her naturalness.

'You, my dear, are a *find!*' exclaimed the director. 'Will you be staying in Dunedin? There are no end of plays we could do with you. Can you sing as well? You know, we will never let you go now!' And Georgiana, laughing and blushing, suddenly knew she was home.

Overnight, Georgiana became the talk of the town. Far from keeping out of the public's eye, she'd become Dunedin's darling. Every night for a week she played to packed houses and was greeted by name in all the shops. Harry would be furious of course, when he found out that she had used her own name, but it had been a spur of the moment decision. All charades were over, no matter what the consequences, and Georgiana had never been so happy. Rehearsals and performances consumed her every moment, keeping her safe not only from Tom, who would never have the chance to approach her, but also from confronting her emotions that had suddenly become tangled and conflicted once again.

Georgiana couldn't wait to see Harry again, of course, but this new life offered something she'd never had before. For the first time since her parents' death she actually belonged somewhere and felt like a complete person. She was loved for just being herself. It was the most extraordinary, unlooked for gift. She finally knew who she was and what she was. Part of her couldn't wait to tell Harry, share it all with him. But another part of her shrank from thoughts too threatening to contemplate.

Harry would understand an actress's joy. But would an earl? If he did indeed claim his title, then what? It didn't bear thinking about and she thrust the niggling worry away whenever it pricked her happiness.

It was after the first act of the Saturday night performance that a note was passed to her in the wings.

Georgie you are incorrigible! I've barely been in town half an hour and have already heard your name mentioned by no less than three people! We will talk, you and I. But this is to let you know that obviously I am returned and with Malcolm Sedgewick in his rooms behind his shop. I cannot wait to tell you all. Will meet you at the stage door at the end of your performance and will take you to meet him. He is most desirous to make your acquaintance – poor man won't know what's hit him when he does!

H.

Her heart soared at the jaunty confidence with which the note had been written. He was back and clearly safe. For two pins she would have fled the stage then and there and gone to Sedgewick's shop immediately. But that was impossible so, drawing in a deep breath, she moved back onto the stage for the next scene. No one in the audience could have guessed that her thoughts had suddenly flown elsewhere, but she was acutely aware that her blood was racing and her heart was light. Harry in just another hour.

It was during the curtain calls at the end that she saw him. There was Harry in the front row applauding. It was hard to make him out properly, of course, for the row of gas lights sent leaping shadows across the faces, but there was no mistaking the height, the set of the shoulders, the thick sweep of hair.

He came to see me, she thought, and sent him a dazzling smile. But at that moment one of the jets of light flared and she saw that the hair was brown and the features, though very alike, were not the same. The man was applauding and smiling but without a flicker of recognition.

Immediately she looked away, forcing smiles to others in the audience and curtseying as her thoughts tumbled over one another. Could it be Harry's half-brother? Impossible. What would he be doing here? Yet there was no other explanation. The likeness was uncanny. No wonder Harry had shocked everyone who knew Phillip. She too was very shaken by their similarity. But what on earth was he doing here? It could only be to make mischief for Harry. She blew a final kiss from her fingertips to her adoring audience, then almost ran off the stage. As usual the cast was standing around to greet her.

'*Georgiana*, that was your best performance *ever*!' cried her leading man. She smiled but called over her shoulder, 'I have a friend at the door. I cannot keep him waiting.'

In minutes she had divested herself of her costume, had dragged on her dress and had scoured off most of her stage make-up. Then, gathering up her skirts, she went straight to the door. She must warn Harry. But when she looked out, no one was there. Now the panic she had felt from the moment she'd sighted his half-brother threatened to overwhelm her though she tried to reassure herself. Harry must have mistaken the time her performance would end, that's all, and was probably still at Sedgewick's shop.

Swiftly, she made her way down the road and around the corner, to the alley which lay behind Mr Sedgewick's shop. Sure enough, there were lights on in the back room and through the thin curtains she could see the shadow of a man crossing the room. She went to the door and knocked. It opened and she looked into the lined face of an elderly man with thin greying hair.

'Mr Sedgewick?' she asked, her apprehension deepening as she noticed a livid bruise beginning to colour his cheek. 'I'm Georgiana da Silva and I—' she faltered as a familiar voice interrupted.

'Come in my dear, we've been waiting for you.'

The door swung wider and there, standing at Mr Sedgewick's side, holding a pistol, was Tom.

Chapter Thirty-Six

Georgiana gave a small scream and fell back a pace, but Tom shook his head and gestured with his pistol for her to enter. 'Oh no, Miss Trent – or should I say Miss da Silva – I would not have you disappear at this moment after all my efforts in locating everyone.'

The room was small and showed evidence of a struggle – a chair overturned, a tablecloth pulled askew. And there, half reclining on a small, shabby sofa was Harry, blood soaking the left shoulder of his shirt and spreading down the sleeve. His face was drawn white with pain, but he managed a tiny smile. 'I'm sorry, Georgie, I would have warned you but I feared he'd shoot Sedgewick.'

'Quite right. I wouldn't have hesitated, you know.'

Tom spoke with his usual quiet courtesy and Georgiana shivered. His face was open and friendly, the expression as affectionate as ever. Only now he was holding a gun, still levelled at Mr Sedgewick. 'Make yourself comfortable, Georgiana – may I call you that? Sarah does not seem right, now, and we are beyond formalities I imagine. No, do not worry about Trent – he is going to die either sooner or later, but if you go to him, it will be sooner.'

Georgiana swallowed and crossed instead to an armchair by the fireplace. It took every ounce of control to remain calm. The approving look Harry flicked her warmed her marginally and she sent him the faintest of smiles. Tom, seeing this intimate exchange, gave a short laugh. 'It appears you two have become better acquainted since our last meeting.'

'We were always better acquainted,' said Harry. His voice rasped, likely from the pain, though he refused to show it.

'I always suspected there was a bond between you – was he the dastardly captain that deserted you in Madeira? Ah, I see from your face, Georgiana, that he was. But there's no time to tell me the full story, much as I'd like to hear it. Sedgewick, no doubt Trent has filled you in on all the details.'

'If you mean that he is the rightful heir to the Elrington estate, yes he has.' Sedgewick had righted the chair and now sat down on it. Tom remained standing next to the door. Georgiana hadn't quite closed it and a cold draught blew in, but Tom did not appear to notice. With a shiver, she drew closer to the flames.

'Why are you here, Tom?'

He looked amused. 'The same reason that Trent is, of course. He was not happy to return from slipping out to the theatre to find me questioning Mr Sedgewick and objected to my methods. Stupidly he launched himself at me. Did you think me such a fool,' he said, turning to Harry whose face was drawn with pain, 'that I wouldn't come properly prepared this time?'

'Perhaps he never thought one man would shoot another who was unarmed.' Sedgewick's voice was acid.

Tom smiled. 'Perhaps – but then it is always a mistake to underestimate your opponent. After our little encounter in Christchurch, I was determined not to be caught out again. Of course, I knew where you were both headed and followed you down, only to discover Mr Sedgewick out of town and Sarah – or Georgiana, I should say – the star of the stage. Yes, I've been here a few days m'dear, but didn't want to alert you to the fact. I had a feeling Trent here would fetch Mr Sedgewick back for me if I were patient. I didn't think he would abandon you, Georgiana.' Tom paused and turned back to Sedgewick. 'Now, we are finally all assembled in one spot – barring your brother, of course, Georgiana, although he turned out only to be a bit part in this drama after all. It is almost funny when you recollect so much of it began with him. But there you are. Mr Sedgewick, you are now in the spotlight. Do you have proof of Trent's legitimacy?'

Sedgewick stayed quiet. Tom's voice sharpened. 'Don't try any games, man. I can outplay you all.'

His eyes strayed with meaning towards Georgiana and in a flash Harry was struggling to sit upright as he swore ferociously. Tom merely turned the pistol on him. 'Stay there. I don't want to kill you just yet.'

'Why kill him at all?' demanded Georgiana. 'If there is proof, Mr Sedgewick here can give it to you. You can destroy it and then there'll be no need to kill Harry. He won't be a threat any more.'

'What do you say, Sedgewick?' Tom cocked a brow.

'No!' said Harry furiously.

'If I give it to you, will you leave us all in one piece?'

'Of course.'

'Don't trust him,' cried Harry, rising, but in two swift strides, Tom crossed the room and slammed a fist into his wounded shoulder. Harry collapsed with a groan.

'You have no choice but to trust me,' Tom pointed out.

Georgiana squeezed shaking hands together as Sedgewick crossed the room and crouched beside the table.

'Careful,' warned Tom, wiping his bloodstained fist across his thigh.

Sedgewick lifted the table cloth to reveal a small safe tucked beneath. Without a word, he began dialling the combination. Harry closed his eyes and shook his head, but it seemed to take all his strength just to stay conscious. The door of the safe swung open, revealing a pile of papers inside. Sedgewick rifled through and withdrew one and handed it to Tom who glanced at it, nodded, then shoved it into his pocket.

'Why did you have it?' he asked with mild interest.

'My lord gave me the marriage certificate on the day he heard that his wife had died – had apparently died. He was afraid his parents might find it and destroy it, thus removing any stain on their name. I thought he was being overanxious at the time, but now I discover they were prepared to go to far greater lengths.'

Tom nodded and smiled. 'The pride of the family is very strong. Lady Elrington even disapproves of Lord Walsingham, although it's his money that keeps her estates flourishing. Well, *your* estates as it turns out,' he said to Harry, 'but you must know it is impossible for you ever to claim them. I'm doing you a favour really. No one would ever accept you as earl and being shot is kinder than being hung, after all.'

He raised the gun and levelled it at Harry.

'No!' cried Georgiana, flinging herself in front of the prostrate figure.

'Georgie, for God's sake,' swore Harry, pushing her out of the way with his sound arm.

But even as Tom cocked his pistol, another voice said, 'I wouldn't do that if I were you.'

Everyone's heads swung towards the door. There stood a man, looking remarkably like Harry, with a gun aimed at Tom's head. Harry drew his breath in sharply. Sedgewick's eyes widened, and for a minute Tom was completely thrown. The two armed men looked unwaveringly at each other then Tom lowered his gun and smiled. 'You must be Phillip. You cannot think how long I have wanted to make your acquaintance, but my father always forbade it. Put the gun down – we are on the same side, you know.'

Phillip held his gun steady, however. 'You have an advantage over me, I'm afraid. I do not think our paths have ever crossed.'

'No, I was raised in the neighbouring county, but I've known all about you these past fifteen years.'

'I don't see why.'

'You are my step-brother – though not perhaps officially, of course.'

'*What*?' Harry and Phillip spoke together then exchanged surprised looks.

'I am Lord Walsingham's son,' said Tom, enjoying the stir he had caused. 'Of course, I was not raised in the same manner as you were, but he provided for me and my mother over the years and visited frequently. He spoke of you so often – his step-son.'

Now the gun did waver and Tom saw it. 'Come, we are almost family. I am here on your business, after all, securing your inheritance. I presume that is why you are here, too. Did your mother send you?'

Phillip shook his head. 'My grandmother.' His sudden rueful smile was disconcertingly like Harry's. 'I don't know quite what is going on,' he confessed. 'I was away but received a distraught letter from my mother because a bas—' he glanced at Harry and Georgiana and coughed—'because an illegitimate child of my father's – a sea captain bearing an uncanny resemblance to me – was out to make mischief and had murdered Iver. She thought I might be in danger. But at the same time I received a curious note from my grandmother telling me not to believe all I heard and imploring me to visit my father's valet, a Malcolm Sedgewick in New Zealand, and learn the truth. She warned others may be searching for him too and that I should keep my head down. You sir,' he said, turning to the elderly man making a little bow, 'must be Mr Sedgewick. I believe you had been my father's man?'

The older man nodded, his eyes on Phillip's face.

'How the hell did you come to be here right at this moment?' demanded Harry, even whiter than before.

Still keeping his gun on Tom, Phillip moved deeper into the room. 'I only arrived in town this morning – I'm a bit behind you all but have been dogging your footsteps all the way, as it turns out. In Christchurch, the man at Mr Sedgewick's old house was mystified as to why I should be the third person in a week asking for him and I was surprised, too, until I learnt one of the men looked exactly like me.' He gave Harry a quick glance, his expression unreadable. 'In Oamaru, the plot thickened when several young men stopped me to demand to know where my beautiful young sister was. You, I assume?'

Georgiana cast her eyes down demurely and gave a modest nod.

Phillip continued, calm and conversational, though his finger remained on the trigger. 'At Mr Sedgewick's shop this afternoon, I knew the question to ask and discovered that yes, my *brother* had been there just days before with a young woman on his arm. When I was informed that Mr Sedgewick was still out of town I decided to while away the evening at the theatre. I'd heard there was a marvellous new actress.' He inclined his head to Georgiana and said, 'You were indeed wonderful.'

She blushed and couldn't help feeling gratified, even though she still did not know on which side this man stood. Harry gave a little growl. Phillip shot him a half-amused, half-understanding glance. 'Imagine my surprise when this same actress gave me a radiant smile as though she knew me. Suddenly I realised that my half-brother must be somewhere near.' He looked at Georgiana. 'I saw you coming out of the stage door and decided to follow you in case you led me to – to the man I've been seeking. And indeed my impulse proved correct for now I find you have brought me to both my brother and Mr Sedgewick.'

Tom spoke accusingly. 'Were you listening at the door?'

'Yes. It's not something I normally do, but I heard Miss da Silva scream and thought it prudent to first see what was taking place inside.'

'So you've heard enough to know. Your mother's marriage was illegal,' said Tom. 'You, dear step-brother, are as much a bastard as I.'

There was savage satisfaction in Tom's voice and suddenly Georgiana realised that he must have hated Phillip all these years – the privileged step-brother who had everything. Phillip drew his breath in. He looked over at Harry who, for a man with a bullet in his shoulder, still managed a good attempt at a shrug.

'Is this what you killed Iver for?' asked Phillip contemptuously. 'Is this what you crossed the world for? The Elrington title?'

'No!' cried Georgiana. 'Tom killed Iver, not Harry. He was framed by Walsingham.'

Phillip looked at Tom. 'Is this true?'

'Does it matter if it is? Of course I killed Iver. He was trying to destroy our father. He was planning to pull down the whole business – he had to be stopped.'

'Your father, not mine.'

'It would have destroyed your mother just as much.'

Phillip paused and Tom pressed home the advantage. 'Think how much this'll hurt your mother. She'll be ridiculed. Trent here will cast her out – he said he would. She's the victim here. She never knew of the marriage until Trent stuck his nose in. My father saw at a glance how to save everything. If Iver died and Trent was taken for his murder, all would be safe. All could continue as before.'

Tom's voice was soft and urgent with persuasion, but Phillip shook his head. 'What? Continue as a lie?'

'No, as it should be. As it still can be. All we have to do is deliver up Trent to the law and—'

'But I will testify for him,' cried Georgiana. 'I will tell the truth in court.'

'Do you think they will believe a young woman – an actress, at that – in love with him?' asked Tom.

'They'd believe me,' said Sedgewick, stepping forward.

'An old man with a grudge against the family?'

'They might believe me,' said Phillip.

Tom stared at him, incredulous. 'Would you throw it all away? All I've done for you? For what? A whim?'

'A principle,' said Phillip. 'The truth.'

'My father always had contempt for you,' spat Tom. 'That's why I became his right-hand man. You weren't up to it, he said. How right he was! Wouldn't ever let me near you but he told me about you. Said how you were at heart the farmer, not me. You had no head for business. Where do you think all the money came from for your land and its projects? Your cottages for your workers? *My* efforts, *my* risks. It was I who helped my father build up the tea business from nothing, yet you profited from it, even though you didn't know the half of how the money was made. He always protected you – I don't know why. I was the son to him. You were nothing. I gave him my strength, my love, my support, but it was *you* who called him father.'

'Not when I was older,' said Phillip, white around his mouth. 'Not when I came to know what sort of man he really was.'

With a howl of rage Tom launched himself at Phillip, knocking the gun from his grasp. The two men crashed over and rolled, locked in a death grip. Then Tom, the heavier, was on top and his large hands were around Phillip's neck squeezing and squeezing as Phillip tore at the fingers. As Georgiana lunged for a fire poker, a shot rang out and Tom slumped forward.

'Is he dead?' cried Georgiana, flinging the poker aside.

Phillip, breathing raggedly, rolled the man off his chest. 'No, there's a heartbeat.' He looked up at Harry, who stood swaying in the corner where the gun had gone spinning in the fray. 'Good shooting.'

Harry smiled grimly. 'Not good enough. I meant to shoot the bastard through the heart.'

'Lucky your aim was off, then,' Phillip remarked as he rose and strode across the room just in time to catch Harry as he collapsed.

Chapter Thirty-Seven

When Georgiana finally fell into bed, she felt ragged with exhaustion. The night's events replayed over and over in her head; a confusing blur of voices, actions, fear, hatred, relief. Now it was all over. Yet sleep evaded her. Instead she lay, staring into the blackness, her throat constricted, unshed tears burning behind her eyes. In her heart she felt a pain so acute it was as though a part of it had been ripped from her body.

'Why?' she admonished herself. 'You should be rejoicing!'

Everything had finally fallen into place. Tom had been taken away to gaol and Phillip and Sedgewick had both assured her Harry's wound was not too serious. Phillip had brought her back to the hotel, saying it was not appropriate for a young woman to be alone with so many men. He'd looked perplexed when she'd laughed. Charlie was due any day now. Just the thought of his happy-go-lucky grin was enough to make her heart skip. All in all, it looked like there were happy endings for everyone. Phillip was adamant that Harry was the rightful heir and must take his place as such. Harry hadn't said a lot, struggling with pain, but as she was leaving he'd caught her hand and said in a low voice, 'I can clear my name, now. Tomorrow we'll talk.'

A lump had risen in her throat and she'd nodded, though she could not meet his eyes, vivid blue in his white, drawn face.

Harry was a free man – more than that, he had a brother, a grandmother and was an earl. He owned a manor and vast estates; it was the stuff of dreams. He loved her and tomorrow he would ask her to marry him. She could become Lady Elrington. It really had come to this, after all.

She'd tried so hard not to think about it, quashing her fears, but now they had to be faced. This past week had changed things – or confirmed them. She wasn't sure which. Yes, she could play the role of Lady Elrington, she knew she could. After all, it would be no harder than playing a cabin boy. But that was just it.

For the first time she could ever remember, she wanted nothing so much as to just be herself, Georgiana da Silva. The only roles she wanted to play now were on the stage. She loved New Zealand. Here she could breathe; here she was already loved and admired. It would be so hard to return to England with its dictates of how one should behave, how one should think.

She thought of Harry, remembering all the adventures they'd shared together. He would still be Harry, even if he were an earl. But it wouldn't be the same. Their lives would be laid out, each day a repetition of the one before, the years layering upon each other. Balls, hunting parties, trips to London to see new plays, but never to act in them. Then she thought of how vividly alive she felt when she was with Harry, of the yearning that only he could quench, and she pressed her hands very hard over her face, nails digging into her scalp. Was she mad? She had promised just a week ago to love him forever. How could she even think of throwing away such love, such passion?

Now, staring into the black night, cold reality squeezed her heart. In the end, love simply wasn't enough. How well she could understand the decision Harry's mother had made to leave Henry. Harry's grandparents had been right. A seamstress just wasn't a suitable wife for an earl.

Nor was an actress.

She could play the part, but deep down she would always know that she was cast in the wrong role in the wrong play. Her true nature would come out, sooner or later. It had to.

That is why her own mother had run away. Harry deserved so much better and, though he would not realise it now, in years to come he would learn to thank her.

The plain fact stared her in the face. In a flash she would have married a salt-stained sea captain of a leaky tub, but she couldn't marry an earl. There would be no happy ending for her, after all. Tears welled and though she ground the heels of her hands into her eyes, they could not be contained.

Turning her face into the pillow, Georgiana abandoned herself to her grief, her body riven by wracking sobs. Harry had not died but she would lose him anyway, would send him away to his new life in which she could never play a part. She wept for all that had been, and what might have been, and for the death of all her dreams of love and laughter and life. Yet, even as her heart was cleft in two, her mind remained very clear that was the only decision she could make.

They were all finally together the following evening when they gathered for dinner at the hotel. Georgiana's fans were disappointed as she would not be performing that night, but the story had already hit the headlines and it did her fame no harm at all.

Earl and Actress saved from Murderous Mayhem

It had been a hectic day, full of arrangements to be made. Tom was in custody and would be taken back to England to be tried for Iver's murder. Phillip and Harry would travel back together to give evidence. Malcolm Sedgewick had given a signed statement, but was also prepared to travel back to England if need be. Walsingham's days were numbered. Harry's shoulder was bound tight, but the doctor said it would heal cleanly. Though Harry was still pale from blood loss, his eyes were as brilliant and clear as a midsummer's sky and all three men were in very high spirits, a close bond having already formed between them. Georgiana put on a brave face so that no one would know how she ached just to look at Harry, how much she dreaded the moment when they would finally talk.

'I have to tell you,' Malcolm Sedgewick said, looking from Harry to Phillip, 'that it's typical of your father that I must still be embroiled in his escapades all these years later.'

The brothers laughed and clinked wine glasses. Now that they were seated together, the differences were more obvious. Phillip was tidier, his face milder, his chin more rounded. His hair was dark brown, his eyes hazel, but still the likeness was extraordinary.

Sedgewick shook his head. 'Henry and Alexander reincarnated.'

Just then there was a cry across the dining room. 'George!'

Her hand, in the process of reaching for her wine glass, stilled even as her heart leapt and she spun in her chair. 'Charlie!'

She flew across the room and flung herself onto her brother's chest, both of them laughing.

'I can't believe I've found you,' she cried as he swept her off her feet in an enveloping hug.

'I can't believe you are here. What the hell is going on, George?'

'I hardly know where to begin,' she said. 'Put me down and come and meet everyone.'

She dragged Charlie over to their table where the men had risen and all were grinning at the exuberant siblings. Introductions were made and an extra place was laid. Charles, in his usual way, seemed to take Georgiana's arrival in his stride, though he did confess to being immensely surprised to discover not only was his sister in New Zealand, but that she was already famous and embroiled in the greatest scandal the little town had ever known.

'That's George,' he said, laughing. 'If you knew what she used to get up to when she was a child—'

'Egged on – no, *led* by you,' she retorted.

'You never needed leading if trouble was nearby,' Charlie said.

'Never a truer word spoken,' Harry added.

Charlie raised an eyebrow and shot Harry a querying look. Georgiana hastened to intervene before her irrepressible brother pursued this promising ground for future teasing. 'So Charlie, are you really fabulously rich?'

He looked abashed as he shook out his napkin. 'Ah, no. Mistake, as it turns out. Soon as I was better I went back and it turned out that it was not a gold seam, after all. The merest thread, in fact.'

'But Charlie, I've had two men wanting to marry me for my fortune if you died. Are you trying to tell me there was nothing after all?' she demanded.

'Nothing,' he said mournfully, but his eyes danced. 'They would have inherited a good deal of mud, however. I'd welcome any partners at this point. Interested, anyone?' he asked, and looked hopefully at his new acquaintances.

The other diners in the restaurant turned around at the resounding laughter that erupted from the table.

'I can't believe it,' said Georgiana, wiping her eyes, her voice still unsteady. 'If you only knew what a cycle of events you set in motion when you wrote such nonsense. And to think all those stupidly greedy men believed it.'

'But Georgie, you still haven't told me which men wanted to marry you,' said Charlie. 'There was no mention of that in the papers.'

They had not been completely forthcoming with all details to the newspaper. When the journalist had arrived, Harry had indicated to the others with narrowed eyes and a slight shake of his head that he did not want everything revealed until he'd had a chance to talk to Phillip alone. So Charlie was given the whole story, with Harry and Georgiana constantly interrupting each other, and with additions from Sedgewick and Phillip. He found the tale immensely entertaining although he was aggrieved when he was told how Tom had described him as a bit part.

'I could have been the hero. Oh how I wish he had come after me. Then I would have been in the newspapers and not my sister. Georgie, you had no business getting involved.'

'There's gratitude after I risked life and limb to save you.'

'And loved every minute of it, if I know you.'

'There were some good parts,' she admitted and gave Harry a smile.

'And there will be even better,' he said with such love in his eyes that her heart plummeted. 'Which brings me to the next point.'

'No, Harry,' she said in a low voice. 'Don't.'

'I have to,' he said, 'it's been burning away at me for far too long. Now your brother is here, I would like to ask him for your hand in marriage.'

Charlie's eyes widened, but though he grinned, he shook his head. 'I'd never speak for George. You must ask her yourself.'

'Gladly,' said Harry, turning to her and looking deep into her eyes. 'Georgie, I love you. Will you marry me?'

She was appalled he had proposed to her in front of everyone – he must be so sure of her answer. Grief choked her and she could not speak. She shook her head.

'But Georgie,' said Harry, his voice coaxing, 'I'm not a wanted man any more. I'm an earl and rich beyond imagining. We'll go back to England and live royally in Elrington Manor and you shall have as many horses as you like.'

Tears brimmed in her eyes as she still made no reply and

just looked down at her hands in her lap. She was vaguely aware of the astonished, uncomfortable silence of the others, but could not begin to explain, pinioned as she was by Harry's unrelenting blue gaze.

'Georgie,' he urged again, 'I'll dress you in fine clothes and beautiful jewellery and take you to all the balls in the countryside.'

Now anger flared, hard and bright, both with Harry and herself. What a fool she'd been. He didn't know her, didn't understand her at all. 'Never!' she said, tilting her chin at him and blinking away her tears. 'Nothing in this world would induce me to become the wife of an earl.'

Harry laughed and turned to Phillip. 'See!' he said. 'I told you. You will have to keep the estates now, dear brother, because nothing in this world will prevent me from marrying Georgie.'

Georgiana gasped. 'It was all a hoax?'

'Not the proposal, not a bit of it. But we've been wrangling most of the day as to who will run the estate. Phillip can't believe I simply don't want it.'

'It's hard for me to believe it too,' said Charlie feelingly.

'Not for me,' said Georgiana with a blinding smile.

'I only embarked on this mad venture to clear my name and to avenge my mother,' Harry explained. 'Well, my name is cleared and Phillip and I are agreed the truth of her marriage will be made public. She will finally get the acknowledgement she deserved.'

Phillip nodded, his face suddenly serious. 'I'm afraid I can't save my mother, poor woman, from scandal. The truth must be told. It will be a double blow when my step-father is arrested.'

Harry reached out a hand and clasped his brother's shoulder. 'But Phillip – and I, if she will have me – will be there to support her. She's a victim in this story and shouldn't be punished. Which is why, dear brother, you must remain in the manor. It has been her home these twenty-seven years. If we play our cards right, hold our heads high, the scandal will eventually blow over.'

Phillip's hand went up to cover Harry's, but he smiled and shook his head. 'It's a generous offer but no, my mother and I will make a new home.'

'Generous be damned!' Harry exclaimed, pulling his hand away and punching Phillip lightly on the arm. 'Don't you see, you've been raised to the role while I haven't the first idea where to begin. I'm a sailor. I like the free life. But most importantly, I came to my senses and knew I couldn't condemn Georgie to a life of luxury.' Georgiana gave a gasp of mock indignation and he turned to her. Laughter and tenderness were both in his face. 'I cannot tell you how much I missed you when I went on alone to Arrowtown. I suddenly realised I've become accustomed to sharing adventures with you. It just wasn't as much fun without you. If ever there was a woman born to be a trial and a tribulation, a companion and a joy to a sea captain, it has to be you.'

He cupped her cheek with a hand. 'Then I came back to find that far from living a sane, safe life, you'd become the talk of the town. What the hell had I been doing to contemplate, even for a minute, making you lady of the manor? Your talents are far, far too great to be hidden away.'

Tears brimmed in her eyes and Georgiana turned her head to kiss his palm. For a second they looked at each other, then Harry turned back to the others and said in that brisk tone she knew so well, that brooked no opposition, 'Georgiana is right, New Zealand fits well. I'll refit *Sally* then get her down here and look for new business ventures while my brother and partner runs the estate in England.'

'But it simply isn't right,' Phillip protested. 'You are the earl, you should have the home.'

'If I may speak,' interrupted Sedgewick, 'I think Harry is right. The fact, Phillip, that you feel it is so wrong and he cannot see that it is, makes his choice all the better. You are of that world, he is not. Of course Harry has to keep the title but, you know, I do not think your father would care much who had the house. He never envied his brother and would have lived just as happily in a cottage with Mary if he'd been able to. If you feel so strongly about it, you can make provisions. One day there will be children to think of, after all. But these things can be sorted out with a bit of imagination. Just because it's not been done before doesn't mean it can't be done. Everything's possible. That's the New Zealand way of thinking.'

'There you go,' said Harry jubilantly. 'If Sedgewick says our father wouldn't have minded, that's good enough for me. And I have to say, I do like the New Zealand philosophy!'

Phillip still looked troubled. 'It's wrong. You must come back and take your rightful place.'

'Very well,' said Harry, 'I'll try again, just to please you, Phillip. Georgie, this is the last time I'll ask. Will you come back to England and marry the Earl of Elrington?'

His face was alight with the wild impudence that was surely his father's legacy. She shook her head, her eyes shining.

'Never!'

'In that case,' he said, suddenly serious, taking her hand in his, 'will you, dearest Georgiana da Silva, marry Harry Trent?'

His eyes, brilliant blue, burned into hers. She saw love there, and tenderness and the promise of much laughter and many adventures. There was also so much more. She saw the strength of a man who inspired loyalty and trust. A man who had fought for, and protected her. Commander and adventurer. Earl and pirate king. A man with the heart of a lion, who could harness the winds.

With a start, her hand went to her throat to where her griffin lay. Of course. How had she been so blind?

'Georgie?' Harry prompted her, his voice at once imploring and demanding, as he squeezed her other hand for the only right reply.

She was an actress, she knew her cue.

'Yes!' she declared. 'Oh yes, and as soon as possible.'

With a laugh of elation, he snatched up both her hands, pressing kisses on them before leaning forward to drop one on her nose. His smile, wickedly, promised so much more later. Then he turned to the others at the table.

'Well, that's it then. She has the final say on the matter. You see, I cannot leave Georgie because it certainly won't be long before she'll have some fiancé wanting to wring her neck. And that fiancé, I am determined, will be me!'

About the Author

Zana Bell grew up in Zimbabwe and studied English Literature at the University of Cape Town. After travelling for several years doing a wide range of jobs, she immigrated to New Zealand where she now lives with her family and cats in a small harbourside community.

She began writing, just for the fun of seeing whether she could actually complete a novel and immediately became hooked. She enjoys writing in a variety of genres but has a particular fondness for all things historical.

For more information visit www.zanabell.com
Follow Zana on Twitter @ZanaBellAuthor

More from Choc Lit

If you enjoyed Zana's story, you'll enjoy the rest of our selection. Here's a sample:

The Road Back
Liz Harris

Winner of the 2012 Book of the Year Award from Coffee Time Romance & More

When Patricia accompanies her father, Major George Carstairs, on a trip to Ladakh, north of the Himalayas, in the early 1960s, she sees it as a chance to finally win his love. What she could never have foreseen is meeting Kalden – a local man destined by circumstances beyond his control to be a monk, but fated to be the love of her life.

Despite her father's fury, the lovers are determined to be together, but can their forbidden love survive?

'A splendid love story so beautifully told.' Colin Dexter, O.B.E. Bestselling author of the Inspector Morse series.

Visit www.choc-lit.com for more details including the first two chapters and reviews, or simply scan barcode using your mobile phone QR reader.

The Silver Locket
Margaret James

Winner of 2010 Reviewers' Choice Award for Single Titles

If life is cheap, how much is love worth?

It's 1914 and young Rose Courtenay has a decision to make. Please her wealthy parents by marrying the man of their choice – or play her part in the war effort?

The chance to escape proves irresistible and Rose becomes a nurse. Working in France, she meets Lieutenant Alex Denham, a dark figure from her past. He's the last man in the world she'd get involved with – especially now he's married.

But in wartime nothing is as it seems. Alex's marriage is a sham and Rose is the only woman he's ever wanted. As he recovers from his wounds, he sets out to win her trust. His gift of a silver locket is a far cry from the luxuries she's left behind.

What value will she put on his love?

First novel in the trilogy.

Visit www.choc-lit.com for more details including the first two chapters and reviews, or simply scan barcode using your mobile phone QR reader.

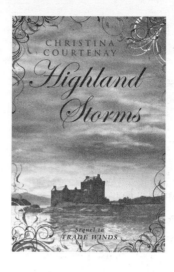

Highland Storms
Christina Courtenay

Winner of the 2012 Best Historical Romantic Novel of the year

Who can you trust?

Betrayed by his brother and his childhood love, Brice Kinross needs a fresh start. So he welcomes the opportunity to leave Sweden for the Scottish Highlands to take over the family estate.

But there's trouble afoot at Rosyth in 1754 and Brice finds himself unwelcome. The estate's in ruin and money is disappearing. He discovers an ally in Marsaili Buchanan, the beautiful redheaded housekeeper, but can he trust her?

Marsaili is determined to build a good life. She works hard at being a housekeeper and harder still at avoiding men who want to take advantage of her. But she's irresistibly drawn to the new clan chief, even though he's made it plain he doesn't want to be shackled to anyone.

And the young laird has more than romance on his mind. His investigations are stirring up an enemy. Someone who will stop at nothing to get what he wants – including Marsaili – even if that means destroying Brice's life forever ...

Sequel to Trade Winds.

Visit www.choc-lit.com for more details including the first two chapters and reviews, or simply scan barcode using your mobile phone QR reader.

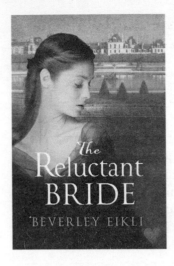

The Reluctant Bride
Beverley Eikli

Can honour and action banish the shadows of old sins?

Emily Micklen has no option after the death of her loving fiancé, Jack, but to marry the scarred, taciturn, soldier who represents her only escape from destitution.

Major Angus McCartney is tormented by the reproachful slate-grey eyes of two strikingly similar women: Jessamine, his dead mistress, and Emily, the unobtainable beauty who is now his reluctant bride.

Emily's loyalty to Jack's memory is matched only by Angus's determination to atone for the past and win his wife with honour and action. As Napoleon cuts a swathe across Europe, Angus is sent to France on a mission of national security, forcing Emily to confront both her allegiance to Jack and her traitorous half-French family.

Angus and Emily may find love, but will the secrets they uncover divide them forever?

Visit www.choc-lit.com for more details including the first two chapters and reviews, or simply scan barcode using your mobile phone QR reader.

To Turn Full Circle
Linda Mitchelmore

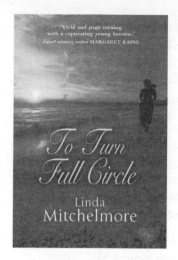

Life in Devon in 1909 is hard and unforgiving, especially for young Emma Le Goff, whose mother and brother die in curious circumstances, leaving her totally alone in the world. While she grieves, her callous landlord Reuben Jago claims her home and belongings.

His son Seth is deeply attracted to Emma and sympathises with her desperate need to find out what really happened, but all his attempts to help only incur his father's wrath.

When mysterious fisherman Matthew Caunter comes to Emma's rescue, Seth is jealous at what he sees and seeks solace in another woman. However, he finds that forgetting Emma is not as easy as he hoped.

Matthew is kind and charismatic, but handsome Seth is never far from Emma's mind. Whatever twists and turns her life takes, it seems there is always something – or someone – missing.

Set in Devon, the first novel in a trilogy.

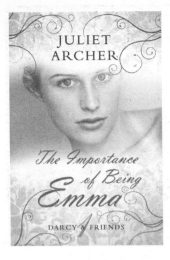

JULIET ARCHER

The Importance of Being Emma

DARCY & FRIENDS

The Importance of Being Emma

Juliet Archer

A modern retelling of Jane Austen's *Emma*.

Mark Knightley – handsome, clever, rich – is used to women falling at his feet. Except Emma Woodhouse, who's like part of the family – and the furniture. When their relationship changes dramatically, is it an ending or a new beginning?

Emma's grown into a stunningly attractive young woman, full of ideas for modernising her family business. Then Mark gets involved and the sparks begin to fly. It's just like the old days, except that now he's seeing her through totally new eyes.

While Mark struggles to keep his feelings in check, Emma remains immune to the Knightley charm. She's never forgotten that embarrassing moment when he discovered her teenage crush on him. He's still pouring scorn on all her projects, especially her beautifully orchestrated campaign to find Mr Right for her ditzy PA. And finally, when the mysterious Flynn Churchill – the man of her dreams – turns up, how could she have eyes for anyone else …?

Visit www.choc-lit.com for more details including the first two chapters and reviews, or simply scan barcode using your mobile phone QR reader.

CLAIM YOUR FREE EBOOK

of

Close to the Wind

You may wish to have a choice of how you read *Close to the Wind*. Perhaps you'd like a digital version for when you're out and about, so that you can read it on your ereader, iPad or even a Smartphone. For a limited period, we're including a **FREE** ebook version along with this paperback.

To claim, simply visit ebooks.choc-lit.com or scan the QR Code.

You'll need to enter the following code:

Q241307

This offer will expire October 2014. Supported ebook formats listed at www.choc-lit.com. Only one copy per paperback/customer is permitted and must be claimed on the purchase of this paperback. This promotional code is not for resale and has no cash value; it will not be replaced if lost or stolen. We withhold the right to withdraw or amend this offer at any time. Further terms listed at www.choc-lit.com.

Introducing *Choc Lit*

We're an independent publisher creating
a delicious selection of fiction.
Where heroes are like chocolate – irresistible!
Quality stories with a romance at the heart.

Choc Lit novels are selected by genuine readers like yourself.
We only publish stories our Choc Lit Tasting Panel want to
see in print. Our reviews and awards speak for themselves.

We'd love to hear how you enjoyed *Close to the Wind*.
Just visit www.choc-lit.com and give your feedback.
Describe Harry in terms of chocolate
and you could win a Choc Lit novel in our
Flavour of the Month competition.

Available in paperback and as ebooks from most stores.

Visit: www.choc-lit.com for more details.

Keep in touch:
Sign up for our monthly newsletter Choc Lit Spread for
all the latest news and offers: www.spread.choc-lit.com.
Follow us on twitter: @ChocLituk and facebook: Choc Lit.

Or simply scan barcode using your mobile phone QR reader:

Choc Lit
Spread

Twitter

Facebook